KILL CODE

A WOLF SIX THRILLER

ALEX SHAW

B

Boldwood

First published in Great Britain in 2025 by Boldwood Books Ltd.

Copyright © Alex Shaw, 2025

Cover Design by Nick Castle

Cover Images: Shutterstock and iStock

The moral right of Alex Shaw to be identified as the author of this work has been asserted in accordance with the Copyright, Designs and Patents Act 1988.

A CIP catalogue record for this book is available from the British Library.

Paperback ISBN 978-1-83678-404-3

Large Print ISBN 978-1-83678-405-0

Hardback ISBN 978-1-83678-403-6

Ebook ISBN 978-1-83678-406-7

Kindle ISBN 978-1-83678-407-4

Audio CD ISBN 978-1-83678-398-5

MP3 CD ISBN 978-1-83678-399-2

Digital audio download ISBN 978-1-83678-402-9

This book is printed on certified sustainable paper. Boldwood Books is dedicated to putting sustainability at the heart of our business. For more information please visit https://www.boldwoodbooks.com/about-us/sustainability/

Boldwood Books Ltd, 23 Bowerdean Street, London, SW6 3TN

www.boldwoodbooks.com

For my wife Galia, my sons Alexander and Jonathan, and our family in England and Ukraine

1

In the darkness, Ruslan Akulov's eyes snapped open. Something shook him awake from his dreams, yet it wasn't a gentle, comforting hand. It was rough, it was rolling, as though he was being battered by waves.

Turbulence.

Akulov was on a plane? But how had he got there?

There was a judder which abruptly threw him from his three-seater couch and slammed him onto the floor. The jet violently jinked to the right and started losing height. Disorientated, head heavy, he lay there for a moment as he felt vibrations coursing through his body.

A voice, sounding distant, asked him, 'Akulov, you OK? You awake?'

Before he could answer a pair of powerful arms scooped him up, and Akulov felt himself being dragged to the nearest seat. The voice spoke again, now sounding louder, 'You OK? Can you hear me?'

As the pain in his head intensified, Akulov squinted at

the man who was strapping him into his seat. He recognised him; Hormann. 'Yes... I can hear you.'

'The engines are out,' Hormann said.

Abruptly the jet dipped, making Hormann stagger backwards. He threw his arms out and clambered into an empty seat, past the sofa.

Akulov only now noted the complete lack of engine noise. His eyes immediately seeking out the wing through the window, he observed the absence of any navigation lights blinking back at him. What noise he could hear was not man-made but the rushing of the wind as it buffeted the fuselage, making the entire airframe shake.

Akulov was confused. 'What's happening?'

Hormann said, 'No idea, no idea at all. You're asleep, I'm having a drink, then suddenly nothing. No bang, no boom, no smoke.'

Akulov had the odd feeling he'd been on the plane before, its interior seemed familiar. Yes, he had, it was the same CIA chartered Gulfstream G280 which had brought him to Canada. But what had happened to it? Something had knocked out an engine, but there was no smoke, no noise. And what about the second powerful Honeywell unit on the other side? Could the jet limp home, or glide on a single power unit? He didn't know. But on no engines at all? His mind was fuzzy. The last thing he remembered was staggering out of the hotel and then there were flashes of Hormann helping him into a jacket, and then going through what must have been an airport, a security desk? Answering immigration questions with short answers before being laid down on the jet's three-seater couch.

Concussion.

The word rolled around in his head. Did he remember

Hormann telling him that's what he had? Yes. He'd been blindsided by someone with a fire extinguisher but how...

'Where are we?' Akulov asked.

'Up in the sky!' Hormann's voice was tense, terse, as he shouted from the other end of the executive jet. 'We had to change course, the pilot said there was a huge storm coming in. Biggest he's ever seen. Shit, I don't know, I think we probably got hit by lightning and it created some type of short, y'know?'

'Planes are designed to survive lightning strikes,' Akulov stated, not knowing how he knew this.

Past two further rows of highly padded leather seats and the walnut bulkhead, a voice escaped from under the cockpit door. It was loud. It was insistent.

'MAYDAY... MAYDAY... MAYDAY... Alpena Tower! I repeat, MAYDAY... MAYDAY... MAYDAY... Alpena Tower!'

Another voice now spoke, Akulov guessed it was the co-pilot, and his desperation was unmasked, 'I've got nothing! Nothing is responding!'

'MAYDAY... MAYDAY... MAYDAY... Any Tower! I repeat MAYDAY... MAYDAY... MAYDAY... Any Tower!'

Akulov's mind was whirling. Where were the exterior lights? Didn't commercial jets have an electronic warning voice imploring the pilots to 'PULL UP... PULL UP...' and more importantly, why weren't they?

Akulov was abruptly jerked to one side as the jet lurched and started to spiral. His head felt heavy, as though he was on a spinning funfair carousel, and it was pinned to his left. And then like it had been caught by a giant hand, the jet abruptly levelled out as Akulov now saw, in weak daylight, ground beneath them. He strained to make out any landmark for reference. He could see nothing made by man. He reasoned it had to be the wilderness, the prairie which ran up to the international border of the US and Canada, but he wasn't an expert. Before he had time to think of any possible action he could take or even to assess his situation, the nose of the CIA jet angled down again.

'Shit! Oh Jesus... oh Jesus... We're really going down!' Hormann's voice was just below a scream.

Outside his window Akulov saw treetops like green fingertips, almost within touching distance, so near he imagined their nails scraping the fuselage beneath his feet. The whole plane began to shake with increased violence, Akulov wasn't a pilot but had been in enough airframes to realised they were carrying far too much speed for a safe landing, for any landing. And then the ground vanished to be replaced by a substance which glittered and glimmered as it rushed past below them.

Water.

It had to be a river or a lake, more than likely one of the Great Lakes, and if that was the case it would be like landing at sea. Akulov fought the increased G-force pressing him back into his seat and managed to bend his body forward into a brace position, his head all but touching his knees and his arms protecting the sides and back of his head, in theory. He screwed his eyes shut. He sensed the aircraft's nose rise, perhaps they had a chance, perhaps they would survive this. But no. He knew it was hopeless.

This wasn't the way he thought his life would end, but then he reasoned, as a killer, he dared not hope for the perniciously kind mercy of a fellow assassin's bullet.

The Gulfstream G280 slammed with a shattering shudder, belly first into the body of water with more violence than anything Akulov had ever felt before. The stricken jet's forced deceleration sounded thunderous as the steel howled and screeched. Akulov's head was cocooned between his arms, yet these were being jolted left and right, the luxury, executive airframe buckling as it ploughed under the surface of the water.

And then there was a sudden stillness. Icy hands seemingly clawed at his feet as water gushed into the cabin. Akulov opened his eyes and inhaled deeply. The false buoyancy as the water took full control of the sinking jet was almost as abrupt as the impact itself. Akulov understood he had to remain calm as the urge to panic gripped him. He had a chest full of air and knew how long this could sustain him on average, but the issue was he was sinking deeper and deeper and was still strapped into his flight seat.

Where was Hormann? Akulov couldn't see him.

The water was rushing up to his neck now as he moved his hands to free his seatbelt. He managed to manoeuvre himself out of the seat, taking a gulp of air, a moment before the water completely filled the cabin. Looking up he could see the daylight dimming with each passing millisecond as he sank.

He had to escape before it was too late. He again tried to relax and let reason, and his training guide him.

Guide.

That was what he needed, a guide. The emergency floor lights, which every commercial jet had to show the way to the exit, were off but he could still follow the seats to the front and the exit. And then he realised why he was sinking so fast; the fuselage had broken into at least two pieces and his part which comprised of the tail section of the aircraft was sinking last. With nothing to lose and everything to gain, Akulov forced himself to swim downwards, past the couch to the last seat he could see as the icy cold water gripped his chest. He reached the seatback, his lungs started to burn from within whilst they contracted from without. Past the seat, in the murky underwater twilight, he could just make out the next section of the jet sinking deeper, moving away, and within the section he could see a figure, arms frantically moving, legs kicking. But Hormann was already too far away from him to be saved.

Akulov grabbed the jagged edge of the fuselage, with first his left and then his right hand, and pulled with his arms, but something snagged his left wrist on the jagged edge. It was his cheap, Casio G-Shock watch. He tugged and the strap was sliced clean through. Akulov kicked out with his feet and pushed past. He was free of the wreckage. He took a pair of strokes with as much power as he could muster away from the still sinking wreckage, then as his vision started to dim, he fancied he heard the voices of the pilots, calling him like sirens as he pushed upwards at the surface and his salvation.

2

COLOGNE, GERMANY

One Week Ago

Akulov exited Cologne's central station and headed directly for what had been the world's third tallest building for ten years, *Kölner Dom* – Cologne Cathedral. Each time Akulov had passed the building he'd admired its heft and architecture. However, he felt its grandeur had been diminished, hemmed in as it was by buildings, many newer and uglier – which included the railway station – on each and every side. It had been Akulov's idea to meet in the German city, but his broker had chosen the location and the time. She was the only person he trusted, since entering his line of work, to do so.

He passed by the cathedral's towering ornate entrance doors as a pack of Asian tourists posed for a group photograph. One of them, probably the tour guide, held a large golfing umbrella, and as Akulov neared he noted it was emblazoned with the Chinese flag. For a nation, whom in the past had actively banned religion, these Chinese tourists seemed extremely happy to be in front of the building which retained the title of the world's tallest cathedral. Ensuring his face didn't appear in any videos being taken by the tourists by turning away, Akulov headed for Burgmauer Strasse and left the square. Walking at a leisurely pace he passed the line of cream-coloured Mercedes taxis parked nose to tail on the right side of the street before he crossed and paused outside the 'Dom Souvenirs' shop. He peered into the window, just another interested tourist, but his focus was not on what lay within the store, rather the reflection of what was outside and behind him. He checked the reflection for anyone who had suddenly stopped walking, was tying a shoelace, or talking on a mobile phone. Years before this would have also included anyone obscuring their face with a tourist map or newspaper but the digital age had made both of these items a standout 'telltale'. He saw a man in a bomber jacket skip a step and then remove his mobile phone from his pocket. Akulov kept his gaze on the man's reflection as he turned to his left and entered the Café Reichard, whose entrance was directly behind him. Akulov carried on walking up the gently sloping street until a set of steps appeared to his right. He abruptly turned right, cutting the corner and taking them down to the lower but parallel Komodienstrasse. Here he turned right again and headed back towards the cathedral, having walked in a circle. He drew level with a McDonalds and crossed the road, now heading for his real destination, the 'Excelsior Hotel Ernst'.

A concierge wearing a black peaked cap and royal blue jacket welcomed him as he entered via the revolving door. Once inside, Akulov crossed the marble-floored foyer to the reception desk, where a blonde woman standing amongst a forest of polished walnut panelling greeted him in German.

Akulov spoke the language well enough but unlike his American English, his accent betrayed him as a foreigner, so he pretended to be American.

'Good afternoon. My name is Chris Bradwell, I believe I am expected?'

The woman took a millisecond to switch languages, and her eyes contracted slightly. 'One moment, sir, just let me check.'

She reached down to an open drawer, in which stood a desktop computer, then tapped several keys. Akulov took the time to assess the room, casually turning his head but not enough that it was obvious.

'Yes, Mr Bradwell,' the woman continued. 'You are expected. You will need to take the lift to the third floor. Room 314 will be on your left.'

'Thank you.'

'Thank you, sir, and have a nice day.'

Akulov smiled at the use of the American salutation, although he suspected there was some sarcasm in its usage.

He crossed to the lift and rode to the third floor, all the while preparing himself to launch an attack, if he needed to, on any sudden assailant. The lift was empty, and the corridor was too. Ignoring the doorbell button, he rapped on the door with his knuckles. A moment later it opened inwards and an immaculately dressed woman bid him to enter. Akulov shut the door behind himself. The room was a suite with bright cream walls and a thick pile biscuit-coloured carpet. Past the large bed were two armchairs each either side of a coffee table on which stood a bottle of schnapps and two shot glasses. Tall windows framed the table and through these the cathedral was almost within kissing distance.

'Have a seat, Ruslan,' Valentina Tishina said in Russian, unscrewing the top of the bottle and filling both glasses.

'Thank you.' Akulov sat on the chair to the left of the table, as she had chosen the seat nearest the bed.

It was the first time they had met since his last contract had concluded, and that had been on another continent in another season. She raised her glass and waited for Akulov to follow. He did so reluctantly. She knocked back her drink and placed the glass on the table. Akulov copied. He wasn't going to drink any more, but was glad of the bottle within grasp which could inflict a considerable amount of damage if he were to use it as a weapon to repel an assailant, and for the Ukrainian assassin this was a constant consideration.

'The places you bring me to, Ruslan.' Tishina was now speaking in English, her accent cut-glass, home counties.

'You chose the hotel,' Akulov replied in the same language, wondering why they were using it to communicate in private.

'You chose Germany, and I spent too much time here in the eighties to be a fan.' She sighed. 'One day you may finally invite me somewhere more appealing.'

'I hear their pork schnitzel is good.'

Tishina let the edges of her lips curl upwards. 'On occasion I wonder about you, Ruslan. I ponder how someone so gifted in certain areas can be so... stunted in others.'

Akulov looked out of the window. This was not the conversation he'd wanted to have.

Tishina refilled both glasses. 'Aren't you going to ask me how I am?'

Akulov frowned. 'How are you?'

'Do you mean since recovering from being held captive?'

'Yes.'

'I am much recovered. Unlike my business.'

'I see.' Akulov understood what she was about to chastise him for.

Tishina said, 'The information you passed to the Central Intelligence Agency regarding our former operations, and my operatives, has been highly damaging to business.'

'I understand. It was my only move. You know that.'

'No. I do not, Ruslan. You should have walked away and left me where I was.'

'Really?'

'Yes.'

'I see,' he repeated.

'Do you?'

Akulov sighed. 'A thank you would be nice.'

Tishina slowly shook her head and a full smile creased her face. 'Thank you, my knight in bloody armour!'

'Bloodied armour.'

Neither spoke for a moment. Akulov realised his throat was suddenly dry. His hand surprised him by reaching for his glass. He downed the second shot. 'We are here. What is the contract?'

'I don't have a full intelligence pack.'

For a second time Akulov frowned. 'Do not tell me this is another rushed job?'

'No. It is not.'

'Then why...' A thought struck Akulov. He looked Tishina directly in the eyes. 'This is not coming from you, is it? This is from them.'

'Yes. Because of the agreement you unilaterally made for my continued freedom.'

Akulov understood. 'Where are they?'

'They are watching us, like peeping Toms, from the room

next door,' Tishina gestured to the door in the wall linking the two rooms. 'They are expecting you.'

'What happens if I go out of the front door instead?'

'Then you will have broken your promise, and I know, Ruslan, you are a man of your word.'

Akulov let his eyes fix on hers for a moment as he thought back to the previous contract, one in which he had agreed to certain demands as well as passing over intelligence on their business dealings for her release from a CIA black site. 'Then as a man of my word I have no choice.'

'That is correct.'

Akulov stood. He let his gaze linger on the towering, gothic building opposite. 'OK.'

'Good boy,' Tishina said.

Akulov headed for the connecting door. He could feel Tishina's eyes on him but did not turn around. He pushed down the handle, and it opened silently as though the mechanism had recently been oiled. Stepping through he saw the corresponding door to the other room was already open. Standing by the bed, facing him, was a man with a blond ponytail. He was wearing a black leather jacket, dark blue jeans and a pair of hiking boots. Akulov shut the door behind himself and stepped into the room.

'Howdy, Wolf Six,' Mike Parnell said.

'Did you know,' a voice, with a slight southern drawl, said from a chair by the window, 'that in addition to being the world's tallest Cathedral, Kölner Dom is also the world's third tallest church?'

'Its full name is Hohe Domkirche Sankt Petrus,' Parnell added.

'I think we all read the same guidebook,' Akulov replied, deadpan.

'Come, take a pew, Ruslan,' Vince Casey of the Central Intelligence Agency said.

Akulov moved past Parnell and sat in the second seat. There was no Schnapps in this room, but three bottles of beer stood on the table. Parnell closed the door then pulled up a third chair from the dresser and took a position at Casey's side.

The older CIA officer was wearing a pair of khaki chinos and a long-sleeved navy blue polo shirt which was tighter at his chest than his waist. He looked a little fitter than the last time they had met, and even more like a 1980s Robert Redford. Casey reached forward and twisted off a bottle top. 'Drink?'

'No. Thank you.'

'Tishina got in first with her schnapps, I know – she can be very persuasive.' Casey raised the bottle to his lips and took a long pull. 'You gotta love real German beer.'

'Kölsch is the local stuff, it's served in those damn small glasses,' Parnell added.

Akulov said nothing.

'How have you been?' Casey enquired.

'Fantastic,' Akulov replied, flatly.

'Now that is great to hear.'

'Heartwarming,' Parnell added.

Akulov made no reply, the CIA duo were a double act, but their aim was not comedy.

'I have a job for you,' Casey stated.

'Non-paying,' Parnell clarified.

'That's exciting.'

'Indeed it is, Ruslan.'

When Casey didn't elaborate, Akulov asked, 'What is it?'

'How's your Chinese?'

'Restaurant menu only.'

'Now that's funny. Listen. We have a job for you, north of the US border. Winnipeg. It's a quick kill with an in and out – insertion and extraction courtesy of Air Casey.'

'CIA charters,' Parnell stated.

'Why not use a scheduled airline? Won't a private jet seem out of place?'

Casey smiled. 'Don't you think they have Gulfstreams in Canada? Look, we need the speed, and we need the control.'

'So, you want this kill to happen when?'

'Five days' time. We have a tight window when the target is going to be in the area, otherwise things start to get messy and complicated.'

'Five?'

'Yes.'

'You obviously have the mark under surveillance. Why are you asking me to undertake this contract specifically, when you have any number of agency assets available?'

'You owe us.'

'And,' Casey said, 'I won't be running you through the books.'

'You're a black asset, Wolf Six, so black you make midnight look grey.'

'That's good, Parnell,' Casey noted, 'you been writing poetry again?'

Parnell tapped his temple with his index finger. 'In my mind.'

'And the Chinese link?'

'The target.'

'You had better give me a briefing pack, Casey.' Akulov's voice betrayed no discernible emotion.

Casey took another gulp of beer as Parnell rose from his

chair and collected a large envelope that had been lying next to the TV. He handed this to Akulov.

Akulov took out a 10 x 8 glossy photograph. It showed an Asian man exiting a Rolls Royce Cullinan. Next, he removed a sheet of paper and speed-read the information printed on it.

Casey stated, 'That's Fang Bai, he goes by the Western name Paul Fang. He's thirty-seven, a dual Canadian citizen and Chinese national.'

'But Article 3 of "The People's Republic of China Nationality Law" states that China does not recognise dual nationality,' Parnell added.

'And here's the issue,' Casey continued. 'If Fang enters China on a Canadian passport, he'll be treated by the Chinese authorities as a Chinese citizen.'

'So?' Akulov looked up from the papers.

'He's CEO of ByteTime.'

'Fin-tech, not food,' Parnell clarified.

'So,' Akulov repeated.

'So, we don't want him back in China.'

'What do you want me to do?'

'I want you to assassinate him, Ruslan. He will have about his person a little, red box. It's roughly the size of a cigarette packet. It is vital that we get that too.'

Akulov looked up from the paper. 'So this is not a simple hit. I have to be close enough in order to take this box from Fang?'

'Correct.'

'And how do I know he'll have this box on him?'

'It never leaves his side,' Casey clarified. 'Did you know, in Chinese culture, the colour red represents happiness, success, and good fortune?'

'White Fang has taken this to heart.'

Akulov looked at Parnell. 'White Fang?'

'The name Bai means white or clear in Mandarin.'

'And Fang means, fang?'

'No, it means square or four-sided.'

'The point is,' Casey continued, 'this box will always be with him. It contains tech which we believe has military implications, and we cannot let it fall into anyone else's hands, especially the Chinese.'

'Why hasn't he given it to the Chinese?'

'He hates China. His father was one of the protesters on Tiananmen Square back in nineteen eighty-nine. He's going to Hong Kong for a business meeting; he's been working on a billion-dollar deal.'

'You want me to kill a man for the tech he has created?'

'Yes, but make no mistake, Ruslan, Fang is not a good guy. He associates with high-ranking Triad members. Within the Triad structure he acts as a "White Paper Fan", that's their term for a financial and business adviser.'

'He's a bad dude.' Parnell folded his arms.

'In addition to this he uses ByteTime to wash their money and to transport certain "live goods".'

Akulov dropped the paper and photograph on the table and sat back in his seat. 'Casey, last time you wanted me to tackle the Russian Bratva, and this time it's the Chinese Triads?'

'You didn't enter this profession to make friends, Ruslan. This time we intend to pin the hit on the Chinese Triads.'

Akulov looked at Parnell and then back at Casey. 'How?'

'You'll be wearing the colours and logo of a rival Triad. Of course, your face will be covered.'

'I killed twelve men for you in Chicago, Casey. How many more am I indebted to you for?'

'Until I say "stop", Ruslan. Until I say, "that's it, that's enough". And then who knows, I may want to retain your services on a paid basis. You and Tishina can no longer fly below the radar, just you remember that.'

'I understand.' Akulov was angry but couldn't back out.

* * *

Warsaw, Poland

The man with the briefcase ignored the lift and took the stairs down into the basement level of the car park. Although the offices and apartments above were clean and modern, the stairwell retained the grimy scent of urine, and the car park stank of gasoline. It was dark too, which was as the man with the briefcase had wanted it to be, in fact it was he who had loosened a connection to the electrical system hours before. This too had prevented the CCTV camera at the vehicle entrance from operating. Posing as a potential customer, he had, the week before, contacted the security company to discuss their products and as a matter of fact had asked about call-out times in case of malfunctions. The sales manager had reassured him their response time for such a call-out, in the rare case of camera malfunction was four hours, which was good for a company of their size operating within the restrictions of a busy capital city. The man with the briefcase had given a Proton email address to which further information could be sent and ended the call. Now four days later, his recent electrical tinkering had ensured that both the camera and the lights in the basement car park were out. He had done this at 3 a.m., a time at which human activity was at its lowest ebb, even in Warsaw. All but the most hedonistic had gone to bed, all but the most fanatical morning runners had not yet arisen and all but the most vigilant security guards were yawning at their monitoring desks. It was his favoured time to strike, but the man with the briefcase had waited for half an hour, just to ensure the building's security staff had not decided to send anyone from the warmth of their office to check out the anomaly.

Walking upright, with an unhurried gait, as though he had a right to be there, and wearing a custom-made, long wool coat over his business suit, the man with the briefcase approached the target vehicle. Just enough light filtered in from the sodium streetlights outside the car park entrance to illuminate his way. This was in addition to the unmolested light in the opposite stairwell, the one he hadn't broken, the one which led to the still closed shopping mall tacked haphazardly onto the side of the residential tower.

Although his head was facing squarely forward, the man's eyes scanned evenly left and right for any hidden assailant, any threat which would impede his mission. His step was soft, and his gait was even, yet at any second the man with the briefcase was ready to spring into action.

The large, luxury German sedan was parked in its own numbered space, the best space in the basement, one which ensured no one could park on either side of it, impeding its entrance or exit or worse still, dinting the door. Although it was just a piece of metal, the man with the briefcase appreciated the workmanship which had gone into this particular Mansory Mercedes. It would be a shame when it was destroyed.

Even though the CCTV was off he needed to be careful.

Placing the briefcase on the ground and crouching down as though to tie his shoelace, he opened the case and removed an IED. To call it an improvised explosive device was an insult to his expertise and the design of the device, he felt. The beauty of his creation would only ever be seen by himself; however, its effects would be felt by many. He slid the device under the car, closed his case and stood. He now retraced his steps towards the stairwell, and that was when the lights switched on.

Except they were not the lights he had disabled. These lights were handheld floodlights, and they were trained directly on him.

The man dropped his briefcase and threw himself to the floor behind the closest vehicle, a bulky, black Range Rover, as abrupt voices ordered him in American accented English, to 'Get on the ground!'

He was on the ground alright, but he was not there to comply with the American's commands. He heard footfall. Transferring his weight to one side, he reached into his coat, and withdrew an HK MP5K machine pistol from a custom-made sling. From underneath the SUV he fired a burst of rounds back across the basement in the direction of the lights and the approaching boots. From the yells, he knew he'd hit at least one of his would-be captors before he sprang to his feet and emptied the remainder of his magazine into the hesitating floodlights. More anguished yells were now joined by return fire. Rounds zipped past his head, tore at his custom-commissioned coat, and made him judder as they were stopped by its ballistic lining. He dropped the empty HK and pulling a Glock 17 sprinted for the ramped exit to the basement. More rounds hit him in the back, again caught in his coat, making him stumble but not stop.

Reaching into his left coat pocket now, the assassin felt for the remote trigger and detonated the IED.

The shockwave was devastating in the confined, concrete cave and raced out to meet him, pushing him forward as he continued to move as quickly as his bulky, ballistic coat would allow up the ramp. He reached the surface, leaving behind him clouds of choking dust, and a team of dying men; and most importantly for him, unanswered questions.

3

TALLINN, ESTONIA

Basson enjoyed the cobbled streets and ancient walls of the Estonian capital; it was a far cry from the barely dry concrete and steel of his adopted home of Doha. The alcohol too was an awful lot cheaper and of course the place was a party town. As he sat in the unusually named 'Bar with No Name', he saw yet another British 'Hen Party' wobble along the winding street. But it was not just the Brits who came to the place, each Friday night ferries from Helsinki brought marauding packs of Finns who could drink to excess, sleep it off in a hotel and repeat, before heading home to Finland on a Sunday afternoon having spent far less than it would have cost in their homeland for the hangovers. Basson liked alcohol, and when he knew he was not working he would indulge more than a man of his age should. His age! He smirked, he was fitter than anyone else he saw in the bar, something that was not wasted on the middle-aged woman who had been serving him large glasses of the local *Saku Tume* dark beer for the past hour. However, he had something else on his mind.

He still had bruises from the disastrous failure of his contract in Warsaw three days before. The ballistic lining of his custom-commissioned coat had halted the rounds fired by the Americans from penetrating his flesh but had not prevented the blunt-force trauma. He had been lucky that it was muscle that had been impacted and not organs. Nevertheless his back, covered as it was in purple and red, reminded him of an abstract painting. Anti-inflammatories had helped and so had booze. He was feeling it a little, the four half litres of beer inside giving him a light buzz, but he didn't care. He wanted to get the anger he had to whoever had tipped off the Americans to his actions out of his system. Beer helped, and of course so did fighting. It was as it had been in the French Foreign Legion, the only way to blow off steam. That and accommodating women.

From where he sat at the corner of the dark bar, he could clearly see the entrance and through its large bay windows the cobbled street outside. The broker from Belfast simply known on 'the circuit' as 'The Irishman', and not 'The Northern Irishman', which Basson believed would have been more geographically, if not politically correct, would be here soon, because if he wasn't there would be severe complications. Basson did not know exactly where his broker called home nowadays, only that it was not far from the medieval capital city.

Fifteen minutes and half a glass of Saku Tume later, The Irishman – Clifford Quinn entered the bar. He was perhaps the same age as Basson; however, his hair showed no sign of greying, which was odd for a man who had sinned so much as an IRA bomb maker.

'Maartin.' Quinn refused to say Basson's name with the

correct French pronunciation. 'I see you have started without me.'

'Oui, I have.'

Quinn waved over the barmaid and ordered two large Saku Tume, with a pair of Irish whiskey chasers.

'What are we celebrating?' Basson asked.

'Your escape from the Central Intelligence Agency.'

Basson turned on his stool and had to place his left foot firmly on the ground for support. As he did so he felt a twinge from his old leg injury. 'You are telling me that it *was* the CIA who attempted to abduct me?'

'One hundred per cent.' The drinks arrived and Quinn raised his glass, '*Sláinte!*'

Basson did not repeat the toast before he emptied his glass. 'Think very carefully now, Cliff. How did they learn of me, and the operation?'

Quinn took a long pull of beer before he replied. 'Rumour has it someone made a deal with them for immunity.'

'Who?'

'Now there's a thing. It was your man, Wolf Six.'

Basson felt his jaw clench. He was unable to form any words for a long moment. Eventually he said, 'How can this be? Wolf Six is a ghost, no one can find him.'

'The Agency got to him.'

A lightbulb went on inside Basson's mind. 'Through Tishina?'

'Correct. Although I am certain it is not as simple as that. I've never met the woman, but I know she's no pushover.'

'She is formidable. She was the GRU's finest operative for many years before she went private. She trained and cofounded The Werewolves.'

Quinn's eyes widened. 'This I did not know.'

'I do not want to believe it, yet given the shared history I have with Tishina and Akulov, it makes sense.'

Basson was bitter. He had been known as a top-tier operator who always completed his contracts, and as such had been taken on by Tishina. However, after undertaking a two-man Amsterdam operation with Akulov, despite the contract having been one hundred per cent completed, he had been, in his opinion, unfairly dropped by Tishina and subsequently ostracised by many on the circuit. Seeking a new broker, he had found Quinn.

'I also have some rather bad news for you, Maartin. Our client was not at all understanding of what happened in Warsaw.'

'Has he taken the contract to another broker?'

'No, it is staying with me, but he is unfortunately insisting that I give it to another asset.'

Basson's eyes narrowed. 'Who?'

'Now c'mon, *mon ami*, you know better than to ask me that. I'm like a doctor; client confidentiality is key.'

Basson took a large, slow swig of Saku. 'You are absolutely correct; it makes no difference to me. What does matter, however, is that my professional reputation has been diminished.'

'Look, there will be other contracts. The Bang-Bang man is always in demand – you know that. Now what you need to do is take some time to recuperate and recalibrate.'

'What I need to do is find the wolf who threw me to the dogs!'

'Wolf Six is a ghost, you said so yourself. Your man is impossible to find, which is why he's so good.'

Basson glared at his broker. 'So good?'

Quinn held up his palms in an 'I surrender' motion. 'I'm not sugar coating this, he's the top dog.'

'Dogs, wolves, it makes no difference to me, all animals die.'

'Now the good news,' Quinn said as he mimed for two more whiskies.

'There is some?'

'The CIA may know where you were, but they do not know who you are.'

'What do you mean?'

Quinn waited until the barmaid had refreshed their drinks before he replied. 'They have the name Maartin Basson, but they don't know anything about the identity you use to travel to and from wherever it is you reside.'

'You are certain of this?'

'I am, indeed.'

'What about you?'

'What about me?'

'Do they know you are my broker?'

Quinn shook his head. 'Absolutely not. I had to reinvent myself after "The Troubles". Do you honestly think I'd put myself in such an exposed situation again?'

'I wondered, which is why I asked.'

'Jesus, Maartin. Let me put this bluntly. If you don't work, I don't eat.'

'No. You just drink.'

'You are my best operator, OK?'

'OK.'

'I have another potential contract on the horizon, but the client is being slow to commit. It'll be something explosive, if you know what I mean. You could be the man in the right place at the right time, because I personally believe you are the only person who could pull this one off.'

'That does sound interesting.'

'Interesting? It's bloody amazing!' Quinn raised his glass, '*Sláinte!*'

* * *

Seven years ago, Monte Carlo, Monaco

Akulov headed east out of Gare de Monaco, climbed Ponte Sainte-Devote then turned down the Boulevard de Suisse. Two- and three-storey residential buildings lined the narrow street, all had balconies, and many were adorned with potted plants adding explosions of colour to the otherwise serene, pastel-coloured buildings. Here and there, between the buildings he snatched glimpses of the harbour. After a while he took a right and made for the sea. Taller residential blocks now rose in front of him. He entered the nearest through the communal front door and without pause exited through the rear. The need for counter-surveillance measures drilled into him years before, he repeated the process with the next building before entering a third block whose exit was, by way of a lift, floors below at promenade level. Akulov continued east along the promenade until he found a bench. He sat, another soul just admiring the view of the bay.

An elderly man wearing a garish coloured tracksuit jogged past as though in slow motion with a look of determi-nation on his red, wrinkled face. He passed a paid dog walker promenading a pack of poodles. The dogs excitedly tugged at their leads, the walker nonchalantly ignored both the jogger, and the dogs' attempt to make friends, and kept her head held high, face shielded behind an oversized pair of sunglasses. Akulov very much doubted he'd live to be as old as the jogger. A line once learnt, or overheard – he forgot from where or who had written it popped into his mind:

'There are old soldiers, there are bold soldiers, but there are very few old, bold soldiers.'

Akulov knew that the chance for an old and bold former soldier turned professional assassin to become elderly was even less.

He watched the old, and probably bold, jogger fade into the distance as a light sea breeze started to brush his skin, bringing with it a heady scent of brine, seaweed, and marine diesel from the myriad of yachts and powerboats. Sitting back on the bench, wearing a pair of mirrored sunglasses, a navy blue blazer, cream polo shirt, blue jeans and tennis shoes, Akulov appeared cool, carefree and composed like the residents of Monte Carlo. Yet, under his calm surface, like the Mediterranean Sea which cosseted the principality, there was hidden danger.

Akulov had not been to Tishina's office before. Meeting there was not their usual protocol. It exposed him to a city state with one of the largest percentage of surveillance cameras per population in the world. It ensured he was safe from violence, however it also meant that he could not be invisible, and for a ghost this was unsettling. But here he was, in Monaco, meeting his broker to discuss his next assassination. It was absurd. But former GRU clandestine operative Valentina Tishina liked Monte Carlo.

And then he saw her. Looking west towards the centre of the capital and the marina, an ash-blonde-haired woman wearing a fitted, emerald-green suit walked a small dog.

With perfect etiquette, she nodded formally at everyone she passed. In the other direction he noted no one who appeared out of place. Eventually the woman with the small dog drew level with the bench. He could now identify the animal as a King Charles Spaniel, but it was so well groomed it looked like a children's toy. Valentina Tishina was twenty years older than him, yet stunning. He'd be a liar if he told anyone, including himself, that he didn't find her attractive. He watched her carry on along the promenade, her skirt shamelessly hugging her backside.

He waited for seven minutes and satisfied that he had not been compromised, left the promenade. He entered yet another apartment building and forsaking the lift he took the stairs to the sixth floor. He pressed a bell on the door of apartment sixty-nine.

Tishina opened the door. She had removed her suit jacket, to reveal underneath a black, silk blouse. In Russian she said, 'Come in.'

Akulov entered. She shut the door behind him and ushered him into the living room. The flat was expensively furnished and commanded a panoramic sea view. Her dog was curled up in a basket, in front of the picture window, warmed by cascading rays of Monaco sunlight which dissected the room.

She sat in a deeply padded floral armchair. There were two others, and she pointed him into one. A low, wooden coffee table separated the two, and a thick, brown A4 envelope lay on the table.

Tishina looked past him, through the window and out into the bay. 'This a favourite place of mine, to sit and watch the world go by. Although what one sees here in Monte Carlo is hardly the real world. Outside the walls of the prin-

cipality, the real world is a dangerous place. And it is our job
to make it safer, for a select few.'

'What is the name of your dog?'

'Milan. I didn't name him. I share him, with a friend.'

Akulov asked, 'So why meet me here?'

'Don't you like Monaco?'

Akulov made no reply.

Tishina smiled. 'You and I have known each other for a
long time now, Ruslan, yet the thought struck me that you
have never been to my office.'

'And this is your office.'

'It is, and a very comfortable one too. I do have other
places dotted around the globe; as you can imagine, I must
not be in the same place for too long.'

'I understand.'

'You are aware that I handle a choice panel of operatives.'

He was but had never asked or thought about her other
assets. 'I am.'

'One of these operatives, a Frenchman by the name of
Martin Basson will be joining us shortly.'

Akulov's eyes flicked to the empty armchair. 'I see.'

'He, like you, is a professional. He is a former Legionnaire and an explosives specialist. In fact IEDs are his
favoured tool of liquidation.'

'The Bang-Bang man.'

'You've heard of him?'

'I've heard of the daft name he is known by. Why is he
coming?'

'Because, Ruslan, what I have for you is a contract which
requires a two-man team, and your individual abilities will
complement each other. In short there will be a positive
synergy.'

'Have you been reading business management books again?'

'No, but perhaps I should write one. How's this for a title – *How to Kill Friends and Influence Bad People*?'

Akulov said, 'What is the contract?'

Tishina nodded at the envelope on the table. 'It is all in there. Basson has already accepted. I've never known him to refuse a chance to make something or someone go "bang", but you I sometimes have to persuade.'

'I see.'

'The fee is high, and the targets are extremely unsavoury.' Tishina stood, causing her dog to raise its head. 'I'm leaving you in charge of the dog. Wait here, I shall return, and then we shall await our guest.'

He trusted Tishina. In fact, outside of the men from his former unit, she was the only person he did trust. And if she said they needed Monsieur Le Bang-Bang for the mission, then that was that. As her heels clacked on the parquet flooring, Akulov reached for the envelope. He shook out its contents onto the table as the front door closed and then locked. There were the usual photographs, 10 x 8s of groups of men and then enlargements of two particular subjects. The individuals in the images looked Eastern European, ethnically Slavic yet not quite Russian. The two men, whose images had been blown up, resembled each other, and this was not because of the way they dressed. One was, Akulov estimated, a decade older than the other yet his hair was a raven black. Was it mandatory, Akulov wondered, for all crime bosses to resemble vampires? In many of the photographs the younger target, and several of the other men, wore tracksuits. Although, Akulov noted, the target's tracksuits were so designer they would have blended in well in Monaco. Meanwhile the tracksuits of the others were identical Adidas outfits, black with the standard three white stripes. The last few photographs in the pack were of a building in Amsterdam, which housed a nightclub.

Akulov moved on to the printed pages. His targets, he read, were a pair of cousins from the feared Dinescu crime family, George and Dragoş Dinescu. The Dinescu family had broken in two, the hold they once had exerted over the Romanian capital city had started to wane as accusations turned to infighting which spilled out into the clubs, bars and streets. The local police were running scared, the power and respect the security forces had wielded in the days of their former dictator president Nicolae Ceauşescu was now long gone. Criminal gangs acted above the law, and in many cases even funded the police, which Tishina's client wanted to stop. There was to be a meeting between the two Dinescu cousins, a reconciliation, which if successful would once more bring Bucharest back under the control of one united family, and whilst crime rates and especially the amount of gang warfare would reduce as a result, the client also did not want this to happen. However, it was not just the Romanian capital that the Dinescu family was operating in. The younger of the two cousins, Dragoş, had recently married a Dutch woman and spent much of his time in Amsterdam. It made sense for a criminal organisation such as theirs to have links with the capital city of a country whose lax laws legalised much of what in Bucharest was highly illegal. And it was because of this that the meeting between the two cousins, and their respective crews, was to take place in Amsterdam.

As Akulov read on he realised that the contract was unusual, and ambitious. It specified that both cousins were to be liquidated at the same time as their travelling entourage. This would consist of their captains and lieutenants. In short, the contract called for the crime family to be wiped out, in the middle of a European capital city, and one constantly full of tourists at that.

Akulov now appreciated why this contract could not easily be undertaken by one man alone. Since leaving the military, Akulov had always worked as a singleton operator, a lone wolf, and he had been highly successful. Soon his call sign – Wolf Six – was whispered with fear. Many wanted to hire him whilst just as many others wanted to hide from him, but being an effective operator meant knowing and understanding your limitations. And on this occasion, he did. It was a two-man job.

Akulov stood, stretched and cast his eyes around the room. He walked to the window, spent a moment staring at the sea. The room was still, apart from the gentle snores of the dog, but then another sound joined this. It was the key turning in the lock of the front door. Akulov tensed then relaxed again as Tishina entered, removed her jacket and placed it on a peg on the wall. 'So?'

'You are correct. It is a two-man job.'

'I'm always correct, and I'll take that as an acceptance.'

'Yet I do not see why we must use explosives. A man with an HK or an Uzi, at close range, with the element of surprise, could inflict the same amount of damage.'

'We will use explosives, Ruslan, because that is what the client wishes us to use.'

'I see.'

'Coffee?'

'Yes. Please.'

'I'll make a pot, not the capsule stuff as there will be

three of us.' She walked towards the kitchen, which was down a short hallway to Akulov's left.

Akulov continued to stand by the window, even though the operator who was about to arrive had been deemed friendly by Tishina, he never liked to meet a fellow assassin whilst seated. It was not a dominance issue, as although he was exactly six foot tall and military muscled Akulov was by no means a huge man, it was a matter of professional respect. Presently, as Akulov ruminated on the practical details of the contract, Tishina arrived with a tray on which was a large pot of coffee and three cups. She looked at Akulov, who took the hint and cleared his briefing pack from the table, before placing the tray down.

'A gentleman would have carried this for me, Ruslan.'

'This gentleman did not want to leave the front door unguarded,' Akulov replied.

'Very noble.'

There was a knock at the door. Akulov instinctively felt himself tense, ready to face and repel whoever was on the other side.

Tishina moved to the door and let in the second member of the two-man team.

Basson appeared older, and perhaps three inches taller than Akulov, and his short hair whilst full, was of a salt and pepper grey. He was clean-shaven with sharp facial features.

'I expect you would like us to converse in either Russian or English?' the Frenchman said before Tishina could welcome him.

'English will be fine,' Tishina replied.

'Of course it will be,' the Frenchman stated. His gaze now focused on Akulov. 'From your reputation I expected you to be larger.'

'Perhaps I have been on a diet,' Akulov replied.

'Martin, take a seat.'

'Merci.' Basson moved to the table, all the while maintaining eye contact with Akulov, and sat in the armchair Tishina had previously occupied. He made no comment about the sleeping dog. Akulov waited until Tishina had taken the third seat and then sat back in his own.

'Martin, Ruslan, as you are aware, the reason you are both here is because I have accepted a contract which calls for a two-man team. And from what I know of your skill sets, you two are the most appropriate pair.'

'Merci, Valentina. It is a great honour to be called appropriate,' Basson said. 'My mother would be proud.'

'How do you suggest this will work?' Akulov asked.

'Are you telling me the great Wolf Six has not already devised a plan?' Basson said, with mock surprise.

'I have, and I imagine you have too.'

'Oui.'

Tishina said, 'Martin, your plan is?'

'An IED.' Basson started to chuckle. 'Unless we can use some sort of RPG, I can't think of a better way to hit a larger target group.'

'Ruslan?'

'I agree. No RPG, unless the meeting is to take place away from the city. We need an IED which is powerful yet directorial in order to eliminate collateral damage.'

'I concur,' Basson added.

'The targets will be arriving in several vehicles, perhaps even a convoy, therefore a single car bomb, or even several will not do,' Akulov stated.

Tishina said, 'I have been told that access to the vehicles will be an issue.'

'So, we need to plant a static IED, once the location of the meet is confirmed,' Akulov said, 'which we may not know until, what? Potentially the same day it is convened.'

Tishina said, 'The client will confirm the exact location. He believes it will be at the Dutch property Dragoș Dinescu invested in three months ago. There is a small hotel opposite; I've booked a room there for you to use.'

'Then we shall bring in our own vehicle, once we have confirmation, park it up and then set it off.'

Akulov frowned at Basson's suggestion. 'Too problematic, if it is in the city, to guarantee a parking space, and in a rural environment it would be spotted.'

Basson sat back in his chair and folded his arms. 'Ah, that is not so for every means of transport. I have been considering the same problem. Wolf Six, *mon brave,* once the location of the meet has been confirmed, you shall take up a position of overwatch – in the hotel, if it is to be at the property. I will then, posing as a bike courier, park up and walk away.'

Akulov wasn't convinced. 'How long can a bike remain before it becomes suspicious?'

'Non, you misunderstand me. What are the Dutch famous for? Their love of the *vélo.* I will be on a bicycle. The Viet Cong put claymores in saddle bags. They were quite effective against the Americans.'

'They were,' Tishina said.

Akulov thought back to his training and the lectures on 'asymmetric warfare' as the Russians had learnt the US called it.

Basson continued. 'I intend to do the same. Two claymores, point sixty-eight of a kilo each of C4, propelling, in total, approximately one thousand four hundred three-point two-millimetre steel ball bearings out in two 60-degree fan patterns. I will of course modify them so I can set them off with a mobile handset.'

Akulov said, 'Isn't that overkill?'

'Would you be happier with underkill? How many men can you shoot after the initial detonation, Wolf Six, and still walk away unnoticed?'

'You have a point,' Akulov conceded.

'Of course I do.'

'But one thing. Do not dress as a courier,' Akulov said. 'A man of your age in Lycra would draw too much attention, and you need to blend in.'

A thin smile appeared on Tishina's lips.

Basson's eyes narrow momentarily. 'You are of course correct. I do not wish to appear as though I am a wayward competitor from the Tour De France! Do not fret, although I am French, I will not be wearing a stripy jumper, nor carry a ring of onions around my neck either.'

4

WINNIPEG, MANITOBA, CANADA

Not since his time operating as part of The Werewolves had Akulov been given a plan to execute without any of his own input. Yet he had to admit that the briefing pack and outline of the operation given to him by Casey had been highly professional. He wondered if this was what it was like to work for the CIA as a deniable triggerman? And if so, it was a lot easier than how he currently operated. Akulov glanced through the window at his reflection as he remembered the last time he had been on a private jet charted by a foreign intelligence agency to get him to a target. That time it had been the British using him, and he had been unofficially partnering with the leader of their deniable 'E Squadron', an SAS trooper named Jack Tate. That mission had led to a savage confrontation with the team leader of his old unit – The Werewolves – who had been working for another Chinese national. Akulov realised his mind was attempting to forge fanciful links between his past and present, and he stopped it.

Akulov focused again on the present and 'the mission', as

Casey had called it. Once they landed and he passed through the cursory Canadian immigration checks for someone arriving on a private jet, using the CIA passport he had been given, he would then be collected by a CIA driver and taken to an address on the outskirts of Winnipeg. There he would 'exchange' his identity for that of an existing 'guest' staying at the same hotel as Fang. The man would be physically similar in appearance to Akulov, yet would have a full beard and glasses. Akulov would wear an identical pair of spectacles and a lifelike prosthetic beard. Akulov's passport would then be used by a second doppelganger, who would book into another hotel, on the other side of the city. The idea was for Akulov's legend to remain intact and that at the time of the hit on Fang, he would be clearly seen on another hotel's CCTV enjoying a meal and a few drinks. Meanwhile, Akulov himself was to change into another disguise – a ski mask and a dark, hooded sweatshirt – and access the floor Fang was staying on by means of the stairs at the same time as the CIA set the fire alarm off. And then he would assassinate Fang and obtain the red box.

On first reading, the plan sounded complicated, with too many moving parts for his liking, but given the resources, and manpower of the CIA, Casey assured him it was 'optimal'. For the very same reasons, Akulov believed it was too complex. And what annoyed him the most was that he didn't have a vote on the matter. All plans were simple, foolproof, until they went wrong.

Akulov rubbed his face, his three-day stubble subtly altered its shape, making his cheekbones less prominent and his jaw not as defined. He didn't mind having a beard, and he enjoyed being clean-shaven, it was the bit in-between which annoyed him. Usually, the itching started after day five or six and then it was another week until he could call the build-up of hair a genuine beard. Just imagining the feeling of the glue and the false whiskers made his face crawl.

The engine note changed as the jet started to descend. Out of the window the seemingly endless pine forests gave way abruptly to the expanse of Lake Winnipeg and the prairie beyond. Akulov knew the city of Winnipeg got its name from the lake, what he hadn't known until he'd googled it was that the lake itself derived its title from the Western Cree words for 'muddy water'. Looking down from above he noted it was muddy enough.

His initial flight in from Germany, aboard a larger CIA charted jet, had been uneventful. He had been the sole passenger, and the flight crew had made no effort to communicate with him, which he appreciated, although they had probably been briefed by Casey not to engage him. As always when he flew, Akulov had managed to sleep. It was the only time when he knew his enemies on the ground could not touch him, unless that was, they knew his exact location and had the necessary anti-aircraft weaponry. He imagined he should be worried about his enemies in the air, which previously had included the CIA, however as the old saying went: 'the enemy of my enemy is my friend', and he was sure both he and the CIA had a least one or two mutual enemies. So, he'd managed to get a few hours' sleep as they crossed the Atlantic before debussing to the smaller Gulfstream G280 in New York.

Speaking to him for only the second time, the captain's tinny voice advised Akulov that they were now on final approach. Akulov straightened up his highly padded chair as he watched the patchwork of green fields flash below them before Winnipeg itself came into view.

* * *

With his newly stamped passport in the name of Ian Rowland, in his pocket and single suitcase in the boot, the black SUV had swiftly taken Akulov away from Winnipeg's James Armstrong Richardson International Airport. Like the flight crews of both CIA jets before, his driver didn't speak.

After nine minutes on the highway, rather than take the main route into the city the Tahoe turned north and took a much quieter road. Ten minutes later it pulled into the drive of a farmhouse. Akulov's door unlocked. It was his hint to get out.

Two vehicles were already parked there. One was a second black Tahoe and the third was a long, Lexus saloon. A man stood by the side of the Tahoe, watching. He was wearing the exact same outfit as Akulov: blue jeans, dark fleece jacket and a pair of hiking boots. Akulov alighted and was reassured that the other man, his doppelganger, was of a similar height and build. The man advanced and extended his hand. Akulov handed him his passport and wallet, which would be returned to him before he exited Canada. The man nodded and passing Akulov got into the black SUV, taking Akulov's place, and drove away.

Another man appeared in the doorway of the farmhouse. He made a beckoning gesture with his finger. Akulov frowned and advanced. Once he was within two metres of the man, he stopped.

'So, you're the legendary Wolf Six?' The man was slightly

older than Akulov, solid looking and his dark hair was worn in a short, neat style.

'Who are you?' Akulov asked.

'You can call me Hormann.'

'Like the garage doors?'

'Just like them, but without the umlaut. I'm taking you to the target's hotel. But first you've got to go inside and meet the Rabbit.'

'Rabbit?'

'It's an in-joke. Just step inside and go right to the back.'

Akulov nodded and entered the farmhouse. Inside it felt colder and damper than outside, as though the place was not lived in, as though it had been left empty, abandoned. His feet made a tapping sound on the wooden floor as he passed the first room. He peered in. It was empty. He then reached the kitchen which had no door, just a space where one possibly used to be. There was a wooden topped island in the middle, a couple of high-backed bar stools to the left, and past all this at the back, a Belfast style sink with a draining board. Outside, through the dirty windowpanes, above the sink, lay what looked like prairie. A man was leaning against the island. There was a suit carrier, with a pair of shoes placed on top of it, a package, an envelope and plate within his reach. The man was wearing a navy suit, a white shirt, a grey and blue striped tie, and a pair of mottled brown glasses. His hair was cut in a similar mid-length style to Akulov's, and he had a full, thick beard.

'You'll find your outfit in the bag, it's the same as I'm wearing now – they even got you a pair of matching shoes – in your size.'

'Thank you.'

'So, the legend they gave me, which you will now take

on, is Ray Hanson. In their wisdom the CIA chose the third most common surname in Denmark for us. You ever been?'

'Yes.' Akulov saw no reason to lie.

'You speak Danish?'

'No.'

'No loss. You're a third-generation immigrant. Your grandparents were from Odense. You're an American HR consultant, based out of Washington. You are here to look for new clients. Do you know anything about human resources?'

'Enough to bore anyone who asks me what I do.'

'Good, because they may – if you go to the bar, which I did not. So, you do not either. You understand?'

'I understand.'

The man picked up a carrot stick from the plate and munched on it whilst he nodded slowly. 'I, so that means we, have been at the hotel for two days. Going out for meetings, and ordering room service when in the room. My breakfast order, delivered at 7.30 a.m. each time by a different member of staff, has been eggs Benedict, coffee and an orange juice. Each morning I've tipped them twenty Canadian dollars – nothing flashy, but enough to seem normal. On the first evening I had a turkey club, and on the second a house cheeseburger. No alcohol, I just drank the complimentary water.'

'Still or sparkling?'

'I had sparkling with the turkey club; I thought I'd live a little.'

'Did you request a side order of carrot sticks?'

'No. I did not.' The man tapped an envelope which lay on the breakfast bar next to him. 'In there you'll find all your docs. There's a wallet, a passport, a hotel key card for room

406, and the burner phone I've been carrying and using for calls – all scripted.'

'And what's in the package?'

'Glasses and a pair of *postiches* – you know the word?' He took another carrot stick and chewed it.

Akulov didn't let his irritation with the man show. 'Postiche? Yes. It is the correct name for a piece of false hair worn on the head; it comes from the French.'

'Good. Anyway, there's two of them just in case. And of course, the stuff to stick it to your face. Good luck.'

'Thank you,' Akulov replied, although he didn't believe in luck, or chance, or for that matter, superstition.

The man pushed forward from the island, took another carrot stick and walked past Akulov towards the front door. Moments later Akulov heard the second Tahoe start up, its V8 rumbling, and then the crunch of tyres on gravel as it pulled away.

Akulov moved to the table. The plate, he now saw, was empty. Rabbit obviously didn't want to share his carrots. Akulov undressed and placed his clothes on the island top. Feeling the chill, he quickly put on the navy woollen suit, and white shirt. He did up the tie and then slipped on the ochre-coloured brogues. The leather felt soft, and the sole was solid, they were expensive. He now studied the passport. Its bearer looked like Rabbit. The photograph however was not that recent, he checked the date of the travel document. It had been issued a little over five years before, so the bearer looked a little younger. However the thick, brown beard and hair remained the same. Akulov flicked through the passport looking for any recent stamps. There was a stamp from six months before for Antigua & Barbuda and previously to that several for various European countries. Akulov put the well-used passport in his inside pocket and now turned his attention to the iPhone. There was no code to unlock the screen and the image on it was a landscape of a sun-drenched Caribbean bay, which he surmised was in Antigua. He tapped the photos icon and saw that there was a selection of shots from Europe and Antigua but the majority, he saw, were geotagged as being from Washington. There were images of Rabbit but none of them were selfies or close-ups, all had been taken by someone else. In short anyone studying the phone would be hard pressed to tell that Akulov and Rabbit were not one and the same, once he was wearing the prop glasses and of course had affixed the beard.

Akulov found the washroom next to the kitchen. He opened the package and found two, individually wrapped, postiches. The colour of the hair was a close match to his own. There was a kit with instructions on how to attach them. He'd worn beards and wigs before, so ignored these. He tore open a packet containing a wipe and cleaned his skin, then he opened a tube of adhesive and rubbed it on his face and neck where the beard was to be placed. He washed his hands before removing the beard from its vacuum wrapping and carefully tapping it in place on his face. He popped on the glasses and stared at himself in the mirror, then back at the passport. He didn't need the resemblance to fool immigration officials, it just had to be persuasive to hotel staff, and for that task he felt his disguise was up to the task.

Once he'd bundled his own clothes and boots into the suit carrier, Akulov left the farmhouse. Hormann was standing by the Lexus. He looked Akulov up and down before getting into the driving seat. Akulov tossed his suit carrier in first then got in the back.

Hormann edged away from the farmhouse, gravel crunching under the tyres. 'ETA twenty-five minutes.'

'Thank you,' Akulov replied and saw the guy's eyes study him in the rear-view mirror.

'You know those old tales, where a guy picks up a hitch-hiker, and they have a conversation only for the guy to turn round and find their passenger gone?'

Akulov didn't but said, 'Carry on.'

'So, the guy, usually, in fact mostly it's a guy in these stories, is travelling on his own. And it's at night, so it's dark, on a deserted road. He sees someone standing by the side of the road, offers them a lift and they chat a bit. He then either turns back to say something and they've vanished, or he drops them off and then looks back and they've vanished – the stories vary depending on who's telling them. So, he pulls over for gas at the next station he sees and gets chatting to the guy, usually a guy, behind the cash desk, and he tells him about his passenger. The guy asks him to describe the person, and he tells them about the long coat they were wearing and their pale skin, etc. Then the attendant explains that the person they picked up died, you know, actually died twenty, perhaps even forty years before. So, all this time he's been driving, and chatting to a phantom, he's shared their car with a ghost.'

'And?'

'That's what I feel like now, Wolf Six. I'm sharing my car with a ghost. I mean I think you're real, but news gets around, you know, about the contracts you've taken and your ability to disappear.'

'Are you concerned that I'll suddenly vanish?'

'Well, here's the thing, I know you will, and it will be right after this mission is done and dusted.'

'I see.' Akulov preferred it when the CIA officers he met didn't talk to him.

'Look, Akulov – can I call you that?'

'You just did.'

'Akulov, I've seen a lot of stuff, and let me tell you, there are an awful lot of perps out there who are above the law, untouchable because our legal system just can't get any evidence on them. So that's where people like you come in.'

'I'm not here by choice,' Akulov stated, flatly.

'Hey, are any of us? It's a calling.'

Thankfully for Akulov, the car fell into silence for the remainder of the journey and eight minutes later, Akulov entered the lobby of the hotel, his phone to his ear to part obscure his face. He headed directly for the lifts. Behind his glasses his eyes took in all those around him. A member of staff helped a newly checked-in couple with their luggage, pushing it on a trolley. Two receptionists tapped away at their desktop computers and three men in cheap-looking suits stood in conversation to his right. The hotel was by no means the grandest he had been in; however, it was the grandest in Winnipeg, and at four stars that was no hardship. He entered the lift and rode up to the fourth floor. A housekeeping trolley was opposite his room and a short, thin woman nodded at him from behind a pile of bedsheets. Akulov nodded back and entered room 406. It was a standard suite, with two rooms, one containing the bed with access to the bathroom and the other the lounge area. The walls were painted magnolia, the carpet was cream with a grey criss-cross print which he imagined was a nod to the original Cree population, but he wasn't an expert. All he needed the place for was one night's sleep and the use of it as a launch point for his assault on Fang the next day.

Akulov dropped his suit carrier on the settee in the lounge and checked his watch. He had less than eighteen hours until it was time to kill.

* * *

Akulov walked cross the hotel lobby ostensibly to use the bathroom but once in the blind spot of the CCTV camera covering the space, he carried on and pushed through the door leading to the stairs. Like many hotels, both the interior decorating and surveillance budget seemed to stop on the other side. There were no marble tiles here, and the stairs had to do with a thin, industrial grade carpet to cover their naked concrete exterior. The walls too were a bland beige. Of salient importance to Akulov however was the fact that there was only a security camera on each door to monitor anyone entering or exiting the stairwell. Akulov checked his watch. He had twenty-two minutes until the fire alarm went off when a minute charge would start a small electrical fire and burn through plugs and power cables in one of the hotel's suites at the opposite end of the hallway to Fang's accommodation. And that would be when Akulov would emerge from the stairwell on the same floor as Fang's suite.

As Akulov continued to climb he thought back on the preparation Casey's team had put into the operation. He knew there must have been some serious surveillance operation undertaken. He had no idea how far it had stretched back to have arrived at the decision to terminate the target on the soil of a friendly state, especially when Fang was a national of that very same state. This was the assassination of a high-profile Canadian, a man who had been photographed in business publications shaking hands with the prime minister, in Canada, by the CIA. And if the Agency's involvement was discovered Akulov imagined the Canadians, and the Chinese, would be outraged, and the wider international community would not be too happy either.

Why was the technology Fang had created so important to the United States, that they could not consider involving the Canadians? It had to be something significant to say the least. Then of course there was the question as to why Fang and his gang were in Winnipeg at all? The man called Toronto his home, it was where his head office was. What had brought him to Manitoba's capital city? The Canadian headquarters of a large US tech firm were immediately next to the hotel, could that be a reason? Akulov chastised himself. He was overthinking this. Did it matter to him at all why the CIA wanted him to liquidate the tech mogul? Akulov was obligated to complete the contract, Fang was the target, and that was that.

Akulov paused halfway between the nineteenth and twentieth floor. He stood statue still and listened for footsteps either from above or below. There was nothing apart from the distant rumble of traffic outside the hotel, and the hum of the lifts ascending and descending. He checked his watch; a black plastic Casio G-Shock. He had six minutes. He removed his long raincoat to reveal the black hoodie he was wearing beneath. It was part of the outfit he had found waiting for him in the hotel wardrobe. A large monochrome design was printed on the front in blood-red ink. It was a fierce looking dragon rearing up at its mirror image, or perhaps it was two dragons – Akulov hadn't worked out which. It was accompanied with Chinese characters, which he couldn't read, but had deciphered with an online AI tool.

It was a name which had meant nothing to him until he had looked it up using the hotel Wi-Fi via a VPN and a burner smartphone. It was pointedly the motto of a rival Triad.

Akulov pulled the burner phone he'd been given from his pocket and tapped the screen to wake it up, and then an app to watch the live feed from the mini surveillance camera in Fang's room. It confirmed that he and his four-man detail were all inside. Positioned in the corner immediately next to the rail for the blinds, the incredibly sleek design made the piece of tech look like a 'stopper', part of the rail system itself. It had a fish-eye lens and a minute microphone, but as the men conversed solely in Chinese when assembled, Akulov didn't understand a word.

Fang sat on a long settee in the three-bedroom suite, with his right arm draped along the edge. Behind him the camera picked up three of his team. Two were sitting on chairs watching the same screen as Fang himself, whilst another was leaning against the arching door frame sepa-rating the lounge area from the master bedroom. Akulov couldn't see what was on the hotel's television set, but what he could see was something in Fang's right hand. It was a little, red box. It was the item Akulov had been tasked to take. The last remaining man was wandering between the two rooms, he was cleaning something and occasionally making comments, which one of the other men was replying to. Akulov recognised what was in the man's hands. It was a 9mm pistol, although he couldn't make out the model. The window blinds were drawn in the master bedroom behind Fang and the seated men, which was good news for Akulov as it prevented the video feed from flaring and losing detail.

This mattered because both the hotel CCTV footage and that from the hidden camera which, when it miraculously found its way to the press, would further muddy the already murky waters of those investigating the hit in Winnipeg, as to who was watching Fang and why. It would implicate the rival Triad for the hit, because even though Fang's branch may reason it was a set up, they could not ignore such a blatant attack on one of their own.

Akulov removed his non-prescription glasses then using the reverse camera setting on his phone, checked his face. The prosthetic beard was still securely glued in place and looked natural. He studied the edges of it, wondering whose hair had been used for the piece, and if that person had ever contemplated the idea that it may, one day, be held fast to the face of an assassin.

Akulov pocketed the phone, noting the time on its screen as he did so. Two minutes to go.

From another pocket he brought out a cream ski mask. It had a pair of horns on top tipped with red and had a printed blood dripping design leaking from the eye holes. Again, it was making a statement, but not a fashion statement Akulov would ever want to wear again. He put it on.

Finally, Akulov drew his suppressed Glock 19 from a specially modified holster under his hoodie. It had a full magazine, fifteen rounds and one in the chamber. Akulov had a spare magazine in his back pocket and reasoned it was better to have it and not need it than to need it and not have it. However, if Wolf Six needed to expend more than sixteen rounds to take down five men, he reasoned it was probably time to retire or be retired.

Akulov now checked the cheap Casio G-shock; he had a minute left. He pulled up the hood of his black hoodie, placed his right hand, still holding the Glock inside the pouch pocket of the hoodie, and waited for the fire alarm to start wailing.

Akulov waited.

Akulov listened.

He could not hear a fire alarm.

He started to breathe deeply, beneath the woollen mask. Calming breaths to oxygenate his system.

Was there an issue? Had the incendiary device failed to go off or had it failed to be detected? Or was the hotel's fire alarm system so antiquated that it took longer for its sensors to register a fire. Casey had been so sure of the skills of his team in Canada that he said it would be impossible for the 'fire-starter' not to set off the alarms. And yet...

Akulov noted the time. A minute had passed. Was he just being impatient? He decided to wait for two more. When the alarm did not sound, he decided to take matters into his own hands. Backtracking down to the nineteenth floor he pushed open the door. Almost four minutes had elapsed from the agree time and still there was nothing. Akulov stepped out into the hallway, saw the fire alarm and set it off.

Less than three seconds later, the unmistakably teeth rattling claxon type siren assaulted his ears. The alarm was loud, not as loud as a gunshot, but critically far louder than the retort of his suppressed rounds would be. Akulov moved back into the stairwell, raced up the stairs to the twentieth floor. There were two sets of stairs, one at each end of the long hallway. The door opened and a single, suited man rushed past him, not noticing the way Akulov was dressed at all.

With no other choice, Akulov entered the hallway hood up and head down. It was less than a minute after the alarm had started, and the guest rooms began to disgorge those who had been inside. They were on phones, talking to each other, wondering if this was some type of unscheduled test, a false alarm, a prank, or the worst thing it could be, an actual fire in the hotel. One couple came out dragging a large hard-shell suitcase each and headed directly for the lift, mindlessly unaware that in the case of a fire the standard procedure was to turn off the power to all lifts.

Akulov turned left, and with the hood still hiding the knitted mask, which had started to overheat his head, he advanced towards Fang's quarters. The suite was three doors away from the stairwell, and Akulov was positioned directly in the way of anyone leaving that room or the others at that end. He knew that two of these were connecting rooms to Fang's, but he didn't know if the remaining two rooms were occupied or not.

Fang's door burst open.

Two of the security detail came out of the room, into Akulov's path. Although they were the muscle, they were shorter than Akulov, if wider by a large margin. Between their heads Akulov could see the hesitating Fang being pushed by the third team member inside the room, and further inside still, the man who had been methodically cleaning his gun was hastily reassembling it as he too attempted to exit, not an easy task and one that took his eyes off his environment and the threat that was Akulov.

Drawing his Glock, Akulov snapped off a quick double tap. Both suppressed rounds hitting the first bodyguard, one in the chest and one in the head. Akulov then shot the second dumbfounded man in the face. Both men were down, categorically dead. Only now did the other two bodyguards realise what was happening as the claxon from the fire alarm had masked the suppressed gunshots. The third man tried to pull Fang backwards, whilst at the same time placing his body in front of his principal as a shield. Akulov shot him, mechanically, once in the head and once in the chest. If the man, whom he presumed was a former soldier, wanted to be a bullet catcher, then who was he to deprive him of this opportunity.

Fang, now in full fear mode stumbled backwards into the suite and into the last remaining member of his team who had dropped his own sidearm and pulled out what appeared to be a throwing knife.

Behind him Akulov continued to feel the heavy footfall and hear the shouted questions of the guests exiting their rooms. Meanwhile, in front, his Glock found the last bodyguard. He fired at the same time as an object flashed past his face, ripping into the hood and pulling it down. Akulov entered the room as the final bodyguard slumped against a chair. Back turned, Fang was noisily scurrying towards the lounge area, on his hands and knees like a child pretending to be a horse. From studying the schematics of the room, Akulov knew there was a bathroom on one side and a balcony on the other. He couldn't let his target fall out of the window, nor could he let him lock himself in another room, which would take time he didn't have to break into.

Striding into the lounge, knowing that the concealed camera would now be picking up his mask and clothes, Akulov raised the Glock and shot Fang in the back. The tech tycoon was pushed prone, his arms splayed away from his torso as blood flowered across his light blue shirt. The man was twitching, not dead yet. Akulov saw the box clutched in Fang's right hand and ripped it away. Akulov thrust it deep into his tight, left jeans pocket. Back to the door, but face to the concealed camera he aimed the Glock at the back of the fallen man's head... when he sensed sudden movement from behind.

Turning, Akulov was shocked to see a heavyset, flaxen-faced man almost upon him wielding a fire extinguisher.

'Oh no you don't!' the man yelled and swung the red, heavy metal canister at Akulov's head.

Akulov twisted and reeled back to avoid the strike but was a millisecond too late, only managing to deflect some of its kinetic energy. The blunt object connected with his skull, on the rear left side of his head, with such force that it took him off his feet and hurled him on to the settee.

If he hadn't already been moving away from the extinguisher at the time it struck his skull, Akulov realised he would have been dead. But he wasn't. The edges of his vision had greyed out, he felt as though he was underwater, and he wanted to vomit. He lay on his back, on the settee, right arm and Glock trapped underneath, looking up at the ceiling. The large man, who Akulov now saw had a regulation-length haircut, loomed over him. His hands were empty, and his left grabbed at Akulov's throat, whilst the right, in the shape of a fist, slammed into the side of Akulov's face. Akulov couldn't feel the impact of the fist, in fact he couldn't feel anything at all, and that was when he knew he was dangerously close to losing his battle with consciousness.

In his diminishing circle of vision, Akulov noted that the right hand had changed shape, no longer a fist but a claw. The claw pulled roughly at Akulov's ski mask, so roughly in fact that it grabbed a handful of beard at the same time. Both mask and prosthetic beard were ripped off in their entirety, exposing Akulov's stubbly, glue-smeared face.

'What the hell?'

The man's grip on his neck lessened as he momentarily studied the masks and beard. Akulov realised this was his only chance. He'd landed on his right side, and his sidearm was still in his hand but just under his right leg. Akulov twisted to the left and managing to free his arm fired a round at contact distance into the big man's abdomen. The man's mouth opened in a silent scream, and he dropped to the ground.

Akulov rolled off the settee and fell on top of him.

And then he heard it, over the cacophony of claxon noise. The anguished screamed words of a child.

'Daddy... NOOO!'

Akulov looked up. A blonde-haired girl was in the doorway looking at the pair of them with eyes as wide as moons, and she was shaking. Getting to his hands and knees, and then to his haunches, Akulov stumbled out of the room and past the grief-stricken girl.

He made it to the stairs without seeing anyone else and then grabbing hold of the railings moved as steadily as he could downwards. Each step brought pain, as his head felt as though it was being hit by hammers in time to the beating of his heart. One flight down, two, he lost track, and it became a blur, but he couldn't stop because if he did he believed he would die.

It was only when he caught up with an elderly couple, he realised he was almost at the bottom. He travelled down with them; they were at the end of the line of evacuating guests and had let faster folks go ahead of them. He followed them through the ground-floor doors and saw he could either head for the lobby or a fire door to his left. He chose the fire door and joined the large huddle of people outside.

Glock now hidden in his waistband, Akulov stumbled

along the pavement and away from the rest of the herd. Rounding a corner, he thrust his hands out against the wall to support himself and vomited. He staggered onwards, the dizziness increasing and his vision still tunnel-like. Tyres screeched and looking to his right he saw a car had pulled up. A man quickly got out and grabbed him under the arms. Akulov tried to protest but didn't have the strength to, and there was something familiar about the man's face. It was Hormann.

Akulov let himself be bundled into the car as Hormann said in his ear, 'Do you have the device?'

'Yes,' Akulov rasped.

Moments later the large sedan moved off. As Akulov lay on his back on the leather seats. Drifting into unconsciousness, he heard Hormann say, 'I'm coming in hot. I've got the asset, and he's injured.'

5

SEVEN YEARS AGO

Amsterdam, The Netherlands

The capital city of The Netherlands was never quiet, especially in and around its centre. In addition to its local residents, it drew a constant, swarming hoard of tourists who had travelled for the culture and the architecture, to visit its canals, museums and the royal palace; or those who came for the clubs, pubs, legal prostitutes and drugs because of the city's world-renowned liberalism. Many visitors arrived in Amsterdam for a bit of both, and that was another reason why, according to his intelligence briefing pack, Akulov's targets wanted a slice of the business cake.

Back home in Romania, the Dinescu family had been amongst the 'investors' who'd had a hand in redeveloping Bucharest's Floreasca district. It was a way to wash their dirty cash, in an attempt to legitimise their activities. The irony that Floreasca itself was built on a former landfill site, was not lost on Akulov.

As arranged by Tishina, the hotel on Kerkstraat was immediately opposite the club which their client knew the younger Dinescu at least part owned. Akulov would have preferred to use a higher floor to perform his function as overwatch for Basson on his approach to target when he planted the IED and then exfiltrated. However, due to the narrow width of the street, if he had been on the top floor of the thirty-room hotel, to have had any view at all of the street below, let alone the ability to snipe at any survivors or other threats, would have meant him hanging – at least in part – out of the window. So, he was reassured to find the room he had been given was on the second floor. He was high enough not to be noticed by those passing at street level, and low enough to engage any targets.

Although working as a two-man team, Akulov and Basson had mutually agreed, there would be no further contact between them either before arriving in Amsterdam or after the hit had taken place. They would be in contact during the operation via WhatsApp on a pair of burner iPhones only. Both assassins were seasoned, professional operators, and responsible for the supply of their own equipment. Akulov did not know, and did not want to know where Basson had been before he appeared on the street below, or where he had procured the explosives and the bicycle. Such was the level of Tishina's vetting process, and the reputation of The Bang-Bang Man, that Akulov knew Basson would not be making amateur mistakes.

Standing a pace back from the window, he peered down the scope of his rifle, his finger away from the trigger as he imagined and planned any shots he might take. The range was too short to warrant a long-barrelled weapon, so he had chosen instead a far easier to conceal HK 416 A5-11. The rifle, without its screw-on suppressor, was a fraction under seventy-one centimetres, which meant he could conceal it in his backpack. At this distance he knew he could dispatch anyone he needed to without using his scope. But he wouldn't, he was not a cowboy. Any shots he did take had to be measured, there could be no collateral damage, no innocent passers-by killed. His shots were to ensure that if not already dead from the blast, targets did not safely leave after the detonation. The client had been extremely specific. The dual principal targets, and any member of their entourage, were not permitted to survive.

Putting the rifle to one side he looked out again at the narrow street. Although there was no canal on this lane, one row over, both behind and in front, there was water, and at either end further away lay wider waterways. In short, to exfiltrate he would need to cross any number of bridges or jump on a boat. Swimming wasn't a hygienic option.

Although Amsterdam was never quiet, at this time of the day at least it wasn't shouting. The washed-out early morning light painted the city like a watercolour, its pleasing architecture further rendered softer, dreamlike. Around him he imagined the other hotel guests to be still sleeping, after long days of sightseeing or partying, unaware of the daylight caressing their windows and of the world awakening.

Akulov felt uneasy. Although he had undertaken similar operations with The Werewolves, these had been in war zones, either official or otherwise, and the civilian population had tended to keep well clear. But this was an undeclared war by his client on the Dinescu family. In taking out the heads of both factions the organisation would implode.

In essence it was a straightforward contract, but Akulov knew that nothing was ever so.

A random thought entered his head, the contract called for the death of George and Dragoş Dinescu. This made a thin smile form at his lips; he was targeting George and the Dragon at the same time, like an omnipotent being taking out both combatants in their fight to the death. However, he didn't believe in dragons, and he knew the meaning of the name Dragoş was 'beloved', which did not seem at all appropriate in this instance. Akulov wondered why he was allowing himself to be so fanciful, perhaps it was Amsterdam, or perhaps the cannabis smoke from the cafés on the street below had penetrated the room and permeated his brain? He liked Amsterdam, but knew that after today he wasn't going to return to the city for a while.

Akulov had arrived mid-afternoon the day before and checked in using an Irish passport in the name of Sean Lerman. Dressed in battered jeans, sneakers and a thick fleece jacket, Akulov had been just another backpacker bumming around Europe. The twentysomething on reception had recognised Akulov's Irish accent and immediately told him where he should go to get the best pint of Guinness. This was information Akulov thanked him for, even if he was not going to use it. His room was clean, and the linen was crisp. The hotel had a two-star rating, yet it was not some vinyl-floored motel with grubby sheets, a lumpy mattress and squeaky bed springs. In fact, it had served him too well so far.

Akulov checked his watch, it was a quarter before eight. The club at the target address didn't open till the afternoon, neither did the steak, Mexican and pizza restaurants further along, so there was minimal risk of unintentional injuries there. The cafés were starting to open, one was next door to the club, and another was its neighbour across the street. Luckily neither had any outside seating. Akulov hoped Basson knew what he was doing and that the blast from the IED would be both directional and directed precisely at the entrance to the target building.

As he watched on, he saw a pair of women arrive on bicycles. Both were young, blonde and wearing baggy jeans, with knitted multi-coloured jackets. One had dreadlocks and the other had long hair tied back to reveal the sides of her head were shaven. Their look, whilst not an official uniform, was a uniform of sorts. Chatting, they dismounted and chained their simple, black bicycles to the metal pole which supported the parking restrictions sign, directly outside the entrance to the club. Without looking back, they walked towards the café next to Akulov's hotel. He lost sight of them a moment later.

Akulov looked to his right, to the junction of the street where it dissected the much busier, and commercial Leidsestraat. Here the brand-named clothes shops and larger independent and novelty emporiums would not open until 9 or 10 a.m. The older of the two principal targets, George Dinescu had arranged the meeting with his cousin for 9 a.m., and Akulov just hoped this timing had mitigated the risk for collateral damage.

Akulov moved his focus away from the street for a moment and grabbed a bottle of Pepsi from the wooden topped table. As he unscrewed the cap, and took a long swig, the burner iPhone in his pocket started to vibrate. He swallowed quickly, the bubbles irritating his throat. Akulov was wearing an earpiece in his right ear but checked the screen nonetheless before he answered. A name was displayed, one he had given Basson, 'MBB'.

Akulov pressed the accept button on his earpiece. The burner iPhone was running encryption software, as was Basson's at the other end, and the line would remain open until after the IED had been set off remotely by Basson. Their conversations, whilst not fully untraceable, were at least safeguarded from all but the most skilled forensic audio technicians. And Akulov doubted the Dutch authorities had anyone of that calibre listening live to the local cell tower traffic, but just to confuse them even more the pair were using an agreed code. It was dull and sounded like everyday conversation.

'Are you at "home"?' Basson asked. Home being the designated name of his overwatch position.

'Yes,' Akulov replied, then confirmed he had the target building under surveillance. 'I can see your "house". When will you be there?'

'I will be at my "house" in a minute.'

'Understood.' Akulov put down the bottle and shouldered his HK. He waited and watched the building. Forty seconds later a man riding a bicycle appeared from the eastern side of the street which housed the target address. He wore black jeans and a blue puffa jacket. Slowly Basson drew to a halt on the cobbles and bumped the bicycle up over the low curb.

'I can see you,' Akulov said, again using regular language instead of military terms.

'Yes, I'm at my house, just locking up my bike,' Basson replied as Akulov watched him slowly, and steadily padlock it next to the two other bikes, left by the women in the café.

Basson removed his helmet, and carrying this in his left hand, wandered towards Leidsestraat.

'I'm getting a "coffee", shall I get you one?'

'No thank you,' Akulov replied. Coffee was the code name of a café on the corner of Leidsestraat which, whilst providing a visual of the entrance to the club, was far enough away that it was well out of any potential blast range of any secondary shrapnel.

More cyclists started to arrive on the street. Most used the previously empty bike stands but one, a man with a bushy, hipster-style beard and jeans that looked as if they had been spray-painted to his legs, tried to place his bike next to Basson's. Akulov felt his concern grow, the hipster attempted to make his chain reach. It didn't so he gave up and used the bike stand a few feet away. Akulov watched him once more pass Basson's bike, and its hidden IED and enter the coffee shop next door to the target building.

Basson's voice in Akulov's ear sounded. 'I think I can see "our friends" arriving.'

Akulov looked to his right. The one-way system meant that the targets' vehicles would have to pass Basson's position to arrive at the target building. He hoped it was the older cousin, and he also hoped he had to wait for Dragoş to open the front door. 'Yes, I think you are right. And they are early.'

A silver Mercedes G-Wagon came to a halt on the street directly outside the target building, in the no-parking bay. A dominating figure, wearing dark jeans and a leather jacket, exited the front passenger side and started to look around. He was meant to be conducting a threat assessment, but he was doing so too quickly, almost cursory, as though the action had become routine, devoid of meaning. Down his scope Akulov made out the man's face. His low brow beneath a head of short, jet-black hair, was furrowed and his eyes narrowed as though scowling, or giving the impression of power. It gave Akulov neither. A second bodyguard emerged. He could have been the twin of the first. Heavy-footed, the second man moved around the 4x4 before he opened the door nearest to the curb. Part obscured by the silver body of the Mercedes, Akulov saw one of his two targets – George Dinescu – emerge. George had run the family business since the death of his father. He was dressed in a suit, which was tight around his torso, as though it was a size too small, possibly because its wearer had put on weight or perhaps, which Akulov deemed more likely, it was worn over a bulky ballistic vest. If he was wearing a vest, it was a wise move, in Akulov's opinion. Most gunshot wounds were to the body, the centre mass. It was only those who were highly skilled or shooting at extreme close quarters who inflicted head shots. Akulov allowed his index finger to rest on the trigger now, not taking any pressure yet but ready to do so in a millisecond.

George looked up and down the street then at his watch. He spoke to one of his men, who made to open the front door to the club but found it locked. George and his entourage were left kicking their heels on the street. George wore an expression of annoyance, whilst his minders looked uneasy, continuously shifting their weight and swivelling their heads. What none of them did, however, was to look up at Akulov, who perched two floors above could take all four out in under ten seconds. But that wasn't what the contract demanded.

'Here comes our other friend,' Basson said.

Another vehicle drew up. It was also a G-Wagon, yet

unlike the first it was not standard. The grey, carbon fibre bulbous body kit attached to its panels and its matte, burnt-orange custom paintwork, stated in Akulov's opinion that its owner obviously wanted to, or needed to be seen, or was a clown.

'Yes. Our other friend has arrived,' Akulov confirmed.

Two large men in black tracksuits, with the telltale white Adidas stripes running down the side, exited the second wagon. Turning their heads slowly, they at least seemed to be more observant than their counterpart from the silver Mercedes. And then Dragoş exited the 4x4. He too wore a tracksuit, it was designer. Akulov noted it was Gucci.

On the pavement now, and directly outside the entrance of the building the two groups of men edged towards each other, like the entourage of two opposing boxers just before a fight. The two bodyguards from each vehicle and their principals. Six men standing and staring at each other, whilst the drivers remained behind their respective wheels. Akulov's briefing pack had informed him that anyone travelling with either of the two cousins was expendable. But of course, six men was far too large a number for a lone hitter to liquidate at the same time. Akulov was a highly skilled sniper, he had been the best sniper in his small, clandestine unit, yet even he realised that even on full automatic, he could guarantee picking off no more than three or four of the six before the rest evaded his scope, and he gave away his position. Then of course there were the two still in the car.

Basson, however, was at street level and comfortably sitting in a café. Akulov imagined that he too was armed with a handgun and could, if needed, also engage the remaining targets. Yet this would draw attention to him, and that was not the modus operandi of The Bang-Bang Man.

'Are we ready?' Basson said, casually.

'Wait. Someone else is coming. In another car.'

'Our friends must have invited them,' Basson replied, without a trace of tension.

Akulov's eyes scanned the new vehicle, a large Mercedes saloon, as it slewed to a stop behind the orange G-Wagon. Akulov eyed the new arrivals and knew that Basson too would be assessing them. Four men alighted. They had dark features, like the Romanians, and were dressed in casual clothes, jeans, and a mixture of bomber and leather jackets. They formally greeted Dragoş before hesitantly exchanging handshakes with George. Did this now make twelve targets in total?

'Looks like more of the family have arrived,' Basson said.

'I agree,' Akulov replied, although none of these men were mentioned in their briefing pack.

'So,' Basson said.

'Too many guests,' Akulov stated. The odds of eliminating all twelve in the initial blast was not good.

'I disagree.'

Akulov blinked, he wasn't used to his professional assessment being questioned.

'Let's open the doors.' To hell, Basson didn't need to add.

Akulov heard a noise, laughter. And now entering the edge of the killing zone he saw the two blonde women who had previously parked their bicycles. One was holding up both arms and shouting happily down the street to Akulov's left, to a group of people on bikes heading their way. It seemed to Akulov like it was some type of bicycle tour group. 'No,' Akulov stated, then switched to military language for clarity and brevity, 'Abort. Abort. Do not proceed.'

Basson sighed. 'You have lost your nerve? We have all twelve.'

The tour group was getting nearer, some were now drawing up next to the target building and dismounting, whilst the two blonde women from the café pointed back at, presumably, the inside of the café. The twelve targets were still standing outside the club, George Dinescu being introduced to the new arrivals in turn by Dragoş Dinescu. 'Abort. We have collateral! I say again, abort!'

'And I say no.'

'ABORT!'

As though he wasn't controlling his own body, Akulov saw his HK move until it was sighted directly upon the head of the Dinescu Family, George Dinescu, and then he felt his finger squeeze the trigger. The suppressed round rocketed from the rifle and all but instantaneously impacted with the skull of the Romanian gangster.

Before the target's body had hit the ground, Basson's voice again sounded in Akulov's ear. 'Execute.'

Akulov spun away from the window, thrusting his back against the wall. Anger and disbelief surged through him as a second later a twin booming explosion sounded. Confined to the narrow street, the dual shock wave rode the walls of the buildings, rising and smashing windows as it did so. Akulov popped back into view and took in the scene below. He now understood Basson had used two explosives, one in each of the saddlebags, in sixty-degree, fan patterns. The direction of the first had shot towards the club's entrance, whilst the second had raced in the direction of the three parked vehicles and anything standing on either side. Eviscerated by innumerable white-hot ball bearings or violently hurled to the ground by the concussive force of the two detonations, Akulov could see no one alive on the street below. Car alarms set off by the rebounding shock wave were wailing, and then the first victims joined in.

Akulov had been at the immediate aftermath of far too many explosions, yet none of them made him feel the way he had now. Bile rose from his stomach, and he battled the urge to vomit. It wasn't the broken bodies and blood that distressed him, it was the knowledge that some of that blood, and a number of those bodies, had been innocent bystanders, and he had been complicit in their deaths. He blinked away the rage, as the dust and smoke rose from below, and squinted down his scope, searching for targets. He saw a figure holding its left forearm and staring at where the hand used to be, stumbling towards the parked cars. Before Akulov could take a shot the man fell flat on his face. Akulov continued to scan, none of the targets were moving. To the left a man had entered his line of sight, he was dressed in a lime green jacket and was shaking a body, laying on the ground, wearing a matching jacket.

'I hear no further shots. Did I get them all?' Basson asked, his voice sounding a little laboured.

Akulov swung his rifle to the right, he saw Basson watching from the end of the street, his black jeans and blue puffa jacket unmistakable.

Akulov moved his mouth, yet no words would come.

Basson started to approach the scene of his own atrocity. 'That was an idiotic thing to do, *mon brave*. Tell me, did I get them all?'

Without thinking, without making any conscious decision, Akulov pulled the trigger on the suppressed HK416. The first round was a little wide and Akulov saw it impact the cobbles. It was unseen by Basson, so Akulov fired again.

A millisecond later the Frenchman jerked to the ground as a small cloud of red mist appeared by his left thigh. In the confusion caused by the aftermath of the bombing, the two suppressed shots had not been heard. Basson lay on his back, unable to move. Akulov watched on, ready to fire again, but his shot was blocked by a pair of men who dragged Basson back inside the nearest coffee shop.

Akulov jerked away from the window. He removed the suppressor and pushed it and his rifle into his open backpack, quickly closed it tight and exited his room. The stairs were busy with guests, some who had just woken up, others who were fully dressed, heading downwards. Akulov arrived at the ground floor. Every pane of glass in the foyer windows had shattered, and the wooden frames were buckled or broken. Akulov crunched towards the open front door and, following the streaming hotel guests, burst out onto the street. Blood, glass, wood, metal and body parts littered the ground. Groups of people sat bewildered; their faces bloodied and blackened. Others cried, whilst others screamed. Akulov pushed his way through the carnage, hoping that anyone remembering him would assume he was traumatised. He could see the bodies of the Dinescu family littering the ground, and smell the scent of burnt flesh and blood.

The sounds of distant sirens reached his ears as he arrived at the strike mark where his first shot at Basson had landed. There was a trail of blood leading into the nearby coffee shop. Akulov followed it inside. The place was busy, the waiting staff frantically giving out water to anyone who needed it. All those seated looked shocked, most were on mobile phones, and several seemed injured. Akulov had been right. This should never have been an explosives job, and Basson had used far too much of it. He ignored the hubbub around him and searched for the Frenchman's blood. There was a trail leading past the counter towards the customer toilets. Pushing through, his backpack making his progress difficult, Akulov saw blood leading to both the toilet door and to a rear exit. He pushed open the door to discover a small walled garden with a back gate which was swinging open. He advanced through the gate and into a twitten that ran between the backs of the rows of buildings. On instinct he turned right and followed it until it dead-ended against the back wall of a large, white-painted town house. Akulov cursed and retraced his steps, this time turning left at the gate. Ahead was another dead end but immediately on his right the alley continued. He followed it and found himself emerging onto another street; this one faced a canal.

The iPhone in his pocket was still there, and it started to vibrate. He hadn't noticed the call had been disconnected, and he had forgotten that his earpiece was still in place.

'Yes?'

The voice that spoke was laboured, raspy. 'Wolf Six, you are a dead man, do you hear me?'

'And you are a terrorist,' Akulov replied, looking around to reacquire the trail.

There was a cackle down the line. 'Why do you care... about those people back there? Did you know any of them? Of course... you did not. What were they... to you? To me they were... nothing worth jeopardising my contract... for. The Bang-Bang Man never fails a contract.'

Akulov didn't reply, his eyes were still searching for any sign of Basson. To his left, by the bridge, a crowd had gathered at the intersection, and there were police officers. To his right further on, he saw several vessels moving away from him on the canal. He squinted and recognised a man wearing a blue puffa jacket. He was slumped back against the gunwale.

'I will find you, and I will kill you.' Akulov's words were whispered, yet resolute.

6

'MAYDAY... MAYDAY... MAYDAY... Alpena Tower! I repeat, MAYDAY... MAYDAY... MAYDAY... Alpena Tower!'

'I've got nothing! Nothing is responding!'

'MAYDAY... MAYDAY... MAYDAY... Any Tower! I repeat MAYDAY... MAYDAY... MAYDAY... Any Tower!'

Akulov imagined he could hear the panicked voices of the pilots repeating over and over in his ears as, gasping for air, he broke the surface. Akulov felt a sudden sense of elation, his body relaxed, and he started to drift, his eyes became heavier and heavier, and the voices of the men faded. Blinking, he fought the urge to let himself float away, he knew it was both his existing head injury and the temperature of the water which had made him vulnerable.

Was he alone? Akulov twisted around looking for anyone else, the two pilots and Hormann, the only other souls onboard, but in the choppy waters he saw no one and nothing bobbing among the waves. He'd seen Hormann sinking, thrashing below him but he'd been unable to get to him. He'd let the CIA officer drown, the man who had saved him in Canada.

Akulov had to move; he had to reach the shore whilst he was still conscious and whilst he could still move. The pain in his head had lessened, he thanked the low temperature of the water for that but not for the pain in his hands at each stroke he took. To his right, which he understood must be the north, he could see black clouds in the greying evening sky, and flashes of lightning. A storm was approaching, Akulov imagined it must be the same one Hormann said they'd skirted earlier, and if he was still out on the surface of the lake when it arrived, he knew he wouldn't make it ashore. In the gloom directly ahead, he could see the outline of trees and a beach. Distance in water was hard to estimate. On land he had reference points, but floating in a large lake he didn't. Was he a mile from the shore, more, less? Akulov had no choice but to continue. He was the Machine, the soldier who had never given up and then as Wolf Six he was the assassin who never died. But there was always a first time for everything.

Akulov kept his strokes rhythmic, as he continued onwards. He'd lost track of time; it could have been half an hour, or it could have been less, and it was probably far less, he reasoned, but either way it was full dark when he dragged his battered body up the gritty shoreline. Out of the water he started to shake as the cold night air nipped at him through his wet clothes. He felt heavy, and his head throbbed. He vomited lake water onto the sand. On his hands and knees, he continued meter by meter away from the dark waters. Around him the only sounds to reach his ears were the lapping of waves against the sand and the rustling of the trees in the wind. He rolled painfully onto his back, collapsing into the damp sand, staring at the dark expanse of lake stretching away from him. The storm had drawn much nearer, raindrops were landing on his face. Looking directly at the moon he saw scudding clouds being pushed south by their darker, stormier brethren. The strength of the wind was increasing, as was the rain which was now noticeably heavier as it splashed against his already wet face. Questions ran through Akulov's muddled mind. What had happened, where was he, and was he the only survivor? He looked back at the lake. If there was anything that gave away the fact it had been the site of a plane crash, he couldn't see it. Once the storm had passed, loose debris would bob to the surface and wash ashore, but in the deep water, it would be difficult to believe what lay beneath: the wreckage of a CIA chartered Gulfstream and the remains, more than likely, of its two-man crew, and Hormann.

But was he the sole survivor? He had seen the cockpit end of the plane sinking below him, and he hadn't even thought to chase it to help, but it had been impossibly far away from him, hadn't it?

There was nothing he could have done for the other men, but what he could do for himself was get away from the crash site. In his mind it hadn't been an accident, because that would have been a coincidence happening immediately after he had completed his mission, his CIA sanctioned hit on a foreign national on the soil of a friendly state. The crash must have been man-made, must have been intentional. Akulov's head felt heavier than ever, he felt a malaise, a dizziness, a lack of focus. Yet, through his concussion a coherent thought entered his mind. Until the jet was found and a full search undertaken, he was missing, presumed dead.

Shaking, Akulov attempted to struggle to his feet, but he was too unsteady and now his neck and back were screaming at him just as much as his head. Whiplash, he imagined, to accompany his concussion. He tried pushing up from his hands and knees to his haunches, but a second wave of nausea surged up from his belly. It folded him over, dropping him, making him retch again. Collapsing onto his side he then found himself once more gazing at the ceiling of stars. Akulov had to move but at that moment the sand felt so soft and welcoming, like the most luxurious bed in a boutique hotel, and the cold rain was like a gentle massage. Akulov's eyes were closing and this time he was powerless to resist.

* * *

Akulov was shaking uncontrollably. Where was he? And then it all came back to him. The mission, the plane, the crash. An animal called out, some type of predator. It could have been a coyote or perhaps even a…

Wolf Six sat up; his eyes open.

The night was still, he could see the storm in the distance, had it missed this side of the lake, or had he just been on its very periphery? Akulov took deep breaths to control his convulsions. He was thirsty. The water of the lake shimmered in front of him, beckoning him forward, inviting him to quench his thirst, yet he knew better than to do this. It may have been a freshwater lake but only natural springs at their source or high-altitude arctic lakes were clean to drink and even these could be tainted by the run off from the land around them. Gingerly he moved forward at a crouch and used the lake water to splash his face and brush back his hair. Akulov blinked away the icy droplets and tried to assess his situation. He needed rest, in a real bed. He'd passed out twice now and had no idea if he would again. He had to find somewhere to lay up, at least until dawn, until he was able to move again. Only then would he leave the immediate area, work out what the hell had happened, and get some medical attention.

Akulov rose to his full height, immediately feeling dizzy. He took several deep breaths, and the pain in his head returned, as did that in his back and neck. It forced him to bend forward like an old man but at least he was able to walk. He trudged away from the shoreline.

Akulov felt as though his mind was drifting in and out of clarity, as he struggled with several muddled trains of thought at once. He and his flight were overdue, and that meant an alarm would have already been raised at Langley, well, within Casey's division at least. But would anyone be sent out to search for him? He was a deniable asset who had been strong-armed into conducting a hit on a dual Chinese-Canadian national. For all Casey knew, Akulov himself could have caused the Gulfstream to crash and used what basic flying skills he'd had to make good his escape. But to what end?

Had it been an accident, or had the plane been targeted and attacked, and if so, how? The mission was over, Fang was dead and his little red box... Akulov realised he'd had it in his pocket when he'd collapsed outside the hotel but now it wasn't there. Hormann must have taken it. In that case it had gone down with the plane. But would the CIA accept this truth? An icy realisation washed over Akulov. Could he have been set up? What was it Vince Casey had said, back in Cologne, when the CIA officer had stated they were using a private jet, *'we need the speed, and we need the control.'*

Or could the CIA be thinking right now, at this very moment in time, that he, Wolf Six, had decided to take the box to sell it on to the highest bidder, or worse hand it over to Russia? Yes, there were those who still believed that once a member of the Russian war machine always a member, but he was Ukrainian, and he had turned his back on the country who had claimed control over him. Or perhaps they thought he'd taken it for leverage? Perhaps to force an agreement that his debt to the CIA had been paid back?

What then of the pilot, co-pilot and Hormann, who may or may not be dead, whose bodies may or may not be trapped in the submerged fuselage on the lake-bed? Surely the Agency would come out looking for them? Then again, they were part of a clandestine operation, be they just chauffeurs or flying taxi drivers. No, Akulov decided, he was on his own, until he could reach civilisation at least.

And then it struck Akulov that he was isolated, with nothing but the damp, dirty clothes he was standing in. Not understanding why he'd failed to check for it before, Akulov reached into his jeans pocket and pulled out a battered, nylon wallet. He opened it up and whilst the cash was still partially wet, at least it was there. $1,000 in varying denominations. Enough to get him out of a scrape, and not enough to create any suspicion. The wallet was empty apart from this. It, like him, had been sanitised before the mission. There was no ID or bank cards or anything that could identify who he was or where he had come from. Even the clothes he wore, with the exception of the Triad hoodie, which he now realised Hormann had hastily attempted to conceal under the Harrington jacket, were generic brands worn both sides of the border. In short, if his body had washed up on the shore, and unless the submerged plane was found, there was nothing to link him to the CIA.

Above him the stars were bright. By looking at the constellations he had a rough idea of where he was, a very rough idea. He knew heading south he'd hit a town sooner or later. He cursed his concussion, damned the man who'd caused it, and swore at his missing Casio. Akulov knew it was easy for him to blend in and blend away into nonexistence in the US, yet first he had to get to one of his emergency caches, and the nearest he estimated was over a state away to the south.

The light from the large moon reflected off the surface of the lake, throwing the trees beyond the shores into stark contrast. Akulov knew he should be moving covertly through them but without any NVG equipment this would be an arduous if not dangerous task. He paused every fifty yards or so and cocked his ears listening for anyone, or anything that was watching him, tracking him, but he was seemingly alone in the wilderness. Seemingly that was because a throaty growl reached his ears, not a natural noise but the mechanical vibrations of a V8 engine, and then it was joined by another. Two vehicles approaching the lake. Abruptly, a hundred metres or so ahead, headlights burst through the brush, illuminating an access road and a jetty which until that moment, Akulov had been unable to see.

The outlines of the vehicles were identical and unmistakable, pickup trucks, the type favoured by those who needed power and something rugged enough to handle the rough terrain. Akulov slunk into the foliage and edged forward, a tree at a time, assessing if the newcomers were a potential threat.

The sound system of one of the trucks was playing what seemed to his untrained ears like a Taylor Swift song. Illuminated by both the moonlight and their own headlights, he watched the vehicles empty. From their size and gait he identified both drivers as male. An additional bulky figure clambered out of each truck, one turned to look back at the woods, as though sensing they were being watched. At that moment the face was illuminated by the headlights, Akulov saw it was a woman. And something inside him said she was dangerous. Four people, two trucks, in the middle of the night. It looked like a meeting of sorts. He observed further, nearer now and hidden in the shadows as Taylor Swift informed the world that she 'cried like a baby' on its way home from a bar, which Akulov thought was an odd comparison to make.

A plastic crate was taken from the bed of the second truck and placed on the ground. The group of four seemed to be chatting jovially, as they drank from the distributed bottles. Under the cover of the noise and shadows caused by the lights, Akulov moved even closer. He noted the nearest vehicle, the lead truck, had a flag on its rear quarter panel, artistically painted as though it was fluttering in the breeze. He couldn't make out whose flag it was.

And then the music abruptly stopped. Two of the party visible to Akulov, illuminated clearly in the headlights, seemed to be facing off against each other. The larger of the two figures was a man, and the second who was just marginally smaller was the woman. Akulov still could not make out any specific words but recognised the venomous tone. A seemingly exuberant gathering by the lake had turned into something far more sinister, and then it happened, something Akulov had not expected, something which changed his entire world view of what he was witnessing.

The man threw out both arms as though attempting to explain something. The woman mimicked his gesture. Abruptly the man dropped his beer bottle then lurched at the woman, with a clubbing, swinging right fist. The woman, taken by surprise, made no move to defend herself and the punch hit her squarely on the jaw. She staggered backwards and fell onto her backside. The other two made no move to protect her, or to halt her advancing attacker. Incredulously, Akulov watched as the woman lashed out with her leg, hitting the man in his shin. He grunted and took a step back, and then she rose to her feet. Slowly and unsteadily, her left hand holding her jaw, her right bent and gripping a dark object. Akulov immediately recognised it for what it was. Without issuing any warning or saying another word, the woman shot the man who had struck her at point-blank range, two shots in quick succession, their dual retorts bouncing off the trees and racing across the water. One in the chest and one in the head. A double tap. An instant kill. The same as he would have done, and the trademark sign of a professional shooter.

The remaining two onlookers didn't react, there were no shocked screams, nor did either back away. The woman took a step forward and spat on the dead man.

Akulov had witnessed death. He had been the creator of a lot of it. He had been the executioner of choice for a myriad of clients, yet the execution he had just been made witness to struck him as highly brutal. Had the victim been lured to the lake to be slain, had the killing been pre-planned or had it been a moment of hot blood, of madness?

And of equal importance why did the others not seem to care?

Leaving the dead man where he had fallen, the woman and the remaining two men clambered back into their trucks, after both men copied her by spitting on the corpse. The music switched back on, pop again but this time a tune Akulov didn't recognise. The pair of trucks rolled off, retracing their route away from the lake. Akulov was both mesmerised and repulsed.

An eerie silence had returned to the lakeside, as Akulov stood, shivering and swaying on unsteady legs at the murder scene. Moonlight illuminated the corpse's features. What was left of the face after the round had exploded into it seemed to have an expression of shock to it, but Akulov knew this was just his mind's interpretation of the facial muscles. It was a myth that muscles retained their memory after death. The man was wearing a padded trucker's type jacket, undone over a thick plaid shirt. Dropping to his knees, and grimacing at the pain shooting up his back, to his neck and now into his head, Akulov manoeuvred the corpse out of the jacket and put it on. It was at least a size too large, but he was glad for both the inherited warmth from the slowly cooling body and the fact the jacket had been open, so the round fired to the chest had not damaged the front at least. He then checked the body for anything else that may be of use, hoping for a cell phone but finding only a wallet. Inside was three hundred dollars, and a Michigan driving licence. It was in the name of Warren Johnson, he'd been thirty-eight. Akulov replaced the licence, took the cash – dead men don't have bills – then buttoned up the jacket and stood. He wondered how many other bodies were perhaps feeding the local wildlife, above and below the water. He turned away from the corpse. He didn't know these people; it wasn't his fight. He had to go.

He followed the track used by the trucks away from the water's edge and into the trees. As he walked, he was acutely aware of his body battling the fatigue and trauma of the events of the past twenty-four hours. Yet he knew it was nothing compared to his relentless, arduous training in the bleak, frozen Russian steppe all those years before. Akulov allowed a smile to form about his lips as again he remembered the time he had been given the nickname 'Machine' by his fellow conscripts because he was the only one of them who had not been broken by the countless miles of marching and running. Yet, as the throbbing in his head reminded him, that had not been done with a concussion nor after surviving a plane crash. He continued. Although the path was much easier to navigate, he stumbled and had to grab hold of a tree branch for support. He paused, inhaled deeply then took another step.

Akulov's mind started to drift back to those training days. After serving less than a year of his stipulated national service, he and just eleven others across the country's entire yearly conscript intake, had been selected to receive advanced specialist training to eventually form the highly classified, deniable unit known as 'The Werewolves'. He may have been given the name Machine by the men around him, but the Kremlin had given him the identity of Wolf Six, and that was a nom de guerre he still used to this day. It was a name which caused fear and awe in equal measure. His near celebrity status within the underworld was based on his results which were due to his abilities. And those abilities had been noted and nurtured by his broker, Valentina Tishina, all those years before when she had been in the

GRU. Then what of Tishina? As yet she would have no reason to contact him, to fear for if not his safety, then at least his status. He'd get to an internet connection, and then he'd get to her, and then he'd decide what to do about the CIA.

Akulov stumbled again, but this time could not break his fall and landed jarringly on the stony track. He lay face down, his brain yelling at him to get up but his body unable to comply. He sensed the air seem to get darker around him, the edges of his vision greying out and then without fully realising what was happening Akulov lost consciousness.

Sleep had always come easily to Basson, regardless of where he was or what he had been engaged in. However, tonight had been different. In the small hours, images from his past had flashed before his still shut eyes. Was he asleep, awake or in some type of state in between? He had invited the memories, playing like a fuzzy home video from the 1990s, a time when he had been in his prime, a time when he had been in the French Foreign Legion and deployed to global flashpoints. It was a highlight reel, and he saw faces his conscious mind had long forgotten, fallen friends greeting him. It had reassured him, and he had then fallen back into a deep sleep until one specific memory resurfaced, and it was the most vivid of all – Sarajevo...

The blood trickled into his eyes from the cut on his forehead, and the sound of incoming Serb shells screeched in his ears. From his observation point, Basson could see the heavy artillery guns of the Army of Republika Srpska firing from the hills above Sarajevo. They were shelling the neighbouring suburb of Dobrinja again, a place where only civilians lived.

'And to think this is what we signed up for when we joined the legion?' The baritone voice of Legionnaire Desange said, at his side. 'To be peacekeepers who are not allowed to fight for peace. Look at us, Martin, we are cowered here in this observation post whilst out there women and children, and the elderly, are being blown apart. And all for what?'

'For power,' Basson replied. 'That is all it is ever about, power.'

'What power? What is the point in taking this place?' the African Legionnaire replied.

'The Serbs want it because it is here, because it is the capital of a country which they can't allow to exist. So, they attack, they lie – saying they will not, and then they attack again. There is nothing we can do, unless we take a side and become combatants ourselves.'

'Which is what we should. Yet that will not happen. We are here, forced to wear these sky-blue helmets and not our kepi blanc, because yes, we are soldiers but we are ordered to just be observers for the UN.'

'Are you saying, my friend, we should be here as NATO?'

'Of course, would that not stop the bloodshed?'

'It would give us a chance to shed blood,' Basson stated.

'How is your head?'

'It stings, that is all, who was to know concrete could splinter like that?' Basson wiped away the blood from the bottom of the field dressing.

A larger boom sounded as a shell landed just past the perimeter fence and made the small concrete room vibrate. 'Putain! This is enough to drive a man mad!'

'But, Martin, are we not already mad?'

Basson glanced at his fellow Legionnaire. 'But of course we are, is that not why we are here?'

Desange started to cackle, and Basson could not help but join in.

Another shell landed, this one nearer to the men of The United Nations Protection Force. The impact and explosion kicked up a wave of dust. Basson felt his eyes become drawn to it, as the wave became thicker, approaching their position. He shouted to Desange, 'Are you seeing this?'

Desange did not reply. Turning his head Basson found his friend laying slumped over his binoculars. It made no sense. If the man from the Ivory Coast had been caught by the compression wave, then why hadn't he? Why was he still breathing? Frantically, Basson checked him for any entry wound or visible signs of injury. There were none. He started to shake his friend, whose eyes suddenly snapped open.

Desange had raised his right arm and was pointing out at the runway. 'Death... death...'

Basson swivelled his head and then felt a chill travel up his back. Open mouthed he saw what looked like a swirling tornado of dust and debris approaching their position. It was changing shape as it rotated, like a living being, and he could see objects writhing within it, their outlines blurred and undefined. Eyes not comprehending what he was seeing, he tried to turn his head yet found he was unable to move, that he was paralysed. A shape started to form within the dust, it was a man, it held a rifle, yet it did not have the head of a man, its eyes were a glowing red, and its teeth were bared... and then without warning there was a blinding flash and he felt something hit his skull and then a huge weight crushing every inch of his body. Basson tried to scream, yet no sound came...

The warble was loud, it was rhythmic, and it was insistent. Basson opened his eyes and had no idea where he was, then as the lined, plastered ceiling of the hotel room came into focus, he remembered. He threw out his right hand and grabbed the telephone. 'Oui?'

The voice was soft, formal, the language English yet the accent was the almost Scandinavian lilt of an Estonian. 'Mr Durand, this is your 6 a.m. wake-up call.'

Simon Durand was the name Basson had used to check in to the hotel, and the same one he would use to fly out of Estonia. 'Thank you.'

Pushing the phone back into its cradle, he brought his hands up to his head and rubbed his face. He'd had the dream again. The same one that used to haunt his nights for years, the one that he used to drink away. The one that had finally been banished, not by booze but by a therapist. The professional he had seen had used hypnosis upon him telling him it was, ironically, all in his mind, and that those with strong minds could overcome such things. Basson had bristled at the notion that he perhaps did not possess as strong a mind as others, so had there and then forbid his subconscious from ever dredging up the memory of that day in Sarajevo when he and his friend had almost died.

In fact, Basson had started to study the mind and learnt to channel his near-death experience, the fear of being blown up into the joy of being the one who initiates the explosions. Back in France, he added to his existing military understanding of munitions by learning all he could about them. He grew to be an explosives expert, eventually becoming the Legionnaire his superiors sent for when an explosive option was required or when an IED needed to be disarmed.

Yet Basson became tired of bomb disposal, even though he was expert enough to do so safely, and save lives. In simple terms there was no fun in any of it, and certainly no financial profit to be had. He wanted to be solely on the other side of it all, devising ways in which he could make objects, targets, and people explode. A decision had to be made. He remembered the adage about men joining the legion 'to forget'. He had simply joined because he wanted to be the best. Now he believed he was. He accepted he had a blood lust, and craved the carnage that war brought with it. Yet, was it not natural for young men full of testosterone, trained to kill, to actually want to do so? He had not joined the French army merely to wander around a parade ground with shiny boots, or whitewash rocks littering the paths leading to the officers' mess, although on Corsica there had been a lot of both. He had served fifteen years in the Rep, in three consecutive contracts, and the time to sign on for another term was almost upon him. Basson chose to walk away. Some thought it was because of age, others who'd asked him were told he wanted to try something else, but what no one knew was that war had fundamentally altered Martin Basson. The day he walked out of the gates and away from the base was the day he stopped being a soldier and became a contract killer. It was the day The Bang-Bang Man was born.

And he'd never had the nightmare since.

Until now.

Basson closed his eyes again and tried to remember the dream. Something was different about it, what exactly he didn't know. Sarajevo, Butmir Airport, the terminal building, the runway, and the Serb guns in the hills. It was vivid, it didn't feel like thirty something years ago. But the swirling cloud of dust, that had never happened, not like that. Basson attempted to remember what he had seen inside the dust. It came to him, gradually appearing in front of his eyes like condensation on a bathroom mirror. The man held a rifle, his head was not of a man, the red eyes, and the bared teeth... it was a werewolf.

Basson angrily threw back his covers and swung his legs off the bed. Pushing himself to his feet he felt his back and his knees complain, as they always did whenever he ventured anywhere away from the heat of the Middle East, but today these annoyances were joined by a pain in his thigh, a niggle which had left him long ago too. The place where the bullet fired by Wolf Six had punched straight through his leg years before. Why too had this returned? He reasoned it could not be physical it had to be psychological, but his mind, and his will, were both too strong to countenance phantom injuries. Weren't they?

No. The only pain he should be feeling now was in his head from unwisely pouring too much dark, local beer down his throat the night before. He stomped across the room to the window. From his high floor he had a view across Tallinn to the sea beyond. The Hotel Viru, had been Estonia's first high-rise building. It had become famous during Soviet times because its nightclub had stayed opened to 1 a.m., which was a whole hour later than clubs in Moscow or anywhere else in the entire Soviet Union. Viru was the Russian word for 'Believe', and as Basson looked out of the window at the city below, he still believed he would be the man to kill Wolf Six.

Basson headed towards the bathroom, but something made him pause and collect his burner smartphone from the bedside table. It was a cheap brand, bought locally. He'd kept it turned off with its battery removed so that he could neither be tracked nor listened to. He popped the battery back in and turned it on as he entered the bathroom and switched on the shower. An electronic tone informed him he had a message; he peered at the screen – expecting it to be from the service provider. He was wrong. It was from the sole person he had given the number to, his broker, The Irishman. It was a three-word message:

Check email. Urgent.

Basson sat on the edge of the bed as he logged in to his encrypted email account and checked the draft folder. There was a message, he read it hoping for information about Akulov's whereabouts. It wasn't; however, his disappointment was part mitigated by the fact it was the offer of another contract. A fastball hit on a banker. Due to the fact it was a fastball, the client had been persuaded to pay double. Basson deleted the message, left his own in the draft folder stating his acceptance and once more powered down the handset. He glanced at the wall clock. If he was quick, he could get a flight out within the next three hours and make the hit the next day. Feeling the rush of adrenalin that came with the thought of planning, designing and using an explosive device, Basson stepped into the warm shower.

* * *

Unknown location

Akulov was at his grandmother's dacha, an hour's drive outside of Moscow by car but longer by the bus they took. The summerhouse smelled of a mixture of wood and home cooking. There was always fresh bread to be had, his grandmother was known especially for her baking and here in the countryside she made pies

with the plums and cherries grown in the garden, which to
Akulov as a child had been a magical orchard. He was still in his
warm bed, and he could hear her in the kitchen talking to herself
as she prepared his breakfast. Since his parents had died her love
was all that he had known, she was all the family he had. As he
had grown older the memories and loss of his parents had faded,
until he realised he could no longer remember their faces, or their
voices. Yet he was never sad, or lonely – his grandmother saw to
this, and it was only when he became an adult, he realised the
entirety of the superhuman effort she had made. And now he was
back with her, in his bed, at the dacha, whilst she made him his
favourite breakfast. He felt loved, he felt comforted, yet something
was wrong, something did not make sense. It wasn't summer, it
was late autumn, a time when she had always shut up the little
wooden cottage ahead of the harsh winter snows. So why was he
here with her now? And whose voice was that? Was she speaking
to someone, or was she listening to the radio as she cooked? No, it
was definitely a conversation... but wait, was that even her voice?
Akulov's mind was trying to grasp at something which was not
quite there, ethereal, like smoke... like a phantom... like a ghost.

A ghost.

And then a realisation hit him. He wasn't with his grandmother, at least not yet...

Akulov opened his eyes.

The ceiling above him was covered with yellowing
cracked plaster. There was a combination light and ceiling
fan, neither of which were on. Sunlight was streaming in
under the edge of a roller blind to his left and on his right,
through an open door he saw a bathroom. Akulov was
laying on a single bed. He pulled himself up on his elbows,
the bed frame creaked, and his head started to pound as
daggers of pain travelled from his temples around his head

and shot down his spine. Akulov squeezed his eyes shut and when he opened them there was a man standing in the doorway staring at him.

'He lives.'

'I do,' Akulov replied, voice croaky yet using his neutral Washington accent.

'I put your clothes in the washer, you can take anything you like from the dresser. Greg was about your size, his stuff should fit. Shower is through there, and you need one. Food is ready whenever you are.'

'Thank you...'

'Needham, the name's Jake Needham. And you are?'

'Adam, Adam Hurst,' Akulov replied pulling a name from a list of possible future alias's he had memorised. 'Where am I?'

'Black River.'

That made matters no clearer for Akulov. He asked, 'What happened?'

'You can't remember?'

'No.' Akulov could not remember anything after collapsing.

'I found you out by the lake. Hell, everything here is by the lake. Wash, dress and we'll talk.' Needham nodded and shut the door as he left the room.

Gingerly, Akulov pulled off the bed covers and swung his legs out and onto the floor. The pain in his back was less as he stood, but he felt dizzy and grabbed at the metal bedhead for support as his vision momentarily blurred. Regaining his composure, Akulov moved to the window and raised the blind. Squinting he peered into the watery autumnal sunlight. Outside the view was of a parking lot, twelve spaces, ten empty with the other two taken up by a pair of vehicles. One was a newish looking silver Chevy Silverado and the other a smaller, older tan-coloured Bronco. To the left Akulov could make out a row of log cabins snaking back into a wooded area. So where was he, some type of camp? And more importantly who was he with? He fought the impulse to grab some clothes and bolt, but that was not the action of a normal person, and that was what he had to pretend to be as Adam Hurst, after all. Akulov checked the door to the room, there was a key on his side in the lock. He turned it and the bolt slid into place. The bathroom was small, looked like it hadn't been remodelled since the 1960s but was functional and smelled of bleach. Akulov assessed himself in the mirror. Under his stubble, his cheeks were hollow, and his eyes looked as though they had sunk into his skull, this along with his matted hair made him look like a 'hobo', or as his grandmother would have said, a *'Bomzje'*. Using the mirror he gave himself a visual check-up. He was bruised, across his chest and legs, and had some scratches, but nothing that needed any medical attention. He took several long, slow deep breaths and was satisfied that the pain he felt in his torso was muscular, not the crackling, stabbing of broken ribs or a pierced lung.

Akulov tried to remember the details of the crash, the pressure on his body as the plane plummeted, but most of all the shuddering impact of the water. He'd tweaked his neck, but couldn't remember exactly when or how. Tentatively Akulov prodded his head, remembering the fire extinguisher blindsiding him. He felt a lump at the rear and to the left. He gently rubbed both hands over the area. He felt pain, but he couldn't feel any abrasion to the skin, and certainly no movement of the skull which would indicate a fracture. So, it was highly likely he was concussed, however an MRI or CT scan would be needed for one hundred per cent accuracy. His head hurt and his balance was off, so as far as he was concerned, he had a concussion. And the best treatment for that was rest, which he hadn't got time for.

Removing his underwear, Akulov stepped into the shower cubicle and closed the door. The water pressure was good and after letting it heat up; he started to wash himself with the half-used bottle of Head & Shoulders shampoo already sitting in the tray. It was minty, and made his head tingle. There was no shower gel. He steadied himself with his left hand against the white tiles as he let the warm water rinse off the lather. The throbbing in his head started to subside a little but the heat of the water made him feel nauseous. He dry-retched and knew it was time to get out and get dressed.

He dried himself with a towel, which mimicked the bathroom in being old yet adequate, before he padded to the dresser. There were six drawers, and he went through them all collecting a pair of jeans and socks – he drew the line at wearing second-hand underwear – a white T-shirt, and a thick, black and red checked shirt. As he retrieved his still damp boots from the floor, he caught a glimpse of himself and realised he looked like a lumberjack. But he was OK. Akulov sat on the bed for a moment as a bout of dizziness hit him. He inhaled and exhaled deeply until it went, then unlocked the door to the room he had been given and exited.

He found himself in a corridor, one way led to a door, which he presumed was the rear exit of the building, and the other took him to something he did not expect, a commercial kitchen. Strip lights illuminated the stainless-steel surfaces and the scent of cooking, which he now realised had permeated his sleep, grew stronger. Akulov took another step and understood what the place was. It was a diner. He could see the dining hall itself through the serving hatch. There was a conversation. He saw the rear of Needham's head, the man's silvery hair neatly brushed back and held in place by some kind of product, gel or wax – he wasn't an expert. Placing his left hand against the wall, Akulov steadied himself as he listened to what was being said. It wasn't interesting, and he wasn't mentioned. After a minute or so Akulov decided to join the two men, but at that moment the second man bid Needham farewell and left through a door which, like an old-fashioned store, made a bell tinkle.

'Thank you for the clothes,' Akulov said by way of an entrance.

Needham turned to observe Akulov as he entered the dining hall. 'Now you just take a seat. One of the booths is probably best.'

All the booths were in the window, and this would mean he was on display to anyone who passed by the diner, but it also meant that tactically he'd have advanced warning of anyone approaching. Akulov sat in the booth furthest away from the door, with a wall against his back and a window on his left.

'How are you feeling?'

'Fine,' Akulov automatically replied.

'Apart from your concussion?' Needham said as he lowered himself into the seat opposite.

'How did you know?'

'I've seen it before, I used to be a military medic many moons ago. When I found you, up by the lake, you were slurring your words and wobbling like a drunk, yet I couldn't smell an ounce of booze on you. And then of course once I got you in the truck, I realised you'd been for a swim.'

'I had,' Akulov said.

'So do you mind telling me, Adam, what the hell happened to you?'

'I really appreciate your hospitality…'

'Jake, Jake Needham.'

'Yes, sorry, I forgot.'

'Concussion.'

'I really appreciate your hospitality Jake, but I need to be going. Can I use your telephone?'

'Can you remember the number you need to dial?'

'Yes.'

'No.'

'No?'

'No, I'm afraid you cannot use my phone because of the storm. The line is down on the landline, and the cell tower must have taken a bash too. No reception in the area at all.'

'I see.'

'Look, you can have whatever you like – on the house, and then once the lunchtime rush is over, I'd be happy to drive you up into town to use a pay phone or to get you checked out by Doc Flowers.'

'Flowers?'

'Yep, and would you believe it he's married to a woman named "Rose".'

"Rose Flowers?"

"Yep, he used to joke he'd name his daughter Petal."

"And did he?"

"No. Oh, I almost forgot." Needham reached into his pocket and produced Akulov's wallet. "Here's your billfold and cash back. They've been in the dryer. I suppose that makes me a money launderer!"

'It does. Thanks.' Akulov's head was throbbing, and he was finding it hard to concentrate.

Needham persisted with the conversation. 'How'd you end up with a head injury, wandering around the lakeside after the largest storm this place has seen in living memory?'

Needham had been helpful thus far, and although his mind was not where it should be, his threat radar had not pinged. The best cover was always a version of the truth, yet in this case even a truth with curated omissions would be unbelievable. 'My boat sank in the lake.'

Akulov saw Needham's eyebrows rise above the frame of his glasses. 'You sank your boat?'

'It was just a small sailboat,' Akulov lied. 'I was a fool to go out in the storm.'

'You certainly were. Where were you heading?'

'I was out getting photos of the storm.'

'One of them, huh?'

'Yes. It's a hobby, and if I can get a unique shot, I sell it.'

'Like to *National Geographic*?'

'Like that, but overseas mainly, Europeans seem to like anything that disrupts this side of the pond.'

This brought a smile to Needham's face. 'They sure do. In a former life, after the army, I became a lawyer, nothing sexy, corporate stuff, but international, so I got to travel all over. And as soon as I opened my mouth anywhere in Europe... well, the looks I got. They hate us. I genuinely believe the Europeans hate us.'

Akulov didn't agree but had struck a nerve which made the older man talk about himself, and whilst Needham was talking about himself, he wasn't trying to pick apart Akulov's cover story.

'Now you need to eat, rehydrate and rest. But first, painkillers. I've got generic ibuprofen and generic paracetamol – I'm not paying extra to big-pharma for the privilege of buying something with a name made up by a committee of admen.'

'Never on an empty stomach my grandmother used to say.'

'True, very true.' Needham got to his feet. 'Right, let me bring you some pancakes, with syrup and bacon and one of my special bottomless coffees, and your painkillers.'

'Thank you.'

'You need to stop thanking me, Adam. It's what we do up here, we take care of people.'

8

FIVE YEARS AGO

Marseilles, France

As the home of the French Foreign Legion, Basson felt relaxed in Marseilles. As the second largest city by population, the French capital of Paris being the first, it was also easy to lose himself in. As a young soldier he had romanticised ideas of finding a local woman and settling down in a little place with land in the surrounding countryside. Now as a man in his late middle-age, he could think of nothing worse. Comfort made people grow fat, and familiarity made the soul shrivel. In his opinion, as soon as one started loving another, one lost the love of oneself. Through his bronze-tinted Ray-Bans he could see it all around him at the old port. Men younger than him walked either hunched over or with stomachs spilling over the top of their waistbands, and the one thing they all had in common was that they were either with a woman, or walking with children or dragging a pet. He wondered from time to time if he was the only person who had it all figured out. You lived, and you died.

What was important was that you enjoyed what you did in between, yet many of the men he saw looked sullen. He did not consider himself to be a misogynist, he liked women, he simply refused to subscribe to the notion that he should spend his life with one. Like all males of the species, he had his needs, and he knew where to go to satisfy these, what he didn't need was to hold hands afterwards and discuss the colour of soft furnishings. His mind flicked back to a memory of his father losing his temper with his mother over the colour of their new curtains. He had been simply satisfied that the damn things kept the neighbours prying eyes out of their affairs and did not in any way hold an opinion as to the best shade for them. This had been one of the only times he had agreed with his father, having always seen his mother's point of view, and deep down for a long time Basson had thought that perhaps it was he, who in however minute a manner, had triggered his father to leave them.

Basson continued to walk. Although it was out of season the place was busy with tourists, and a surprising number of them were American. Basson, however, was not in Marseilles as a tourist, he was here on business to meet one of his suppliers, a former Legionnaire like him, who had gone into business for himself. Basson paused and looked at the yachts pulling at their moorings in the gentle breeze. He raised a burner iPhone in front of his face and slowly started to take a panoramic photograph of the port and the boats, and also of course the people around him. Whilst the panoramic image distorted faces of those who moved, it would also show him if anyone was paying him any undue attention. It was far from foolproof as a counter-surveillance tool, but he lost nothing in using it and there was always the chance that he may take anyone watching him by surprise.

Satisfied, as much as he could be, he started to walk again along the Quai du Port until it became the Quai de Neuve Rive, this time at a meandering pace, the type favoured by the elderly or the unfit, and not a pace he could ever countenance in the real world. He paused outside a restaurant. It was named The Queen Victoria and was an established eatery selling British pub food. He was hungry but could not bring himself to eat any imported tourist fare, he'd have something after his meeting. He passed several more international restaurants, a museum and a theatre before he increased his pace and crossed the street. Glancing back, he could see no one following him, which either meant no one was or that they were professionals. He carried on at his increased pace, uphill, thankful for the opportunity to stretch his legs after several days without the ability to undertake his daily swim.

On reaching the Sofitel Hotel, he entered the lobby directly behind an Asian family of four who had just alighted from a large Citroën saloon. As he had no luggage, just his brown leather courier style bag slung across his chest, and had not arrived by car, the staff paid him less attention than the family heading to the reception desk, whose designer luggage was being placed on a wheeled trolley. Basson removed his sunglasses and took a seat on a long, low-slung, caramel-coloured suede sofa, in the low-ceilinged, white-walled, lounge area, and observed the scene. The father was nodding at the receptionist, the mother was smiling. Meanwhile their offspring – one boy and one girl – who seemed to be in their late teens, but already towering over their parents, leant limply against the counter, like sticks of celery, their eyes solely on their smartphones.

Basson remained where he was for another ten minutes, watching those who entered, crossed, sat in and exited the hotel lobby. From his sofa, which was too soft for his liking, he could see the road sloping upwards, the one he had taken earlier to the entrance of the hotel. There was no cover for an operative to lurk and watch. Anyone wishing to keep tabs on him would have had to either use this same path or use one of the side entrances to the hotel, but either way Basson would see them entering the foyer. He retrieved his burner smartphone and tapped a curt, confirmation message to a number he had memorised and then sent it. Less than a minute later he received a reply. It was an address. He checked the location, ensuring he knew where it was, and abruptly stood.

He strode towards the lifts, passing a rubbish bin he subtly dropped the smartphone inside. If anyone had managed to track him, they would still believe he was in the hotel. Rather than take the lifts he took a door which led to a side exit and was back outside the building.

Eight minutes later, and after taking several turns, again to flush out any followers, Basson arrived at the address. The apartment was on the top floor of an ornate, sandstone, five-storey building immediately opposite Plage des Catalans and next to a small, whitewashed, private hotel. The communal door to the building was wood – stained a dark red colour – and next to this was a standard intercom panel. Basson pressed the correct button for the penthouse and moments later the door lock buzzed open. Inside there was no lift, and this was no hardship for Basson who took the stairs up without issue. On reaching the top floor he saw the door was already open and his contact was standing in it, arms crossed.

'Come inside, old pal.' The man was wearing cream-coloured cargo trousers, a baggy, white cotton shirt, and his accent was Scottish.

'Merci, *mon brave*,' Basson replied.

The interior of the apartment was so bright, Basson was tempted to keep his Ray-Bans on, but took them off, nevertheless. He knew nothing about interior design but could tell that the place had undergone a recent renovation, which whilst impressive, was incongruous with the character of the building.

'Can I get you a drink, Martin?'

'Just water for me, I am working.'

'Really, and here's me thinking this was a social visit.' The Scotsman pointed to a white marble-topped table, on which there were four glass bottles of Evian. 'I heard Tishina dropped you?'

'Yes, she did.' Basson unslung his courier bag and placed it on the white, tiled floor, next to the table.

'How so?'

Basson let out a long sigh in an attempt to control the anger he still felt towards his former broker. 'Someone tried to prevent me from completing a contract and then attempted to kill me.'

'Do you know who?'

'Yes.'

'Who?'

Basson selected a bottle, twisted it open and took a long sip. He smacked his lips and said, 'Wolf Six.'

'He's a ghost. He attacked you?'

'He claimed the contract was his. He told Tishina it was either him or me.'

'She chose him?'

'Oui.'

'Fils de pute!'

'You never did master the accent,' Basson replied, as he moved to the window. 'This view looks expensive.'

'Ei, it was. It's like having my own private beach.'

'Do you have what I ordered?'

The Scotsman shook his head. 'Martin, of course I have it, what do you take me for?'

'A Glaswegian thug?'

Slowly a smile started to split his contact's craggy features. 'You know me too well, pal. Take a seat.'

Basson nodded and sat on the large, white settee which hugged the wall. He sipped his mineral water as the Scotsman left the room. Seumas Gallacher had already been a five-year veteran of the Rep when Basson had joined. Now in his sixties the hard drinking, hard fighting Glaswegian looked to be at peace. His bunk and his belongings had always been the cleanest and neatest amongst their regiment, and even during deployment dirt gave him a wide berth. Over the years they had known each other, his close-cropped hair had gradually gained more salt than pepper until the present when it was as though the deeply tanned Scotsman had been dipped headfirst into a tub of flour.

Eyes darting around, Basson surveyed the space. It was clean, it was clinical, it was white. There was a complete lack of anything to hint at the owner's age or character, but Basson guessed if a woman lived here there would be several statement items to introduce colour, probably cushions of some sort. And curtains.

Gallacher returned holding a leather pilot's case in his hand. He handed it to Basson then sat in a white armchair, which was placed at ninety degrees to the settee. 'Everything you asked for, and another option, is in there. Take what you want and leave what you don't.'

'I will.' Basson opened the case and rummaged inside. He pulled out a shoebox-sized hard-shell, black rubberised case. It had a manufacturers logo imprinted on it. Clicking it open he revealed a Sig Sauer P365X, a micro-compact 9mm handgun. He placed this on the marble table in front of him. Next, he took out a similar sized box and opened it too. This contained another sub-compact handgun; this one was a Mossberg MC2c.

Gallacher said, 'That's me giving you an option. In terms of performance both are similar. I personally prefer the Sig as it's easier to conceal, but the Mossi is better for those with larger hands, and obviously the extra rounds over the Sig may come in useful.'

Basson said, 'If I have to use fourteen rounds, I need to go back to firearms school. I'll stick with the Sig.'

'Good choice.'

Next Basson removed two smaller but longer boxes, suppressors for each of the handguns. Finally, Basson clasped his hand on what was to him the most important part of his order. 'Now this is what I wanted.' This time the box was larger and had steel clips keeping it shut. He flipped up the clips to reveal a pair of hand grenades. They were identical and dark green in colour with a hint of bronze. Basson had often thought it was a better choice, rather than Racing Green, for a sports car.

'I couldn't get the HG85, so that's the one used by the British, the L109.'

'The only difference is the safety clip on the L109,' Basson said as he lifted out the grenade on the right. He noticed Gallacher momentarily tense, and rightly so.

'Ei, it's a little beauty.'

Basson rolled the abrasive, textured, spherical, bulblike body in his hand, it was designed in such a way that it was easy to hold and would not slip from a sweaty palm. Yellow markings on the side stated the manufacturing details, the letters 'SM', an abbreviation of 'Swiss Munitions'. It always struck Basson as odd that a peaceful country such as Switzerland, famed for its chocolates and mountains, was also notable for its Swiss Army knife, but far less so for the munitions it produced.

'*D'accord*. Merci as always, *mon ami*.'

Akulov had attempted to go for a walk outside the diner. On unsteady legs he'd navigated the exterior wall, past the windows facing the road and then turned on the path leading to the cabins. He'd eschewed the stolen jacket, which was hanging on a peg on the back of the door and was letting the chilly air reinvigorate him. It was working and his head was starting to feel a little clearer, but he knew he was in no fit state to head out on his own. He peered in the window of the first cabin and saw a bed and armchair draped in plastic sheeting. He walked to the next cabin and this one he noted was full of boxes, and several large plastic drums. He imagined it was storage or supplies but whatever it was there seemed to be a lot of it. He leant against the wall as his head started to spin. Taking several deep breaths, Akulov knew he had to get back to his room and rest.

However once back in the room Needham had lent him, he found he couldn't sleep even though he knew his body needed rest to repair the injury to his brain, which he hoped amounted to nothing more than bruising. If there was any bleeding, well that was a different matter, and one he couldn't let himself worry about now. He'd found some reading material in a drawer amongst the clothes belonging to the previous occupant, a tourist map and a brochure. His head throbbed as he studied the map which he used to confirm his exact location on the shores of Lake Huron. The old brochure was for the diner and attached wilderness campsite, which as far as he could work out consisted of the eight log cabins in the land curling back from the parking lot. The leaflet was at least twenty-five years out of date, and it listed fax and telephone reservations numbers. There was no website, nor anything related to the digital age. It struck Akulov that his was the last pre-digital generation, and even he had found it odd that Needham had no internet access, yet he was aware there was a growing percentage of the population who had eschewed the digital to disconnect and return to analogue. And this appealed to him. It was a way, perhaps, for him to finally escape the cycle of contract killings which had hounded him for the past two decades. He lay on the narrow bed staring at the ceiling, his eyes tracing the cracks in the plaster, his mind attempting to rationalise the random lines and shapes into recognisable images. He was tired but didn't want to sleep; was injured but couldn't rest here. He got up and left the room.

Needham's breakfast rush didn't happen, but what did happen was three customers arriving mid-morning. Akulov remained in his booth, in the corner, nursing a bottomless coffee, and not wanting to return to his room. It was a tactical advantage for him to see who was approaching before they arrived, and he had seen the trio of late middle-aged men arrive from half a mile away. They were clearly regulars known to Needham, and apologised for being so darn late. The road had been blocked by a fallen tree and a power line, and how was Needham's power? Needham explained that his was fine, he had his generator anyway, but his phones were out. The others said theirs were too, but they'd be damned if they were going to miss a Needham breakfast.

Akulov observed the three friends as they chatted, he was witnessing something he knew he would never have. These men seemed to have known each other for a long time, and reminisced about this and that, explaining to Needham – who they called a newcomer – where they needed to for the story. Akulov had lost contact with his school friends, the Russian children he had been at school with, and he had lost contact with all but one of The Were-wolves. And he very much doubted that he and his mountainous friend, Bato Dorzhiev aka The Beast, would be sitting in the European equivalent of a diner, sharing break-fast, when they were in their seventies.

Presently the three men left, and Needham came back over with a piece of apple pie. 'You know there's nothing as American as a piece of apple pie.'

Akulov accepted the plate. He wasn't going to be pedantic and tell Needham that in fact the first written record for a recipe for apple pie was published in the late thirteen hundreds in England. 'Thank you.'

Needham sat opposite him in the booth. 'You don't look much like a pie eater to me, I mean a guy who's in the shape you are in.'

Akulov finished his mouthful and said, 'I have a gym membership.'

'So, what do you do when not sinking boats? Do you work on the water?'

'No.' Akulov slowly shook his head and wished he hadn't. 'Human Resources.'

Needham repeated the response as though the words were in a foreign language. 'Human Resources? You mean personnel?'

'Exactly.' Akulov pushed more pie onto his fork. He'd use the same cover story as the one given to him by the CIA. 'It's boring but every company needs an HR department, or someone to run their HR function for them, and that's where I come in.'

'So, you're a consultant?'

'Correct. I consult. I tell my clients what they need, and on occasion do the work for them in the interim until together we can hire the right people.'

'Well, I don't need an HR department.'

'No, I suppose you don't.' Akulov allowed himself to smile. 'This is the best pie I've tasted since I was a kid. My grandmother used to bake. My favourite was her cherry pie.'

'Now a good cherry pie is a work of art. You know who taught me to bake?'

'Your grandmother?'

'My grandfather. My grandmother was great at cakes, but at pies, well it was always Pops. They've both been dead fifty years or more now, but they live on in my kitchen, and on your plate.'

Akulov heard a sound outside, the burble of an engine, a guttural, heavy sound. He looked up from the plate to see a pickup turning off the road. 'More regulars?'

'They regularly come here, yes,' Needham replied, his voice sounding tight.

Akulov watched as a weathered, red Ford F150 stopped in the car park and swayed on its springs as four bulky men clambered out. Something about them looked familiar. Akulov sipped his coffee as they drew nearer.

'Excuse me,' Needham said, standing. He headed to the counter and stood behind it by the cash register.

The first man entered. He had a wide, ruddy face, and a low brow topped with brown, wavy hair which in Akulov's opinion looked like a floor mop. He was six foot tall, and almost as wide, almost square. He swivelled his head and squinted at Akulov, as though not understanding why he was there, before he turned back to Needham.

'You got peach pie, Needham?'

'Only apple today, Ted.'

Ted grunted. 'Then make it four pieces of apple pie, big slices with cream. You hear?'

Needham nodded. 'I hear.'

Ted's three associates stood a half step behind him, in an almost reverential manner, not like bodyguards but more like followers. The tallest had ginger hair and Akulov estimated he was about six foot five; he was also obese. Ted glanced over at Akulov again, and his followers did too, like a Greek chorus. The second one had light brown hair, slicked back, much like Needham's, and small pig-like eyes which seemed to have sunk into his face. The last had a round face and a thick head of blond hair with a jagged fringe. It looked to Akulov like an accident, but it was probably fashion. Ted continued to stare.

Akulov's eyes were not on Ted, they were on the road outside, but he was adept at using his peripheral vision, it had been the only thing that had saved his life back at the hotel in Canada. If he'd not moved, he was under no illusions that the fire extinguisher would have cracked his skull at the very least. He had a sudden flashback to the little girl, screaming, and his chest became tight. She should never have seen what she had, yet there was nothing he could have changed. Her father had wanted to stop what he had seen happening, and in doing so had brained Akulov. But, Akulov reasoned, there was nothing to be gained from dwelling on the fact that he had survived, except in analysing how he had missed the large man approach him in the first place. A half-smile appeared on Akulov's face. It had been the ski mask, of course it had, it had restricted the very edges of his vision.

'You see something funny?'

Akulov turned his head, looked at Ted, said nothing.

'You answer me when I'm talking to you.'

Akulov raised his cup, drank some more.

'That's right, you hide behind your coffee cup.'

'Ted,' Needham interjected, 'why don't you four take a seat and I'll bring your pie right over?'

Ted turned back to face Needham. 'What? Do I take orders from you now?'

'Come on, I was just meaning the quicker you are settled comfortably, the faster I can serve you your pie. Extra cream for you, Dave, right?'

The red-haired follower nodded, the fat on his wide neck wobbling. 'Oui, for me the extra.'

Akulov cocked his head on hearing the Québécois accent, they were close to the Canadian border, and weren't a million miles away from Quebec, it was certainly a lot nearer than France. Yet what was most notable about the voice was that it seemed too high pitched for a man of his size.

'Have you taken care of that little job for the boss, Needham?' Ted asked, a sneer forming about his mouth.

Needham cast a quick glance at Akulov. In his opinion he seemed furtive. 'I got it all sorted. She knows she can trust me.'

Ted pointed a large finger at Needham. 'She'd better know it.'

Ted moved with a rolling gait across the expanse of the diner, followed by the other bulky men, and took the booth at the opposite end to Akulov. Ted sat with his back against the wall, Dave squeezed in facing him, whilst Pig-Eyes and Haircut, who were almost as large as Ted, sat on either end. They looked like a sub-par NFL team, muscled, but fat with it, sturdy but slow.

Akulov's threat radar hadn't pinged yet. Whilst something at least a little unsavoury was going on here, it wasn't anything he deemed pertinent to his own safety. Thugs were thugs, they were not trained, professional killers, and he was. Akulov took a deep breath and realised for the first time that his head wasn't pounding, in fact he felt nothing more than a vodka hangover level ache. From his pocket he popped more of the pills Needham had given him, although his head was feeling a little better now, he needed to keep a steady flow of analgesics into his system to keep it that way.

Needham brought a tray with the four-piece pie order, then delivered another tray on which stood milkshakes – two pink-coloured, one light brown, and one yellow. Ted took the yellow one. Akulov didn't need to imagine the flavours, it was obvious. His own coffee had finished again, and he waited for Needham to bring him a refill, not that he needed more coffee but because he had questions.

'I'm sorry you had to see that,' Needham said, in a hushed tone. 'Ted is a bit of a character.'

'I imagine in a small place like this there are a few.'

'That's for damn sure.'

'So,' Akulov asked, 'who is he?'

'A local kid with issues. His great-grandfather started this diner, then passed it on to his grandfather, and then his father lost it because of his drinking problem.'

'Let me guess, he dislikes you because you bought it?'

'He hates me for it, yes. He thinks it's his by right, his birthright, his inheritance.'

'It is just a diner,' Akulov said, perplexed.

'Yeah, well, he doesn't see it like that. One man's diner is another man's castle.'

Ted shouted across the dining hall, 'Hey Needham, more pie over here.'

Needham closed his eyes and pursed his lips before he returned to the kitchen. Akulov now saw that Ted was looking at him, whilst talking to his friends. And then, as Akulov had half expected, Haircut stood and moved away, making room for Ted, who struggled to his feet and exited the booth.

Needham took a diagonal course, complete with a tray, towards Ted, who was scowling at Akulov and heading directly towards him.

'I got your next piece of pie, Ted.'

'Put it on the table. I want to chat to your friend.'

'C'mon Ted...'

Ted sidestepped Needham and continued. Akulov took a couple of long, deep breaths to relax his body and felt his chest and back protest. He turned his body to face Ted full-on and held the younger man's gaze. Ted slowed, perplexed by Akulov's actions but continued forwards nonetheless.

Reaching the booth, he sat heavily directly opposite Akulov, which tactically was an extremely unwise course of action. Ted folded his arms, which was even sillier. He was holding Akulov's gaze, and Akulov was holding his.

'Don't you know who I am?' Ted asked.

'I'm guessing your name is Edward?'

The low, wide brow of the bulky man furrowed. 'Only my ma calls me that. I'm Ted, Ted Lehnert.'

Akulov said nothing.

Ted said, 'You not heard of my family?'

'No. I have not.'

'That accent, what's that, Washington?'

'Yes.'

'Now I understand. You're from out of state.'

'I am.'

'Well, that gets you a break.'

'Thank you.'

'Yeah, I'm thanked. See, we don't like strangers getting involved in our affairs.'

'I'll be gone tomorrow. I just need to get to a phone, and then I'll leave.'

'I see.' Ted rubbed his ruddy face with his right hand as though he was buying time to think. 'Where'd you park? There's no truck out front.'

'I came by boat.'

'Now that's a goddamn lie. We been to the lake and there isn't a boat.'

'It sank in the storm. I swam ashore.'

The narrow brow furrowed again. 'You swam ashore?'

'I did.'

'When?'

'Last night.'

'When, last night?'

'I don't know, I lost my watch.'

'You got any ID?'

'Why?'

'Why what?'

'Why are you interested if I have ID or not?'

'Because I need to know who you are.'

'Why is that?'

Ted looked incredulous, as though he couldn't understand why Akulov didn't understand. 'Because I asked, and I'm Ted Lehnert.'

'Are you a police officer, Ted?'

Ted's chest seemed to swell. 'I'm an appointed deputy. So is my man, Dave.'

'That's a lot of manpower,' Akulov said with thinly veiled sarcasm.

'It is. We got important things to take care of around here.'

'Like knowing who everyone is?'

'Exactly. It's like national security. This close to the border anyone can try to get in.'

'I've never met a sheriff's deputy before; can I see your badge?'

'Guy wants to see my badge,' Ted shouted back over his shoulder, 'he thinks he's "him".'

'Handcuff him,' Dave mumbled, with a mouthful of pie.

Akulov waited for Ted to speak again, still a little unsure as to what his game was.

'So, you have any ID?'

'No.'

'Mind if I search you?'

'Yes.'

'Good.' Ted started to rise from his seat.

'Yes. I do mind if you search me.'

Ted looked down at Akulov. Confusion flashed across his broad face for a moment before it turned to annoyance. 'Who are you?'

Akulov didn't think it was an existential question Ted was posing, so gave him the same name he had given to Needham. 'Adam Hurst.'

'What kind of a name is that?'

'The best kind, my mother would say.'

'So, Adam Hurst, you were on your boat and it sank?'

'I heard it was the worst storm in living memory?'

'Yep, it was. Where's your boat moored, when it's not sunk?'

Akulov pictured the map he had found that morning which showed Lake Huron in detail, both the US and Canadian sides. 'Lion's Head.'

The furrows came back again. 'Lion's Head?'

'Yes.'

'That's in Canada?'

'You are the local.'

'Not to Canada. You were crossing from Canada?'

This was a truth, but there was no reason for Akulov to give any information to the thug. 'The boat was moored, at Lion's Head. I was out for the weekend.'

'On your own?'

'I don't like people,' Akulov replied, giving Ted an actual truth.

Dave called out, 'Pie's getting cold!'

Ted slowly straightened up. He started to walk away, then half turned back, his right index finger raised. 'When I see you again, you have your ID.'

Akulov held Ted's gaze, and made no reply.

Akulov remained where he was for the next ten minutes

until Ted and the others got up and left. He noted that none
of them made any move to call for the bill, neither did they
leave any cash. He watched Needham clean the table then
got to his feet. His head was a little woozy, but the pain had
lessened further. Slowly, gradually, Akulov was starting to
feel more like himself, although he wondered, with so many
changes of identity he was likely to forget who he really was
one day. He leant against the stand-up bar, more questions
now in his mind but neither their subjects nor their answers
anything to do with him. Whatever was happening in this
odd little place, and whoever Ted and his group thought
they were had nothing to do with him.

Needham finished loading the plates and glassware into
the washer. 'No one talks to Ted like that.'

'They should. Ted is a bully.'

'Look, he's just bad news. Now how about you give me
five and I'll meet you out the front? I'll take you into town
and you can find a phone.'

'That sounds good to me.'

Akulov exited through the front door. Needham locked
the door behind him then pulled down a shutter which said,
'back soon'. Soon was a relative concept, in the grand scale of
things, Akulov thought. Times needed to be absolute, he
wasn't one for vague notions, in fact this was the only part of
his job he had ever found frustrating. If he knew he had to
lay in a cold, muddy ditch for a day – twenty-four hours –
then fine, he could accept that. Yet tell him he had to lay in
that same ditch until sometime in the afternoon, well, that
was a different matter. As he let the lunchtime sun brush his
face, he remembered how his grandmother used to call him
'impatient'. He'd watch her gather the ingredients, make her
dough, and then he'd ask her how long it would be until it

was ready. So, she'd tell him that first the dough had to rise, and then she would divide it up into smaller pieces for rolls or leave it as it was for a loaf, and then it would need to be baked. So, he would repeat the question, and after a while she realised that 'soon' wasn't a scientific enough reply for her grandson. So, she took him to the library where she asked the librarian to help him find a book on baking. Akulov remembered taking home that red covered book and devouring every work and instruction until he knew how long each and every type of dough took to rise, dependant on ingredients and ambient temperature. He'd then watch his grandmother, giving her advice or chiding her when her timing was off. However, as a child what he could not understand was how, even when she did not follow her recipes or his timings to the letter, her bread was always perfect. She told him there was one thing his books didn't account for. Puzzled, he asked her.

Her simple reply was 'Love. I bake my bread for you with love.'

Akulov shivered, and not because of the ambient temperature. It was the cold shadow of grief falling upon him again. After his parents had been killed in a car crash, she had taken him from Kyiv to Moscow and raised him as her son. She was all he had. He remembered back to the day she had been murdered; the day Chechen terrorists had bombed her apartment building. That day he had died inside, to be reborn as a weapon of revenge. However, that was another time, another place, and another country, but was he still the same? Who was Ruslan Akulov, what was Ruslan Akulov? The young boy fascinated by the process of baking bread, the teenage conscript wracked with grief, the special forces soldier killing for the country which had claimed him, or the assassin known as Wolf Six who stood here now. At the moment he was none of them. He was Adam Hurst, and he had to get to a phone.

Akulov sensed movement to his left. Ted and two of his party of four rounded the corner. Akulov noted it was Dave who was not with them.

Ted's eyes narrowed as he met Akulov's gaze, and his chest puffed out. 'So, Hurst, you find any ID in the last five minutes?'

'Go home, Ted. You are making the parking lot look untidy.'

Ted stopped in his tracks. He frowned, as if trying to understand someone speaking in tongues. 'What the hell did you say to me?'

'Don't take that, Ted,' Pig-Eyes urged, speaking for the first time.

'Yeah, teach him a lesson,' Haircut added, with a grin on his round face.

'I think I will, and now,' Ted stated.

As the trio edged towards Akulov in a V formation, with Ted in the lead, Akulov wasn't impressed.

'We take care of people around here,' Ted stated, 'and now it's time to take care of you.'

Perhaps a small test was exactly what Akulov needed to assess his current operational effectiveness. He said, 'Go ahead, Ted.'

The flat-faced local scowled and lurched forwards, his shoulders hunched and his fists up. It was a classic boxing stance, except for the fact that Ted's footwork was wrong. His legs were straight, as though made from unyielding steel. He threw a left jab at Akulov. It was an obvious feint as he retracted it before it was anywhere near landing, and launched a right hook. Bringing his left arm up in an L shape to protect his head, Akulov stepped into the incoming arm, letting it slam against his shoulder, with a jolt, to gauge Ted's strength, before swinging his hips, he drove his right knee into Ted's stomach. Ted started to fold at the waist and Akulov pushed him away. Ted stumbled towards the diner. Without pause, and noting he had enough space, Akulov now struck out at the third man – Haircut, with a crescent kick. His booted foot caught the unsuspecting heavy on the side of the head and immediately sent him toppling sideways and down into the dirt. Akulov hadn't put his full strength into the move yet feeling dizzy he understood it was not a manoeuvre he should attempt again until he had fully recovered. Akulov now faced Pig-Eyes, who stood open mouthed with his palms up in a defensive manner.

'Walk away,' Akulov said.

Pig-Eyes shook his head, then closed his mouth and charged forward. His arms were splayed outwards, like a wrestler attempting a heavy takedown. Akulov tried to move out of his reach, but the younger man was deceptively quick and his right arm collided with Akulov's stomach. The momentum behind the move forced Akulov backwards. Boots slipping on the loose gravel, he fell yet managed to twist as he did so and landed on his attacker with a jarring thud. Akulov threw his left elbow into the man's face for good measure before he rolled off and away. Back on his feet, he felt even dizzier than before. Akulov took a deep breath, as he swayed, and attempted to blink it away.

Ted was still doubled over. His right arm outstretched and supporting his weight against the wall of the diner. He angrily pointed at Akulov before abruptly convulsing and vomiting up his recently consumed pie and shake. Wiping his mouth on his sleeve he said, 'You'll pay for this!'

'You didn't pay Mr Needham,' Akulov retorted, as he assessed the other two thugs. Pig-Eyes was sitting up and moaning with his head in his hands, whilst Haircut was slowly crawling away. Akulov was satisfied the force he had used had not been excessive. He was also glad he had not needed to be in a prolonged fight. Akulov said, 'I do not know, and I do not care about whatever it is you get up to here. As soon as I can get to a phone I will be gone.'

Ted staggered towards his two friends. Regaining enough composure to spit at Akulov. Raising his arm, he pointed and said, 'This is not over!'

Akulov sighed. 'Edward, this did not even start.'

Ted stopped and stared at Akulov before helping Pig-Eyes to his feet, whilst Haircut had now managed to find his own. Shoulders hunched, body language screaming dejection, the trio trudged away from the diner, onto the access road, and headed towards the bend and whatever lay beyond it.

'We ready?' Needham rounded the corner of the diner. He was looking down at a bunch of keys. As his eyes met Akulov's, surprise spread across his face. He then spotted Ted's gang just before they disappeared from view. 'What happened?'

Akulov shrugged. 'Ted had questions.'

'And?'

'I gave him answers.'

Needham chuckled then gestured to the truck. 'Hop in.'

Akulov crossed to the truck, and reaching up for the passenger door, found it was open. He climbed inside the double cab Chevrolet. He half remembered being in there before.

Needham clambered into the other side and started the engine. 'Now the best place to take you is going to be north to Alpena. Apart from the lake, the only thing we've got around here are the trees of the Thunder Bay State Forest. And let me tell you, at the best of times, even when the cell towers haven't been flattened by a storm, the cell reception there is patchy.'

With a burble, the pickup started, and Needham pulled away from the tarmacked lot. They rounded the bend and Akulov saw a smaller path leading through the trees and the back of Ted's head as he walked along it. They continued on the access road, which became a slightly wider, yet still narrow, tarmacked strip seemingly going nowhere until they burst out of the trees and Akulov saw a line of large wooden framed houses, each facing the lake and set back in their own secluded pieces of land.

Needham explained, 'Mostly left empty. Rich folks from out of state buy them, use them for maybe a month or two a year, and that drives up the prices for the locals who, unless they want to live in a tent, can't now afford waterfront footage.'

'That's capitalism,' Akulov replied flatly.

'It sure the hell is. You know sometimes I think we'd all be better off living in China.'

Akulov's eyes narrowed at the mention of the country whose citizen he had just assassinated. 'Really?'

'Of course. The American factory worker has grown lazy, whilst the Chinese are flourishing. Look, I'd love me some American made, but ninety-nine per cent of all global manufacturing takes place over there, in communist China.

And don't tell me that they've taken our jobs, because they have not. We didn't want them.'

Akulov didn't know what to say so he remained silent. If Needham was happy to blather on, he was happy to listen.

'Look, Adam, I think we need to get your head checked out. Get you a scan or whatever they do nowadays. There's a large medical centre up in Alpena.'

Akulov agreed but he couldn't risk appearing on any records, especially without any form of ID. He knew he was far enough away from Winnipeg not to be caught up in any investigation into the Fang assassination, but that wasn't to say there wasn't anything else he'd be put in the frame for. In short, even though he was playing an American, and being aided by an American, he had to function as though he was on hostile ground in enemy territory. 'I'll get myself checked out once I get home. I've just got to contact my wife.'

Needham cast him a quick glance sideways. 'Jesus, you'd better had, she'll already be raising hell with the authorities trying to find you.'

Akulov thought quickly, it was Tishina he was referring to. 'I doubt it. She was on an extended spa weekend. She's not expecting or wanting to hear from me.'

'Even with a concussion and a capsized boat?'

'Well, the concussion is one thing, but then she always said I had a hard head, and the boat is another. It belongs to a friend who lets me use it, and once he's back from vacation he's not going to be too happy.'

'For your sake, Adam, I hope he has insurance.'

They continued on the narrow two-lane Black River Road, west, with nothing but verdant trees on either side. The road was empty, and it was as though they were deep in the wilderness. 'We'll take the "twenty-three", not really any other direct route, unless you like off-roading?'

'Not the way I'm feeling,' Akulov replied. Then a thought crossed his mind, he looked over at Needham. 'What were you doing up by the lake when you found me?'

Needham wet his lips, and behind his glasses Akulov noted the corners of his eyes pinch. 'I've got a hunting shack out there; well, some may say it's a lake house. Anyway, I wanted to check if it was still standing after the storm.'

'Was it?'

'More or less. The roof leaks, if I'm lucky or have a mind to I may be able to get it up and inhabitable for those "back to nature" types by the start of the tourist season.'

'Do you get many tourists through this part?'

'We get a fair share, I have to take on extra staff during the summer – hence the room I put you in, and if pushed another of the huts can be used for staff. You know, because I call them "chalets", I can rent out each of those cabins three times over in high season.'

'And that's another reason why Ted wants the diner?'

'I expect that's the only reason Ted wants the diner.'

'And he's a sheriff's deputy?'

'Ted was, once, and his fat pal Dave still is. A couple of years back, a guy went missing, some corporate big-wig from Boston – don't ask me why he came here to get away from it all rather than the Caribbean, but he did. Anyway he goes missing so the sheriff needed more manpower to look for him, like a search party type of thing, so Ted was one of the party, and to give them some teeth – to persuade people to let them search their property, they deputised some of them – this included Ted and his French pal Dave.'

'Dave is French not Québécois?'

'No he's from Québec City, and likes to tell everyone so. But it's the same difference, European roots so I don't like him.'

'Isn't Needham a European name?'

Needham started to laugh. 'Way to go to win friends and influence people, Adam.'

'It's a talent,' Akulov replied.

'You're right it is European. If fact, it's "Olde English". Before the seventh century, "ned" was the word for "need" and "ham" was short for "hamlet", or village, etc. So, the name Needham meant that the guy needed a home. When I arrived here twenty-five years ago, I needed a home. And that's why I bought the diner.'

The incline of the road started to increase and as they crested the hill another diner could be seen on the junction with the twenty-three. This one was larger and, from the colour of the clean and well-maintained timberwork, seemed a lot newer.

'That's the competition. Well, it's the nearest, best bar to my diner, so no competition at all, to be honest. Would you believe that place has been there since 1937?'

'It looks newer.'

'That's because it was constantly burning down – being made of wood – so they had to keep rebuilding it. Hence the brick. It's owned by a nice couple.'

They joined the twenty-three and turned right to head north, but as they did a police patrol vehicle pulled out from the restaurant's parking lot and started to follow them. It was a black Ford Explorer wearing heavy-duty bull bars and had the word *'SHERIFF'* and a shield stencilled on its side in gold. It kept a short distance behind, making no attempt to close the gap or to overtake.

Rounding a bend, the road started to climb. They passed a large one-storey white building set back with its own parking lot. Old Glory fluttered high above from a free-standing flagpole, and a sign on the gabled entrance proclaimed the place to be 'Alcona Township Hall'. Still the Explorer was behind them. Further ahead they passed white, wooden cabins set back amongst the trees on both sides of the road. The grass verges on both sides started to rise and as they crested the top of the hill, Once away, Akulov noted, from any onlookers, the Explorer's lights flashed on. Akulov readied himself for a physical confrontation.

Needham sighed. 'I am not a fan.'

'Of law enforcement?'

'Of this law enforcement officer in particular.'

Akulov looked back, via the vanity mirror on his sun visor, he couldn't make out who was driving, so how had Needham?

Slowly reducing his speed on the otherwise deserted highway, Needham brought his pickup to a halt, at the edge of the grass covered verge. The sheriff's vehicle stopped a safe distance behind, and a large, solid figure got out, a woman. Her uniform consisted of a taupe pair of trousers, and a chocolate brown shirt fastened with a taupe tie, it wasn't flattering. She adjusted her belt, and slipped a taupe, wide-brimmed hat on top of her mop of brown, wavy hair. She approached the truck on Needham's side.

'Hello, sheriff.'

'Mr Needham,' the woman's tone was gruff. 'I need to speak to your friend here. I need to take him back to the office.'

Akulov felt the pang of recognition as he saw the sheriff's

face. It was the same woman who had murdered the man by the side of the lake. The woman who had executed him like a professional hitter. And what did this mean? She was an assassin? Improbable. That she had advanced military training? Highly possible.

'Why is that, sheriff?'

'Because I received an "E-Tip" via the website saying he may be linked to some unsavoury criminal activity.'

Akulov remained silent, Needham said, 'I see.'

Akulov didn't need this. He weighed up his options. He was unarmed and on the wrong side of the truck cab to drive it away. He could open the door and sprint across the road and into the woods but how long did he have before the sheriff managed to loosen off a shot? He'd seen her shoot, and knew she was highly trained. So, then what? If she missed, he'd go on the run through the woods until he could find another vehicle? It was possible, but not preferable. And if he remained and let himself be taken in for questioning, what about the questions she was going to ask him? He did have genuine ID for the Adam Hurst legend he was using but this was not with him, it was in a cache he had created a state away, and then of course there would be an issue if they attempted to fingerprint him. Akulov balled his fists feeling his smooth fingertips against his palms, smooth because using an old soviet trick he had carefully filed away his fingerprints with very fine sandpaper. It wasn't a technique he favoured as it was all too easy to scar the dermis to such an extent that it left another type of unique mark. When he couldn't wear gloves, he used liquid silicon to fill the papillary ridges, but silicon wore off, it needed to be reapplied, and it left traces of its own. So, on this occasion he had not used silicon. His skin would recover, growing back within ten days or so but for the moment the question asked by the police would be 'why had he done this?' and that of course would raise red flags. And then of course he had seen the sheriff murder a man by the lake.

As if reading Akulov's mind, the sheriff abruptly raised her service issue Glock 17 and adopted the 'Weaver stance'. 'Mr Needham, get out of the truck.'

'B... but why?'

'Because you are in my goddamn way.'

Akulov had no choice, his hand was being tipped. Needham undid his seatbelt, raised his hands, and started to open the door. When he was halfway out, and part obscuring the sheriff, Akulov bolted. Pushing open his door, he landed on his right foot and tried to power away. But his movement was slower than he realised, his steps leaden. One step, two steps, three... a single shot rang out and a round slammed into the tarmac by his right foot.

'Try me!' The voice was controlled and confident.

Akulov stopped. No one could outrun a bullet, and with a concussion he now realised he couldn't outrun anyone. Head throbbing and heart racing, he raised his hands.

'That's it, nice and slow, you just stay there,' the sheriff said as she approached.

Akulov estimated how long it would take for her to reach him, and at which precise point she would be overreaching to place a pair of cuffs on him. He was about to turn when a sharp sensation, like innumerable needles puncturing his skin, made his body convulse and every muscle contract. His mouth froze open as he dropped face first into the dirt. Before he could regain his motor functions, his arms were dragged behind his back, and he felt the cold steel of police handcuffs fastening his wrists together.

'Sheriff Lehnert, please...' Needham said.

Lehnert? She had the same surname as Ted, so was she a relative? In a place this small and sparsely populated she had to be. And of course, that explained why he was being taken in.

'Mr Needham,' the sheriff said, as she removed the two steel barbs from Akulov's back, 'I'm going to need you to come with me too. Now do you also need a set of cuffs, like Mr Hurst?'

'No... no.'

The sheriff patted Akulov down for concealed weapons and 'sharps'. She dug his wallet out of his back pocket and then pulled him to his feet. Akulov noted she was unusually strong. He blinked, he had a headache again and could taste blood in his mouth. Most of all he noted his body felt heavy and hard to control, this was a sensation which he knew from experience would wear off within minutes, but he'd play up its effects. At the moment the sheriff thought he was one thing, whilst Needham believed him to be something else. Meanwhile Akulov knew that neither of them could ever imagine what he really was.

'C'mon, Mr Hurst. Don't make this thing any harder on yourself.' The sheriff led him by the elbow towards her police vehicle. 'But attempting to evade arrest, well that's gotta be added to whatever it is I charge you with.'

'What... is it you are... charging me with?'

'Larceny.'

'Larceny,' Akulov's brain still felt a little muddled, 'larceny? Of what?'

'Of a sailboat.'

They reached the Explorer, and the sheriff nodded at the

back. 'Mr Needham, if you'd be so kind to open her up, and get in.'

Needham nodded, Akulov noted his hand shook as he pulled the door handle. 'Y... yes, sheriff.'

'You are on your own,' Akulov stated.

'I am. Do not try anything. If I pull my service weapon on you a second time I won't miss.'

Akulov could well believe her. He wouldn't let her draw her weapon.

Needham clambered into the Ford, and then the sheriff pushed Akulov in next to him. Climbing back into the driver's seat, and separated by a safety mesh from her passengers, the sheriff's eyes locked onto Akulov's. He sensed anger simmering within her. Did she know he had seen her kill a man? If not, was she this hostile to every suspect she apprehended?

She strapped herself in, started the SUV and performed a U-turn. They once again passed the houses, the hall and the restaurant and this time they did not take the fork for Black River, the Explorer continued south, downhill, on the twenty-three in the direction of Harrisville.

'Why do you need to take me in?' Needham asked, his fear now replaced with outrage.

'Ya gonna keep whinging all the way to Harrisville, Needham?'

'I just want to know why?'

'Why? A – because I say so, and B – because I need you tell me everything you know about Mr Hurst.'

Akulov said, 'I am not a very interesting person.'

'Oh, I see. Are you a failed comedian, as well as a failed escapologist?'

Akulov thought that was a witty response but made no reply.

'Sheriff, I found Adam by the lake and brought him back to the diner.'

'Whoa, save it for your official statement, Needham. We gotta have it on the record.'

Needham closed his mouth, and the interior of the Ford became silent.

Akulov attempted to get comfortable whilst being forced to sit on his own cuffed wrists. He slowly started to test the cuffs, checking as to whether they would give at all. They didn't. They were on, and they were tight. Akulov remembered the last time he'd been cuffed six months earlier. On that occasion they'd been a little loose and by using an old yet risky technique of dislocating a thumb he'd managed to free himself. However, on this occasion there was no such luck. Next, he started to slowly move his wrists independently to each other in a winding motion, winding the chain which connected the modern-day manacles, getting the metal to twist against itself before he pulled the knotted chain apart. In time, with luck and enough force he could weaken a link and that would in theory enable him to free his arms. That was if the sheriff didn't notice what he was doing.

Outside the passing countryside was a myriad of verdant green spruce, and well-maintained grass on both sides of the single lane road. Dotted here and there were driveways leading to houses, larger than the ones Akulov had seen earlier and further back from the hum of the passing traffic. The size of the trees and the sheer proliferation of them hemmed in the road, giving a sense of isolation, of claustrophobia. It also meant the place was easier to get lost in, and harder to control. And then the trees thinned out and they passed a vineyard. Apart from the tourist map he'd studied, Akulov didn't know the area but estimated he didn't have more than another twenty-five minutes maximum until they reached the sheriff's office. And he knew that was nowhere near enough time to defeat his bonds.

Akulov's estimated arrival time at the sheriff's office had not been too far off the mark, and without another word passing between the trio the Ford Explorer pulled into a parking lot bordered on two sides with single-storey, flat-roofed, red-brick buildings. The place looked like a middle school with the exception that the windows here were much smaller and several tower arrays protruded from the roof. The sheriff parked in a reserved space outside the larger of the two buildings. A mesh fence, which became a cage at one end, surrounded half of the facility. The sheriff's office was in amongst residential buildings and looked out of place. Akulov halted his attempt to torque his handcuffs and relaxed his shoulders. A figured emerged from the main entrance. He was tall, rail thin with a pinched face and although he looked to be pushing seventy, still had a schoolboy head of chestnut-brown hair parted to one side. Not physically intimidating more someone who demanded respect. He approached the Explorer and opened Needham's door.

'Jake, what you been up to, jaywalking?'

'Jim, that's enough,' the sheriff growled as she exited the vehicle. 'Needham has some questions to answer, so take him inside and put him in my office.'

'Yes, sheriff.'

The sheriff now proceeded to open Akulov's door. 'Get out. Do not try anything.'

Akulov followed the order. He stood, facing her, perhaps just an inch taller than the flat-faced woman. It was the first time he had noticed her eyes. They were dark, small and lifeless. It was something he had seen in innumerable killers, but never in a law enforcement officer. She stared back at him in silence. Akulov waited for her to give him his next order, and he imagined she was waiting for him to show his nerves or to do something stupid. He did neither.

'Follow Deputy Grant. I'll be a couple of steps behind you. Walk.'

Akulov turned his back on the woman, although every instinct told him not to do so, and strode after the two men. Grant held open the door for Needham and then let it close behind them. With his head facing directly ahead, Akulov moved just his eyes to scan the area. The sheriff's office sat in a lot, on a grid system surrounded by respectable looking white, wooden-clad houses on three sides separated by tarmacked roads. The remaining side occupied by the utilitarian twin building to the sheriff's office had a pair of signs on it. One read 'Alcona County Clerk' and the other informed him that the facility also housed the 'Alcona County 81st District Court'.

Akulov arrived at the entrance door, it was pulled open from inside by the tall, thin deputy.

'Yes. Go inside,' the sheriff stated with a voice devoid of any warmth.

Akulov entered. Deputy Grant moved to the processing desk and picked up a sheet of paper. Behind the desk was an open-plan squad room containing two rows of tables with low wall dividers separating them into workspaces. In one of them, with his uniform straining to retain his girth, was a gingered-haired deputy. It was Dave. He was eyeing Akulov with what looked like amusement. Akulov looked past him to the glass walled office at the back, in which he could make out Needham about to sit down.

Deputy Grant said, 'I'm going to need you to hand me all your belongings, Mr Hurst.'

'I'm a little confused,' Akulov said. 'I am not under arrest.'

The furrows of Grant's brow grew deeper. 'Are you not?'

'The hell he's not,' the sheriff said, as the door electronically snickered shut behind her.

'I have not been read my Miranda rights.'

The sheriff moved past Akulov and handed Grant the wallet she had taken from Akulov's back pocket. 'This is all he had on him.'

'No watch and no phone?'

'That's what I said.'

Grant asked, 'There's blood on your face. Are you injured, Mr Hurst?'

Akulov decided to keep quiet about his concussion. 'Just a scratch.'

'He cut his pretty face trying to run away.'

'Ah.'

'Turcotte,' the sheriff raised her voice, 'escort Mr Hurst to room two.'

Dave pushed himself slowly up from his workstation and ambled towards them. He squeezed his morbidly obese frame through the gap between the front desk and the wall.

Instinct and training told Akulov the most opportune time to escape captivity was as close to the point and time of capture as possible, whilst the opposition was still in motion, their assets out of place, their plans still being constructed or their base not yet reached. However, he had been prevented from escaping out on the twenty-three, and now handcuffed, with a closed door behind him and three law enforcement officers around him, Akulov's chances of escape were even less. So, he made no bid for freedom, because that was what was most expected of him. He became placid and compliant.

Dave Turcotte's large, fleshy right hand clamped itself around Akulov's left elbow as he manhandled him forward, past the desk and into the open-plan interior of the sheriff's department. They walked the entire length of the room before Turcotte led Akulov through a door on the left and down a short flight of stairs. The room was a corridor with half windows on the left and three steel doors on the right. The first door was closed, and the second was open. Turcotte stepped sideways, pushed Akulov inside then locked the door.

A solitary fluorescent bulb protected by a wire cage, flicked on. It was too powerful for the space, but Akulov imagined this was part of the theatre such rooms were used to create. A metal table and a pair of matching metal chairs were bolted in the centre of the room, into the uncarpeted concrete floor. A half glare reflected from the unpolished steel tabletop. Akulov moved to the window. It was the same width but half the height of a standard office window, and thin steel wires ran through the glass. Outside the view was of a neighbouring house, part hidden by well-established trees. He'd had worse views. It was only now that he noticed drain holes in the corner of the room to facilitate the sluicing out of any liquid spillages. This was normal in a mortuary, but he'd never seen such channels in an interview room.

Akulov ignored the security camera, mounted high in the corner next to the door and protected, like the light, behind a metal safety cage, and sat in the chair facing the door. Arms behind his back, he started the process again of torque turning the chains between his cuffs, waiting to feel the resistance as the links became interwound, before sharply moving his wrists apart. It was an art, and one that would have been so much easier if he'd had his hands cuffed out in front. He could in theory pull his arms under his legs and step over the cuffs. However, as he was being monitored this would be seen and further detrimental actions, he imagined, would be taken. Akulov knew his chances of successfully defeating the metal links was low, but it was better than accepting defeat. That was something not in his nature.

After forty-five minutes or so, just enough time he knew that was mandated to make him jumpy, a key turned in the lock and the sturdy, metal door opened. Deputy Turcotte squeezed his fat frame through the entrance and only now did Akulov see a second visitor – Deputy Grant had been behind him, hidden by the girth of Turcotte's torso. Akulov allowed himself a thin smile, seeing the two men of equal height standing side by side was like a 'before & after' advert for a weight loss drug.

'What are you smiling at?' Turcotte spoke directly to him for the first time, his voice was childlike, singsong, almost squeaky.

'Come on, David, be polite,' Grant said. 'Now, Mr Hurst, I've got to take your prints, if that's OK with you?'

Akulov knew his cover didn't check out, and that it wouldn't hold. Adam Hurst did have a Washington driver's licence, which did appear on the relevant website, but that still did not account for his presence by the lake and of course his lack of fingerprints. And then the question remained in his head, why had he not been Mirandized? Akulov said, 'It is not OK. I've not been legally detained.'

'What the sheriff says is law, is the law,' Turcotte stated.

'I'm sure there is a genuine reason for it,' Grant said attempting to sidestep the question, 'and talking from my considerable experience it's always best to be courteous and polite.'

'I cannot argue with that,' Akulov stated.

Turcotte locked the door and took a step towards the table. 'Lean forward and push your arms back. I'm going to undo your cuffs. But don't try anything.'

'I'm sure Mr Hurst won't be rash. Will you, Mr Hurst?'

'I will behave.'

Akulov complied with Turcotte's request. Now would be the time to attempt to escape but now would be the time it was also expected. Turcotte had both the key to the handcuffs and the interview room, and Akulov had no doubt he could overcome both him and the much older Grant. Without a concussion, all it would take would be a couple of seconds and a couple of moves. Yet that would give him away, and show the Alcona Sheriff's Department that Adam Hurst was more than an HR Consultant. Currently the sheriff had nothing on him. The boat he had claimed to have sunk was fictitious, and so was its owner, meaning no charges could be brought against him. So that meant either he was being framed for the theft of another real vessel, or the sheriff just wanted to hold him. The latter seeming far more likely. However, if this was the case, the question was why did she want to hold him? Did she suspect he had witnessed her execution of the man by the shore of the lake? Or perhaps Ted had gone crying to her?

Turcotte placed his large hand on Akulov's back and

pushed him lower in the direction of the tabletop. 'Do not move.'

The steel felt cold through his checked shirt, and then his hands were freed. Again, Akulov resisted the urge to attack.

'Now place your hands palm down on the table and sit up straight,' Turcotte said.

Akulov complied.

Grant had a US letter-sized black plastic case in his hand. He sat and placed the case on the table. Opening the case, he took out a card. There was a table printed on it, consisting of columns wide enough to take the inky print of a digit. 'Mr Hurst, please turn your hands over.'

Akulov did so, aware that within seconds he'd be seeing confusion on the veteran deputy's face.

Grant removed a piece of shaped sponge from the case. 'I just need to ink your fingertips.'

Akulov remained still as Grant painted the ends of his fingers.

'I need you to now roll each of your fingertips in turn on the corresponding space provided on the card. Make sure you get the full print. Roll your finger slowly, and only once, left to right.'

Akulov was interested to see the results and also the reaction of the two deputies. Once he'd finished Grant blinked as he stared at the smudges on the card.

Grant said, 'Now that is unusual.'

'What?' Turcotte stepped forward and peered down.

'No discernible ridge lines.'

'No fingerprints?' Turcotte's confusion had made his voice squeakier.

Grant looked Akulov in the eyes. 'Now this I have never

seen before, but I have read about it, and well, to be honest, I thought it was something that in today's modern world technology would have prevented from happening.'

Akulov said nothing. If Grant knew why, or he suspected why he had no fingerprints that would lead to harder questions and questioning, prompting Akulov to act.

Grant nodded and folded his arms. 'Are you fond of photography at all, Mr Hurst?'

Akulov now understood what Grant was thinking and felt a sense of relief as this did tie in with what he had told Needham. 'Yes. Old school analogue, not this new digital nonsense.'

Grant nodded again, as though he knew exactly what had happened. 'And do you have a dark room and develop your own film and prints?'

'I do. That is all part of the fun.'

The question was leading, which was not an effective way to elicit objective information. 'You don't wear gloves when you develop your prints, do you?'

'No. I do not.'

'I don't understand,' Turcotte said. 'What has any of this got to do with taking his fingerprints?'

'The chemicals used to develop photographic prints can, on occasion, eat away at the top levels of the dermis – that's the skin, David. The result is that for a time, until they regrow, the fingerprints can disappear or become far less easy to take a print from.' A crooked smile cracked Grant's pinched face. 'So making one print appear can make another disappear.'

To assist with Grant's narrative, Akulov added, 'I like to take photographs of natural phenomena, mainly. Mostly black and white.'

'Like Ansell Adams?'

Now Akulov nodded. 'Exactly. I was trying to get some images of the storm front when, well it got too close and I lost the boat, and of course my equipment.'

'Taking photos of the rain? What an idiot,' Turcotte said.

'Hey, David! That's enough, show Mr Hurst some respect here. OK. I'm afraid I have to leave you in here until Sheriff Lehnert calls for you. I hope we can get all this business cleaned up; you don't look like a boat thief to me.'

'Thank you,' Akulov said.

Turcotte shook his head, still amused by Akulov's misfortune as he followed Grant out of the door. The lock thudded shut and Akulov was left alone with his inky fingertips. He wiped them on his borrowed shirt.

10

FIVE YEARS AGO

Monte Carlo, Monaco

Akulov was tired. He'd driven for seven and a half hours, overnight from Rome after Tishina had informed him Basson had been sighted. He stifled a yawn and stretched as he looked out of her picture window at the impressive view of the sea and promenade below.

'Coffee?'

Akulov turned and said to the woman he had always worked for, 'Thank you.'

She sat with her back towards the window, and he sat across the coffee table from her. Tishina pulled out her mobile phone from the pocket of her slacks and studied the screen. Akulov let his eyes linger on her features as the rays of Monaco morning sunlight illuminated her from behind in what he remembered photographers calling *'contre jour'*, meaning against daylight. Her hair glowed, and the outline of her body was visible beneath her blouse. For a moment he forgot himself.

'It is rude to stare, Ruslan,' Tishina said, now meeting his gaze.

'I agree, it is. I apologise. I was thinking.' Akulov reached for the nearest coffee cup and took a sip.

'Do tell?'

'I was trying to work out where Basson was headed.'

Tishina sighed. 'Ruslan, I thought for once you were going to say you were thinking about me, or about us?'

'No,' Akulov lied, 'I was not.'

'Well, I can't say that is not a disappointment.'

Akulov didn't reply.

'Ruslan, this "side quest" of yours has tied up quite a few of my resources.'

'I understand.'

'Favours have had to be called in.'

'Thank you.'

Tishina looked down at her iPhone and swiped at the screen. 'The tracking app says that Basson has just left Marseilles and is heading east.'

'He's coming this way.'

'Perhaps.' Tishina looked up and met his eyes. 'Tell me your plan?'

'I'll intercept him and kill him.'

'Simple.'

'It is.'

'You have no qualms in liquidating a fellow operative?'

Akulov frowned. 'You and I both know he is nothing of the sort. He is a murderer.'

Tishina nodded. 'Yes, he is. Some of those deaths are on me, as much as they are on you, which is why I agreed to help. There is a limit, however, as to what I can do, and how much time I can spend on this.'

'Because time is money?' Akulov asked, thinly.

'I have a business to run. If you are not working on a contract for a client, neither of us are getting paid.'

Akulov had never let money sway his decisions, not for several years at least. He said, 'I wonder why Basson has reappeared now?'

'My contacts don't know. He was spotted in Marseilles which meant Gallacher. A meeting with Gallacher meant he wanted tools which he couldn't bring into the country.'

'So that implies he has not been in mainland Europe.'

'Or simply needs resupplies. I spoke to Gallacher.'

'Can he be trusted not to warn Basson?'

'I warned him to keep quiet, or I'd send you after him.'

'Charming. What did Gallacher sell him?'

'Two L109s, and a Sig Sauer P365X plus suppressor.'

'Hand grenades?' Akulov frowned. 'That means messy, and messy is loud. Yet a sub-compact handgun, especially with a suppressor, says stealth.'

'It whispers stealth,' Tishina added, 'and concealment.'

Akulov drank more coffee then asked, 'How long can you track him for?'

'As long as we need to. He will not get away, Ruslan.'

'Good,' Akulov said, already feeling energised.

* * *

Basson enjoyed driving, and on occasion, in between contracts, would drive from Qatar via Saudi Arabia to the UAE. Going by plane it was a quick hop of less than an hour from the one Gulf state to the other yet Basson much preferred the drive, especially so when he was able to push his Bentley Bentayga to its limits. Traffic and the standard of driving in Saudi was dreadful and he got a thrill each time he traversed the country and avoided any incidents. Driving in Qatar was safer, if no less chaotic, whilst driving in the UAE was safer still.

Basson's drive today was from Marseilles to Nice and would take him a little over two and a quarter hours – according to his rental car's built-in satellite navigation system. He knew in peak tourist times the roads in the region became clogged, especially nearer to Nice, Monaco and of course the border with Italy. As a Frenchman he was proud of the country he had been born in and had killed for, but living there was not for him. He loved the food, and the wine but it was the sullenness of serving staff and the grime which annoyed him. People were not proud of their jobs, and certainly did not take pride in their towns, yet he mused, in general, France was cleaner and its population less lazy than the Italians. Basson's target was Italian, which he preferred to killing a countryman.

As the kilometres slipped past, he found himself both enjoying the views and the music he had on the Peugeot 2008's over-complicated sound system. It was a mixture of French pop music, which he hadn't heard for a while. Idly he wondered if Vanessa Paradis still sang about taxi drivers, and he found himself humming along, and tapping his hands on the steering wheel even though he didn't know the words. Each time he returned to France, in fact most parts of Europe, he was always struck by how green the countryside was. Although, he realised, he no longer felt as though he connected with the people of his home country, its customs and its lack of civility. No one country was perfect, but in terms of privacy and respect, and respecting privacy, Qatar was hard to beat.

He passed signs with turn-offs for routes into San Tropez, Cannes, and Antibes. As he neared Nice the traffic started to slow and bunch up. Basson sat amongst the traffic patiently strumming his fingers to French pop and edging forward when he was able to. He was on a schedule but knew that he had at least six hours yet to assassinate his target.

It was a messy job, something he specialised in, and who else could his broker – The Irishman – call upon to proceed with such a hit? The client wanted the target destroyed, obliterated, unable to fill a coffin let alone be presented in an open casket before weeping friends and family. This was perfectly fine with Basson. The man he had been sent to wipe from the face of the earth was an Italian industrialist by the name of Antonio Lombardi. He was fifty-eight and now on his second marriage to a woman who was twenty years his junior. An internet search had brought up hits on his first divorce, his then wife being an Italian soap opera star, and subsequent second wife being a weather girl. Basson had chuckled to himself; it was all very Italian. Lombardi would be spending the weekend at a boutique hotel in San Remo at what he had seen online was a yearly meet-up of a car lovers' group named 'Esotico Italiano'. Photographs from the hotel's own website from the year before included an image of Lombardi standing at the edge of the photograph with a blonde woman who was not his second wife, and did not appear to be over the age of twenty-five. The nose of a dark blue Ferrari Dino was visible just in front of them, whilst in the foreground there was a red

Ferrari F40, a 458 Italia and gate-crashing the Ferrari crowd a DeTomaso Pantera in a subtle burnt orange hue. Other posts on the hotel's website were of visits from a Porsche owners club and several events with Italian and French influencers. In short, the hotel was the place to be, and to be seen, for those who wanted to be flashy.

Basson knew Nice, and he knew that it was far enough away from his target in Italy to make the perfect place for him to leave his hire car. He left Autoroute 8 at the exit for Nice and headed south. Minutes later he was driving along Promenade des Anglais. The sparkling Mediterranean Sea was on his left and in front of this lay the promenade itself, it was busy with locals and tourists taking in the unseasonably warm air. He passed the famed Hotel Negresco, and the Villa Massena Museum then turned into the access road for an underground car park. Inside the car, over his polo shirt, he slipped on a cotton field jacket. It was a custom-made item. It was reversible, one side navy blue and the other a brick-red. It had eight large pouch pockets, four on the inside and four on the outside, and was loose around his torso, thus allowing Basson to carry items in the pockets without them altering the line of the jacket. His explorer trousers were off the peg, and these had two sets of zip-off sections on the legs enabling the trousers to become knee-length or thigh-length shorts. And for footwear he wore a pair of black, supportive, Brooks running shoes. Exiting the car, he took a courier style satchel from the boot. He locked the Peugeot and left.

It was an uphill walk to the SNCF railway station, and Basson zigged and zagged, taking streets that sometimes backtracked before eventually arriving at Gare de Nice-Ville. Now he retrieved, and put on, a distinctive black and gold

'Dallas Cowboys' corduroy cap. He was certain that he had not been followed so went directly to the ticket office and bought a return to Menton, the last French town before the border with Italy. He had ten minutes to wait before his train was ready to depart so went to the platform and sat down on a bench. A new burner phone was in his bag, and he fought the impulse to grab it, switch it on and send a message to his broker asking for any news on the search for the elusive Wolf Six. Finding Akulov was an obsession, it had already been two long years, yet the Ukrainian assassin had remained like a flickering shadow on a summer's day, ever present yet out of reach. Basson took three long, deep breaths as the assassin's face swam into his mind. The man had attempted to abort the contract they had worked on together, shot him and made him a pariah. Akulov was going to die, of that he had no doubt, and he would be the one to do it. Internally he was seething, and this anger mani-fested itself as a sneer about his lips. Basson watched his train pull in. He stood up and boarded it.

The high-speed TGV service ran from Paris to Menton, stopping at first Cannes then Nice on the way. In summer travellers were packed in like sweaty sardines, however now, in the spring, seats were available. He sat facing forward, looking out of the window at the passing landscape, his childhood memories of that last summer holiday as a real family played like a film behind his eyes. Occasionally in the small hours when sleep would not come, Basson wondered whatever happened to that twelve-year-old boy, and his hopes and dreams. Basson closed his eyes and shook his head. NO. He was no longer that child. Life had made him into something else, and that was one of the finest contract killers on the planet. Now that was something of which he was proud.

The train sped through the French coastal countryside giving all those onboard tantalising views of picturesque bays and beaches but not stopping at any of the smaller stations. The train arrived in Monaco via a tunnel and many of the passengers alighted. With nothing to see out of the window, except for the dark, half-lit interior of the part-underground platform, Basson's reflection looked back at him, however this time it wasn't him. It was a man with the head of a wolf. Of course, Tishina, the mother of werewolves was here, in Monte Carlo. A mere leisurely walk about the pavement from the railway station and he'd be at her flat. He should change his plans, go there now, and put a bullet in her skull, or better still plant a small explosive charge on her door handle. The imagined image of Tishina begging him to spare her, brought a thin smile to his lips.

* * *

The tracker on Basson's hire car had flickered and then stopped sending its location in central Nice. By then however a contact of Tishina, Akulov did not ask who, had been tailing the vehicle at a safe distance. He confirmed that the former Legionnaire had entered an underground car park and left his car. On foot the man had then tailed Basson to the SNCF railway station, where a second contact took over surveillance duties and confirmed that he had purchased a return ticket from Nice to Menton. The contact bought a ticket for Monaco and took the same train, he advised Tishina that she had just twenty minutes to intercept it. Ten minutes later, Akulov stood at the very end of the platform in Monaco, awaiting the arrival of Basson's train.

Akulov had made mistakes in his professional life, and innocent people had died, but what had happened on that morning in Amsterdam because of The Bang-Bang Man was inexcusable. Basson was a maniac. He had crossed the line from highly skilled operator to mass murderer, and in the time since the 'bicycle bombing', it had been rumoured the Frenchman had become a tool for those whose morals were even looser than his own. Several apartment bombings in Southeast Asia, a couple of car bombs in Central America and the daylight assassination of a young politician in Brussels were amongst the hits attributed to him. Many on the circuit took questionable contracts, yet the majority were both human and professional enough to have a modicum of moral fortitude. Akulov understood the profession he was in was evil, yet he did all he could to ensure that his own acts were not. He had a moral compass, a kill code, and those whom he carried out contracts upon deserved to die. The American tourists Basson had blown up in Amsterdam had not. Akulov was not given to whims of personal vengeance, in part because those who went against him invariable wound up dead, but this was different. As Akulov waited for the incoming train, he was sure that he was not the only interested party looking for the Frenchman.

The train glided to a halt, the doors opened, and passengers alighted. Directly in front of Akulov, a middle-aged man with messy grey hair in need of a trim, looked straight into Akulov's eyes and said, as he passed, 'Second to last carriage. Rust-coloured field jacket.'

Akulov made no facial expression to acknowledge the intel. He stepped up and onto the high-speed train. Dressed as a scruffy tourist, in a battered blue baseball cap and denim jacket and green combat trousers, Akulov boarded the TGV hoping his quarry, confirmed as sitting at the other end of the train, had not spotted him. Taking an aisle seat facing backwards, on the half-empty first carriage, Akulov kept his jacket buttoned up to aid in the concealment of the Glock 26 holstered under his left armpit and its suppressor concealed beneath his right. His baseball cap was as low as it could be over his eyes without looking as though he was consciously hiding his face, which he was. Akulov understood he was being taped by the train's internal CCTV system so any thought of taking Basson whilst he was still sitting in the carriage was a non-starter. Akulov was resigned to wait until both he and the Frenchman had alighted at Menton.

A little under twenty minutes later and after hugging the coast, the train deposited both assassins in Menton. Akulov had stood by the door and waited until the last possible moment before stepping off. He immediately put on an oversized pair of black Oakley's. Ahead, he saw a man wearing a rust-coloured coat had also held back. They were both employing the same counter-surveillance drills. Akulov quickly turned his back and stepped towards a large information stand, it provided him with the only possible cover available on the deserted platform. He slowly counted to thirty before turning around casually. Basson had gone. Akulov headed towards the exit, hoping he hadn't jumped into a taxi. Outside he was reassured to see the man identified as Basson taking the sloping road down to Edward the Seventh Avenue, which Akulov knew from studying a map on his burner phone, would take him directly towards the seafront.

Menton was the last town in France before the Italian border, and an ever-growing proportion of its residents were wealthy French from other regions who had decided to retire there. As Akulov slowly followed Basson he understood there were worse places to live out one's retirement. A thought struck him, had Basson moved here to retire, its location after all was convenient for France, Monaco and Italy? But it didn't matter a jot to the Ukrainian if Basson had or was planning on retiring or not, as it would be he, Wolf Six, who would permanently retire him.

Although it was mid-morning on a spring Sunday, the town was not empty. Pedestrians were on the pavement, entering and exiting cafés and the tennis court he passed on his right was busy with what looked like a coaching session. The narrow, treelined avenue continued down a gentle incline, Akulov crossed to the other side, where the foliage was thicker, and hung back a little. Basson had not once looked back, doubled back or checked for a tail, which either meant he had become sloppy, or that he knew he was being followed and did not want to alert his follower to the fact that he knew. Akulov hoped it was the former. Basson arrived at the end of the avenue where it gave way to the coast-hugging Promenade du Soleil. Akulov stopped, part hidden by a tree and watched as Basson crossed the road and stood by the railings looking out to sea. Akulov remained static. The fact that Basson had halted could be a tactic, a counter-surveillance tool and at any moment Akulov imagined he would turn around in an attempt to catch anyone watching him.

* * *

The air was fresh, something which admittedly Basson missed in Qatar. He retrieved his burner phone from his bag, powered it up then logged into a US-based Uber account he had created under the name of Bill Yates. He requested a pick-up from his current location and gave the destination address as San Remo, Italy. And then he waited. He casually turned around to watch for any watchers, not that he imagined he was being followed in Menton, but it would have been bad tradecraft to completely ignore all counter-surveillance measures.

Ten minutes later an eager looking man wearing a suit, and black framed glasses, glided to a halt by the side of the road in a silver, Tesla Model S. He powered down the window and asked, 'Monsieur Yates?'

'Hi there,' Basson said, speaking English with a passable Texan accent. 'That's me. Are you my ride to San Remo?'

Above his glasses, the man's brow furrowed, and he switched to English. 'Yes. Hello. I will take you to San Remo. Grand Hotel Londra, yes?'

'Yes. That would be great.'

Basson entered the Tesla, waving away the idea that his bag should go in the boot. 'I like to keep my belongings with me.'

The driver nodded and made no reply. Basson understood the man's English was not great, so he made no further effort to talk.

The Tesla silently wound its way out of Menton and back onto the A8. It was an easy forty-minute drive across the border to San Remo, however as they neared the edge of France they encountered roadworks. One lane on either side of the A8 autoroute was closed and construction workers were to be seen in their high-visibility safety wear. Abruptly an older model Renault Clio with an aftermarket body kit indicated and immediately attempted to squeeze into the narrow gap in front of Basson's Uber and an articulated lorry ahead. At that same time the Uber had started to move forward. Slamming on his brakes the Uber driver sounded his horn at the Clio, and muttered obscenities in French, which of course he believed his ride did not understand, at the three twenty-something looking men inside the Clio. The lorry pulled away, but the pimped-Clio did not move. The Uber driver honked the horn again. The Clio abruptly reversed, then jerked to a stop within centimetres of the Tesla's front bumper. As the Tesla's screen showed a warning, an internal alarm rang in Basson's head. He prepared himself for action, his left hand taking his satchel, whilst the right pushed inside to find his silenced Beretta. And then the Clio driver's left hand appeared from the open window and flipped them the bird. Immediately the two passengers did the same. The Uber driver cursed again, this time louder and with arm gestures of his own. Basson was angry too. In Qatar, this type of behaviour was intolerable and illegal. Expats who had digressed and given in to such acts were fined and imprisoned or in some cases deported. In France, the yobs in the car in front did it with immunity.

Basson took several deep breaths, meanwhile the Uber driver brought his hands together and started to slow clap, then shouted at the Clio, 'Bravo on being brainless bastards!'

The Clio accelerated to catch up with the truck. The Tesla moved too, but the driver pressed his pedal with less urgency. They entered a tunnel in the hill, which then became a bridge spanning a deep valley at the other end. On the right the Mediterranean Sea sparkled and on his left a scattering of whitewashed houses, in amongst the myriad of green and brown trees, hung on to the hillside. In front a large sign informed all those who read it that the road they were travelling on, which up until now had been the French Autoroute 8, was now called the E80 Autostrade and this particular stretch was also, confusingly, named the A10 – Autostrade dei Fiori. A hundred metres past this sign on the motorway of flowers, was in Basson's mind a far more important sign. It was a blue square with a circle of gold stars around the edge framing the word 'ITALIA'.

As someone who was used to criss-crossing borders on a regular basis, the complete lack of border control on this stretch of road was welcomed. Now in Italy Basson started to feel the excitement of the upcoming kill. In his mind he had planned it over and over, using Google Earth and Street View to scout the area around the hotel. San Remo was not a town he had been to before, and that risk of operating somewhere new, on an 'in and out' operation, was highly exciting.

Twenty minutes later after exiting another tunnel in the jagged hills, Basson saw the sprawl of San Remo and its outlying areas below. From the motorway of flowers, it looked in his mind typically Italian with its narrow, winding, chaotic roads, lined with misshapen whitewashed houses. The Tesla left the A10 and headed for the coast. The roads up close and personal were even narrower than he had expected. Basson felt his pulse increase as his excitement mounted at nearing his target. The driver muttered to himself as he negotiated the switchbacks and narrowly avoided a Fiat barrelling at him in the other direction, but they reached the entrance to the hotel without incident. Just to reinforce the fact that he was an American tourist, Basson handed the driver a twenty-dollar bill as a tip and told him to 'have a nice day' as he exited the taxi. No one had come to meet his car, which was a plus as he was not actually going to stay at the hotel.

* * *

Akulov's own Uber came to a halt at the entrance to the hotel. He stepped out in time to see the back of Basson's head as the Frenchman put his satchel over his shoulder and took the sloping exit ramp away from the hotel. Puzzled, Akulov followed at a leisurely pace. Outside the hotel grounds he rejoined the main road and saw that almost immediately opposite, and sloping downhill, was a wide access route for another hotel, one that looked a lot more upmarket. He watched as Basson crossed the road at the traffic lights and paused at the crest of the hill facing the grand, white building. Akulov had to admit it was much more ornate than any of the other surrounding buildings he had seen thus far in San Remo, its location seemed incongruous to its surroundings. Staying on the north side of the road, Akulov continued to observe as Basson in turn observed the hotel. From his elevated position, Akulov noted there was a VIP car park in front of the hotel's grand entrance and a larger, he imagined overflow car park, was to the left which was part hidden by well-established tall trees. The VIP car park however was completely on display to anyone who cared to pass on the street. Like many grand, or boutique hotels the area acted both as a secure location for the highly expensive vehicles and secondly as promotion for the hotel itself. On this occasion, in pride of place for everyone to see, was a collection of supercars. Akulov identified an Alfa Romeo 4C, two Maserati MC 20s, a single Lamborghini Huracán, and four Ferraris, each a different model. One of these, Akulov noted, was a highly unusual blue, Ferrari Dino. As he looked on, Basson checked his wristwatch then carried on walking past the hotel and took a right, entering the park area next door. From the other side of the road, Akulov noted the area had several paths crossing it and a restaurant on one side. He felt his stomach rumble as he caught a waft of cooking. But he wouldn't eat now, of course. Basson sat on a wooden bench, placed his bag on his lap and delved inside. Akulov saw that he turned his head to look left and right whilst his hand rummaged inside. At this distance, although Akulov had a good view of his target, he could not see what Basson was doing with the bag, and given his penchant for explosives it was worrying. Maintaining his visual on Basson, and casually leaning against a wall across the street, Akulov pulled out his burner phone and starting up a secure, encrypted app, called Tishina.

'How was the magical mystery tour?' she asked.

'Not very magical in a ten-year-old Prius.'

'Where are you, exactly?'

'Overlooking a park on the outskirts of San Remo.'

'Italy?'

'Yes.'

'There's an exquisite boutique hotel there, the "Falconi", you can't miss it. It's white, faces the sea and is very grand.'

'I'm next to it. There's a collection of supercars outside.'

'That makes sense. When I stayed there the rest of the clientele were either young influencers or older, extremely wealthy Italians. Both sets liked their bling.'

'And why were you there?'

'I was with an extremely wealthy Italian gentleman. Don't be jealous.'

'I am not. They are short and have hairy arms.'

'Wait a moment, I'll call you back.'

Akulov kept his phone out now as a prop. An elderly couple approached Basson's position but stopped one bench short of his and sat. Akulov noted that Basson immediately closed his courier bag and started to fiddle with his own phone. Akulov enjoyed studying body language, and could also lip-read; however, he didn't speak Italian. What he could understand, by the way both the man and woman were expressively waving their arms, was that they were having either a heated, or impassioned conversation. Akulov's burner screen informed him Tishina was calling him back. 'Yes?'

'I've just checked on their website. This weekend the hotel is hosting an Italian exotic car club. There is going to be a charity presentation by the pool at three this afternoon, and after that the owners of the exotic sports cars will be leaving to drive in convoy through San Remo before they each head home. Could the club and its members be Basson's target?'

Akulov checked his watch, it was a little before two. He said, 'Would anyone arrive on target with such a tight time limitation?'

'No one sane.'

Movement. Basson was on his feet. Akulov said, 'Can you check the members of this club for me? Tell me if anyone stands outs.'

'In the sense that they may have a contract on them?'

'Yes,' Akulov replied and ended the call.

Basson had started to walk further into the park before he turned right onto another road. Akulov now entered the park and followed. Half a minute behind, Akulov could see the path Basson was now on lay parallel to the main promenade and ran up against the garden walls of the hotel. The route had both lanes for cyclists and pedestrians and at this point was two metres lower than the palm tree lined boundary of the hotel's pool area and gardens. The beat of some type of modern music, Akulov wasn't a connoisseur, reached his ears. Basson drew level with the hotel itself and stopped and looked up and into its territory. He held up his phone, as though recording the spectacle above him.

Akulov undid his denim jacket and reached his hand inside, ready to draw his Glock. However, he soon realised his position on the pedestrian walkway was too exposed. The hotel was above him on his right but below on his left and next to the Ligurian Sea was a busy access road to the private paid beaches and car parks. In essence the hotel's patrons could see him, but not the ugly access road, whilst those on the access road could see him but not the hotel's pool and garden area. He imagined the well-heeled hotel residents enjoyed sipping overpriced cocktails whilst looking down on the poorer passers-by. Even now, out of season, he could see hotel guests sitting on sun loungers and day beds, enjoying some of the first weak sun of the year. And at least two were looking in his direction. He kept his right hand where it was and moved forward at a slower pace than before as he drew closer to Basson.

* * *

Basson was enjoying the music. It was a cross between jazz and euro-pop. Still recording he checked the time on his phone. It was three o'clock. A PA system was switched on and, with the usual initial screech of feedback, the master of

ceremonies started to talk about the charity they were
raising money for, the exotic car club and then a few words
about their host – the hotel itself. And he then introduced a
guest of honour. Basson recognised her as an Italian pop star
from the late eighties and the beat of her biggest hit started
to pump out. Amused he watched on as she moved like
someone half her age on the small stage, which was
surrounded by three huge, suited men. He imagined these
were her 'boys, boys, boys'. The small crowd to his left and
right grew larger as an increasing number of nosey passers-
by stopped to watch and listen and then recognised one of
their most beloved icons. They could all see the day beds
nearest the edge of the terrace, and just make out some of
the congregation of people further away on the grass. Via
the PA, Basson heard the name of his target being called, as
chairman of the exotic car club. Basson knew this was his
time to move.

He left the hotel behind and walked, at a hurried pace to
the west. He took a set of concrete steps up and entered a
narrow residential street, with whitewashed villas on either
side of a single-lane tarmacked road. Halfway up, he took a
right into a courtyard at the back of a four-storey apartment
block. All the windows had blinds pulled down to protect
the occupants from the harsh sunlight. Basson noted there
were no obvious security cameras. He took a single step up
and pushed the communal door. It opened inwards. There
was a door on either side of him and a flight of stairs directly
ahead. He again checked for cameras and saw none. He took
the stairs, walking confidently, as though he belonged there,
to the top floor and then up the extra flight of stairs which
abruptly ended at the access door to the roof. Stopping mid-
floor, he quickly removed his jacket and turned it inside out

to reveal the wearable dark blue reverse side. Next, he unzipped the leg sections of his cream-coloured explorer trousers, making them thigh-length shorts. He neatly folded the zip-away sections and stored them inside two pouch pockets of his jacket. He now emptied the contents of his courier bag, carefully placing the two grenades, and the suppressed Beretta, onto the tiled floor. He unclipped the bag from its strap, it too was reversable, and turned the black bag inside out to reveal its garishly coloured, green interior. He then reattached the strap and put its contents back inside, this time including his NFL cap. He checked his watch. He was ready.

Basson hurried back down the stairs, trying to make as little noise as possible and exited through the front door. Once out of the courtyard he continued to head up the street knowing from his scouting of the area via Google Maps that it led back to the main road, Corsa Matuzi which ran past the front on the Falconi Hotel.

Basson appeared on the pavement directly next to an ice-cream parlour and started to walk east up the slight incline. He passed a Mexican restaurant, two estate agencies, another hotel, and finally a podiatry centre, until he was level with the access road to the target's hotel. He checked his watch – half past three. He crossed the road and back-tracked slightly walking past the stripy pedestrian crossing. Directly behind this, and hidden by a thick stone wall, was the entrance ramp for the Grand Hotel Londra, the place the Uber had dropped him off at less than two hours before. He casually leant against the wall, one foot up, feeling the reassuring weight of his bag pulling at his shoulder. He studied his phone screen, as though he was just passing time as the occasional local or visitor went by on both sides of the street.

At this time of day on a Sunday, San Remo was quiet, and
that was all the better for him.

* * *

Akulov was furious. He had been held up by the crowd
watching and listening to the charity presentation so had
only managed to catch a glimpse of Basson turning right and
taking the steps up onto another street. Walking as fast as he
dared, by the time Akulov reached the narrow side street, it
was deserted. Whitewashed villas and garden walls lined
both sides of the narrow street, and Basson could be in any
of them or none of them. He slowly proceeded up the slope
towards the main road at the top, understanding that as
choke points went, this was, as the Americans were fond of
saying, a 'doozy'. At night, or in bad weather or even if he
had been wearing a long coat, Akulov would have been able
to have the G26 in his hand and its suppresser screwed
firmly into place. But it was a Sunday afternoon, with a
cloudless sky. Akulov completely undid his jacket now,
letting it hang open and loose. It would take him less than a
second to retrieve his Glock, but any draw was slower than a
shooter who had already pulled their own trigger.

He continued to climb, passing closed gates and doors in
walls and seeing windows of villas above, some shuttered,
some not, some curtained but none of them open, so far. An
open window in his mind meant a shooter set up to take the
shot. He reached halfway and took the opportunity to turn
into a courtyard. The sidewalls of gardens made up two sides
and the last was the back of a five-storey block of flats.
Akulov studied the windows of the building, all were closed.
Fluidly he pulled out his Glock, and then the suppressor,

which he threaded onto the short barrel of the sub-compact 9mm handgun. He now thrust the silenced Glock back into the inside of his jacket, not into the holster, rather his large inside pocket. He did his jacket up again, now at least the weapon would not fall out, and left one button undone to allow him to draw the Glock if needed. It wasn't a perfect solution and may perhaps add an extra half a second to his draw, but at least any rounds he now fired would be suppressed. It was then that his burner phone rang again.

'Yes.'

'None of the members of the exotic car club have criminal records or any obvious links to organised crime, but they are not a group of nuns. At least three of them are on their second or third wife, and two others have just finished hostile takeovers of rival businesses.'

'So, any of them, or all of them could be Basson's target?'

'Yes, or none of them. Where is he now?'

'I don't have a visual.'

'Explain?'

Akulov did. 'I'm going to head back to the front of the hotel, and I'm going to go dark.'

'Call me when it is done.'

'I will.'

Akulov rejoined the street and continued to climb back up to the main road. He turned right and started to walk back towards the hotel. And then he heard loud, powerful, throaty engines start up.

* * *

Basson heard engines; they were revving, and they were loud. This had to mean the exotic cars were about to move off. He swung his bag round to his left side and unzipped it. He retrieved a grenade with his right hand and held it at his side, his body obscuring the item. The engines continued to rev and now changed tone; he took that as a cue they were moving off. Basson casually looked both ways, up and down the street. There was no one on his side of the road for at least a hundred metres, and thirty metres away on the other, a pair of women were standing on the pavement, outside a shop and behind a row of parked cars, and further behind them a single man wearing a baseball cap and sunglasses was walking in his direction. Looking left now, towards the access road to the target's hotel, Basson saw the red nose of a Ferrari appear. The car turned slowly then fishtailed, as the accelerator was blipped. It was a 458 Italia. A second red Ferrari followed a moment later, this was a 599, then came the Alfa Romeo, the two Maseratis MC 20s, and the Lamborghini before the last three Ferraris appeared. Moving at a more leisurely pace the 1971, blue Ferrari Dino 246 GTS, belonging to Basson's target – Antonio Lombardi, brought up the rear. Basson tutted. Although a number of motor enthusiasts had referred to the Dino as a lesser Ferrari or 'a Fiat in drag', Basson loved its curves. And the classic car market had started to agree with Basson because prices were currently surging.

It was a pity to destroy such a beautiful car.

Lombardi was in the driving seat, gesticulating with his left hand, as his right held on to the wheel. His passenger was a blonde woman, who looked twenty-five and was neither his first nor second wife. The Dino had its targa top removed to allow Lombardi and his female friend to enjoy both the sunshine, and the adulation of passing motorists. Unwittingly, this also aided Basson.

The procession passed Basson's position without pause and continued along the Corsa Matuzi. Basson waited for the last of the Ferraris to pass before he quickly stepped out onto the pedestrian crossing. Simultaneously he removed the pin from the first grenade. The Dino halted abruptly. Basson waved cheerily with his left hand, the one holding the pin, and threw the grenade in an arc at the historic car.

Neither passenger nor driver reacted. They had three to five seconds left to escape as the grenade landed in Lombardi's lap. Basson turned and sprinted back across the road the way he had come. Pulling off his bag, he threw himself behind the thick, stone wall separating the road from the grounds of the Grand Hotel Londra. Basson lay supine and waited for the malicious sound he loved more than anything else, it heralded death, destruction, and pain. In the aftermath of his actions a myriad of car alarms would sound together, creating a techno dance track from hell. Cries, screams and shouts would drift over the wall from the injured, the shocked and the outraged. The sneer was back on his face, and his heart pounded in his chest, the expectation was electric...

And then nothing. Five long seconds and nothing. Basson rolled up to his feet. What had happened? Was it a dud? He pushed his crushing disappointment and disbelief aside and took a breath. Never mind, this was why he had the second grenade as a backup. He just hoped the target was still near enough for him to catch him.

Basson pulled the second grenade from his bag and advanced around the corner.

* * *

Akulov saw the supercars growling towards him, but the last one had stopped, locals on the pavement were staring, and the passenger was screaming. In a flash, a figure in a dark blue field jacket, and shorts stepped out from the pavement and threw an object into the last car in the procession, a blue Ferrari Dino. Instantly recognising the man as Basson, Akulov started to sprint towards the scene, zigzagging around a pair of women standing metres in front of him and blocking the pavement. The blue Ferrari remained immobile in the middle of the road as the female passenger continued to scream, and then the male driver yelled. Both occupants now all but leapt out of the classic car, half falling, half running back the way they had come towards the steep access road of the Falconi Hotel. The man shouted, *'Bomba! Bomba!'*

Akulov knew it was one of the two grenades Gallacher had sold Basson that had landed in the Ferrari, and he also knew, unlike Basson, that the L109s grenade had been rendered inactive by Gallacher upon Tishina's request. Impossible to tell unless the casing was opened and examined, and it looked as though Basson had trusted the armourer enough not to do so. In Akulov's world trust was an illusion.

Akulov drew level with the entrance to the drive for the Grand Hotel Londra, the same place Basson had been dropped off by his Uber, and the exact same place he had now darted back into. Akulov drew the suppressed Glock and spun around the thick, stone wall. Basson was already running to the opposite end of the wall, the other gap in the semi-circular driveway, which also led back to the main road. Wasting no time and not having any qualms at all about shooting the Frenchman in the back, Akulov squeezed the trigger, sending a round racing after the assassin. It hit him in the side yet seemed to have no effect. Akulov understood it must have simply sliced through his billowing jacket. Akulov's next round missed altogether as Basson, suddenly realising he was under fire, threw himself down and around the corner of the wall.

Akulov upped his pace, he had to get to Basson before he could get in a position to return fire. He had eight rounds left in his standard ten-round magazine so could not afford to use any as covering fire. Akulov went wide and low around the end of the wall. Basson was already on the other side of the road and sprinting towards the Falconi Hotel. What few pedestrians there had been on the street, had now formed a group of perplexed onlookers and more had seemingly swarmed like ants, out of apartments overlooking the whole scene. All thought of concealment gone, Akulov acquired Basson and fired again. The round missed the man's head by the smallest margin and shattered a window in the building across the street. Now the onlookers started to scream and at that exact same time the sound of an approaching police siren reached Akulov's ears.

Basson was now hurtling down the Falconi's steep driveway. Akulov heard the faintest of 'pops' and realised that Basson was using his suppressed Sig Sauer. Yet he hadn't turned around to engage him. Akulov understood he wasn't the target. He suddenly felt his chest tighten with anguish as he realised that Basson must be chasing down his targets. Akulov reached the start of the driveway. Basson was already at the bottom, and a body lay on the tarmac between them. It wasn't the woman from the car, nor the driver. It was another man those white shirt had now been stained crimson with his own blood. Wracked with guilt, Akulov had no time to stop to check on the fallen hotel busboy, he had to reach Basson and eliminate him before he could cause any further casualties.

Basson turned as he raced for the front door of the hotel but then he abruptly skidded to a stop, as though he had been struck by lightning. He had recognised who it was who was chasing him.

'Wolf Six!' Basson roared, raising his Sig.

Akulov dived to his right, behind a bush, as a pair of incoming rounds sparked up off the tarmac where his right foot had been. A second round zipped past through the leaves. Akulov crawled to his left, and using the foliage for cover got to his haunches then ran to the side of the hotel, putting the building between himself and any possible angle Basson may have to take a shot. He reached a terraced area, set out with tables and chairs and next to this was a door leading into what he imagined was the dining room. Several perplexed guests and a lone waiter stared at him as he rushed past them, weapon up, and into the building. A second later the screams started again. As Akulov tore through the obstacle course of tables and chairs in the completely monochrome room, another waiter appeared and held his arms up as though attempting to stop him. However as soon as he saw the Glock his eyes became wide, and he pushed himself back against the charcuterie table. From outside Akulov could hear nearing sirens, and from further inside the hotel, along the hallway, he heard voices shouting in Italian and an anguished scream. He exited the dining room and advanced down the hallway, where white walls with matching marble greeted him. A figure flashed past at the end, Basson. Akulov had no shot so didn't take one. He burst into the hotel foyer; the reception desk was to his immediate right but to his left a body was sprawled across a white leather settee. It wasn't the target, it was a bald man, wearing a flowery shirt, and there was a single, precise entry wound in his forehead.

At that moment Akulov caught movement in his peripheral vision, and turned just as a huge form landed on him. Akulov slammed into the unforgiving marble floor, landing on his right shoulder, his Glock sliding from his grasp. A meaty fist made contact with the side of Akulov's head and then a forearm was pressed hard across his throat. Eyes bulging Akulov stared up at who he could only presume was a bodyguard, and one attempting to throttle him at that. Akulov attempted to buck but the man was too heavy, so Akulov relaxed his body then brought up both of his arms and in a swift, vicious movement performed a bat strike, slamming the palms of each of his hands against each of his assailant's ears. It was a move that did disorientate and could perforate eardrums. Immediately the bodyguard released Akulov's throat, and his hands shot up towards his ears. Akulov bucked and rolled onto his side, sending the 'heavy' sprawling. Getting up to his haunches he searched for his Glock and saw it just in front of an armchair. He scrambled towards it as a large boot collided with his stomach. Akulov felt the air leave his body and once more he slumped on the cold marble. A second bodyguard now bent down and collected the Glock. He pointed it at Akulov. His hand was too large for the grip of the sub-compact 9mm handgun, making it look like a child's plaything, but at this distance just squeezing the trigger would ensure a kill.

And then the man's head jerked sideways, and a puff of red mist filled the air. The bodyguard dropped and landed on the outstretched Glock, the silencer of which took the brunt and was bent between the dead weight of his body and the marble flooring. Akulov darted behind another piece of furniture, a sturdy marble-sided credenza, as he heard a familiar voice.

'No one kills you but me! I have waited for this moment ever since that day in Amsterdam, Wolf Six.'

Akulov said nothing and assessed his options. He heard the squeak of rubber soled shoes as Basson moved.

'Stand up, and raise your hands above your head, Wolf Six. This time you have really lost. I am going to end you. After that I am going to the room on the top floor to complete my contract by executing Lombardi and his young mistress. The Bang-Bang Man does not fail.'

A voice roared in Italian and then Basson's Sig snapped twice, two rounds, yet the voice continued yelling. Akulov got to his feet. He saw the first bodyguard, whom he now assessed was easily double his own weight, embracing Basson in a bear hug. At least one of Basson's rounds had hit the man as blood was flowing freely from his thick neck, his collar already made scarlet, yet his strength had not seemed to wane. Basson's arms were trapped by his side. His trigger finger started to pump, and random rounds exploded as loud thuds out of the end of his suppressor slammed into the furniture and the floor. One, two, three and a fourth. And then, grip unwavering, the bodyguard dropped to his knees, forcing Basson backwards onto a second white settee, before he finally fell forwards and pinned him. Akulov sprang to his feet. Ignoring his own damaged sidearm he tore across the room towards Basson and his Sig.

Before he could reach it, a barked warning filled the foyer. This one was a command. A pair of Carabinieri officers, had entered, and their service Berettas were drawn.

Basson's Sig popped twice in quick succession and the policemen dropped. With a sneer on his face, the Frenchman now turned his suppressed micro-compact 9mm handgun on Akulov.

'Now where were we?' Basson squeezed the trigger, and the Sig Sauer clicked.

'We were at the part where you discover your twelve-round magazine is empty, Basson.'

Basson's face contorted as though it was folding in on itself. 'No!'

Akulov sprang at him, landing a heavy knee in his chest, the momentum of which caused both men to fall over the back of the settee. Akulov rolled off, but Basson, gasping for air, managed to grab the leg of a table, causing a large vase to drop and land on Akulov's chest. As the water and pungent smelling flowers fell about Akulov's face, Basson staggered to his feet and ran towards the back of the hotel. Akulov rose, the vase smashing, and raced after Basson.

Although panting for breath, Basson was fast, but slower than the younger man. By the time they had reached the entrance to the terrace Akulov was close enough to launch himself from the top of the wide, white, steps leading down to the pool and garden. He slammed into Basson's shoulders and both men tumbled forward heavily, slamming into and then rolling down the concrete steps. Akulov tasted blood, as he painfully struggled to his feet.

Basson was on his hands and knees, blood pouring from a wide gash on his forehead. He cursed Akulov in French. *'Nique tes morts!'*

Akulov said nothing as he took a step forward and launched a powerful kick into Basson's side, causing the former Legionnaire to drop. Akulov took a breath and then

bent down, grabbing Basson by the back of his neck and
hauling him to his feet. Basson's face was a bloodied mess,
and he blinked away rivulets of blood. He looked defeated,
yet Akulov knew better than to relax just yet. The anger he
felt towards the man at that moment was possibly the
greatest he had ever felt, only matched by the hatred he had
felt for those who had murdered his grandmother decades
before in Moscow. Both times, Akulov realised, the focus of
his wrath had been a bomb maker, a terrorist.

Akulov swung his right fist upwards at Basson's face, he
was going to shatter his nose and send shards of cartilage
into his brain, but Basson jerked to one side and at the same
time his left knee connected with Akulov's unprotected
groin.

Feeling as though his stomach was being yanked out of
his abdomen, Akulov fought the urge to double up and
managed to deliver a headbutt, which caught Basson on the
side of his head. Basson pushed forcefully at Akulov,
creating space before he fell once more onto his hands and
knees and dragged himself onto the sloping grass. Akulov
dropped to his own knees and, panting, watched as slowly
and painfully, almost like an ancient, giant tortoise, Basson
tried to escape. The Frenchman's hands gave way, and he
slipped onto his side, and started to roll down the grassy
verge.

Akulov looked around. Inside the hotel grounds the residents had scattered but there were still curious faces
watching from the path below, past the edge of the hotel's
territory. Back on his feet and breathing deeply to dissipate
the pain in his groin, Akulov followed Basson. He kicked
him again as the man continued his slow downwards roll.

Basson came to an abrupt stop against a low retaining

wall, no more than two bricks high, which separated the grass from the stylish, white anti-slip tiles surrounding the hotel's matching white, rectangular pool. Finally, Akulov could stand this no more. Using his left foot, he stomped on the man's abdomen and then sank to one knee to deliver a killing blow to Basson's throat. Arm shaking, Akulov stopped, his knuckles all but touching the man's throat. He realized he was breathing heavily, and he saw that Basson was defenceless. He was about to become a monster to kill a monster. He drew his arm back again but then fate, and the Italian police, intervened.

An abrupt sharp, stinging sensation, as though ten thousand barbs had been plunged into his skin, forced his body to convulse as every muscle contracted. Akulov's mouth was frozen open as he dropped sideways over the retaining wall and onto the tiles.

Stern voices in Italian gave commands around him, which he didn't understand but recognised the tone of, and then a voice spoke in English, with an American accent.

'Please, you gotta help me! This guy's a maniac! He shot those poor people in there and then tried to kill me!'

Akulov managed to raise his head, as Basson, now sitting up, made eye contact with him. Akulov felt his hands being dragged behind his back and a pair of cold, steel cuffs attached to his wrists. And then a hand pressed on his back and removed the steel barbs of the taser which had taken him down. Strong arms then dragged him to his feet, as Italian was barked at him. Meanwhile Basson was being helped up by a male police officer, whilst his female colleague secured a field dressing to his forehead. The male officer now put his arm under Basson's and helped him walk back up the slope. Akulov tested his cuffs. They were on tight. He'd lost Basson, but he could not lose his liberty. He spun around, breaking the grips of the hands on his arms. Two members of the Carabinieri faced him, they seemed shocked by and unprepared for his rapid actions. Akulov's right foot slammed into the right knee of the officer on his right, causing the man to howl and fall sideways. Meanwhile, Akulov had noticed that the Carabinieri officer on the left, unlike his colleague, did not have a pair of handcuffs hanging from his belt. Using one of the only moves he could manage in his shackled state, Akulov copied Basson's earlier attack and kicked the man in the groin. As the officer doubled over, Akulov fell on top of him, and placing his back against the officer's front, managed to work his right hand into the man's trouser pocket. His fingertips snaked around a small key. Akulov then frantically rolled away and inadvertently dropped into the large pool. It was unheated and the water was frigid. He let himself sink, as like Houdini he struggled with placing the key into the lock for the left side of the hinged handcuffs and releasing his arms. His feet hit the bottom, followed by his buttocks and then moments later he was pushing up and away, his arms separate again. He reached the far end of the pool and dragged himself up and out, with the handcuffs still attached to his right wrist. In a state of confusion and shock the two Carabinieri were still squirming on the grass, and the other pair who had hold of Basson had frozen, protecting the man claiming to be a victim and not quite knowing what to do about Akulov.

Feet squelching in his trainers, Akulov stood. A third pair of police officers were running at him from the rear gate at the end of the sun terrace, blocking his path. The first drew his service weapon, and then the second copied. Akulov knew there was no escaping any rounds they may fire, and the fact that two of their own lay dead or dying back inside the hotel gave him little reason to believe that they would not hesitate to shoot. Akulov did the only thing he could, he raised his hands above his head.

Angrily shouting in Italian, the two men he had attacked and escaped from, advanced. One grabbed Akulov's arms once more, whilst the other snapped the cuffs shut and removed the key. Out of the corner of his eye, Akulov now saw Basson being led away, around the side of the hotel. An order was barked at Akulov and then one Italian pushed him in the back whilst the other gripped his left elbow with far more force than was necessary and, under the still drawn Berettas of their colleagues, frog-marched him back up the steps and into the hotel.

The aftermath of the fight with Basson sickened him, not because it was anything he had not seen before but due to the fact that several innocent men lay dead. Men that he would have been able to save if he had got to Basson faster. The group crossed the foyer, as more outraged Italian was hurled at him, before he was half pushed down the entrance steps and into the car park. To his immediate right there was an ambulance, and Basson was entering it. The ambulance doors closed, and the vehicle moved away, siren sounding. Akulov pulled at his cuffs, testing their integrity. They were solid. The four men in uniform herded him towards a dark blue Carabinieri liveried Alfa Romeo Giulia. One of the officers opened the passenger door and then bundled him inside. Moments later Akulov was sandwiched between two law enforcement officers in the back whilst the other two, who had their weapons drawn, were in the front. One started to speak animatedly on his radio whilst the other put away his pistol and drove them up the entrance ramp and out of the hotel grounds.

Akulov had no doubt once the various handguns had been tested it would absolve him of any of the killings, however it would not excuse him for tearing through a boutique hotel with a suppressed Glock and battering Basson. He'd be questioned, hard. And he'd be remanded in custody whilst a case was built against him, for whatever crimes the Italian legal system decided he had committed. He imagined this would include attempted murder. And then of course there was the ever-present risk that other previous contracts he had undertaken in both Italy and the rest of the EU would be linked to him. Akulov had to escape. And he had to do so as quickly as he could. He had no illusion that Basson would also be attempting the same.

Akulov assessed his surroundings. The two Carabinieri in the front were tall, and their seats were pushed back in their runners, whilst the men either side of him were shorter, and wirier. The only one talking was the passenger in the front, the three others sat in stony silence, perhaps in shock as they attempted to process what they had witnessed. But this was good for him. The Alfa Romeo turned off the main road through the town and took a steeper, narrower route away from the coast. On one side the ground fell away, offering views of the glistening sea beyond. Akulov had no idea where they were headed, or how far away from the hotel the nearest secure cell was, but he imagined he didn't have long until they would arrive. Uncomfortably leaning back in his seat, his full weight pushing against his wrists, which in turn were digging into the upholstery of the bench seat, his hands had started to become numb. Yet he welcomed this. He slowly attempted to pull his wrists apart, once more gauging the strength of his shackles. He now realised that the left cuff, the one that had been reclosed, was tighter than the right. In fact, the cuff securing his right wrist, whilst not loose, did allow his hand a little more space. Akulov had only one possible move he could make. He'd done it before, yet that had been during his specialist training, and in that instance the cuff had been the older US style chain-linked type not the secure, hinged version favoured by many European law enforcement agencies. He had nothing to lose and his freedom to gain. Akulov relaxed his shoulders, set his jaw tight, and then violently twisted his right wrist and hand. A momentary white-hot poker of pain stabbed him in his hand to be all but instantly replaced by a cold wave washing up his arm as he dislocated his thumb. Pulling with all the power he could muster, Akulov forced his contorted, right hand through the cuff as his flesh ripped open. At the same time, he threw himself to the left, all but on to the lap of the unsuspecting officer, as he managed to bring his right foot up and slam his heel into the face of the man sitting to his right. Before any of his four Carabinieri escorts had time to react, Akulov then swung his right elbow up into the face of the man he was squashing. Now the driver understood something was happening. The Alfa swerved across the narrow road, and the front passenger attempted to turn in his seat. Akulov shot his left fist into the front passenger's throat. Reaching forwards, Akulov then snaked his left arm around the neck of the driver and squeezed as hard as he could. Hands leaving the wheel, and clawing at Akulov's arm, the Alfa Romeo jinked left and across the road. Akulov let go and hunkered down behind the passenger seat as the Carabinieri vehicle left the tarmac and dropped down into a deep, grassy gully. Arms protecting his head, Akulov felt the sedan roll twice, and airbags explode around the cabin. And then they came to a sudden halt. Before the four stunned Carabinieri officers could move, Akulov pushed away from the back of the car and scrambled across the unconscious front passenger. Unlocking his door, Akulov fell out of the Alfa headfirst and onto the grass outside. Struggling to his feet, and cradling his bloodied right hand, he hobbled away through the small olive grove, which the Alfa Romeo now found itself entangled in.

11

HARRISVILLE, MICHIGAN

Akulov sat back in the metal chair with his eyes closed. He was just resting them, ready to snap them open if he needed to. His head now felt almost normal, and apart from a few lingering aches from his other bruises he assessed himself as being functional. To allow himself to be held by the sheriff was a mistake, he knew that. He should have escaped earlier, yet something had told him to stay where he was, it was a sixth sense, and he found it was seldom wrong.

Weak afternoon sunlight filtered in from the half-sized security window and he could hear birdsong. He didn't know what type; he just enjoyed their tunes. He'd always liked listening to the birds, there had never been a wide variety in the Moscow suburbs, the dacha however was a different story. On a summer's day he'd sit on the lawn with his grandmother, drinking *kompot,* and watching the birds jump in and out of the forest as though they were playing a game of dare. He'd always wanted to feed them, and to stroke them like he had done with the stray cat who had claimed his grandmother's dacha as his territory. His grandmother wasn't a fan of cats and told him not to encourage the 'gypsy cat'. Back in Moscow, he'd had a friend whose father had smuggled a grey parrot into the country. The bird lived in the flat with the family and ate its meals with them. When he told his grandmother about this, she had instructed him to always wash his hands thoroughly after visiting that apartment. Akulov looked down at his inky hands, his grandmother wouldn't approve.

He heard footsteps outside and the key turn in the lock. Deputy Turcotte stepped inside, again followed by Deputy Grant. The older man was holding what looked like a sleeping roll and a pillow.

'Mr Hurst, look I'm sorry to say Sheriff Lehnert is not going to be able to see you until the morning.'

Akulov stood. 'That's fine. I'll come back.'

'Ah, no,' Turcotte squeaked, taking a step forward.

'That means we've got to keep you in overnight, Mr Hurst.'

'I understand,' Akulov said, noting the unmasked joy on Turcotte's face.

'I'm sorry we don't have a spare bunk. The other room is occupied. So, I'll just put this down over here, on the floor.'

Akulov took a pace backwards, whilst every instinct told him to advance, to attack and to escape.

'Now I think I'd better show you to the bathroom, it is just at the end of the hall.'

Turcotte pulled out a taser. 'Don't you try anything, the sheriff told us you attempted to run once already.'

Akulov nodded, yet inside he wondered what was up with this sheriff's department.

Grant left the room and turned right. Akulov followed with Turcotte bringing up the rear – taser at the ready. In the narrow space he could have attacked Grant with ease, but the man was just doing his job and Akulov had an aversion to attacking non-combatants. If it had just been Turcotte, Akulov would have kicked him in his massive gut and taken a chance. They passed another locked door on the right before arriving at the entrance on his left.

'We'll wait here. Don't you try anything,' Turcotte squeaked again.

The bathroom consisted of a urinal on the outer wall, directly below the window, a pair of sinks and a pair of toilet cubicles. Akulov used the toilet then washed his hands and face as he stared at his reflection in the mirror. Apart from several broken blood vessels in his eyes he didn't look too awful.

'Time, Mr Hurst.'

Akulov exited to find the men standing either side of the exit, again Turcotte was behind with the taser and Grant was leading the way back to the interview room. Again Akulov thought about barging past Grant and bolting for the steps up to the open-plan squad room and freedom, but he didn't. He entered the room.

Grant said, 'Do you like pizza?'

'Everyone likes pizza,' Turcotte added.

'Yes,' Akulov said. 'I like pizza.'

Turcotte locked the door and Akulov looked around his five-star accommodation. He unrolled the bed and lay down. It was better than laying on the floor and more comfortable than many cheap hotels he'd been forced to stay at, and at least here he had no fear of being found by the Triads. He looked at the cracked ceiling and felt his eyes starting to get heavy when the door opened again.

Akulov was up and standing by the time Grant had

placed a deep crust takeaway pepperoni pizza pie and a large bottle of Coke on the table.

'Enjoy your meal, and sorry again,' Grant said as he left, and Turcotte once more locked the steel door.

* * *

Montreal, Canada

Mickey Martel wiped his forehead with a towel and admired himself in the gym mirror. He'd definitely made some gains. He took off his sweaty singlet and tossed it onto the weights bench. Turning sideways on, he pushed his chest up, grabbed his right wrist with his left and twisted at the waist back towards the mirror. The 'side chest' was one of his favourite poses, and he popped it whenever and wherever he saw his reflection. Next, he turned fully back to the mirror, placed his hands either side of his waist and flared his lats. With a self-satisfied expression growing on his face, he raised his arms above his head, flexing his wrists and bending his arms to pull a 'front double bicep pose', or 'the coat hanger' as an ex-girlfriend had called it. He held his stance and in his mind's eye saw himself as his favourite Canadian wrestler, 'The Model' Rick Martel, whilst the crowd booed. Although both men shared a surname, unlike the former professional wrestler, whose 'arrogance' was just a gimmick, Mickey Martel was a 'heel' in real life, as the main muscle for Jean Gagnon and his 'syndicate'.

The bleeping of his phone dragged Martel away from his daydream. He picked it up off the incline bench, his thick fingers tapping in a code to unlock the screen. It was a WhatsApp message from a number which should have only been contacting the group in an emergency. The message was a close-up of a driving licence, the focus on the holder's name and face. What struck Martel the most was the intensity of the subject's eyes peering back at him electronically.

The text of the message read:

> Found this fils de pute snooping. He won't tell us who sent him or who he works for. Can you ask around?

'Can I ask around?' Martel repeated the question to the empty gym. 'What am I, directory enquiries?' He inhaled deeply, he'd better head upstairs with this. Pulling on a grey Gold's Gym hoodie, Martel exited the underground gym and took the lift to the top floor of the office block. Stepping out onto the landing he was greeted through the floor-to-ceiling picture windows with a panorama of downtown Montreal. He turned to his right and knocked on the door of the corner office.

'Entrée!' a gruff voice shouted from within.

Martel entered to find the half-brothers Jean Gagnon and Piere Cote glaring at him. He shut the door gently behind him.

Cote said, 'Mickey, you see that photo?'

'How could he?' Gagnon asked.

Cote, the younger half-brother, looked back at Gagnon, who was relaxing in his large, leather desk chair. 'It's a group chat, Jean. You, me and Mickey are on it.'

'Ah oui, you told, me,' Gagnon nodded. 'Mickey, you got any ideas?'

'Not yet,' Martel remained by the door.

Gagnon held up his phone. 'Should I know who this is?'

Cote leant back in the visitor's chair. 'You should, if

Squeaky-Dave thinks it's important enough to send it to us. We've got to do our due diligence, right?'

'Ask around, Mickey, send it to the circuit guys, see if they know.'

'Shall I include The Irishman?'

'Especially The Irishman,' Gagnon said.

All three men's phones buzzed as a follow-up message arrived, from SD – Squeaky-Dave.

Gagnon squinted at it. 'Is that a photo of a hoodie?'

Cote read the text.

> This is what the guy had on when he was found.

'Only an imbecile would wear that,' Gagnon stated.

'Found?' Cote repeated. 'What does that mean?'

'Ask Squeaky.'

Cote spoke as he tapped out a message.

> What do you mean, SD, by 'found'?

Martel said, 'I think I've seen that design somewhere before.'

'Where, the noodle bar?' Gagnon allowed himself a smirk, before pointing at Martel's legs. 'Anyway, why are you wearing shorts, have you been to the beach?'

'I've been in the gym in the basement.'

'I know where the gym is, Mickey. So, I'm listening?'

'That guy's face meant nothing to me, but now I've seen the hoodie I'm thinking maybe it does.'

'Meaning?' Cote replied, looking up from his smartphone.

'I'm sure that's the Long-Zi Triad emblem.'

'Longzy?' Gagnon said, a smile appearing. 'That what you boys wear in the gym?'

'I see where this is going,' Cote said.

'Where?' Gagnon did not.

Mickey continued. 'That hit in Winnipeg. The hitter was wearing the same hoodie.'

'Was he now?'

'Yeah, and I've been hearing that the Long-Zi say it wasn't them, not their style.'

'This hoodie is not their style?' Gagnon asked.

'The sign is theirs, and the face – gimme a minute.'

'Sure, take your time, we have all day, isn't that right, brother?'

'All day,' Cote confirmed.

Mickey fiddled with his phone and pulled up the news website he wanted. A computer-generated image of a man's face filled his display. This one however showed the subject with stubble, shorter hair, and the eyes were dull, but he knew he wasn't wrong. On the balls of his feet, he advanced towards the large, wooden desk and held his iPhone in front of both bosses. 'See this? It's the video-fit of the hitter – given by that guy who whacked him on the head.'

Gagnon frowned. 'The "have a go hero"?'

'Oui.'

'He's still in hospital, took one to the gut,' Cote said.

'Oui. That face Squeaky-Dave sent us sure looks like the photofit to me!'

Gagnon snatched the phone, eyes narrowing as he peered at it at arm's length. He compared it to the photograph of the guy Squeaky-Dave had sent. 'Could it be a match?'

'Looks like it,' Cote agreed.

'Then there's the footage at the hotel. The hitter wore the same hoodie.'

Gagnon was not entirely convinced. 'You could get one of these hoodies at any dollar store.'

'No way,' Mickey said, emphatically. 'The Long-Zi will kill anyone who wears their sign who is not Long-Zi.'

'So, anyone wearing this was Long-Zi or wanted the world to think they were Long-Zi,' Cote stated.

'Yes.'

Gagnon nodded. 'See, Mickey, in spite of what others say, including medical doctors, I know you've got something up there between your ears apart from muscle.'

'Merci, Jean.'

Cote said, 'We've got a huge opportunity here.'

Gagnon rubbed his chin. 'Oui. We have. Who was the hit on, Mickey?'

'You don't watch the news? It was on Paul Fang – the Tech Guy. He was a money man for the Yee Kwan Triad.'

Gagnon folded his arms. 'Here's what we do. We know where this guy is, and that's privileged knowledge, and that means leverage. So, we tell the Yee Kwan we've found their man, for a finder's fee.'

'You think they'll go for that?' Cote asked.

'If they want the hitter they will negotiate, for sure,' Gagnon replied.

'Do we wait until we hear back from the circuit?' Mickey asked.

'Nope. We get this out,' he waved Martel's iPhone, 'the face goes to the circuit now, someone has to know who this shooter is. At the same time as we open discussions with the Triads.'

'I'll tell Squeaky-Dave to keep him alive and under wraps,' Cote stated.

'For sure,' Gagnon said. 'Mickey, how well do you know the Yee Kwan? I mean I recognise the name but you're more "operational" than I am.'

'I know a senior guy.'

'Bon. Then, Mickey, you get a hold of him. Tell the guy what we have, and tell him to contact me to negotiate. Give the guy my "business" number. Then you get yourself down there to Squeaky-Dave's and you take a look at our mystery hitter.'

There was another 'ping' as a message was added to the chat, it was from SD. Cote read it out.

> He was found by the lake.

Mickey said, 'That makes no damn sense. I mean by the lake—'

'Whatever,' Gagnon cut in. 'Who have we got down there as sheriff, with Squeaky, Mickey?'

'Sue Lehnert.'

'Then you get down there *tout de suite*, I don't trust Squeaky with guarding something this important. Take the jet, then have it come straight back. Now, you just ensure sure you have those calls. This could be the making of you, Mickey.'

'Merci,' Martel replied.

12

MONTE CARLO, MONACO

The supercars of Monaco no longer impressed Basson, so used to, as he was, the very same models and even more outrageous editions revving along the small man-made streets of Doha's Pearl. But they had impressed him once, and that had been during his first trip to the principality as a boy. His parents had brought him by train all the way south from Paris and along the coast. It had been a long summer holiday. They had spent time in Nice, then Monaco and finally taken in a few sights in neighbouring Italy before finally wrapping up their time and returning home to Paris. It had been his favourite holiday; it had been the last one he had ever been on where both his mother and father were present. Two months after the holiday had ended, in a wetter than usual Paris September, his father had walked away from his marriage to his mother. And for a twelve-year-old boy, this had broken Basson's heart.

Now as he rode the bus into Monte Carlo from Nice, catching glimpses of deserted out of season beaches, he also had anger and disappointment in his chest. It had been five years since he had failed to kill the man who had insulted him, the man who had shot him, the man who had destroyed his reputation, Ruslan Akulov the assassin known as Wolf Six. Five long years of searching for the man without a single sighting.

Basson listened in to the conversations around him, most were in French with a smattering of English, and Italian. The French speakers were workers heading into work, whilst the others were excited tourists. Basson was dressed as a tourist in sneakers and jeans. A polo shirt and windbreaker covered the thin ballistic vest he was wearing. The combination was enough to defeat small calibre rounds, and of course the occasional breeze blowing in across the Mediterranean. It was never very cold in Monaco, indeed the coldest aspect of Monaco was the entitled stares of the Monégasque when a lesser visitor failed to give way on the promenade. They amused Basson, in much the same way as the Qataris did. Both were small countries; both were wildly wealthy, and both were fighting above their weight on the world stage. Bravo.

The bus stopped opposite the entrance to the marina and Basson followed the other passengers off and onto the pavement. Immediately cameras and camera phones were raised, and fingers were pointed, accompanied by excited statements about it being 'just like in the films'. Basson wished he could relive that happiness; that of an excited boy promised glimpses of the world's finest cars. Cars had been his thing at twelve, that naive, carefree time before the world, and ultimately he, had turned cruel.

Basson left the tourists to their revelry and made for the promenade. He felt the autumnal sun on his face, as he passed locals and residents out for their early morning

constitutional strolls. None of the people he saw were overweight, these were people who knew how to take care of
themselves, these people were winners and not the fat
oligarchs nor minor millionaires who would surface later for
a sugary, buttery breakfast of coffee, cakes and croissants. In
the distance he saw a pink figure moving slowly towards
him, and subconsciously Basson increased his pace to
ensure the crossing of their paths happened sooner. As
Basson's eyes fixed on the approaching figure, he felt almost
a sense of relaxation overcome him. Was it happiness? The
elderly man in the designer tracksuit was jogging in slow
motion, not a power walk but an actual run and Basson
found the way he moved mesmeric. This was who he wanted
to be when he was in his dotage, to hell with sitting at home
or worse still, residing in a home for the old and lazy, this
would be him every morning without fail, either swimming
or running or both. The runner nodded at Basson as he
passed and the two men shared a single, respectful,
'Bonjour.'

Basson walked on until he drew level with the next free
bench. He sat, casually leaning back and seeking out anyone
who may be paying him too much attention. Now he could
see a young couple strolling with what he expected would
be a designer buggy for their little one. The father was pushing, with an expression on his face which Basson had last
seen on his own father's, pride. The mother meanwhile was
wearing oversized sunglasses to hide, he supposed, her
weariness. Basson had never wanted children, and he'd
never met a woman he wanted to stay with for long enough
to warrant them. It was the same with pets, what was the
point? Cats wandered around nonchalantly demanding
food, whilst dogs did nothing but wag their tails and defe-

cate. He had no need for anyone or anything; except his reputation, that was.

A part-remembered Shakespearian quote came to mind, one he had been taught not at school but by an Englishman serving alongside him in the French Foreign Legion.

> *He that filches from me my good name Robs me of*
> *that which not enriches him,*
> *And makes me poor indeed.*

Basson remembered looking up the word 'filches' and assigning it to his memory. He'd taken pride in his command of the English language. And it was Akulov and his broker who had filched his reputation from him. He was The Bang-Bang Man, known as an operator who always completed his contracts, yet Amsterdam had changed all that, even though the contract had been one hundred per cent completed, and the client was happy, he had been made a pariah on the circuit. Tishina had paid him what he was owed. However, she had also disowned him, stating that their business relationship was forever severed. This had forced him to seek out other, far less well-paying and less ethical contracts with clients who cared little for the loss of human life.

Yet, as he sat on the bench, enjoying the weak autumnal sun, Basson had enjoyed it all. Word had spread of him to new clients until he had been approached by The Irishman, who had now for almost five years, been his broker. Initially Basson had believed his time in the wilderness was over, yet however much he had tried, he had been unable to shake off the outrage of Akulov's shot, and Tishina's actions. As an assassin he had achieved much, and had made enough money that he no longer bothered to ask what fee a job paid.

Yet what he had not achieved, what had been demolished, as though by one of his own IEDs, was his reputation. He'd failed to kill Wolf Six, Ruslan Akulov, during the San Remo fiasco, but he would try again. Now, however, his patience at an end, he would do the next best thing to slaying the Werewolf, he would kill the woman who had helped create and train Akulov's unit, the woman who had been both of their brokers, the only woman, with the exception of his mother, he had ever respected. He was going to kill Valentina Tishina.

He would take great joy making an unexpected entry into her apartment, and then he would toy with her, he would make her suffer and make her apologise before he finally snuffed out her life. With a sneer about his lips, which he knew from experience others took to be a smile, he rose from the bench and carried on along the promenade. He took a set of steps up and onto a narrow street set between high-rise and high-cost apartments. All had boutiques or cafés occupying the ground floors, the Monégasque and Monaco residents deeming themselves too important to occupy the lower floors. From memory of that day seven years ago, Basson found Tishina's building. He had searched government records to confirm that it had not changed ownership.

He took a seat in a café across the road from Tishina's tower. The place was on a bend, and he knew her building, which perched on the edge of the rise, was one of the lucky few whose sea view would forever remain uninterrupted. He ordered a black coffee and ignored the small almond biscuit which was presented with it. He knew he was taking a risk in not setting up an OP and conducting surveillance on the building to confirm Tishina's presence, but knew that this was a very difficult task to accomplish given Monaco's high percentage of CCTV cameras per capita. He was a Legionnaire, and a Legionnaire never allowed indecision to delay an attack on an enemy, and for the past seven years, Wolf Six and his broker had been his enemies.

He noticed a white-haired woman exit the building. She was perhaps eighty, maybe older, and in her hand she carried a shopping bag. It was a simple thing, not the type to be taken into a boutique. Basson now had a plan. He followed her with his eyes around the corner knowing in that direction there was a boulangerie which, at this time, would be having one of its busiest periods for its regular customers. Basson ordered a second coffee accepting that if he asked for a third, he would start to appear conspicuous. Minutes passed and he drank slowly. He'd started to reach for his wallet to pay when he saw the old woman reappear, a pair of large baguettes protruding from the top of her bag and a second bag, this new one plastic with gaudy images of vegetables printed on it, in her other hand. Her pace was slower than before.

Basson placed enough cash on the table to cover his caffeine and then started to walk away. After several paces he crossed the street and addressed the woman.

'Madame, please allow me to assist you. A lady should never carry her own shopping.'

The white-haired woman looked up and squinted. 'Thank you, young man. With each year it seems to me there are fewer and fewer gentlemen left.'

'Alas, we are a dying breed,' Basson replied as he deftly took both bags.

The old lady nodded. 'This way, I'm just in here.'

Moving at the slowest walking pace he possibly ever had,

he following her, pausing at the door as she tapped in a four-digit code, making no thought to hide it. They entered.

She said, 'Luckily for me I am only on the second floor, and of course there is a lift. On occasion I take the stairs, and on occasion I do not. It all depends on the weather.'

'Such is life,' Basson replied, with fake sincerity.

They took the lift, exiting on the second floor and Basson waited whilst she opened the front door. Immediately a pair of cats appeared and started rubbing against her legs.

Basson hid his disgust and handed her the bags. 'Voila.'

'Thank you. You are a true gentleman. Would you like to come in for a coffee and perhaps a warm pastry?'

Basson smiled. 'That does indeed sound very nice, but I am sorry my friend upstairs is expecting me.'

A smile also appeared on the woman's face. 'Then you had better not keep that young lady waiting!'

Basson retreated as the woman shut her door. He could hear her talking about him to her cats. He took the stairs upwards, five more floors, to get to Tishina. He reached the next landing and paused, cocking his head and listening. He could hear the squawk of a seagull outside and from one of the apartments a piano was playing. He supposed the other residents either could not hear it or did not mind, even now before 9 a.m. on a Saturday morning. He continued to climb the stairs, the rubber soles of his casual sneakers not registering much of an audible sound. Four steps down, from her floor, and out of the sightline of any spyhole or security camera he retrieved his micro-compact Sig P365X from his messenger bag. Next, he took out a simple, shaped device with enough C4 to defeat the door lock, which he would detonate with a basic command wire. Basson listened to the sounds of the building again. He knew he was being paranoid; no one was expecting him.

With a rapid, yet smooth motion, Basson ascended the last remaining stairs. He reached out for the door and placed the device firmly over the lock, moving away to the side of the door. Before the potential concussion wave, he heard a telephone ring. He paused and listened. He heard Tishina speaking French and thanking her caller for the information. Basson felt his expectation and excitement build like never before. He was going to take great delight in killing Tishina. And now he had it confirmed she was in the apartment. All but giddy with excitement, left hand holding the detonator, his right holding his silenced Sig, Basson took a long, deep calming breath and pressed the button.

There was a muted thud as the shaped, breaching charge went off. Yes, it would be heard by other residents and by those passing outside, even the café customers opposite, but it would take either a professional or someone with a very keen ear to pinpoint the exact direction, especially if he were to casually walk out of the building less than two minutes later.

Basson spun into the space left by the door which now hung suspended by a single hinge. Weapon up he searched the interior of the flat hunting for Tishina. He advanced into the living room which, Basson noted from memory, had not changed. It was empty, even the dog was nowhere to be seen. He turned right and slowly moved along the hallway. There was a sound no louder than that of a hardback book landing on a tiled kitchen floor, immediately followed by another. Instantly Basson felt himself jerk backwards. The rubber soles of his trainers gripping the parquet floor prevented him from falling flat on his back, and his ballistic vest prevent the twin, suppressed, 0.38 calibre rounds from penetrating his skin and slicing into his internal organs. Basson was shocked. Even though he had donned the thin vest, and endured being hot and sweaty because of it, it had not actually registered in his mind that Tishina may shoot back, let alone shoot first. This train of thought took no longer than a second to flash through his mind. That was enough for the woman, shooting at him from the other end of the hallway, to fire again. This round also hit his chest, but higher, and this one did knock him off his feet. He landed heavily and the back of his head slammed into the floor. With his vision greying out, Basson scrambled backwards, feet frantically attempting to push him away, arms rising in an attempt to bring his Sig to bear. He got a pair of shots off and Tishina howled as both slammed into her chest. She crumpled, falling against the wall at the end of the hallway and slid down until she resembled a rag doll propped up in a sitting position. Basson tried to pull himself up, yet before he could fire Tishina did again. Twice. One round embedded itself into the wall and the other round hit his right forearm, instantly making his hand spring open and for his Sig to clatter to the floor. At the far end of the hallway, he saw Tishina's own hand was shaky, like a weightlifter struggling to raise a barbell. She fired again, once more striking his chest before she dropped her suppressed G42 and her head fell forwards.

Chest on fire, head spinning and right arm not responding to any instructions, Basson used his left hand to reach out and grab his Sig. He pointed it and pulled the trigger; the round struck Tishina in the midriff making her fall sideways like a sack of discarded clothing. Basson dragged himself backwards and around the corner before he turned onto his stomach, pushed up to his haunches, and staggered out of the flat.

He thrust his silenced Sig back into his courier bag and stumbled down the stairs, unable to grip with his right hand and having to rely on his left to steady him. He burst out of the front door. There were already people on the street pointing at the building. They may have heard the charge, or less likely so, they may have heard the exchange of suppressed rounds, but what they did see was a man with a bloodied arm staggering. He heard a whistle blow, and looking right saw a police officer. Basson was armed but injured, and certainly didn't have enough rounds left in his Sig to get into a firefight with the Monégasque police. There was no way he could commandeer a vehicle before the police fell upon him, which left only one option. Pumping his legs as quickly as he could, Basson raced around the bend in the road and down the steps to the promenade. Locals and tourists alike stopped or moved out of the way as he raced towards the water. More shouts now were levelled at him, as Basson launched himself into the water in amongst the yachts of the rich and infamous berthed in Monte Carlo's Port Hercule harbour.

The sound of the door being unlocked awoke Akulov from a dreamless sleep. Sunlight once more swam into the room, it was morning, and quite early. He stiffly stood and, moving to the centre of the room, awaited his visitors. Deputy Turcotte entered but this time he was accompanied by the sheriff.

'Sit.' She pointed at the chair facing the door. Akulov sat and she then sat opposite and folded her arms, whilst Turcotte stood in the doorway.

'You are a mystery man, Mr Hurst. What is the real reason for your presence in my county?'

'Am I being officially questioned?'

The sheriff's left eye twitched. 'Why are you asking?'

'Because you haven't charged me, I haven't been allowed a phone call, and I can't see any recording device. It seems to me my rights are being ignored.'

'Uh-huh. Are you au fait with the procedure of law enforcement in the state of Michigan?'

'No.'

'Well, I am the law here. Now tell me, why are you in Alcona County?'

'By accident.'

'Explain.'

Akulov saw no reason not to repeat the story he had told Needham about borrowing a friend's boat and then being washed ashore.

'That's what Needham told me. You lost everything, huh? Except for your wallet?'

'Yes.'

'A wallet containing no ID, no credit cards, just cash?'

'That is correct.'

'When the boat you "borrowed" got into difficulty, did you radio for help, or set off a flare?'

'The radio was broken, and I couldn't find any flares.'

'No life jackets either?'

'No.'

'What was the name of the boat?'

Akulov plucked a name from memory of a yacht he'd seen in Monaco. '*Fino*.'

'*Fino*?'

'It's a type of wine.'

'Fancy. Who is it registered to?'

'Phillip Kemp,' the name of a Canadian he had once met on a plane.

'You get that, Turcotte?'

'Yes, sheriff.'

'Be sure to run it for me later.'

'I will.'

'Now about your fingerprints. Old Jim Grant tells me they were chemically eroded, burnt off by the photographic development process? Is that so?'

'Yes.'

'Where were you developing photographs?'

'At home.'

'Where is that?'

'Washington.'

'You got an address?'

'It's on my driver's licence.'

'Of course it is. What were you taking pictures of?'

'I took a series of landscape last week.'

'Where?'

'Lake Ontario.'

'I see a theme. Lake lover, huh?'

'I like the great American outdoors.'

'Mr Hurst, you have an answer for every question.'

'Isn't that what is expected?'

'It is, Mr Hurst, from a liar, or a criminal.'

Turcotte snorted. Akulov's eyes tracked to him. He looked as though he was enjoying the show. In his hands he was holding a brown, cardboard, document file. Akulov presumed it was a prop to be introduced.

'The thing is,' the sheriff continued, 'I don't believe any of your answers. Don't get me wrong, we found a District of Columbia driver's licence on the DMV DC database with a photograph which looks a lot like you, but I don't think you are Adam Hurst, and I don't believe you borrowed a boat named *Fino* from a Phillip Kemp. So, who are you, and why are you here in my county?'

Akulov made no reply.

'You're not going to answer that one?'

'You already have the answers.'

'You see, Mr Hurst, I believe that I do. Why did you try to evade arrest?'

'Am I under arrest?'

The sheriff sighed. 'Why did you attempt to run off?'

'Why did you attempt to shoot me?'

'It was a warning shot. Do you think I could have missed at that distance?' She raised her right hand and Turcotte speedily stepped forward and handed her the file. She opened it and retrieved a 10 x 8 photograph which she placed on the tabletop and pushed over to Akulov. 'Who is this?'

Akulov looked down. The image content didn't distress him, but the person who was in it surprised him. Akulov made himself recoil, as though he was seeing something a civilian would find distasteful. 'Why are you showing me a photograph of a dead man?'

'Because I believe you killed him.'

'What?' Akulov pretended to be shocked.

'This unfortunate gentleman washed up on the shore not too far from where Jake Needham found you.'

Akulov glanced at the photograph again, it made sense. It was Hormann, the CIA operator who'd been with him on the doomed jet. He said nothing and waited for the sheriff to continue.

'Our county coroner says he drowned, but there are other premortem injuries on him consistent with say a fight or some kind of attack.'

Again, to Akulov, this made sense. Hormann had been in a plane crash and would have attempted to fight his way out of the sinking fuselage, just like he had. However, this was not something he could tell the sheriff.

'Would you like to know the darndest part of all this?'

'I would.'

'This gentleman had no ID on him, just a wallet

containing cash. This sound familiar to you? He also had a little red box, sealed in a waterproof case, zipped inside his jacket. Do you have any idea what that might be?'

'No. I do not.' Akulov still had no idea what the device was, he'd had it in his possession for less than five minutes and within that time he'd been missed by bullets and hit by a fire extinguisher. He did however know that the CIA wanted it, which meant that he had to get it back.

'Lucky for us he wasn't in the water that long, the coroner estimates no more than eighteen hours, so AFIS managed to get a match to his prints. Does the name Brett Wayne mean anything to you?'

'No.' It didn't.

'That's the guy's name.'

Akulov made no reply. He presumed this was Hormann's real name, or perhaps just another legend, but either way it made no difference to him.

'Tell me about the jacket you were wearing when Needham picked you up?'

'It was warm.'

'Was it yours?'

'No.'

'Whose was it?'

'I don't know.'

'How come?'

'I found it. By the lake.'

'Huh. Kinda careless of the owner, don't ya think?'

'I agree.'

'I have the jacket in my office, and I've examined it. I know who the real owner is.'

'Then please return it on my behalf.'

Sheriff Lehnert's eyes narrowed. 'That jacket belongs to

Deputy Johnson. He went missing the night of the storm, the same night you appeared, by the lakeside wearing his jacket.'

'What are you saying, sheriff?'

Lehnert sounded incredulous. 'What am I saying? D'you hear that, Turcotte? What am I saying? I'm saying you know something about the disappearance of one of my deputies. I'm also saying you know something about the death of Brett Wayne.'

The sheriff was correct. He did.

'You materialise and we've suddenly got two dead men.'

'Is Deputy Johnson dead?'

Lehnert's eyes flickered. 'You tell me?'

There was a shrill, electronic trilling. It was coming from Turcotte. Akulov noticed the sheriff's eyes momentarily widen, as though in shock. Without a word Turcotte felt inside his uniform slacks and pulled out a smartphone. When he spoke, his voice was higher and squeakier than ever. 'We've gotta take this! We gotta take this now!'

Sheriff Lehnert abruptly stood, she pointed at Akulov. 'Stay.'

Turcotte had the phone to his ear. 'Oui?'

Turning, the sheriff bundled the large man out of the door and once more locked Akulov in.

Akulov sat for several seconds wondering what he had just witnessed, and wondering if Lehnert knew he was also a witness to her assassination of her own deputy.

* * *

Doha, Qatar

As Martin Basson entered the dark waters of the Persian
Gulf the sound of the Fajar prayer reached his ears, broad-
cast from the mosque a street away from his villa. Basson
was a non-believer residing in a Muslim country yet found
the melodic voice, with words he did not fully understand,
comforting. It reassured him that in everything there was
balance and order, even in the chaos his work inevitably
created. Basson liked to swim. It was his exercise of choice
for cardiovascular conditioning. As always there was a slight
twinge in his left thigh as his body registered the difference
in temperature between air and water, the lasting memento
of Wolf Six's bullet, fired in Amsterdam, which had failed to
kill him. This he lived with, and embraced, it reminded him
to never make the same mistake again. His leg had recovered
years before to such an extent that he wondered if the
twinge was real at all or, like the man who had created the
injury, a ghost. Nevertheless, it was something he felt when
the colder weather came. He was sure an expensive surgeon
would be able to rectify the nerve damage, but then what
was the point of forgetting a mistake he had learnt from?
Now the phantom twinge in his thigh was accompanied by
the real stabbing pain in his right forearm. Tishina's bullet
had hurt him like hell, yet luckily it had not reduced his
mobility and, cleaned up, and given three months or so of
physiotherapy, would become a second phantom injury. It
was a badge of honour for him, a permanent reminder that
it had been he, Martin Basson, who had ended the life of
Valentina Tishina. Now all he had to do was to kill Akulov.
Basson studied the waterproof dressing. Today he was going
to push his arm, and the rest of his body.

At this time of year, the sea around Doha had a chill to it
which he appreciated, even if his joints did not, as there was

nothing more distasteful than being forced to forge ahead in a body of water as hot as a bathtub. He'd never forget his first time in the Middle East more than twenty-five years before. It had been a quick forty-eight-hour stopover, a respite in between training operations with the Legion. His team had landed in Doha and no sooner had they received the keys to their hotel rooms, were hot-footing it through the scorching sand towards the inviting sea. Diving and crashing into the water it had struck Basson that both air and sea were of an equal temperature, and his body had no idea whether it was wet or not, submerged or on the surface.

He and the rest of the men from the '2e Régiment étranger de parachutistes' – the 2nd Foreign Parachute Regiment known as the 'Deuxième REP' – swam and splashed for forty minutes before heat and hunger led them to the hotel brunch. Basson enjoyed the memories of his bawdy comrades drawing looks of disdain from the business people and the very few tourists who had visited the Qatari capital all those years before.

At this hour of the morning, the sea and the giant buildings which overlooked it were peaceful. It was the period just before dawn, a magical time where anything and everything was possible. He continued to plough on through the gentle waves from his private beach on the man-made Pearl Island, to the deeper waters of the Katara bay, an Olympic standard swimmer he maintained, with pride, to anyone who ever asked. Basson remained vigilant crossing the lanes used for pleasure craft, jet-skis and sail training boats, aware that in his black wetsuit he was as visible as a shadow at midnight. He increased his stroke rate as he pushed out into the much choppier waters at the mouth of the bay. Once clear of the artificial trench separating The Pearl from the

Persian Gulf, the water was colder and darker. Basson had no fear of what may be lurking in the depths, if it ate him then so be it. Yet he knew the only man-eaters this close to land patrolled the nightclubs. Navigating the man-made headland to circumnavigate the yacht club. He now made for the private beach of the grandiose St Regis Hotel. Reaching the rope indicating the start of the safe swimming zone for the hotel guests, he dived under it and into the hotel's private waters.

On reaching the shore, Basson powerfully strode out of the water. The beach had not yet been set up for the day and he knew that would happen imminently, the sand would be raked smooth, any lingering litter taken care of and then the day beds arranged in rows which pleased the patrons. Basson rinsed the sand from his feet, then took the steps up to the poolside area. The lights of the impressive full Olympic-sized swimming pool threw a spectral glow across the pre-dawn scene. At the far end of the pool, dwarfed by the towering hotel, was a white hut-like structure where the beach concierge was located. Here lazy tourists would instruct the hotel staff to find them the best spot by the pool or on the sand, and cover their loungers with thick, soft, striped hotel towels.

A figure wearing a dark blue windbreaker over a white uniform stood behind the counter at the concierge desk. He was, habitually, an hour early for his shift but as a fellow former French Foreign Legionnaire, always ready for whatever the day threw at him. As Basson gave him a nod the man spoke.

'Impressive, I have been timing you. That was faster than last week.'

'No headwind today,' Basson replied taking the towel his

friend held out to him and quickly patting himself dry. The African security manager then exchanged the towel for a cup of coffee. 'Merci, Desange.'

Desange raised his own cup in a salute to his former comrade. 'And how is life from the expensive seats?'

Basson let a thin smile appear on his lips. 'Expensive. Something is always going wrong. Perhaps I should come and work with you?'

'And what, my friend, give up your multi-million Riyal villa for a shared staff apartment?'

'You are right. I've had enough of listening to your snores.'

'It was your farts that were far worse,' Desange replied.

Both men sensed movement as a hotel guest huffed into view. He was wearing a lime green T-shirt and matching shorts; both were tight around his rotund frame. On reaching the counter he placed his arms on it for support.

Desange switched from French to English and asked, 'Good morning, sir, how can I help you?'

The accent of the voice which replied was Russian, and the words were slurred. 'The drink in my room is finished. What time does the bar open?'

Basson disguised his disgust at the man's wobbly body. He took an immediate and vehement dislike to anyone who failed to look after their physique, even at the age of fifty-five he knew he was fitter than many men more than a decade younger.

'The bar?' There was no surprise in Desange's voice. 'It will not open until after ten. You could perhaps order a drink from room service or something to accompany your breakfast. Perhaps a Mimosa?'

'Mimosa? Pah, that is for the women. Real men like me, like us three, we drink vodka.'

Desange nodded whilst Basson's face remained stony. The guest retraced his steps without saying another word.

Basson said, 'Tell me you continue to enjoy it here?'

'After what we have been through? Of course I do. It is highly relaxing knowing that no one is going to shoot me. And you, what about your consulting?'

Basson's cover was that of a security consultant, and if his old friend had any inkling as to his real post-legion line of business, he had never alluded to it. Working as an assassin for hire was not a job that instantly sprang to mind in the party game, popular amongst expats of asking 'where are you from originally and what do you do in Doha?'

'I am as happy as I can be in a job that is not at all interesting. I fly to see clients who have too much money and then advise them how to prevent others from taking it.'

Desange finished his coffee. 'Business-class travel does sound highly boring.'

'It is, and private jets are just tedious.' Basson passed his cup back. 'Thank you, as always, for the coffee.'

'Same time tomorrow?'

'Of course,' Basson replied. 'I'll see you tomorrow, if I'm not dead.'

Basson retraced his steps back down to the beach as the horizon started to lighten. Entering the water, he powerfully pushed away from the sticky sand, wanting to see how quickly he could get back to the villa. Behind him lights had started to come on in the hotel rooms of the early risers and in the distance the residential towers on The Pearl started to sparkle. He could make out the headlights of vehicles moving, ferrying maintenance teams in one direction and businessmen in another.

Twenty-five minutes of hard swimming later brought Basson to his beach as the sun started to rise, and he felt the first rays of warmth drying his back. Apricity it was officially called, the warmth of the sun on a winter's day, yet winter in Doha was still warm. So, was there a more relevant term? He'd look it up, once he was indoors.

Turning, Basson looked back across the strait at the towering hotel once more before he walked the few steps from the wet sand to the edge of his garden and then followed the stepping stones inside. The live-in maid had a steaming pot of black coffee waiting for him at the table on the terrace upon a silver tray. Basson lived alone and hadn't hired Rose, from the Philippines, because he needed the house cleaned, he'd hired her so the place was never empty. Crime rates in Doha were so low to be almost non-existent, and he'd had top of the line CCTV cameras installed both inside and out, yet the presence of a maid – who would talk to the maids in neighbouring properties – made him seem somewhat more respectable, a member of the community, and less remarkable. And as a contract killer that was what he wanted.

Basson pulled off his wetsuit and speedos and slipped on a thin towelling robe. He sat on his wooden chair and poured a coffee. He sensed Rose appear behind him in the doorway. She collected his swimming attire. She was discreet and only addressed him when a matter needed attention.

'Sir, phone ring in office. Maybe ten minutes ago.'

'Thank you.'

Basson was in no rush. Only one person had his number

– The Irishman, and he would only call to alert him of a message left in his secure account. It was a quarter to seven when Basson, still wearing nothing but his robe, unlocked the door to his office. He held his hand against the small scanner on the office desk and the custom made, shallow drawer clicked open. It was deep enough for just an iPhone. He retrieved the handset, logged in to a secure email account and opened the message in the draft folder which, as it had never been sent, could never be traced by a third party.

The draft contained two lines of text and a JPEG. Basson's eyes were immediately drawn to the image. It was a photograph of a Washington DC driving licence in the name of Adam Hurst. He recognised the face, the fire in its eyes made him shiver. The subject was unmistakable. It was the man who had shot him in the leg. It was the man who had tried to kill him, twice.

Basson sat in silence as he studied the face. Images, as though taken by an outdated cinecamera, flickered in front of his eyes. Memories of the operation they had been on together, the contract which had gone wrong, and Italy. Basson realised his breathing was heavier than usual. He closed his eyes and inhaled and exhaled, long and slow. Opening his eyes once more he read the text above the photograph:

Image taken by a former client.
Please confirm identity.

Basson deleted both the image and text then typed in a two-word reply:

WOLF SIX

14

THE PERSIAN GULF

Basson always flew business class into the US, not because he couldn't afford first-class, but rather he would be singled out further as being something or someone special, and he didn't want that. He wanted to be less memorable, and so he joined the high-flying execs and wealthy tourists in the larger, yet just as opulent – if truth be told – business class cabin of the jet. He travelled into and out of Qatar using an alias, an identity which he had purchased, and then nurtured. His French passport, which was genuine and supplied by a contact in Lyon, used his photograph but did not bear his name. It was this passport, which was the basis of his identity, his life in Doha. It carried his Qatari visa which had been used for him to receive his Qatari Identification Card, known as a QID, which all residents had to carry. As far as the Qatari authorities were concerned, he was a Frenchman by the name of Richard Tournai.

Basson leant against the inflight bar and enjoyed his cognac whilst the overly made-up flight attendant fixed a sugary cocktail for an overweight American woman from

Memphis, he only knew she was from Memphis because she told anyone who would listen her entire life story. Basson was surprised the woman had managed to enter the aircraft through the passenger entrance, and even more surprised that she had squeezed into her Qsuite seat. He could not understand why anyone would allow themselves to become that obese. Smiling, he brought his glass to his lips as he remembered correcting a woman who had once told him she had a medical condition. He'd replied that her condition was the inability to close her mouth when passing a patisserie. She hadn't been happy. Basson found it highly annoying that he was only sharing what everyone else was too polite to express. It was the same with ugly people, they had their place too, and that was behind their own closed doors. He sipped the last of his drink, he'd allow himself to relax a little on the flight before the fun and games started in the US. The fat woman, believing his sneer to be a smile, and this to be amusement at her anecdote, now widened her audience from just the flight attendant to include him.

'...then I said, Geoffrey, you may have padlocked the stable doors, but the horse has already bolted!'

The flight attendant smiled warmly, well trained as she was to be both waitress and confidant to her passengers.

Basson indicated that he wanted another drink and said, 'They are difficult animals to control.'

'Grandsons?' the woman said with a wide, wobbly smile.

'They are the same. Headstrong until they have been shown who is boss. My grandmother was a very stern woman, but she made the best cakes. So, for me it was like the carrot or the stick.'

'Perhaps it was the carrot cake or the stick?' the large woman quipped in return.

'Oui, *exactamont*.' He nodded at the flight attendant as she placed a new glass on a paper coaster in front of him.

'Nuts?'

'Aren't we all?' Basson said, with a wink.

The seatbelt sign switched on, and the cabin crew asked Basson and the woman to either return to their seats or fasten themselves into the bench seats against the bulkhead, facing the bar. The large woman chose to return to her own seat, Basson imagined this was because she had a seatbelt extender. He remained in the bar area as he watched the woman in uniform secure the loose bottles before she retreated into the galley. He would attempt later to get her number and could perhaps impress her with his villa on The Pearl.

Basson's mind switched to the contract he had accepted. Once he'd confirmed the identity of the subject in the image as Wolf Six, his broker had immediately informed the Long-Zi Triad, and the Long-Zi had immediately agreed on a contract to kill Akulov. Basson wondered why the Triad had chosen to use his broker rather than one of their own in-house assets. Could it be, he pondered that they feared the semi-mythical assassin? Was it that if they failed it would further tarnish the Long-Zi name? Whatever the reason was, Basson did not care. He cared solely for the fact that it would be he, Martin Basson – The Bang-Bang Man – who would end the life of Wolf Six. He was excited, and he was ready, he was just frustrated that he could not get at Akulov sooner. The direct flight from Doha to New York, JFK, was just over fourteen and a half hours, and in that time, he was aware that anything could happen. It was enough to drive a man mad, but he knew better than to worry about something that he could not control. What he could control was his itinerary. Once he landed in JFK it was then another four and a half hours, and a change at Detroit before he arrived at Alpena County Regional Airport. Basson had made arrangements with a contact, paying him over the odds, for the specialist equipment he needed, which was a lot easier to get in the United States than in Europe. His contact would be ready and waiting for him in a car at the Alpena airport parking lot, where it was thankfully a short forty-minute drive to the target location. Although he liked to announce his presence with a 'bang', on this occasion Basson had chosen not to use an IED to decimate his target but, if needed, to gain entry to where he was being held. He was going to exact his revenge in a leisurely and cathartic manner, and this of course would be the most painful. He had it all planned out in his head. Basson slowly swirled the last of the cognac around his glass before savouring it in his mouth. This was going to be his final drink until it was all over, until he had killed Ruslan Akulov, Wolf Six. As the smooth fire of the cognac warmed his chest, before his eyes he saw the Werewolf of his nightmares once more, yet this time the figure was howling, trapped in a vortex of swirling flames.

* * *

Harrisville, Michigan

Akulov had fallen asleep. He didn't know how long for but what he did know was that he was still in the same damn room. This was starting to get old. He knew there was no way out of the cell, that the interview room had become. The window was far too small for anyone larger than a child to squeeze through, and then that was only possible if they could break and remove the glass first without being stopped by whoever was watching over the surveillance camera.

The training manuals of the Russian army had not been up on mindfulness, his instructors had not taught him or the other Spetsnaz conscripts what to do with their thoughts, and their doubts, if they were ever to be captured by the enemy. Resistance to interrogation was an art within itself, and it had only been later under Tishina's tutelage, within the GRU and the Werewolf program, that these techniques had been taught. The whole focus of the army's training had been on how to avoid the enemy, escape from them or, and this was the most preferred option of his instructors, how to eliminate them. But Akulov had not been at war, he had been detained by a small-town sheriff. No doubt other men in his position, and with his training, would have taken the easier option and attacked, and they may have succeeded, or they may have not, but Akulov was sick of taking lives that he did not have to. His past had been littered with the bodies of those who got in the way, who had been in the wrong place at the wrong time. Ninety-nine per cent of these people he had been paid to kill, but it was the one per cent which haunted him. They had been victims of incomplete intelligence, incorrectly identified or were simply collateral damage. Simple. There was nothing simple about killing an innocent bystander by mistake, and it sickened him. These people he had murdered. His victims were the men and women whose faces he saw in his darkest hours. And now alone in this makeshift cell, he was battling to banish them from his thoughts. Akulov had never considered that the black dog of depression could bite him. He was a Werewolf;

he would scare it off before it had the chance to even snarl. However, for some reason he was finding today challenging. He reasoned it was the concussion, perhaps as his brain healed the contusion it had received, it was somehow misfiring and sending out the wrong commands, and these were manifesting as irrational and intrusive thoughts? But what did he know? He wasn't a brain surgeon. What Akulov did know was that head injuries could change a man, he'd seen it happen, and read about it too. He remembered a TV report on a Dutchman, whom after being struck on the head with a falling brick had found that he needed only three hours of sleep a night and had more energy than before. It was as though the blow had unlocked some sort of enhanced ability. Yet Akulov knew these types of cases were extremely rare, more often than not soldiers he had seen had lost memories, movement, and emotion, or simply their humanity.

He stood and started to pace. Perhaps if whoever was monitoring the cell saw him acting agitated they may come in to check on him, and then he would, this time, attack. Akulov felt like a caged animal, and of course he was, he was a Werewolf, he was Wolf Six.

He moved to the window, and stretching up, put his fingertips on the ledge. Raising his legs he let himself hang as he stretched his back, the muscles complained and then they started to relax, and to lengthen. Hanging with his right hand now he banged on the glass with his left palm, it made a dull thudding noise, and he started to see miniscule, threadlike cracks appearing. He continued to pound, and they became larger. The best lie contained a truth, and if the deputies believed he was attempting to escape they would try to stop him, and of course he would then strike.

There was noise outside, heavy footsteps on the concrete floor. Akulov needed to time this right. He heard the key in the lock, the scrape of it engaging and the mechanism dropping into place, the bolt sliding back and then as the door started to open, he pushed himself away from the wall and bounded on the balls of his feet for the door.

Turcotte ambled into the room, a satisfied expression on his face, and a baton in his hand. Akulov's swinging left elbow slammed into the side of his large head, as his right hand grabbed the extendable baton. Turcotte fell, mouth open, stunned, not understanding what had happened. Akulov stepped over him and out of the room that had been his cell. He turned left, for the stairs, and immediately was confronted with another bulky obstacle – Ted Lehnert. He had an iPhone to his ear. Akulov jabbed the baton into his large stomach, forcing him to double over and drop the phone. Akulov now swept his legs away and the oaf fell face-first to the floor. Akulov grabbed his phone, the speaker still talking away on the other end. He ended the call, took two steps away from Ted, and tapped in an agreed distress message to a number he'd memorised.

Delayed whilst shopping

He then shared his location via google maps before dropping the phone. It was no good to him, he'd grab another from somewhere else.

Behind him Ted was starting to moan, and beyond him there was no sound coming from Turcotte.

Baton in his right hand, held by his side, Akulov advanced up the stairs with his left arm up and ready to engage any possible opposition.

And then he saw them.

Sheriff Lehnert and a large man, whose checked, sports jacket was straining to contain his biceps. They were walking side by side and equidistance between the front door and Akulov. It took a second for the pair to comprehend what they were seeing. They both reached, seemingly, for sidearms. Akulov pivoted and turned to his immediate left. There was a short corridor leading to a back door, it was opening, and Deputy Jim Grant was stepping back inside. Their eyes met and Grant froze.

'Stop or I'll shoot!' Lehnert shouted, and at the exact same time opened fire. There was a thunderous retort and a round tugged at the side of Akulov's shirt. It continued on and missed Grant by the smallest of margins before sailing on and out of the building. Grant was still motionless, but his mouth was now open.

Akulov yelled, 'Move!'

Another retort and a round pinged off the door frame. Grant ducked, and Akulov pushed him to one side as he tore past and through the doorway.

Outside now, Akulov found himself in a caged area with green, wooden fencing on one side screening the rear of the law enforcement building from the neighbours. Turning left at the end of the building was an open door in the cage leading to the smaller parking lot, a stretch of lawn and the suburban street beyond. Akulov raced for the exit.

A large figure spun round the corner from the other side, completely filling the mesh door. It was the man in a sports jacket, and he had a sidearm in his right hand. He started to raise it, a snarl on his face. But Akulov was too close and batted it away with his left arm whilst his right whipped the baton into the man's torso. The large man grunted but didn't fold like Ted had done. He staggered to one side and was able to swing a left hook back at Akulov, who was already attempting to move past him. Even though it was a glancing blow, Akulov felt the strength behind it as it struck him on the right bicep, making his hand release Turcotte's baton. Off balance, Akulov stumbled into the unforgiving brick wall of the sheriff's facility. His adversary was fast and came at him, left fist up and out – ready to jab or parry, whilst his right now poised to strike. Akulov, pivoted, ducked and then rising to his full height shot out a quick, right knee which slammed into the attacker's unprotected groin. As the large man doubled up around his leg, Akulov saw the sheriff exiting through the same door he had used less than twenty seconds before. She fired another round at him, this one missed his head by the narrowest of margins and struck the wall sending shards of brick into his face.

Sheriff Lehnert slowly approached him, keeping her service issue Glock aimed directly at his head. 'Get on the ground, pretty boy!'

Akulov complied, he had no choice.

'*Putain de bordel de merde!*' On his hands and knees, the large man was swearing in Canadian accented French.

'Get up, Martel, I doubt there's much there to hurt.'

'*Va te faire foutre, Lehnert!*'

Akulov understood but was not inclined to translate Martel's instruction for the sheriff. She was probably the best shot he had seen in a long time, and he was puzzled enough to want to know how and where she had been trained. He would have said the US army, yet in a country with a constitutional right to bear arms almost anyone could train until they mastered the art of shooting a handgun. However, range firing was one skill, shooting at a living, moving target and missing purposefully by miniscule margins was another.

'Who the hell do you think you are?' Martel had switched back to English. 'I said, who are you?'

Akulov remained silent, and motionless.

'Can you hear me? Or are you deaf as well as stupid?'

There was a slight scraping of gravel against the sole of a shoe and Akulov tensed his body, sensing what was going to come next. The kick struck him with force in his left side almost lifting him up from the ground. Akulov grunted and rolled in an attempt to mitigate the damage to his muscles and internal organs.

'Enough!' Lehnert said.

'Je m'en fous!' Martel spat back at her.

Lehnert tossed a pair of cuffs at Akulov. 'Put these on, Mr Hurst.'

Laying on his back now, Akulov put the cuffs on quickly, at the front of his body, before both the sheriff and Martel noticed their mistake.

'Get up, you piece of American garbage!' Martel said as he hauled Akulov to his feet by his arm. 'If you were not so damn valuable to me personally, I would break your face right here!'

'We need to get back inside, now,' Lehnert said.

Akulov let himself be dragged back to the door. He saw onlookers standing in small knots watching the scene unfold. It had been reckless of Lehnert to use her firearm in a residential area like this, a wide or misjudged round could have easily found its way inside any of the neighbouring, white wooden houses. Akulov assessed his options. He'd not escaped, but he had sent a message to Tishina, his broker, with his exact location. He couldn't guarantee that she would come for him, but the chances were that the CIA would want him to at least ascertain what had happened to the red box they had ordered him to kill Fang for.

Back inside he saw Grant handing Turcotte an ice pack. The larger man snatched it and held it to the side of his head.

Ted loomed in front of them, he was holding a tissue to his nose. 'He attacked me ma! Ya gotta charge him with that!'

'I will, Edward,' Lehnert replied. 'Now move so we can take him back downstairs.'

Ted lurched forward and threw a wild haymaker. Akulov twisted and ducked, and the fist missed his jaw and struck his shoulder.

'You little bitch!' Ted yelled.

'Enough!' Lehnert got between the pair.

Martel pushed Akulov away and down the stairs. 'You've got a lot of talking to do!'

'Lock him in,' Lehnert said.

Martel all but threw Akulov back into the interview room. He broke his fall on the nearer of the two steel chairs. It hurt. 'When we come back you better talk, or you are going to be in a world of pain!'

The door shut.

Akulov moved back to the mattress and lay down. There was no point now in using any extra energy. He took several slow, deep breaths to assess how much damage Martel's kick had done. He groaned, but didn't feel any stabbing or sharp pain in his side, and that meant the strike had merely bruised his abdominal and oblique muscles. He'd had worse, and something told him he was about to receive something a lot similar, and very soon. He closed his eyes; he needed the rest.

* * *

Martel was angry. Hurst had made him look like a fool. He glared at himself in the washroom mirror and suppressed the urge to smash it. Whoever this guy was he had some training, and it had only been Lehnert who had managed to stop him. Martel took a deep breath; he had almost lost what was a valuable asset to The Syndicate. He needed to keep hold of Hurst until he heard the results of Gagnon's discussion with the Triads. He was shrewd enough to know that it wasn't just money that they would be getting from the Yee Kwan but respect as the people who had tracked down the man who had dared to dishonour their Triad by assassinating Fang. Hurst escaping would have meant not just losing any fee the Yee Kwan may have agreed to pay, but also his position within The Syndicate and potentially his life. Whilst the half-brothers had been known to give second chances, the Yee Kwan did not. They were black and white in both their decision-making and their actions.

Martel straightened up and winced. He still had a gnawing pain in his lower abdomen from Hurst's knee strike, but as he wasn't pissing blood, he knew it was going to be OK. But Hurst would get a receipt for that, and Hurst would not be so lucky.

Jacket off, Martel pulled a couple of poses, ignoring the pain and letting the tightening of his cotton shirt against his muscles elevate his mood. How could Hurst ever hope to compete with him in a true test of strength, in a true gladiatorial fight? The answer was that he could not. No, he would go into that interview room and would do just enough damage to the man to find out exactly who he was and what he knew before the Triads arrived to claim him.

He took a deep breath, there was something here that was not right, it was something that made no sense. How had Hurst managed to undertake the hit on Fang and then appear at Needham's facility the next day? How had he arrived? Had it really been by boat, as Needham had told Lehnert? Had he been delivered by car? It didn't make much difference, yet the question that no one seemed able to answer was, why was Hurst in Alcona County at all?

Unless...

Unless he had come to target the facility? Was that it? Was Hurst here to take out Needham and the others who ran business here for The Syndicate? That had to be it. There was no other explanation. Hurst had not magically just fallen out of the sky.

Martel adjusted his hair, put his jacket back on and left the washroom. He held his head high and tried to forget about his embarrassment. He needn't have. The room was empty. Grant had gone outside to reassure the townsfolk that there was nothing further to worry about, and Squeaky-Dave and Lehnert's son were nowhere to be seen. In many sheriff departments the lack of staff would have been an issue, but Harrisville was a sleepy place out of season. When, of course, the sheriff was not loosening off her firearm.

Lehnert was in her office. Martel pushed the door open and entered, as though it was his, and in a sense it was. As was the norm, she had been elected sheriff by the local community. She had been the best candidate, and that was partly because she had been recommended and supported by the previous incumbent – Sheriff David Kennedy, another 'Dave' but this one not at all squeaky. Kennedy had been a Vietnam veteran, and Martel had respected him for that. In turn Dave Kennedy had respected Sue Lehnert for her service, in the United States Army Military Police Corps. So, with Sheriff Kennedy's endorsement, and that of other senior local government officials, she had been elected. Two other respectable candidates had decided to withdraw, and a third had gone missing. Lehnert owed Martel and The Syndicate for that.

'You OK, Martel?' There was neither concern nor sarcasm in Lehnert's words.

'I'll survive, which is more than I can say for that son of a bitch.'

Martel noticed a plastic evidence bag on the desk, and sitting on top of this was a red box about the size of a packet of cigarettes. 'What's that?'

'I have no idea. It was found on a body pulled out of the water near Needham's place.'

Martel's furrowed his brow. 'Near Needham's place?'

'That's what I said. Close to where Needham found Hurst.'

Martel sat. 'You think Hurst killed the guy?'

Lehnert shrugged. 'Looks that way to me. The guy drowned, and he had premortem abrasions on his arms, torso and legs.'

'Premortem?'

'It means they were inflicted before he drowned, the coroner said it looks like he was in a fight.'

'That's it then, case closed,' Martel said, with authority. 'Cut and dry. Hurst killed him. We know that's what he does for a living, right? Perhaps our John Doe was part of his team, and they had a falling out. A falling out of their boat!'

'Is that meant to be funny?'

'I enjoyed it.'

'Death is never a joke. Anyway, he's not a John Doe. We got an ID. The guy's name is Brett Wayne, and he lives in Washington DC.'

'So, what are you saying?'

'I'm not saying anything, just stating the facts. The guy is from Washington DC, Hurst is from Washington DC. So yeah Mickey, I think Hurst killed him, and I haven't got a clue why.'

'So why is that box not in the evidence bag?'

'I wanted to try to understand what it was.'

'What is it?'

'Like I said, I don't know. There's no obvious way to open it, but the doc had it X-rayed and it's full of electronics.'

'It's a hard drive.'

'Could well be just that, but there's no port.'

'So, it's Bluetooth, or something.'

'Something, yeah.'

'Can I see it?'

'No.'

Martel shook his head. 'Ooh, sheriff. You are very commanding.'

Lehnert narrowed her eyes.

Mantel said, 'You paid the coroner his usual fee to forget about our John Doe?'

'I did. As far as the world is concerned Brett Wayne was never here.'

'That's good because the last thing you need is some sort of federal investigation.'

'Hello? Hello?'

Martel stood. He saw Needham entering from the reception area. 'You should lock the door.'

'What's there to steal, paperclips?'

Needham crossed the empty squad area and stood in the office doorway. 'It's awfully quiet here.'

'Now it is,' Lehnert clarified.

'Someone told me there were gunshots.'

'She shot Hurst.'

'What?' Needham looked shocked.

'I discharged my service weapon in his direction to prevent him from escaping.'

'But you hit him?'

'I wasn't aiming for him, and didn't hit him.'

'He got out past that buffoon Squeaky-Dave,' Martel said, dismissively.

'Yeah, I know,' Needham nodded, 'Dave and Ted arrived at my place demanding pie.'

'I'll have a word with Ted,' Lehnert replied, 'but he was a little shaken up. Hurst hit him.'

'Yep, Ted told me that too. He also complained that Hurst bust the screen of his cell phone.'

'When did Hurst have his phone?'

'He took it from him, and then he just dropped it on the floor.'

Lehnert gave Martel a quick glance before she retrieved her own cell phone and started a call. 'Edward, yes. Everything is fine here. Yes, Needham has just told me about your screen. Look, I don't know, buy yourself another one. Now listen, I need you to do something. Check your call register. Did Hurst try to call anyone before he dropped your phone? No. Right but what about... yes? He did? Forward the message to me. Yes, alright take a screenshot and WhatsApp it over. Thanks. Oh, and Edward, stop being a dick to Needham. Got it? Thanks.'

'What did he say?' Martel asked.

Lehnert raised her left palm. 'Wait one.' Her cell phone pinged. She tapped the screen and opened WhatsApp. 'OK. Our guest didn't call anyone, but he did send an SMS, and he attached this location to it.'

Martel held out his hand. 'Give.'

Lehnert rolled her eyes and handed over the cell phone.

Martel studied the message. 'This is some kind of code.'

'Ya think?'

'What does it say?' Needham now was curious.

Martel read out the short message. 'Delayed whilst shopping.'

'That's all?'

'That and this location. It had to be a call for backup or help, like an SOS.'

'We could trace the number,' Lehnert held out her hand, 'but it'll be a one-use burner.'

'What makes you so sure?'

'He's a professional.'

'Wait now,' Needham leant against the door frame, 'am I missing something? Is this why you're here, Mickey?'

'You are, and it is. Hurst is the guy who hit Paul Fang in Winnipeg.'

'Hurst? Him? Really?'

'Yes, really.'

'Wait, and the other guy, the one I've just collected from the morgue, he was with Hurst?'

'Oui.'

'That accounts for his concussion then,' Needham stated. 'They fought, one died and the other didn't.'

'No,' Martel corrected, 'Hurst was given the concussion when a guy hit him with a fire extinguisher in Winnipeg.'

'Oh. So, who are they?'

'It doesn't matter who the dead guy was.'

'Brett Wayne,' Lehnert stated.

'It doesn't matter who he was because he is not a threat. What matters is who Hurst is and why he is here.'

Needham looked perplexed. 'It's always the quiet ones. Sheesh, and to think he was there sleeping in my spare room. I actually liked the guy. He's a professional hitman?'

'The Triads may be coming for him,' Martel continued, 'and if they are I need to get as much out of him as I can before we hand him over and they take him away.'

'I wouldn't want to fall into the hands of the Chinese!' Needham shook his head.

'Needham, have you got any pie with you?'

'Yeah, I've got a family sized peach one in this pocket and a cherry one under my vest. No, I have not. At my place, yes.'

'Too far. Look, get some from The Dockside Café and bring it back here. We're going to try the carrot before the stick.'

'I like to be the stick,' Martel said, a smile forming about his lips.

Martel watched Needham walk away and out of the building before he heard his cell phone ring. It was Gagnon. He put the phone to his ear. 'Oui, boss!'

'Have you secured the hitter?'

'Yes. He's cuffed in a cell here at Lehnert's place.'

'Bon. Now you keep him there, OK? It's important nothing happens to him. The Yee Kwan want him in one piece and completely untouched. You got me?'

Martel's jaw dropped. 'Wh-what do you mean, untouched?'

'They have a very specific way of exacting revenge, and

they don't want it messed up by handing over a guy who's already been battered. *Comprends-tu?*'

'*Oui, je comprends.*'

'Don't tell me you've slapped him about already?'

'No, he's fine.'

'Bon. Now I've got a question for you. When this Hurst guy whacked Fang he stole something from him. The Yee Kwan want to know if he has it?'

Martel's eyes flicked to Lehnert's desk and the red box sitting upon it. 'Was it a small, red box?'

'That's exactly what it was. Do you have it?'

'Yes we do. It was found on another guy who washed up lakeside.'

'Listen to me, you keep that box just as safe as Hurst. *D'accord?*'

'OK.'

'Right. I'll call you back once I've done the deal. In the meantime, send me a What-Is-Up photo of the box.' The call ended.

Martel stood and moved his phone above the desk. 'Gagnon needs a "What-Is-Up" photo of the box.'

'Why?'

'Because he calls WhatsApp "What-Is-Up".'

'No. Why does he want a photo?'

'Because it was stolen from the Triads.'

15

HARRISVILLE, MICHIGAN

Laying on his side, facing away from the surveillance camera, Akulov had continued to work the chain on his cuffs. Physically he now felt more or less fine. His head was a lot clearer. If he had to grade himself in terms of operational effectiveness he would say eighty-five per cent, but of course concussions were nebulous. Dizziness and loss of balance could reappear at any time until he was fully healed, but he was encouraged that during his short-lived escape attempt his body had responded to his commands without complaint or fault. Akulov was hungry, and he was angry. It wasn't a good combination. He needed fuel. He hadn't eaten since the pizza he'd been given by Deputy Grant the day before. But the hunger he could manage, what he was now struggling to control was his anger at himself.

The daylight outside his small window had now turned to night, and the bulb had been turned on. He'd lost, what, two days so far being held in his cell by a sheriff's department who clearly had little or no regard for the law. When the sheriff had first taken him in, he knew that at his usual fitness levels, he could have got away, but even though he sprinted as fast as he could out on the highway, his steps had been leaden, and his head had swum. And then when he was outside, he should have fought back and to hell with the consequences. He felt like he'd lost his edge, and he hoped it was solely because of the concussion. He jerked the cuffs in frustration, still nothing.

Akulov heard footsteps outside, the first there had been for what he estimated was at least two hours. He got to his feet, he was ready, and this time in spite of the cuffs and even though they'd anticipate it, he wouldn't hold back. The door opened slowly, and a voice said, 'It's me – Jake Needham, and I bring pie.'

Akulov remained still, but ready to strike.

Needham entered the room; he was holding a paper takeaway plate and cup. 'I brought pie, and coffee.'

Deputy Grant was behind him. He said, 'Now you sit yourself down, Mr Hurst.'

Akulov's eyes darted to the door, the large shape of the other man who had grappled him was there too.

Martel said, 'You want to try again?'

'Now come on, Mickey,' Grant replied, 'he's not going to do anything, are you, Mr Hurst?'

Inwardly Akulov cursed. He could go through Needham and Grant like nothing, but then the Quebec meathead would just shut the door. He sat. 'What type of pie?'

'Peach.'

'I still prefer cherry.'

Needham placed the plate on the table, and to Akulov's surprise, sat on the chair with its back to the door. Grant exited and the door snickered shut again. 'They want me to talk to you.'

'Why?'

Needham sighed. 'Look, they know what you did up in Winnipeg.'

Akulov hid his surprise. 'I don't know what you are talking about.'

'Look, Adam, I'm not a cop. I'm the guy who found you, and took you in.'

'Thank you.'

'You're welcome. It's like I said, we take care of people around here. Now tell me about the other guy they found on the shore.'

'What guy?'

'The dead guy who had a red box in his jacket pocket.'

Akulov felt his eye twitch, the fatigue giving him an uncharacteristic tell. 'How would I know?'

'Look, this isn't for me. Listen, if you could clarify a few things, which would help the sheriff with her investigation, well I think you'll see we can get this all cleared up.'

'You told me you were once a lawyer.'

'Yep, sure was.'

Akulov raised his hands and rattled the cuffs. 'Does any of this seem legal to you? A suspect is brought in, with a suspected concussion – I'm sure you told the sheriff about that?'

'I did, yes. I did.'

'Yet he gets no medical attention whatsoever, no phone call, no official statement is taken and no real food.'

Needham pointed at the pie. 'That's real pie.'

Akulov's stomach rumbled. 'I'm going to need a phone so I can call my lawyer.'

'Is that who you texted when you grabbed Ted's cell phone?'

Akulov made no reply.

'Look, you are not who you say you are. We know that.'

'It's "we" now?'

Needham paused and wet his lips. 'Look, we have an operation here. We need to know who sent you, and why.'

'No one sent me here, therefore there is no why. I am here by accident, and as you well know I was trying to leave when you delivered me to the sheriff.'

'Greg, the guy whose clothes you are wearing, he was the last person to just drop in on us. Claimed he was looking for work, and it turns out he was just looking into us. He was a Fed. We took care of him.'

'I see all pretence of being a model citizen has gone now, Jake?'

Needham sighed. 'That is the stage we have reached, Adam, although I doubt your real name is Adam. What is it?'

'It would make no difference.'

'I'm sure your parents wouldn't agree.'

'My parents are dead.'

'I am sorry for that.'

'Thank you.'

'Look, I'll tell you what we know, hell I'll even tell you who we are, it may make a difference. Have you ever heard of The Syndicate?'

'No, I have not.'

Needham seemed surprised. 'Really, with the circles you must operate in? I mean it's you, and people in your profession, who make up a good percentage of our business.'

'What profession is that, Jake?'

'Physical elimination. Adam, you are an assassin.'

'You think I came here to carry out a contract on someone?'

'Bingo.'

'Interesting.'

'For sure. Now, who are you here to "hit", Adam?'

'No one. I am here by accident.'

'Yeah, I know, the boat you borrowed blah blah blah.'

'What does The Syndicate do?'

'We're pan-national. We offer certain consulting services, and specific, how can I put this, "waste disposal options".'

Akulov now understood. 'You take care of people.'

'Exactly.'

'Why here, why this place?'

'Why not? It's quiet – off season – and there is a long border just across the water.'

Akulov no longer had any fear of the camera feed being recorded, as it was clearly both inadmissible and incriminating for Needham. 'Tell me what you know about me?'

'We know you assassinated Paul Fang and took his little red box. We know the dead guy was part of your team, and we know you both ended up here. We know what you are but not who you are. That's the issue, no one on the circuit knows your face, and so we don't know your name.'

'I am a man of mystery.'

'Yes, you are. Why don't you eat your pie?'

'Is it poisoned?'

'No.'

'Prove it?'

'Heck, why not.' Needham used a plastic knife and fork and cut off the tip of the triangular shaped pie piece. He held it up, like a surgeon then popped it in his mouth. He chewed, swallowed then opened his mouth to show that it was empty. 'Delicious, and now I suppose you want me to taste the coffee?'

'You suppose right.'

Needham removed the plastic top from the paper cup and sipped it. 'There.'

'Thank you.'

'So, eat, drink, be merry.'

'I will, in a while.'

'Who are you, Adam?'

Akulov said nothing.

Needham said, 'You see, I kind of liked you.'

'You don't know me.'

'True, but I think I saw who you are, inside. You could have jumped me when I came in, but you didn't. And why was that? Then the way you spoke to Ted, the way I could tell you were ready to defend me, if he'd got violent. You're a good person.'

'Good people don't kill people.'

'Unless the people they kill are bad people.'

'Are the people you kill bad, Jake?'

'I don't kill 'em, they come to me already dead. I'm the "cleaner"; I just dispose of them.'

'I am still sitting here. What does The Syndicate want from me?'

'Nothing, but the Chinese do.'

'The Chinese?'

'The Triads. You killed their boy, they want revenge.'

'That's logical.'

'That's business.'

'It is.' Akulov started to eat the pie. If the Triads were after him, they would want him alive, and that meant the food was fine.

'The big boss is discussing terms with them, and once settled he'll tell Martel.'

'Is Martel the muscle?'

'That's exactly what he is.'

Akulov finished the pie and started on the coffee. The mixture of caffeine and sugar would give him the energy boost he needed. 'How long will I have until the Triads arrive?'

Needham shrugged. 'If we come to terms, I have no idea. I don't know who they'll send. Will it be the Chinese from Winnipeg or their associates on this side of the border? They won't fly commercial, so that'll make things faster. But I can tell you one thing, it won't be before morning, this is a kinda out of the way place to get to.'

'I see.'

'Now, come on, just between the pair of us, why are you here?'

Akulov saw no sense in withholding the truth any more, the sheriff had him, and she had the red box. 'I am here by accident, and I arrived by plane.'

A look of triumph appeared on Needham's face. 'A-ha! So, you did fly here on purpose!'

'No. I did not. My plane crashed in the lake. The man you found died in the crash.'

Needham's mouth went slack but then he started to laugh, a deep slow chuckle.

The door opened. It was Martel. 'Needham, come with me.'

Needham got to his feet and moved to the door. 'Can you believe this guy? He says his plane crashed in the lake!'

'I do not give a crap.' Martel met Akulov's eyes. 'If you were not so valuable I would break your face.'

'Thank you,' Akulov replied. 'I am relieved.'

The door locked once more and Akulov was left alone,

and this time the light was switched off. In the gloom he wondered how long he had left before he had to face whoever it was who came through that door next.

* * *

Martel was too wired to rest, and of course he couldn't sleep. He was on edge, and the midnight black coffee wasn't helping. This was a huge deal, and he was the one who either made it happen, or messed it up, and messing up a deal with the Triads would be fatal. Members of the Yee Kwan were inbound, and once he'd handed over both the assassin who'd whacked their man, and the red box they were so hot to get back, he'd get his cut. The finder's fee Gagnon had arranged was seven million, US.

Gagnon had told Martel that the Yee Kwan liaison officer, known as the 'Straw Sandal', all but bit his hand off to accept the offer – which in Martel's experience didn't sound like the Yee Kwan at all – only knocking him down from ten million, which Gagnon knew was optimistic. Yet seven million was still much more than they had hoped for, and not bad at all for a day's work. It was an unexpected windfall for The Syndicate. Now to keep the stepbrothers happy, and to get his own one and a half million, he had to make it run smoothly. And that meant getting rid of anyone who may suddenly start to take their oath to upholding the laws of the USA more seriously than increasing their retirement funds. He knew Grant was a potential problem. The old deputy had been a fixture in the department before The Syndicate arrived, and that even pre-dated Needham starting the facility, and Lehnert being appointed sheriff. Of course, Deputy Johnson had already been dealt with, Lehnert carrying out her orders without complaint or hesitation, and that impressed Martel.

Over the top of his Alcona County Sheriff's Department mug he eyed Lehnert again. She wasn't the type of woman he usually found appealing, not dainty in anyway, yet there was something about her he liked. She was tall, and she was strong.

Lehnert caught him in the act. 'Don't they have women in Quebec?'

'They do, but they are all sticks.'

'Look, let's get something clear here? I'm happy to take The Syndicate's cash, hell I'm even happy to do little jobs for them here and there to protect Needham's facility, but that does not include entertaining their performing gorilla. You understand me?'

Martel tried not to laugh. 'Such fire.'

'Shut it! Sheesh it's like I'm sitting here with Pepe Le Pew!'

'Seriously, if this all works out it will be your biggest payday. You could do a lot with one hundred and fifty large.'

'Yeah well, who couldn't.'

'What are you going to do?'

'I hadn't thought about it. I'm a realist. I tell you what I'm not going to do, and that is blow it all on a new truck, which Ted will claim as his own and then total.'

'He's a good kid.'

Lehnert pointed her pen at Martel, 'Now I know you are definitely sleep deprived. He is a crap kid.'

Martel tutted and shook his head in mock disgust. 'What kind of a mother are you, Sheriff Lehnert?'

'You've just answered your own question. I'm a sheriff, and I'm trying to do the best for my kid. But what have I done? He should be on the corporate ladder by now, or at least working in a trade, but what does he do? He's an errand boy for The Syndicate. Hell, even Squeaky-Dave has an actual job.'

'Make Ted a real deputy.'

'Yeah, that would look "above board". With the cash I'll set him up with something. Something he can't mess up; something that'll make him grow up.'

'Such as?'

'I have no idea.'

Martel yawned.

'You can't cut the night shift?'

'You get me wrong. When I am up all night there is usually action, on the dance floor or in the boudoir. It is inaction that fatigues me.'

'It's a skill you have to learn, patience, the ability to wait.'

'Is that the army talking?'

'Yep. In "The Sand Pit" once we had to catch this guy in the act in order to bring him in.'

Martel leaned forward in his seat. 'What was he up to?'

'He was in supplies. We suspected he was stealing and selling to the locals.'

'What Uncle Sam cannot spare a few tins of Spam?'

'There was a racquet over in Afghanistan. First the Taliban find a lowly, susceptible target – a mark. Then over time they'd persuade him to steal larger items until they used blackmail to get him to give them something they really needed.' She took a swig of her own black coffee. 'Anyway we couldn't follow the guy because he'd see us a mile off, so we had to dig in and watch this one compound for five days until our "mark" turned up, which he did.'

'I could not do that.'

'I'm guessing that Hurst is ex-military, and that he was not some type of "regular soldier", and if that's the case then he's just like me. He has been trained to wait and then strike at the most opportune moment.'

'He tried, you stopped him, and we cuffed him. What can he do now?'

'Anything, he's desperate.'

'It pains me to say this, but nothing can happen to him until the Triads arrive, our cash and your cash is counting on it.'

'True.'

'Gagnon told me no one knows his face, no one knows who he is – even The Irishman said he did not have a clue. Now this either means he's so good that he's never been caught, or he's so new to this that he hasn't been photographed before.'

'He's good.'

'You think so?'

'I do; it's a sense I have.'

'*Je m'en fous*, I do not care. He will be gone by morning.'

16

ALPENA COUNTY, MICHIGAN

The SkyWest Delta flight landed a little earlier than expected at Alpena County Regional Airport, which Basson appreciated. The cabin had been less than half full, and although he could have been the first off, Basson let several other passengers pass him to get more time to assess the arrivals hall. He wasn't expecting anyone to be waiting for him except the contractors he had taken on, and they would be at the prearranged spot in the car park across the road. However, vigilance cost nothing and saved everything. He was using another ID, this time he was American and his name was Justin Vernier. His US accent was passable, and any remaining French inflection could be explained away by his surname, although he didn't believe he'd need to do much in the way of any in-depth philosophical discussion with the locals. With his carry-on luggage held in his left hand he smiled at the flight attendant as he exited the cabin.

The terminal was small, clean and functional, he'd been in far worse, but he'd also been in far better, both Singapore's Changi and Doha's Hammad came to mind. But this was a regional airport catering mostly for regional people and of course domestic tourists. At a regular pace, he negotiated his way past other passengers and out through the exit.

Outside the steel and glass fronted terminal building he crossed the cracked, concrete road and saw a black Chevrolet Tahoe sitting a couple of rows back, in amongst the other SUVs, sedans and pickups. The man who was waiting for him was a trusted contractor he had utilised before. Ryan Kelly would, for the right price, happily supply both weapons and munitions, and also pull the trigger to complete the contract. He stepped out of the Tahoe. He was, as instructed, wearing a dark suit. There was another man with him, whom he'd vouched for, by the name of Ross. Basson didn't know if this was his first name or his surname or if it was his real name at all. If Kelly said he was solid, well that was all that mattered.

'Welcome to Michigan,' Kelly said, his southern accent making the name of the state sound like 'Meeshigaan'.

'You couldn't get a black Crown Victoria?'

'A Crown Vic, especial black or midnight blue screams "Feds" or "DEA" or hell, any number of agencies, but this thing not so much. Plus, it's more useful – more space.'

'The Bureau uses them too, when transporting high value individuals,' Ross said.

'He knows from personal experience,' Kelly said with a wink.

Basson wet his lips, he'd started to feel excited. 'Where's the stuff?'

'The equipment you requested is in the back, including the C4 and the detonators,' Kelly confirmed. 'Your suit is on the middle seats.'

'OK. I'll change en route.'

'You're the boss.'

Basson climbed in the back. In front Kelly retook the driver's seat and Ross rode shotgun. The Chevy V8 rumbled as the full-size SUV headed for the exit of the lot.

'Good flight?'

'Any flight you walk away from is good.'

'Where d'you fly in from?'

Basson furrowed his brow as he started to pull off his lightweight, navy blue travelling chinos. 'Why do you want to know?'

'Hey, Bang-Bang, I'm just making conversation, you know, like a normal person.'

'And are we normal people?' Basson replied, as he slipped on the black, suit trousers.

'No, we are not. Point taken.'

Basson removed his light blue chambray shirt and started to put on a plain, white one. 'Any issues I should know about?'

'Nope.'

'What about the other vehicle?'

'I've parked that at the property we scouted, by the water,' Ross confirmed.

'Concerns?'

'Nope,' Kelly shook his head, 'well, OK. What if the sheriff or her deputies refuse to hand over this guy you're so hot about?'

'The sheriff is a woman?'

'She is. I checked the Alcona Sheriff's Department website. Sheriff Sue Lehnert.'

'Then I shall charm her.'

Kelly shook his head, 'Ah, yeah. Drop your American accent for a French one and tell her about your chateau.'

'Something like that.'

'But still, what if they smell a rat?'

'Then they will no longer smell.'

Ross said, 'Law enforcement officers? You're saying we'll be taking out law enforcement officers?'

'Needs must, when the devil rides.'

'Yep, he's riding behind me right now.'

'Merci, I shall take that as a compliment.' Basson took a grey, black and red striped tie from the jacket and inspected it. 'This tie however is quite insulting.'

'Hey, it's better than plain black; you need to look a little human.'

'Oui, more human and less hitman.'

Before they reached the town of Alpena, Kelly cut across smaller, residential streets then turned south on the twenty-three for Harrisville and the target address. They travelled on in silence for a while as Basson now enjoyed the greenery of the passing countryside, not as delightful of course as his native France but certainly more welcoming than the bleak sands of the Middle East.

Ross broke the silence. 'I've a question.'

'Continue.'

'Who is the mark?'

'Someone who let me down.'

'Right.'

Basson started to think of what he had to do, and how it would pan out. Ideally, he'd like to batter Akulov to a bloody pulp and see the fear and regret in the man's eyes as he took his last breath, but he knew that was wishful thinking. Akulov was his junior by almost two decades, and like him had been part of an elite unit. Both men had been highly trained in hand-to-hand combat, and for the first time

Basson accepted that in a fair fight he would not win. Wolf Six's reputation had been built on his results, and the fact that he had never been stopped, yet Basson knew the truth. Akulov's weakness was his own humanity, and for one who saw himself not as a human but as a Werewolf this, the Frenchman thought, was both ironic and comical.

'ETA in ten,' Kelly said.

'Do you have the IDs?'

'Yes, boss. They will pass inspection, none of this plastic toy store crap. Yours should be in the jacket – Tom Oliver.'

Basson found the ID and checked the name. 'It's "Olivier" – like the actor.'

'Who now?' Ross asked.

'He was in that film about the dentist,' Kelly stated.

'*Finding Nemo?*'

'That was about a fish,' Kelly said.

'A fish who escaped from a Dentist's office,' Ross countered.

'Nah,' Kelly shook his head, 'that guy from *Jaws* was in it too.'

'*Marathon Man.*' Basson sighed. 'Now as I outlined it. I go in first with you and do the talking. Ross, you stay with the second vehicle ready to roll, if we need it.'

'Sure, I got it. This isn't my first rodeo.'

Kelly asked, 'Have you ever been to a rodeo, Ross?'

'No, but I've been to the circus a few times, and let me tell you, small-town sheriffs are usually clowns.'

'Let us hope so.'

The Tahoe turned east before Harrisville on a road which led in the direction of the lake. There was a T-junction, and they turned left passing several large homes with lakefront views.

'The house is round a bend at the end of the street,' Kelly explained. 'These places are mostly empty at this time of year.'

'Mostly?'

'It's as near to being invisible as we can be driving this lump.'

'Then it will have to do.'

They passed four more houses, each was larger and more secluded than the previous one before they took an unpathed drive which wound past mature trees before it stopped, with a turning circle in front of a large, white, wooden panelled house.

'This reminds me of *The Waltons*,' Kelly commented.

Basson didn't understand the reference so made no reply. To the left of the house and parked so that it was ready to drive directly back up the track was a rust-coloured F150. Kelly brought the Tahoe to a stop then jumped out. Basson saw him give the area a quick three-sixty visual sweep, although he imagined if anyone was there, they would have known already.

Wearing the same pair of black New Balance casual leather work sneakers he'd travelled in, he trusted no one to select shoes for him, Basson stepped out of the Tahoe and crunched on the gravel towards the back of the vehicle. He opened the tailgate and saw two dull, olive green equipment bags inside.

'Bon. We have work to do and not much time to do it. We'll go inside, go over the plan – thoroughly, I'll prepare the C4, and then we go in.'

* * *

Harrisville, Michigan

'Tom Olivier, Federal Bureau of Investigation.' Basson knew his accent was good, but to his ears there was still the faintest hint of French about it. He raised his badge at the deputy behind the reception desk in a relaxed manner. On the deputy's uniform shirt was a badge which read 'Grant'. 'You're holding a person of interest to us, and I'm here to take him back to Chicago.'

'I was not aware of this,' Grant replied, and Basson noted the man's attempt to mask his surprise as he looked down and squinted to check his computer screen. 'The only perp we have here is a guy we brought in for allegedly stealing a sailboat. In fact, he's not officially been charged yet.'

'Is that so?'

'Yes.'

Basson pulled out a piece of paper from his pocket, on it was printed a photograph of Akulov, the same one The Irishman had sent him. 'This guy?'

'Yes. That's him. Adam Hurst, right?'

'Right,' Basson agreed, cheered on by the fact that the dopey deputy had given him the name of the man they were holding. 'You see, as soon as someone from your department logged a search for that name, well it raised a flag on our system. So here we are. It's an alias he's been known to use. We've been looking for the guy for the past six months.'

'Are you saying his ID is a forgery?'

'Nope. It's real, but he's not.'

Deputy Grant seemed puzzled, like he didn't quite understand. 'Can I ask, what do you want him for?'

Basson decided to use a truth to conceal a lie, and amongst the underworld it was common knowledge that

Wolf Six had been responsible. 'Look, I'm not meant to say anything really, so keep this between us – one old timer to another – but do you remember that big bank job in Chicago?'

Grant looked to be ten years his senior, but didn't quibble this, rather he leant forward a little, as though his interest had been piqued. 'You mean that one with the dead Russian mobsters?'

'The very same.'

'Those Russians killed a cop.'

'Yes, they did, and it seems our guy here took great offence to this and thought he was "The Punisher". Now, we cannot allow that.'

'Are you sure this is the same person?' Grant frowned and read the screen. 'Adam Hurst, with a residential address in some suburb of Washington?'

'The same.'

'Wow.'

'I know.'

'I'll have to see your paperwork, and clear this with Sheriff Lehnert.'

'Hey, I understand, you've got to follow procedure, right? I get it,' Basson said in a tone he imagined sounded sympathetic. 'I've got a paper copy here for you. There's some kind of glitch back at Chicago. A digital request from the Bureau should be on your system by the end of the day.'

Grant looked down again and tapped a few keys on his computer. He nodded. 'I don't see it yet.'

Basson put his hand in his inside pocket and took out a folded piece of letter-sized, white paper. 'Here.'

'Thank you.' Grant took the paper, popped on his

reading glasses and inspected it. 'I've not seen one of these for a long time, I kind of forgot what they looked like.'

'These things are always changing, being redesigned for no damn good reason.'

'I hear you,' Grant said removing his glasses. 'So, this guy, I mean we got an anonymous E-tip that he stole a sailboat, but he seemed, I don't know, like one of the good guys to me.'

'Good at killing perhaps.'

Grant visibly paled. 'Yeah, well he did try to escape last night.'

'Did he now?' Basson felt a twinge of concern.

'Yes, siree.'

'And you stopped him?'

'Well not me, our sheriff.'

'I see.'

'So, just to be clear you think he killed the Russians?'

'He took them all out, allegedly.'

'Jesus.'

'I know right? So that's why we've got to take him back.'

'We?'

'My partner is by the car.' Basson gestured over his shoulder and through the glass door. He saw Grant follow his hand in the direction of Kelly who was leaning against the side of the Tahoe with a cigarette in his hand. 'What can I say,' continued Basson, 'he's addicted. He's got to get his smoke in now before we have our perp in the back. We've all gone "clean air crazy", the FBI can't be accused of subjecting any citizen to secondary smoke.'

Grant said, 'Goddamn rules. The rest of the department make me go round the back on my breaks, like I'm some kind of health hazard leper. Let me take this to Sheriff

Lehnert and have her check and sign it. Shouldn't be more than say, ten minutes?'

'That's fine.'

'You can take a seat if you like.'

'I'll stand, I'll be sitting enough when I drive back to Chicago.'

Grant made no reply as he turned, paper in hand, and walked through the deserted squad room to the glass walled office at the back. Basson hoped the document was indeed authentic enough to fool the sheriff. From studying the schematics of the 'Sheriff's Office', Basson knew that a narrow corridor leading to the rear exit separated the actual sheriff's office from the steps down to the cells. He gazed in their direction imagining that he could hear the black heart beating of the man who called himself Wolf Six held in one of them. He knew there were three cells, and he guessed for the sake of convenience, his prey was being held in the cell nearest to the steps.

Basson picked up a tourist brochure from a pile on the desk and turning away slightly, pretended to browse it whilst he checked up on Kelly outside who was watching the front of the facility and the two entrances to the parking lot for any threats or surprises.

* * *

It was already past nine and Martel had been told the Triads would be with them by eleven. He cursed them for not telling him this sooner. If he had known this, he would have at least taken a few hours to sleep and refresh, rather than having to camp out in Lehnert's office dozing on her short couch. Martel bit into a protein bar, from the stash that he'd brought with him and washed it down with cold, bitter coffee. Whilst he felt like crap, and was shaky as hell, Lehnert looked exactly the same as she always did. The more time he spent with her the more he liked her, and the more he liked her the more likely he knew he would be to make a fool of himself.

'You're staring again.'

'What is art if one cannot appreciate it?'

Lehnert scowled. 'Are you quite right in the head?'

'No,' Martel conceded, 'but I will be when I get my money.'

There was a knock on the glass door. Both Martel and Lehnert turned to look.

'Come in,' Lehnert said.

It was Grant. 'Sheriff, we have an unexpected visitor, well two of them to be precise.'

'What?' Martel said.

Grant addressed Lehnert. 'We've got a pair of FBI agents waiting to take Hurst back to Chicago.'

'The hell they are!' Martel said, jumping from his seat and spilling coffee on the carpet tiles. He stared at the reception area to see a man with salt and pepper hair, dressed in a dark suit inspecting a tourist information brochure. 'Where's the second one?'

'By their vehicle, he's smoking.'

'Is that the Bureau request?' Lehnert asked, gesturing to the papers in Grant's shaky hand.

'Yes.' Grant handed it to her.

Lehnert read the document quickly before handing it to Martel. 'This makes matters complicated.'

Martel couldn't believe what he was reading. 'Are you telling me this is real? The FBI can just take him like that?'

'They are the FBI,' Lehnert stated.

Grant said, 'He's wanted for something big. Do you remember that bank job six months back in Chicago? The one where a cop and team of Russians wound up dead?'

'That was him?' Martel asked.

'The FBI thinks so.'

Martel thought back to the news coverage, and the swirling rumours, which had even reached Canada, about the sole operator who had prevented the bank heist by taking out all but one of the Russians. Some of the wildest ones were that the mythical Wolf Six had been involved, but Martel knew the man didn't exist. He was a fabrication. Martel pointed at the CCTV monitor in the corner of the room showing the feed from the cells. 'Then Hurst is definitely worth the price.'

'What do you mean?' Grant asked.

Lehnert stood. 'Jim, I need you to go home now – that's an order. I'll handle this.'

'I've only just started my shift.'

'Go,' Martel said. 'Special one-day vacation.'

'Well, if you insist.' Grant left the office, shaking his head.

'Is he going to be a problem?'

'He's a busybody but he knows when to look and walk the other way,' Lehnert stated.

'He'd better.'

Lehnert held her hand out for the paper. 'What do we do? I have to sign this; I can't mess with the Feds.'

'What we do is we categorically do not give Hurst over to the FBI.'

'Do you really want to take that chance?'

'For this amount of cash? Yes, I do.'

'How are we going to get rid of them?'

'Simple, we get rid of them. Have you forgotten what it is Needham does here for The Syndicate? We whack 'em, and then Needham processes them like all the others.'

'Martel, they're the friggin FBI! There will be records, logs of where they were and what they were working on!'

'We make it look as if the guy they came for was responsible for their disappearance. Hey, no bodies means no proof.'

'If this goes south!'

'Relax, we got it all covered. Now give me one of those deputy badges of yours, I want one to flash it when you introduce me.'

Lehnert reached into a drawer, then tossed it over. 'Here.'

Martel caught it. 'Thanks, chief. Have you got your taser?'

'Yes.' She removed it from a charger.

'Got a spare one for me?'

'There.' She nodded to a filing cabinet. 'There's an extra one in there, I charged it yesterday.'

'Bon. Now sign and stamp that piece of paper, and let's take the Feds to our "golden boy".'

Lehnert took a pen from a desk tidy and signed the second printed sheet, then retrieving her ink stamp from a drawer put her official mark just below her signature. She got to her feet and adjusted her belt. 'We're doing this?'

'You getting cold feet?'

Lehnert handed Martel a pair of cuffs as she strode out of her office. 'Nope, they're always toasty.'

Martel followed. 'When's Squeaky-Dave and Ted due in?'

'They should be here now, but they probably stopped off for doughnuts, or pie.'

'That figures,' Martel replied.

As they neared the front desk Martel noted the Fed had to be a senior agent, due to his age which he estimated was somewhere between mid to late fifties. The time in his career when he was either happy to coast, and impart wisdom down the ranks, or gunning for that big result to propel himself up the pay scale before he reached retirement. Martel noted the agent's suit was tighter across his chest and shoulders than his waist, just like his own jacket, which meant the guy still lifted, and this of course Martel approved of.

'Hello, I'm Sheriff Lehnert.' She held out her right hand.

'Agent Olivier.' The Fed took the proffered hand and shook it.

Martel raised his newly acquired badge. 'Deputy Martel. We got called out late last night – hence the jacket and pants.' Martel shook Olivier's hand too. Martel noted his grip was firm and there were callouses on his palm.

'It's good to meet you both,' Olivier said.

The door opened behind Olivier and the second Fed entered. He looked to be in his late thirties, and like Olivier he too seemed fitter than average. The pair were definitely field agents, and not desk jockeys.

'Hi, I'm Agent Williams.'

'Here,' Lehnert handed Basson the transfer paper, 'he's all yours.'

'Then let's go and introduce ourselves,' Basson replied.

Martel stepped to one side to let Lehnert, and the two FBI agents pass, but as he did so he saw a second black Tahoe arrive outside. For a long moment he felt his chest tighten as he thought it was the Triads arriving earlier than expected but then two men alighted. One had light brown hair tied back in a ponytail and the other, who seemed older, had blond hair. Both were wearing windcheaters with the same three gold letters emblazoned upon them 'FBI'.

* * *

Basson heard the main door to the sheriff's office open. He turned his head and noted that Deputy Martel was not following them, so he stopped walking. He glanced towards the reception, which given the angle of his head, was where Martel was looking too, and saw two men approaching the desk, both were wearing FBI windbreakers, one had dusky blond hair and the other had his long hair worn in a ponytail.

It was too much of a coincidence to be anything else, in a small place like this the odds were astronomical. Basson felt his rage rising within him as he immediately understood what was happening. It had all been a fabrication. Akulov was not here, and why would he suddenly materialise in such a backwater type of place? No, he was certain of it, he Martin Basson aka The Bang-Bang Man, had been lured here by the American intelligence apparatus, namely the CIA. They had failed in Warsaw, which meant they would be determined not to fail now. If he needed any further confirmation of this, the bodybuilder who claimed to be a sheriff's deputy was reaching for his sidearm.

In the opposite direction the sheriff had continued to lead Kelly to the back of the building but was now turning her body to face Kelly and her right hand was moving towards her waist. To her left, two men, the one in front resembling a giant sumo wrestler, entered from the back of the building.

Basson was trapped in the middle of a sheriff's office.

However, that did not mean he would give himself up. The CIA had come for The Bang-Bang Man, and that is exactly who they would get. He slipped his right hand into his jacket pocket and took out one of the two M67 fragmentation grenades Kelly had supplied him with. Pulling the pin, he twisted to toss it towards the reception area.

The sheriff shouted, her warning was as loud as it was abrupt. 'Bomb!'

Basson's eyes locked onto those of the sheriff, at the other end of the room, as a flash exploded from the end of her service weapon. Instinctively he jinked sideways, mid-swing as the round whistled past his hand and the grenade flew from his fingers. It launched in the opposite direction to the one he had intended, sailing towards the office, and the corridor.

The fragmentation grenade had a standard four to five second delay fuse. He saw it hit the floor at the same time as he rolled under the nearest workstation. He pushed the palms of his hands hard against his ears. Two seconds later the explosive force of the HE grenade tore through the interior wall of the office and out into the corridor and the path of the two men entering from the back, reducing the area to rubble.

An eerie silence occupied the room, as though all the air and sound had been sucked out, which in part Basson knew it had. Now, in the dust and confusion was the time to move. Silenced Beretta up and seeking out targets, Basson sprang from his hiding place and advanced towards the carnage. He could hear murmurs, at least one person had survived. He drew level with Kelly; it wasn't him. He couldn't see the sheriff, but she had been standing at the top of the flight of stairs. Perhaps the concussive force had hurled her down them?

Either way it mattered nothing to him. He pushed on, through the debris. There was movement ahead, a figure had pushed up on its elbows and was dragging itself backwards, trailing its shredded legs and entrails. It was the sumo wrestler. Basson raised his Beretta.

'Pl... please... no...' The voice was croaky, and high pitched. 'Please...'

'It's kinder this way, for everyone.' Basson put a round in the fat man's head. He stepped over the corpse and saw the second man lying face down and unmoving. Ignoring him he reached the exit. The door was hanging from its hinges, he pushed past and out of the building. Gulping in lungfuls of fresh air, he negotiated the cage at the back of the facility, having to use another round to shoot off the heavy padlock. He started to reach into his pocket for his burner phone but then saw the F150 idling further down the street outside a neighbouring house. He waved it over and the truck roared towards him, churning up the grass before skidding to a halt ten paces away.

Basson sprinted across the rear lot for the truck, dragged the door open and jumped in. 'Drive!'

'Where's Kelly?'

'Kelly's dead!'

'What?'

The window next to Basson shattered, showering him in glass, and on the other side Ross' head exploded. Basson pushed himself sideways as another round tore through the thin metal of the truck next to him, gouging his skin on the right side of his torso. He grunted and clambered over the body of Ross, depressing the belt release, he opened the door and pushed him out. A third round hit the truck, this one causing the windscreen to spiderweb. Basson pushed the stick shift into drive and pushed the accelerator hard into the floor. He spun the truck to the left to aim for the main road they had come in on and he saw her, the sheriff, she was walking towards him and firing. First the front then the rear tyres were shredded and the truck dipped to the left and ploughed deeper into the grass. Then the rear windscreen was hit. The Ford continued to move until it bumped back down onto the tarmac, the remnants of the tyres slowing the rotation of the wheels. There was no way he could get away in this truck, but that had never been its true purpose.

A second handgun now joined in pelting the stricken F150. With everything to lose, including his life, Basson turned the Ford back towards the source of the gunfire and stamped on the accelerator, urging it to if not pick up speed, to at least make it back to the building. Basson knew it was time to bail. He pushed the door open and half jumped, half fell out and onto the grass. He scrambled up to his feet and scurried away as quickly as he could. He took out his burner smartphone and tapped open an app. He glanced back, seeing the sheriff advancing, joined by Deputy Martel. His jacket was off, and in his shirt sleeves Basson could see just how large his gym muscles were. Martel pulled the sheriff out of the path of the ambling truck. Yet none of that would make any difference. Basson threw himself to the ground and pressed a command on the app and milliseconds later the detonator attached to the C4 on the truck's large gas tank transformed the rust, red Ford 150 into a bright red fireball.

Ears ringing, Basson stood. He wanted to see the fruits of his manic labour. He could see Martel, he was laying on top of the sheriff, smothering her with his body. Basson didn't know if either of them were alive. A sneer appeared on his face, and he felt the sickly sense of elation as he saw the smoking, crumbling ruin he had turned the back of the law enforcement building into. Then he saw the two real FBI agents. They were approaching tactically, seeking out targets. They spotted him at the same time. One shouted a command, which he chose to ignore and seconds later they opened fire.

Basson ran, pumping his legs he pelted away from the scene of destruction and was almost mown down by a pair of pair of black Cadillac Escalades swinging off the road and into the lot. Basson jinked past the SUVs and careered downhill towards the main road and the lake beyond. More rounds snapped after him, but he dare not look back. The Bang-Bang Man was furious, but at least he still had his freedom.

* * *

Martel raised his head, and looked on as two SUVs came to a stop in the main parking lot. A man climbed out of each. Both were wearing suits, and wraparound sunglasses, and both were Asian. The two FBI agents were approaching them, weapons in one hand and badges in the other. As though they were a pair of synchronised swimmers, each man speedily climbed back into their shotgun positions and the twin Cadillacs wheel-spun backwards, leaving dark rubber tracks on the concrete hardstanding, before turning and racing off. Martel watched on as his one and a half million disappeared around the corner. He let his head fall back into the grass and started to wail.

17

HARRISVILLE, MICHIGAN

Akulov jerked his wrists apart, the chain finally gave, and his hands were independent once again.

He coughed the dust out of his mouth and wiped his eyes. Through the locked steel door, he had heard the footsteps of at least two, perhaps three people and, although the words were unintelligible, what sounded like curt commands. But then suddenly, gunfire and an explosion. Not understanding whether it was because of the deal going bad with the Triads, or perhaps, but less likely, someone attempting to rescue him, he'd had no choice but to remain in his locked room.

But not now.

Now there was a hole in the outer wall, left after a second explosion of such force had ripped the steel table from its fixings and impaled it against the steel door. Akulov realised where he had been standing in the corner he must have been protected from the direct percussive wave of the blast, even though it had knocked him from his feet and thrown him against the hard, cold concrete.

His ears were ringing, and he worked his jaw in an attempt to regain his hearing. Unsteadily he made for the hole and clambered through and out onto the grass at the side of the facility. He stumbled away for several steps before he put his hands on his thighs as he took long, deep breaths of fresh air in an attempt to clear both his lungs and his head. He looked back and to his right, and saw the burning remains of what he identified as being some type of truck, and then he realised that the room next to the one he had been kept in had taken the brunt of the explosion. He now also saw something else on the ground, in fact there were two of them.

A pained voice growled, 'Just stop right where you are!'

Sheriff Lehnert was pulling herself up to her haunches, and by her side Martel was helping her. His white dress shirt had now been blackened and was part ripped off, making him look to all intents and purposes like Lou Ferrigno's Incredible Hulk. She pushed him away and Martel got to his feet. He extended his right arm and pointed directly at Akulov, in a manner which Akulov imagined was supposed to make him scared. Akulov scanned the ground around the pair for any type of weapon, and saw none. He knew he should just turn and run off but something inside him, call it annoyance, he hoped it wasn't pride, made him stay. So he said, 'You can still walk away Martel.'

'After this you will not be able to walk. You know how much you have cost me?'

Lehnert was on her feet, yet instead of joining the brewing confrontation, she was hobbling back towards the sound of the nearing fire sirens coming from the other side of the building.

Martel approached, the expression on his face a mixture

of anger and what Akulov took to be joy. 'Just you and me now, little man.'

Akulov nodded, Martel was perhaps two inches taller than he was and quite a few inches wider. Akulov's muscles, whilst resembling those of an elite four-hundred-meter runner, were unimpressive next to the hulk. Yet Akulov knew his muscles had not been created in the gym alone, and whilst he imagined Martel may have been trained to fight, he had been trained to kill.

The two men were standing on a sloping grassy piece of landscaping, it would be softer to land on yet harder to stay upright.

Martel edged forward, turned his head and spat. In French he said, '*Bâtard, tu vas me le payer!*' – You'll pay for this!

'Why don't you apologise and run away whilst you still are able to do so?' Akulov replied before switching languages, '*Martel. Tu as merdé.*'

Martel blinked hearing French, and he snarled an obscenity in return, '*Mange tes morts, Hurst!*'

'My name is not Hurst.'

Martel's left eye twitched, and this was followed by a miniscule movement in his right hand, and then, as Akulov knew he would, Martel attacked.

Swinging his hips, Martel telegraphed his initial move. He shot out his left leg in a straight, karate kick, and then rather than extending it fully, he brought it back and, threw a straight right fist. As feints went, it was different, and it wasn't the worse Akulov had seen but he had still seen it. Akulov stepped outside the incoming punch, batting it away with his own left hand then pivoting around Martel he slammed his right fist into the back of the man's head as hard as he could. Martel lurched forwards, down the short slope, and Akulov now delivered a stomp kick to the man's lower back to help him on his way.

Martel staggered but managed to regain his balance. He turned, eyes narrowing. His slight height advantage had now been more than negated. Akulov preferred to counterstrike rather than attack, so he patiently waited for Martel's next move. The man came back at him, fists up, changing styles and stances, now resembling more an MMA fighter than one of The Karate Kid's adversaries. Akulov had no doubt that if Martel succeeded in making contact, it would hurt. And then he found out his assumption had been correct.

Movement caught Akulov's eye, a momentary loss of focus but that was all Martel needed, and his right fist hurtled towards Akulov's solar plexus, bypassing his guard and landing with such force that he lost his footing. Akulov fell backwards, landing hard on the grass, forcing the air out of his lungs. Akulov saw the expression change on Martel's face, as though he was sensing victory. He advanced, but Akulov twisted to his right, and kicking out swept the larger man's legs from under him. Martel landed heavily, the back of his head striking the ground. Rather than going in for the kill, Akulov took a step back and looked again at what had distracted him. Two figures were approaching, both wearing FBI windcheaters.

Martel got to his feet, he seemed groggy then suddenly all pretence was gone, and fists up, he charged at Akulov. Akulov took a step forward, to meet the French Canadian and launched a side kick into the large man's abdomen. Martel folded forward, yet still attempted to grab him. Akulov sidestepped and slammed his right elbow against the side of Martel's head. Martel dropped to his knees on the grass. Akulov once again stepped back, this time he took a large breath.

'Need a hand, Wolf Six?' Vince Casey asked, in his relaxed Deep South accent.

'You seem a little tired, Akulov,' Mike Parnell added.

Martel was back up to his hands and knees. He looked around wildly. 'Wolf Six?... Akulov... Ruslan Akulov?'

Akulov addressed the two CIA operatives. 'Thank you, very clever. Why not tell the whole town who I am?'

Casey spread his palms. 'Hey, we're just here to help.'

'Get up, big man, you're embarrassing yourself,' Parnell said to Martel.

Shakily Martel got to his feet and raised his hands. 'Okay, I give up. Arrest me.'

Parnell asked Casey, 'Do we have powers of arrest, I thought we just shot people?'

Casey shrugged. 'It's discretionary. I mean, we're not actually really here, are we?'

'Who... who are you?'

Parnell said, 'Who's this meatbag?'

'Some Québécois mobster's muscle.'

'I am Mickey Martel, *the* Québécois mobster's muscle!' Martel added, indignantly.

'Just cuff him,' Akulov said. 'You do have cuffs?'

'Only from my personal collection,' Parnell said with a wink as he took a set of flexi-cuffs from his pocket and then pulling Martel's arms behind his back, secured them.

'Would you care to tell me what just happened here?' Akulov asked.

Casey and Parnell exchanged glances, before Casey said, 'I was hoping you could tell us?'

'Who rammed the building with a truck bomb?'

'No idea,' Casey said, 'but the Chinese were here.'

'The Triads came for me, and the red box.'

'You have the red box?' Casey asked.

'No. Hormann had it.'

'Well, it isn't on his body. That's in a hut next to some diner in Black River.'

'How did you find me?'

'We found Hormann. He was fitted with a subcutaneous micro-tracker. An old guy we tied up, named Needham, said you were here.'

'I know where the red box is,' Martel said, 'but I want a deal.'

'Yeah?' Parnell replied. 'What sort of deal?'

'Two million dollars, US.'

Parnell started to tap his pockets. 'Sure. I've got three right here somewhere.'

Casey said, 'Here's what's going to happen, you take us to the box, and we put you on a flight back to where, Montreal?'

'Oui.'

'Then we forget we met you, *d'accord mon ami*?'

'*D'accord*. It is in Lehnert's office. Locked in her gun safe.'

'Lead on, Martel,' Parnell said, pushing Martel towards the front of the building.

As though sensing that Akulov had questions Casey said, 'We'll talk on the plane, later, Ruslan. We both need some things answered.'

Akulov nodded, noticing for the first time a crowd of onlookers had appeared on the main parking lot, which was shared by both the sheriff's office and the courthouse. Next to the courthouse and across the road was the Harrisville Fire Department, which accounted for the tender that had now arrived by the small rear lot and was starting to hose down the smouldering truck. The howl of a siren joined the chaotic scene as an EMT team arrived at the front of the facility. Deputy Grant was waving away townsfolk in an attempt to reassure them. They entered the reception and negotiated the debris which included the reception desk. Akulov now saw for the first time the extent of the damage.

'*Tabarnak!*' Martel exclaimed, in French Canadian. 'And see, there is my jacket!'

'First he chucks a grenade and then drives an IED into the back wall, the guy was a maniac,' Parnell stated.

'And we have no idea who he was?' Akulov asked.

'Presumably he was here for you, and perhaps for the box,' Casey stated. 'Yet, as a lot of people want you dead that doesn't narrow it down any.'

Unable to keep quiet Martel said, 'He was also pretending to be FBI. He was nothing to do with us. That was the first time I have ever seen that *putain*.'

They picked their way towards the office. Its interior walls had been demolished, leaving it as just another section of the open-plan floor. The EMTs pushed past them with a stretcher. Akulov saw further on there were a pair of bodies. Lehnert was kneeling over one of them. She moved back to allow it to be manipulated onto the stretcher. Akulov recognised the blackened, flat facial features, it was her son Ted Lehnert. As they reached the office area the EMTs raised the stretcher and quickly, but carefully started to take it outside. The sheriff herself passed Akulov, her face wearing a blank expression, as she followed the stretcher.

In the office area, Martel jutted his chin towards the gun safe.

'Fantastic,' Parnell noted, 'looks like we'll need another grenade to open that.'

'The key is in the top desk drawer.'

Parnell moved to the overturned desk, found the drawer and key. 'Got it.'

Casey held up his hand and Parnell tossed him the key. He stepped over more rubble and opened the safe, which was fixed in concrete to the outer wall. Casey reached in and when he pulled out his hand it was clasped around a plastic evidence envelope.

'The Yee Kwan agreed to pay seven million for that and Hur... Akulov. What is that thing?'

'TV remote,' Casey said, as he zipped it into his jacket pocket.

A red-faced man in a firefighter's outfit approached them. 'You people need to get out of here before the whole place comes down around you!'

'Got that, sir, and thank you,' Casey said. 'Right, let's go, and I'd better call the real FBI now.'

Parnell grabbed Martel by the arm. 'Come on, pal, you're coming too.'

'Where?'

'The airport, we'll put you on a flight.'

'My passport is in my jacket.'

'We'll sort something out.'

'No, look, that's my jacket by the door.'

'Fine.' Parnell grabbed the sports coat from the floor, and checking it did not contain a weapon, proceeded to drape it over Martel's shoulders.

Outside Deputy Grant hurried over, he addressed Casey, 'What the hell is happening here?'

'No idea, but it looks like you're in charge.'

'I'll see you around, Jim,' Martel said, with a wink.

They left Grant slack-jawed. Parnell opened the Tahoe and pushed Martel into the cramped, third row of seats, then got into the driver's seat. Casey held open the back door. 'After you, Ruslan.'

Once both men were in, Parnell edged the full-sized SUV out of the lot and down the street. Casey made his phone call, and Akulov took a bottle of water from the chiller and drank greedily. He sat back and rested his head against the padded, leather headrest, there was a slight pain still from the concussion, he hoped this was just the exterior bruising. He closed his eyes, and they travelled on in silence for a while.

'I want to say that I apologise,' Martel said out of nowhere, 'for the way we treated you, Wolf Six.'

Akulov spoke without opening his eyes. 'Yes, you should.'

'I am sorry. What you did in Chicago to the Russians is a thing of legend.'

'It was a job,' Akulov said, thinking back to the events of half a year before, 'nothing more than that.'

Casey asked, 'Who do you work for?'

'The Syndicate.'

'Never heard of them,' Parnell said, deadpan, from the front.

Casey stated, 'You tell your boss, Jean Gagnon, his operations here are closed, permanently. OK?'

'Oui, I shall pass on the message. You have to understand he is a violent and powerful man.'

'And we're just Sunday School teachers,' Casey replied.

The interior of the SUV went quiet again until Parnell said, 'We've got a tail. Two of them.'

Akulov opened his eyes and looked back. A pair of black, Cadillac Escalades were following them.

'Ruslan, there's a tactical field pack in the back. I think now's the time to open it,' Casey stated.

Akulov climbed into the back, and leaning over the bench seat next to Martel, hefted out a heavy, black kit bag. Unzipping it, he was cheered to see two sets of Kevlar ballistic vests, helmets, and a pair of short-barrelled HK 416 A5 assault rifles with extra magazines. Akulov slipped on one of the vests and took a rifle before passing the same to Casey.

'I'm going to see how eager they are to party,' Parnell stated, 'so hold on.'

Akulov sat down in the rear seat, and made sure the HK was both safe and the business end was not pointing at anyone. The Tahoe increased its speed, the sound of the Chevy V8 battling with the soundproofing. Akulov glanced back, the two Escalades were growing smaller, falling back. Parnell increased their speed again. The Escalades held their position, further away but still following. They looked like usual traffic, except for the fact there were two of them, driving in formation and they were the only Escalades Akulov had seen since being stranded in Michigan.

Parnell appraised Akulov of the situation, 'Two identical Escalades pulled up outside the sheriff's place, they left sharpish when we showed our badges.'

'We may be OK,' Casey commented. 'Let's just run to the airport. Remember the best fight to win is the one you don't have to have.'

'Wise words, boss.'

'Thanks, Mike.'

Akulov allowed himself to relax, but he wasn't convinced.

Martel said, 'So you whacked Paul Fang for the CIA?'

'Who says we're agency?' Casey said, bluntly.

'All this,' Martel replied, 'and you cannot deny it. I used to believe Wolf Six was a myth.'

'Like the tooth fairy?' Parnell asked.

'More like Baba Yaga.'

'Baba Yaga was a witch who lived in a forest,' Akulov stated. 'I have never ridden a broomstick.'

'Shit,' Parnell said.

'It wasn't that bad,' Casey replied.

'No. Possible contact front.'

Akulov now saw what Parnell had spotted. On the long straight road ahead, a third large, black SUV was approaching them. At their current closing speed they'd pass it in perhaps fifteen seconds. Akulov noted from the Tahoe's GPS screen there were no turn-offs on either side for the next mile or so. Parnell powered down all the windows.

'Three black SUVs converging on a fourth on a deserted road? That can't be coincidental,' Casey noted.

'And here's their play,' Parnell said.

Akulov saw the single SUV slow and then stop diagonally across the centre of the two lanes.

Twisting in his seat to look back, Martel stated, 'The other two are speeding up! We need to ram or scram!'

'Thank you,' Casey said, 'advice noted.'

'We'll go for scram, but it may become a ram.' Parnell kept the pace of the Tahoe steady and swerved into the middle of the two lanes. Akulov understood what he was doing, he was giving himself an equal chance of going left or right of the obstruction and thus making it harder for the other SUV to guess where he would attempt to pass.

'On the plus side,' Casey noted, 'they think we're FBI. They're expecting us to stop.'

'Fools!' Parnell said theatrically. 'Mad fools!'

The rear Escalades were still gaining, and Akulov imagined they would stop when they were within safe range of small arms fire.

'Here goes.' Parnell pushed the gas hard, the V8 growled, and the wind buffeted them all.

Abruptly, rounds started to impact the back of the Tahoe. The first couple sounded like stones hitting the bodywork, and then the rear windscreen shattered. And then more rounds tore into the Tahoe's interior.

'*Merde!*' Martel roared, as he slid sideways on the bench seat. 'I think I've been hit!'

Akulov swivelled back in his seat, he ignored the large French Canadian and rested the HK between the rear headrests and sent a short three round burst back at the Escalade on the left. It swerved but continued on. Casey joined him, and this time a line of impact holes appeared across the bonnet of the same vehicle.

'Hold tight!' Parnell shouted.

Eyes front, Akulov hunkered down as the Tahoe jinked left and then sharply to the right. There was a screeching of metal as it flew past the back end of the Escalade, Akulov held his breath – had they made it? And then what seemed like minutes later, yet in reality was milliseconds, there was a jarring impact as the Escalade reversed and struck the rear end of the Tahoe. The back tyres were pushed onto the grass and lost traction, the Tahoe fishtailed and then the front tyres abruptly dug in, forcing the

Tahoe to change direction, topple over and land on its passenger side. The stricken Chevy slid, grinding against the tarmac until it half dropped into the grass filled ditch on the other side.

There was silence and a complete lack of motion for several seconds. Akulov had landed on top of Martel, who was jammed up against the door. Meanwhile Casey was in the footwell, and Parnell was suspended by his seatbelt.

'We all OK?' Casey asked, standing on the door, which had become the floor.

'Peachy,' Parnell replied.

Akulov grabbed hold of the side of the front passenger seat and levered himself up. Looking down now at Martel he saw the man's head was hanging at an unnatural angle and his eyes were glazed. 'Martel's dead.'

There was a skidding of tyres, either the two pursuing Escalades or genuine traffic, Akulov hoped for the latter yet imagined it was the former. Loud retorts from Parnell's Glock confirmed his assumption.

'We got three... no, make that four sighted tangoes. Six you got your HK?'

Akulov's eyes darted around. His rifle was laying under the front seat, balancing on the guide rail. He dipped back down and tugged it free. 'Got it!'

'Vince, what d'you have?'

'No HK, just my Glock.'

'Six, suppressing fire, now!'

Akulov clambered into a firing position and sought out targets through the shattered rear windscreen. He saw three men advancing past the wreck of the Escalade which had rammed them. All three were Asian. Akulov sent two, three-round bursts into them. The first hit one in the legs and made the other two dive for cover, and the second burst finished off the injured tango.

'Moving!' shouted Parnell, as he levered himself out of the door and dropped down onto the grass behind the body of the SUV.

'Casey, go!' Akulov instructed.

Without a word, the veteran CIA deputy director followed Parnell's lead and escaped through his door. Akulov heard Parnell sending single shots back with his Glock. Akulov fired another controlled burst through the rear of the Tahoe then climbed into the trunk.

Below his feet, the vehicle's right side now becoming the floor, was the tactical pack. He ducked down as more rounds zipped past him. The thin sheet metal offered limited protection, but more than thin air. He rummaged in the bag, grabbed two magazines and found a second Glock 17, which he stuffed into his jeans pocket, and also a smoke grenade. He pulled the pin and threw it out of the void that had once been the rear windscreen, and shouted, 'Smoke out!'

He changed magazines, as he counted to three, heard the pop then waited another three seconds before he followed the grenade.

Akulov jinked left, and ran deeper into the ditch, in an attempt to flank the attacking Triads. The smoke from the grenade floated above him like mist. He drew level with the Escalade which had struck them. The rear was a mass of twisted steel, but behind it were three men in suits, two had handguns, and one had a cell phone to his ear. Akulov opened fire. The man nearest to him convulsed as the white-hot lead entered his upper body, and was dead before his back hit the ground. The second man started to turn, his gun tracking with him. Akulov caught him in the chest with two rounds. That left the guy on the phone, who suddenly threw his arms up. Akulov shot him in the head.

The next two Escalades had slowed to a stop with perhaps twenty feet between them, and were angled like anti-tank berms. The first of the two that had followed them was directly to his left. HK up and seeking targets, Akulov crept forward. The driver's door opened, and a suited Asian man dropped out. He banged on the back door with his hand, and it started to open. He retrieved a handgun from a pancake holster, and then he suddenly saw Akulov, and that was the last thing he saw as a single round from a pistol struck him in the head, spinning him sideways.

He heard Parnell shout, 'Yeah! That's a three-pointer!'

Akulov charged at the SUV as the rear door started to open wider. A large Asian in a tight-fitting suit was clambering out, and he had an Uzi machine pistol. Akulov sent a trio of rounds into his centre mass, his large frame wobbled and then he fell out of the Escalade, landing flat on his face.

A burst of automatic rounds zipped past Akulov, sparking on the tarmac at his feet, he threw himself backwards into the ditch again. Rolling onto his stomach, he attempted to bring the HK to bear on the new shooter. Advancing directly towards him was a woman. Her jet-black, long hair billowing behind her like a cape, and out in front of her, held in a classic two-handed grip, was another Uzi. The machine pistol had an incredible rate of fire but was inaccurate at this range. She let go another blast from the 'spray & pray' weapon. This one landed so close to Akulov that it sent up clods off earth into his face. As if in slow motion, Akulov's finger squeezed the trigger. His rounds slammed into her chest, propelling her backwards and onto the hood of the last remaining Escalade. He watched as she slid off and landed in a heap on the tarmac.

Akulov changed magazines again and rose to his feet. He tactically moved towards the Escalade. Its engine was still running, and the doors were open. Holding his HK up at the windows he circled it, checking for any more shooters before he pulled the rear, offside passenger door open. An elderly Asian man with white hair and a matching long beard stared defiantly at him. With a speed that was almost too rapid to deem credible, the old man shot out his right hand. Akulov saw no sign of a handgun, just the glint of sharpened steel. Instantly, instinctively, he inclined his head as the traditional shuriken harmlessly whizzed by. Akulov's rounds however found their mark.

Akulov moved away from the Escalade and yelled, 'Clear!'

Casey and Parnell appeared through the rapidly dispersing smoke.

'Like a goddamn one-man wrecking machine,' Parnell said, shaking his head in disbelief.

'Thank you for the assist,' Akulov replied, feeling his body begin to shake as his adrenalin levels started to fall post-action. He knew he still was not one hundred per cent operationally fit.

Casey pulled out a cell phone from his pocket. 'I'm gonna need to make a couple more calls and send for the cleaners.'

18

ALPENA COMBAT READINESS TRAINING CENTER

Akulov stepped out of the shower. It was the first time he had washed in several days. He studied his clean-shaven face; he was gaunt yet at least he looked more human. He took a white towel and dried himself before he crossed to the wooden bench and started to dress. After making a phone call, and flashing an appropriate badge, Casey had got the three of them into the Alpena Combat Readiness Training Center. The place was immediately next to Alpena Regional Airport and was a training and support facility for the Departments of Defense and Homeland Security. The liaison officer had found Akulov some clothes which, as he dressed, he realised almost fit him. He thought back on the events of the last few days with confusion. He still did not understand what Needham, Lehnert and Martel's organisation had been up to in Alcona County, and he didn't know why his jet had crashed into Lake Huron, yet perhaps most importantly of all he had no clue as to the identity of the man who had been sent to kill him.

The door to the changing room opened. Parnell entered. He had two large cups of takeaway coffee. 'He scrubs up well!'

Akulov said nothing.

Parnell held out the cup in his left hand, and placed it on the bench. 'This is for you.'

'Thank you.'

'Look, I saw you pause, when that woman came at you.'

'I was surprised.'

'That she was a woman?'

'No, that she had an Uzi and was using it at that range.'

'I see. I thought perhaps there may be some humanity left in your Werewolf brain.' He winked.

'Anyone who points a weapon at me dies, that's non-negotiable.'

'That's cold, man.'

Akulov picked up the coffee and sipped it. 'And that's hot.'

'The bird is here. Wheels up in ten.'

'OK.'

Parnell threw a quick, mock salute and left the room.

Akulov moved to the window and looked out across the base, the shared runway beyond that and then the local, civilian airport. Even though it was a small, regional place, thousands of people used it in any given month. That was thousands of lives, thousands of hopes, thousands of dreams. Akulov himself often felt as though he was looking out at life, and not a participant in it.

He thought again about those he had killed today. Parnell was correct, he had hesitated, if only for the briefest of moments when he'd seen the woman with the Uzi. It was his humanity; it was an ingrained belief he'd held since he could ever remember that women were to be cherished, treasured, honoured and were, above all else, more than equal to any man walking this earth. This was the reason, he knew, why he would always be alone. He would never let himself form a relationship with anyone who could someday be targeted because of him. That was how the CIA had reeled him in, by taking Tishina, his broker, the woman who during their fleeting affair he had more than cared for. Yet she was not his only weakness. His mind switched to his only living relative, the man who was now languishing in a secure location at the hands of who knew. Family was all that really mattered in the world, Akulov finally understood, be it by blood or by bond.

Finishing his coffee, Akulov exited their commandeered officers shower room and followed the signs for reception. Casey and Parnell were waiting. A boy, who looked too young to be in uniform, hastily showed them into a dark blue Crown Victoria and drove them directly to the airstairs of their CIA chartered Gulfstream G280. Casey thanked the young airman and the three of them climbed the stairs and took seats, spaced around the cabin.

Akulov felt an uncharacteristic sense of unease as the jet started to taxi. He knew it was irrational, given the sheer improbability that two out of two airframes he'd taken, within the space of a week, would crash. However obtrusive, irrational thoughts were just that, irrational and obtrusive. Akulov closed his eyes took a deep breath, opened them again and watched the ground rush beneath the wing as they pushed back.

Five minutes later they levelled out to their cruising altitude. Diagonally, across the small aisle, Parnell raised his legs and stretched, then let out a long yawn.

'You're getting old, Mike,' Casey said, getting to his feet from further down the fuselage.

'OK, Boomer!'

Casey shook his head and tutted, before taking a seat facing Akulov. 'Now you can tell me what happened.'

Akulov frowned. 'Do you mean before or after that CIA jet you chartered decided to nosedive into Lake Huron?'

'That was wild, and it's miraculous that you're sitting here. So, the last I heard, you received a concussion?'

Akulov sighed, and rested his head against the seatback, again he felt a twinge. 'That damn mask you had me wear, it cut down my peripheral vision. I didn't see the guy coming, until it was too late.'

'His name is Jacob Wray; he's a detective with the Royal Canadian Mounted Police.'

'Hang on.' Parnell sat up. 'Jay Wray was on horseback at the time?'

Casey ignored the interruption and continued, 'He was on a staycation with his wife and daughter, for his wife's birthday. Unfortunately for all parties, the hotel was over-booked, and he was upgraded – the hotel thanked him for his service, to the room next to our target Paul Fang. His video-fit of you was bang on.'

'He pulled my mask off, and that damn fake beard came with it.'

'He'll make a full recovery, by the way.'

Akulov said, 'I was concerned for his daughter.'

'She'll be fine,' Parnell said.

'Yep, well she can tell everyone her daddy is a hero,'

Casey added. 'They gave him some type of award for gallantry. Moving on, what happened next.'

'I acquired that little red box and managed to exfiltrate the hotel. I was about to pass out when Hormann found me on the street. The next thing I remember, fully, is waking up on that Gulfstream and falling off the couch.'

'Tell me about the jet.'

'Like what?'

'Before it crashed, what was happening?'

Akulov shrugged. 'It was gliding, it was falling then it was trying to glide again.'

'The engines were off?'

'Yes, both of them.'

'Was there any noise at all, any smoke?'

'No, it was as though they had been switched off.' Akulov glanced at Parnell then back at Casey. 'Don't you tell me that little red box is what I think it is?'

'It is and now it's sitting in a secure Faraday cage.'

Anger and remorse started to overwhelm Akulov as he was transported back five years to the time he was contracted to a Russo-Chinese private military company. He had been contracted to carry out a series of assassinations over the course of twenty-four hours, starting with a retired US Senator and culminating with the British Ambassador to the United States of America. These had taken place after his employer had detonated the world's first tactical, non-nuclear EMP – electromagnetic pulse bomb – in a terrorist attack over the continental United States. The attack had knocked out anything with a circuit board causing what had since become referred to as the 'Total Blackout'. Akulov said the company's name aloud for the first time in several years, and felt a shiver, 'Blackline'.

'Yes.' Casey fixed his eyes on Akulov's. 'Fang was part of Blackline. He was a prominent, public figure, working out in the open, hence his activities were overlooked for far too long. Unbeknownst to any of us intelligence agencies, he had continued to carry out research and develop a man portable EMP device. Forget the crap you see on TV or at the movies like the EMP 5000X, this thing is real. This thing brought down your plane.'

'You knew about this, and you put me on a plane with it?' Akulov wasn't angry, he was past that, he was incredulous.

'We knew he had created a device. We believed this to be his little red box. We had credible intelligence he was going to provide a demonstration by somehow using his device against the Canadian headquarters of NORAD in Winnipeg, however it seems plans changed. We learnt that rather than "shop window" his technology in Canada he decided to do so in Hong Kong as part of an auction to a select group of bidders. Can you imagine bringing down a plane there? Just think of the global financial chaos it would cause? What we did not know was that the box had a biometric tamper switch.'

'Meaning it would discharge if he was not next to it?'

'That is what we now assume to be the case. The EMP was set off approximately one hundred and twenty minutes after you removed the device from his possession.'

'You didn't think something like this might happen?'

Casey shrugged. 'Not that it's any comfort to you now, but Hormann had strict orders to put it in a Faraday cage – like the one it's in now, for safe storage during the flight. I guess he forgot or chose not to do so.'

'Because of me.'

'You cannot take that blame, Ruslan. You did your part; we messed it all up.'

'After we crashed, I saw Hormann below me. The fuselage had broken in half, and his part was sinking faster, I just couldn't get to him.'

'You had a concussion.'

'Hormann is dead, the two pilots are dead.'

'It comes to us all, padre,' Parnell said.

'You adapted. You took out Fang, and you acquired the box. Mission accomplished.'

'After almost getting me killed in a plane crash, this does not just make us "even". You now owe me, Casey.'

'OK, OK. Your debt is paid, in full. When we land at Reagan, you're free to walk away. And I'll "owe" you one.'

'We promise we'll pay you next time, if we are in need of your services again.' Parnell winked.

'Right,' Casey said, 'moving on. Tell me about Harrisville.'

'What do you mean?'

'There's a lot happening there that is not normal.'

'That's an understatement,' Parnell noted.

'Go through how you came to be locked up.'

Akulov gave the short version. 'After I reached the shore I saw two trucks, Sheriff Lehnert was in one. I saw her kill a man.'

'The sheriff?' Casey asked.

'She left him where he fell. I took the guy's coat, and later found out it was one of her deputies.'

'Now that is brutal,' Parnell said.

'I passed out and when I came round I was at Needham's diner. I rested up, he fed me and told me the storm had knocked out the cell towers and the landlines. Later, he drove me – allegedly into town – but in fact delivered me to Sheriff Lehnert, who had me held in her facility until today.'

'They interrogated you?' Casey asked.

'More like angry questioning. They wanted to know who I was, what I knew, why I was there and who I was working for.'

'You said what, exactly?'

'That I was the world's number one assassin, contracted to the CIA, and I was there to make friends, influence people and shoot bad guys.'

Parnell smirked.

Casey said, 'Answer the question, Ruslan. This is a debrief, and all information is relevant.'

'I told them I'd borrowed a friend's yacht, and it sank in the storm.'

'Which they bought?'

'Lehnert wanted to charge me with larceny of a motor-boat, so perhaps she did.'

'Tell us about Martel.' It was Parnell who now asked this.

'It seems like Martel's organisation was running Need-ham's facility as well as the sheriff's office.'

'That's our opinion too.' Casey nodded. 'We think the sheriff sent him details of your ID – one we didn't know about, and Martel recognised you from the video-fit.'

Akulov agreed. 'That makes sense.'

'As you know, we tracked Hormann's body to the diner at Black River. It was in one of the log cabins around the back.'

'He rents them out as summer chalets,' Akulov added.

'Yet not this one. This one had been dug out and had a tunnel system beneath it.'

Akulov frowned. 'So it's a smuggling ring?'

'Nope, try again.'

'Tell me.'

'It's a disposal plant,' Casey stated. 'Needham uses vats of sulphuric acid to dissolve bodies.'

Akulov blinked. It was an urban myth; it was something he'd read about, but never encountered. 'Needham did tell me they were into "waste disposal".'

'Yep, I know. Quite hard to believe. Anyway, the real FBI will be taking over now.'

'It seemed like such a quiet, little place,' Parnell said.

There was an electronic trilling.

'Sat phone,' Casey explained, moving back to his original seat.

'Busy few days, huh.' Parnell put his feet back up on the opposite seat and closed his eyes.

'You could say that.' Akulov looked out of the window at the world below. He remembered the first time he had ever been on a plane; it was during his time as a Spetsnaz conscript in the Russian army. It was also the first time he'd jumped out of a plane. Those days seemed so far away now, and both he and the world had moved on. Akulov sighed, he wanted to retire but somehow knew that however hard he tried, that decision would constantly be taken away from him by fate and circumstance.

'Update.' Casey sat again opposite Akulov. 'It's odd news.'

Parnell sat up. 'Give it to us.'

'The guy who set off the IED, who arrived before us pretending to be FBI, had a two-man team with him. One who entered the sheriff's department as a bogus Fed, and the other who was found outside on the grass – the sheriff confirms she shot the second guy. Well, the real FBI have run their prints and have positive IDs for them. They are both independent contractors, both former Army Rangers who seem to have embraced the dark side.'

'Sith for hire.'

'Just like that, Mike. The younger guy was one Zach Ross and the older contractor was named Ryan Kelly.'

'I've not heard of them.' Their names meant nothing to Akulov.

'Yep, not in your league, not even the same game. However, Kelly has been around for a while and is known to have worked with Martin Basson.'

Now the IED made sense. 'The Bang-Bang Man.'

'The what?' An amused expression appeared on Parnell's face.

'Basson is a former legionnaire who gets off on explosives,' Casey explained.

'Ah, Monsieur Le Bang-Bang.'

'It's a stupid name,' Akulov replied. 'However, he is deadly serious.'

'His broker is known as The Irishman.'

'Him I know,' Parnell confirmed.

'Looks like there's a contract out on you, and he has it.'

'Not necessarily, we have a history.'

'How?' Casey's eyebrows arched.

'I once shot him.'

'That'll do it.'

'He was responsible for the Amsterdam "Kerkstraat" bombing.'

'Yep, we had an inkling,' Casey held Akulov's gaze, 'and?'

Akulov nodded. 'It was a contract to take out the Dinescu family, we were contracted as a duo via Tishina. I was overwatch. There were civilians in the area. I told him to abort. He didn't. I tried to kill him. I didn't.'

'And people died.'

'Yes. Innocent people died, and I can never change that.'

'The same as your work for Blackline.'

'Yes. The same as my work for Blackline.'

Casey said, 'I heard a rumour Basson was contracted for a hit in San Remo that was unsuccessful. He failed because a second unknown hitter stopped him. That was you again, wasn't it?'

'Yes, it was.' Akulov saw no reason to lie. 'I should have killed him.'

'Akulov, you really need to stop The Bang-Bang Man,' Parnell stated.

'Is this a contract?'

Casey sighed. 'No. Look, I didn't want to tell you this until we were back on the ground and perhaps had more of a handle on the situation. However, in light of this new intel.'

Akulov noted a tone in Casey's voice he'd not heard before. He sat up straight in his seat. 'Tell me.'

'I'm sorry. Valentina is dead.'

Akulov felt as though the plane had abruptly depressurised, and the air had suddenly been sucked away, but he managed to say, 'What?'

'Whilst you were being held, Basson assassinated Valentina.'

'How?' The word erupted from Akulov's mouth before his brain had fully processed what his ears had heard.

'Basson made entry to Valentina's Monaco apartment. There was a firefight. She managed to wing him but unfortunately, he killed her. She died of multiple gunshot wounds to the chest.'

Akulov heard a rushing of blood in his ears, his vision blurred around the edges. He felt both his fists contract and his body start to quiver. It was as though he had been struck again with a taser, and in a sense he had. The interior of the CIA charted jet fell silent, apart from the gentle hum of the powerful engine on each side of the fuselage. Akulov knew that nothing he could do or say would bring her back, and he even understood the reason why Casey and Parnell had kept the news of her death from him. Eventually Akulov said, 'That favour the CIA owes me, I am cashing it in right now. You are going to help me find Martin Basson.'

Casey nodded. 'We will, Ruslan, we will.'

19

TALLINN, ESTONIA

The bar was the same, and so was the woman who served him, but Basson was not. He had arranged a meeting with The Irishman, and this would decide the fate of both men. After escaping Michigan, Basson had taken a very indirect route to get back to Europe via Canada. The long journey had given him the space to contemplate, and time to understand.

Thinking back on the contracts he had accepted from The Irishman since the man had agreed to become his broker, Basson started to understand that there was a pattern, of sorts. In his entire professional career as a hitman, he had never been in a situation where he had been intercepted, yet now this had happened twice within the last six months. However, this recent development was not the only pattern he saw. The actual jobs, the contracts, had been getting smaller and smaller, seemingly requiring less skill. It was as though his broker no longer trusted him to undertake the big jobs, the 'spectaculars' which were the talk of intelligence agencies and the envy of the circuit.

There had been a contract out on a major Indian steel magnate, who had died when his yacht exploded with him in it, off the coast of Thailand. That had been a perfect job for him, and he would have taken great delight in undertaking it, yet he had only heard of it after the fact. Then there had been the hit on a minor Saudi royal whilst he had been visiting Salalah in Oman for the brief rainy season. His highly modified, off-road Lamborghini Urus had fallen into a ravine and exploded, yet whoever had conducted this had used the incorrect amount of explosive and the timing had been off. It had been a shoddy job on an important target. The Bang-Bang Man should have had the contract, yet it had been given to a younger, far less experienced operator who was one of the many Russians gone AWOL from their own army during the war against Ukraine.

Basson drank his beer, in an attempt to wash away the anger so that logical reasoning prevailed. It wasn't working. Basson knew The Irishman was guilty of diminishing him, attempting to make him irrelevant, and of course now betraying him. Basson sighed, what an idiot he had truly been. The Irishman was a former IRA bomb maker, and as such wanted by the British, yet Basson was expected to believe that the man had been allowed to live happily and conduct his business from a state within the EU? Now that stretched believability, especially when Cliff Quinn looked exactly the same now as he had done two decades before.

Why had he not seen it before? The Irishman had been a wanted man in the UK, and an Interpol Red Notice had been issued, and who were the only people with enough pull to override this, to make it all go away? That would be the Americans in the guise of the Central Intelligence

Agency. Basson finished his half-litre and ordered another two as The Irishman returned from the bathroom.

'Take my advice, Maartin, don't ever go to a cheap Chinese takeaway when you're pissed-up. That stuff didn't just clean my pipes, but I reckon it fixed the plumbing in this place too!'

'Are there many Chinese in Tallinn?'

'You'd be surprised.'

'I was surprised by the number of Chinese in Michigan, if you remember, and the Americans.'

'Look, I'm glad you managed to get yourself out of that one. The Triads however are far less than happy. They do not accept failure.'

Basson's eyes narrowed. 'What do you mean, Cliff?'

The Irishman seemed oblivious to the venom in Basson's words. 'I mean, they won't work with you, or me again. Look, I'm not saying this is your fault, but well, they part-paid for a service which they never received.'

'I imagine you didn't pay them back?'

Quinn bristled. 'What? No, don't be daft, Maartin, you know it's all non-refundable. Sheesh, this isn't Radio Rentals they've contracted.'

'What are you saying to me?'

The Irishman took a large slurp of beer before he replied, 'I think it's best if you retire.'

Basson made no reply, his eyes bore into those of his broker, a man who was no stranger to intimidation himself. Eventually Basson said, 'What would I do?'

'You'd live, Maartin. Sheesh. that's what I want to do. You know this is a young man's game, there are not many old and bold soldiers left, but look at us? We are still here. You know as well as me that each contract we take is another chance for us to lose our own lives. Just you imagine what I go through brokering the number of assets I have.'

'How many?'

'What?'

'How many of us are there?'

'I have a stable of five. That's five times the stress, five times the danger.'

'Five times the money.'

'Which is why it's been such a hard decision to give it all up.'

'You are retiring?'

'That's what I'm saying.'

'So that is it? You decide to retire, and you expect me to do so too?'

'I don't expect anything of you, Maartin. But you know it makes sense. These mistakes, would you have been making them if you were younger, more focused?'

Basson closed his eyes and started to count down from ten in his head. He had not made any mistakes, and the other man knew it. Yet he said, 'You are, of course, absolutely correct. This is not a game for us, any more.'

The Irishman raised his glass. 'Now that's the spirit. Look you've made more than enough money to do whatever you damn well want with the rest of your life. You could even set yourself up as a king on some remote island in the Far East. Like a retired Bond villain.'

'Bond villains never get the chance to retire.'

'Exactly, but we can.' Quinn finished his beer and ordered a pair of Irish whiskies. 'Look, you and I are the same. Hell, we've even done the same things, which is why I respect you, and I hope you respect me?'

'I do,' Basson lied. They were not alike. Quinn was not a

highly trained commando. He had been a thug working as a motor mechanic who had then been forced to learn how to create IEDs to eviscerate British soldiers.

The barmaid placed the two glasses on the bar. Quinn raised his and said, '*Sláinte!*'

Basson nodded, not repeating the word.

'This is goodbye, Maartin.' The Irishman stood, extended his hand and waited for Basson to do the same.

Basson stood, shook Quinn's hand then pulled him closer for a man hug. 'Bon Chance,' Basson said, as his left hand dropped a button-sized tracking device into the outer, patch pocket of The Irishman's coat.

'If we were in any other business we could meet up as friends, for the craic... but...' Quinn took a step backwards, saluted then left the bar on unsteady legs.

Basson watched him pass the window and head uphill.

'Can I get you anything else?' the barmaid asked.

'Another beer please, but unfortunately it will be my last here for a while.'

* * *

Half an hour later Basson was on the street, with his messenger bag slung across his shoulder, and walking uphill away from the bar, towards the *Raekoja Plats*, the main square which was the focus of old medieval Tallinn. Pulling out his smartphone he opened the tracking app. The Irishman had crossed the same square and was now stationary in a building three hundred yards away downhill via another narrow street. Basson moved to the address along the confined, cobbled street. The pavements were busy with locals and visitors alike, which Basson welcomed as it meant that he did not look out of place. In fact, the vast majority of those who were out for the night paid him no attention at all. He passed the old KGB headquarters, which in Soviet times had been the most dangerous building to visit in Estonia. Now it was just another government building and had both the flags of the EU and Estonia flying proudly from poles protruding from its heavy stone walls.

The GPS showed he needed to take a left and then follow the road for another fifty metres or so. Up ahead he saw a gaggle of men walking in the same direction as he. They stopped outside a door which a very large man was guarding. He was dressed in the de rigueur 'Bouncer' outfit and had a shaven head. The men spoke to him and after a few questions were answered they were let in. Basson carried on walking and when he drew level with the door, he noted it was a nightclub with a dubious name. The tracker said The Irishman was inside. The bouncer glared at him, Basson made an obscene hand gesture and carried on walking.

Basson knew the range of the tracking device, so decided to find somewhere quiet to wait. Further along the street and around the corner he discovered another smaller bar. Stepping inside he took a seat at a little table by the window and ordered a beer, he'd developed a taste for the local stuff. It was a shame that after tonight he would have no reason to visit Tallinn again.

Two large, lingering beers, and an hour of listening to jazz music later, Basson left the little, dark bar and followed the tracker. As he thought, The Irishman was on foot, and he was moving slower than he had expected. The man was heading back uphill towards the central *Vanallin* area. The very heart of Tallinn's old town. Basson slowed his pace too as he saw that he was starting to gain on The Irishman.

The tracker had become stationary again. Basson looked up. It had stopped at the corner of small street, a junction where several streets met. On the very corner of the street, nestled between two other, taller buildings was a three-storey house. It looked almost like a small church with its sharply pointed roof. Basson saw The Irishman up ahead, and on either side of him a woman was holding his arm.

'Merde!'

As Basson looked on, the trio entered the foyer, a dim light switched on, and then a minute or so later a light flickered on at a second-floor window of the otherwise dark house. He saw The Irishman at the window draw the curtains. This hadn't gone to plan.

Basson moved back into the darkness of a doorway. Lurking in the shadows, he bided his time, waiting for when the man would finally fall asleep. He was happy it was not winter, waiting outside in minus twenty was not fun at all. Subconsciously Basson touched the tip of his nose as he remembered the frostbite he had suffered at the Foreign Legion's Alpine training camp.

Exactly an hour passed, and the streets were visibly emptier as all, but the serious partygoers had gone to bed. Basson moved into a narrow alley and urinated over the edge of a drain cover, he imagined he was not the first to have done so. He leaned against the wall and looked back at the house he presumed The Irishman rented. Like all the buildings in the area it was old enough to have outlived generations of its residents, their lives and loves imprinted on its walls. He wondered, however, if the act that was about to take place was one it had witnessed before, or if this would be a first?

A light appeared behind the front door, the same hall light he'd seen earlier, probably on a motion sensor or timer. Swiftly Basson left his observation point and hustled across the cobbled street. He reached the door moments before it opened, and two women tottered out smelling of pungent perfume. They were speaking Russian, and not Estonian. He held the large wooden door open for them, as they passed without acknowledging or thanking him. Basson muttered, '*Merci Beaucoup.*'

Basson entered the building and closed the door. Quickly checking for any security cameras, he found none. The building consisted of three floors, and the room he had seen Quinn in was on the second floor. There was no lift. He climbed the stairs, slowly, carefully, one at a time. With only one flat per floor, he was in no doubt that he had arrived at the right residence. The door was not original. It was the sturdy, reinforced type of the 1990s he had encountered many times before in Eastern Europe. It consisted of a steel panel and carcass to which was attached a padded wooden board, which itself was wrapped in a thick PU imitation leather. It was meant to be opulent, and may even have been bulletproof, which he knew had been a sales feature of it, especially during the Wild East days of the early nineties. This mattered little to him. The weakest point of any door was always its hinges. Basson knew that using shaped breaching charges on these, and the lock, would have the barrier falling inwards as though it was made of cardboard. But he wasn't going to make an explosive entry into the flat.

In the gloom, illuminated solely by moonlight falling through a window in the outer wall, he pressed the bell. He

waited, with his finger over the spyhole. He heard nothing.
He pressed again, this time holding his finger down on the
buzzer style button. Releasing it, he heard muffled sounds
from within. 'Fek!' A light switched on inside and the door
opened. 'Yeah?'

Basson pushed his foot into the gap and stared directly
into his broker's eyes. 'I've got more questions for you.'

The door closed a fraction, pushing his foot before it
hesitantly opened fully. The Irishman was naked and there
were smears of lipstick around his mouth and on his chest.
He squinted at Basson. 'Sheesh, I'm glad it's you and not that
duo of *geebags* coming back for more money.'

Basson pushed past Quinn and entered the flat. The dim
hallway light illuminated halfway towards a room on the
left, casting shadows across the parquet flooring.

'Where can we sit?'

The Irishman closed the door and wandered past Basson
and into the lounge at the far end of the hallway. The light
switched on and Basson now followed.

Picking up a pair of mauve boxer shorts from the floor
and putting them on, Quinn said, 'I don't know what you
want to discuss. My mind is made up.'

Basson pointed to the large, cognac-coloured leather
settee where the rest of Quinn's clothes lay. 'Have a seat.'

'That's grand of you, thanks.' The Irishman pulled his
shirt back on and flattened down his wild hair.

Basson took a seat in a deeply padded armchair of the
same colour which faced the settee across a glass covered
coffee table. 'This is a nice place you have here.'

'It's an Airbnb.'

'That's a wise move.'

'Look, Maartin, I'm retiring. You need to find another broker, or retire as well.'

'It's my retirement I wanted to discuss.'

'Oh, well no time like the present, although what is it, three in the morning?'

'Someone tried to retire me permanently, if you remember. The Triads shot at me and the FBI attempted to grab me.'

Quinn said, 'I'm glad you got out.'

'How did they know I was there, Cliff?'

'I don't know.'

'I see. How did you know Akulov was there?'

'I can't say – like a doctor – confidentiality and all that.'

Basson pulled a micro-compact 9mm Sig Sauer P365X from his pocket, and a suppressor from his messenger bag. It was the same handgun he'd used to kill Tishina. He slowly started to connect the two tools of his trade. Fear and confusion were great allies at 3 a.m., and now both of these were helping Basson. 'How?'

'C'mon, Maartin, this is me you are talking to.'

'Then you should just answer my question. I'll shoot anyone, you know that, although killing you would upset me a little.'

'I've got an informer in the Yee Kwan Triad. His boss did a deal with this Québécois gangster named Gagnon who had Akulov's location.'

Basson was confused. 'Who was paying my contract?'

'The Long-Zi Triad. Akulov was wearing a hoodie with their emblem on when he hit Paul Fang.'

'The idea was to get the two groups fighting each other?'

'That's the way I think it was dreamt up. But I'll tell you this, neither side knew the hitter was Akulov. If they'd known they were up against Wolf Six they may have tried to recruit him.'

Basson fired a suppressed round into the remaining empty armchair in anger. 'I am sick of hearing about Wolf Six.'

'There... goes my... deposit,' The Irishman stammered.

'It is better than your life.' Basson let out a long sigh, he'd started to feel tired. 'Why were the FBI there?'

'How do I know?'

'Hazard a guess.'

'Perhaps to detain the Triads, maybe to arrest Akulov? Or what if it wasn't the FBI? It could have been a CIA SAD team sent to rescue Akulov.'

'You think he's working for them?'

Quinn shrugged. 'Why not? He's fully deniable and well, he's the best.'

Basson raised his handgun, then thought better of it. 'I found you here, you know I can find you again.'

'Maartin, I'm not hiding.'

'Don't.' Basson stood. 'You enjoy your retirement.'

'You also. Now you get back to the Gulf – Abu Dhabi, or wherever it is you live.'

Basson's left hand formed into a fist. 'Abu Dhabi? Have you ever heard me mention Abu Dhabi, Cliff?'

'I... don't... c'mon you must have done.'

'No.' Basson put a round into The Irishman's left thigh. 'Think.'

Quinn roared with pain and immediately clamped both hands to his leg. 'C... Christ! W... what the... hell... Maartin.'

'Who told you I live in the Gulf?'

'No... no one. I just guessed... by the timing... of your messages.'

'Don't lie to me.' Basson now aimed at The Irishman's chest. 'The next round will kill you. Who told you?'

'The Americans.'

'Which Americans?'

'The CIA.'

'Thank you.'

The Irishman spoke rapidly, his chest rising and falling quickly, a sure sign of hyperventilation. 'They said... they had reason to believe... you lived in one of the Gulf States... They asked me if I knew where... I said I had no clue, because I don't... Sheesh, I don't even know the name you use to travel.'

'This was a meeting with the CIA, a sharing of information?'

'Sheesh, Maartin...'

'First Tishina and now you?'

'I'm sorry. I had no choice.'

'Head or heart?'

'Exactly,' The Irishman said, pleadingly, 'exactly like head or heart.'

Basson cocked his head. 'No, Cliff, you misunderstand me. Where would you like the next round, in your head or in your heart?'

The Irishman started to shake; he raised his hand's defensively. 'Please... Maartin... PLEASE!'

'Let's do both.' Basson fired a double tap, the first round exploded into Quinn's chest, then whilst The Irishman was still trying to comprehend what was happening, the second entered his skull between his eyes. As the gunpowder started to tickle Basson's nostrils, he shook his head slowly. He now definitely needed a new broker.

20

MARSEILLES, FRANCE

Akulov had not felt grief like this since his grandmother had been murdered. It had been three months since he had learnt of the death of his broker, Valentina Tishina. In that time, he had gone through the initial stages of denial, and anger. Basson had murdered Valentina Tishina, and of that fact there was no doubt. Akulov's anger had hardened into a rage which had then become a conviction to kill the man.

Akulov had then reached the stage of, according to the Kubler-Ross theory, 'bargaining' where he had started to constantly question and reprimand himself. If he had only been a better or a faster shot, he would not have missed Basson in Amsterdam, why had he not taken another shot at him on the barge? Why had he not tried harder to persuade Tishina that Basson posed a threat to her? And most of all why had he not been there to prevent it from happening? Yet Tishina had been, like himself, an elite operative. She was well versed on safety and personal protection. Akulov just had to accept that Basson had been better on the day.

The fourth stage of grief, 'depression', had hit Akulov at

the same time. It was an emotion that was new to him. He had felt remorse before and anger at himself for actions he had taken in the past but never truly believed that he had ever been depressed for any true length of time. What had helped Akulov had been the fact that he did not have a classic, close domestic relationship with Tishina. He was not sitting at home expecting her to suddenly come through the front door. What also helped him was that whilst many, if not all of those grieving for someone who had been murdered, resolved to find and take retribution against the killer, Akulov knew he actually would.

He had found it curious that her death had affected him as much as it had, and he'd finally come to terms with the realisation that he had never stopped caring about her even though the brief physical relationship they'd shared had ended almost a decade before. He'd ended it, and she had accepted it as though she knew it was coming. He knew he should not think of what might have been, only what he could do now. And that was find and execute Martin Basson.

Akulov had become driven, obsessed in his goal to locate Basson. Vince Casey had shared what they knew of the man, which was better than nothing but not much at all. This had, however, included a list of known associates. The top of this list had been his broker, 'The Irishman' whom the CIA had previously been in contact with. He however had ended up dead in a Tallinn Airbnb a week after Tishina's death. The CIA believed there had been some type of falling out between broker and operator, yet without any witnesses this murder could not be positively linked to Basson. What they were able to share was the belief that Basson did not reside in the US or Europe. They had hazarded a guess that the Frenchman lay low somewhere in the Middle East, perhaps one of the Gulf States where he was either protected by someone with influence or had successfully crafted a legend – a false identity so good that he had managed to leave no trace. Casey said he was not at liberty to divulge why the CIA were of this opinion.

Akulov had started to work down the list with little success. Yet it was this list which had led him to the starkly refurbished apartment he was sitting in now in Marseilles which overlooked Plage des Catalans. He'd helped himself to room temperature glass bottles of Evian, one of four that had sat in a neat square on a white, marble-topped table.

Akulov checked his watch. He'd been waiting for two hours already. He had become growingly impatient since Tishina's death, and he put this down to the fact that he was not working on a contract for a client rather he was on a quest for himself. He now started to understand how others in his profession, who let their passion run roughshod over their logic, made errors. And errors in his business were deadly. Akulov stood and moved to the window. Below, across the narrow street, locals and those he assumed must be visitors, passed on the promenade. Some wore light jackets, others, usually the elderly, wore thicker coats. It was by no means cold outside, yet it was not warm either, the sun and blue sky giving the illusion of a summer's afternoon on a March day. Past the promenade there were people walking on the sandy beach, and even knots of friends sitting there and chatting. He was again reminded that this was the life he would never have, one where he could simply meet friends, relax carefree and share a coffee.

And then Akulov saw a solid looking man with a ruddy face and chalk white hair approaching with a pair of shopping bags. It was the person he had come to see, Seumas

Gallacher, armourer to the underworld. Gallacher was wearing cream-coloured cargo trousers, and a white puffa jacket, which in Akulov's opinion gave the impression he was a much-aged nineties-era 'boy band' member. Akulov collected his silenced Glock from the table and moved into the hallway. He had already scouted out the best position in which to conceal himself when the Scotsman entered.

It took longer than Akulov had expected for the owner of the apartment to reach his front door, but then he reasoned the man was in his sixties and was carrying two large shopping bags. He heard the key enter the lock, the security bolts slide back and then the heavy, wooden door move inwards. From the small recess next to a wall, where he was hidden from view whilst the door was open, Akulov waited. He heard the front door close and then heavy footsteps walking across the white, marble tiled floor and into the kitchen.

Akulov pushed himself out of his cover, softly stepped towards the kitchen and came face to face with the now angry looking Scotsman. What impressed Akulov was that the man's right hand was held aloft and firmly holding a meat cleaver.

Akulov raised his Glock. 'Do not bring a knife to a gunfight.'

'Who the hell are...' The surprise in the older man's face was tangible, as was the sudden recognition in his eyes.

'Put the cleaver down, Gallacher.'

Keeping eye contact, the Scotsman's right arm moved backwards until he dropped the cleaver with a thud onto a wooden chopping board.

'It's Wolf Six, isn't it?'

'Yes.'

Gallacher sighed, 'Can I at least take my coat off and put my shopping away? It'll spoil if I don't get it in the fridge.'

'By all means,' Akulov said. He took a step to the side to be able to cover the entire kitchen, including the large Smeg fridge, which was also white.

'Ta, pal,' Gallacher replied.

Akulov looked on as Gallacher removed his coat, to reveal a white pullover, and put the coat on a space on the worktop. He then opened the fridge and proceeded to transfer the contents of the first bag to the shelves. He paused as his hand entered the lower, fresh produce tray.

'It is not in there,' Akulov said, 'the sub-compact Beretta you keep under the lettuce. I removed it.'

'That's me told then,' Gallacher said, as he continued to pack away his salad items.

Akulov nodded at the second bag, which contained a large fish, bread, cheese, and two bottles of wine. 'Are you expecting company?'

'I'm just expecting dinner,' Gallacher said. 'May I?'

'Go ahead.'

Gallacher carefully lifted out the fish. It looked like a trout, to Akulov's eyes. Its own eyes were glassy in death and its mouth was open as though it was either mid-scream, or mid-yawn. Gallacher put this on a plate then popped it in the fridge. Next, he put the cheese in there too before placing the bread in a steel bread bin and the wine on the worktop. 'I'm reaching for the bottle opener in the drawer.'

'I know.' Akulov allowed Gallacher to retrieve the corkscrew, open the bottle and then collect two glasses from a clear-fronted cabinet. He filled one glass and then pointed at the other.

'No thank you, I'm working.'

'I see. This is not a social call then?'

'Take your wine and go into the lounge.'

'Will do.'

Akulov let Gallacher pass then followed him, several steps behind. Gallacher sat on the large, white settee which hugged the wall. Akulov took a chair, which was at a right angle to it.

'Cheers!' Gallacher raised his glass, and took a gulp of red wine. Akulov noted the shake in his hand.

'I am looking for a client of yours.'

'Which one?'

'How many do you have?'

'A few.'

'He murdered Valentina Tishina.'

Gallacher took another gulp of wine, this one was larger. After he'd swallowed, he said, 'I'm sorry. I know she was your broker.'

'She was more than that,' Akulov replied, surprising himself with his frankness.

'I don't know where he is.'

'Who?'

Gallacher looked puzzled. 'Bang-Bang.'

'So, you know that Basson assassinated Tishina?'

Gallacher let out a long sigh. 'I suspected it. I know about your history, and I can't think of anyone else who would have taken her out. It's not good for business, is it, if we run around killing each other off?'

'You were in the Legion, is that how you met Basson?'

'Yes. He was an exceptional Legionnaire. I was surprised when he left, but something changed in him, after the head injury.'

Akulov frowned. 'Head injury?'

'In Sarajevo, at the airport. He and Desange almost got splatted when the concrete bunker they were in collapsed. From then onwards he was more determined, more focused, and he trained himself to become an explosives expert. I reckon what didn't kill him made him stronger. The Legion tried to keep him, they even offered him a promotion, an extra one, which is unheard of. And he walked away to become Mr Bang-Bang.'

'You've been supplying him ever since?'

'Not solely me, mind you I wouldn't know if I wasn't. He comes to me when he needs something and when presumably it's not too far out of the way.'

'You don't know where he is?'

Gallacher shook his head. 'No. He's like you, he appears like a bad rash overnight – no offence.'

'None taken. How does he contact you?'

'Via WhatsApp. He has my number. He uses a different burner each time.'

'How do you know it's him?'

'He uses a code phrase; we change it regularly.'

'So, you're telling me you don't know where he is and you can't contact him either?'

'That's right.' He finished the last of his wine. 'I'm not much good, am I?'

Akulov said, 'I have a list of associates – you're on it, hence the visit.'

'Can I see it?'

Akulov fished a piece of paper out of his pocket with his left hand, whilst keeping the Glock fixed on the Scotsman, he saw no point in not sharing it. 'There.'

Gallacher slipped his hand into his pocket and removed a slim pouch, he took out a pair of thin, folded reading glasses, put them on and scrutinised the list. 'How many of these people have you seen?'

'I'm up to "G", hence you.'

'Desange is not on the list.'

'The same Desange from Sarajevo airport?'

'Yes. They were as thick as thieves. Always together – before and after what happened.'

'Where is Desange?'

'I haven't a clue. Look, his full name is Lucas Desange and he's originally from the Ivory Coast. His mother brought him to France as a kid. That's all I've got. If anyone knows where Bang-Bang is, it'll be him.'

'Is he on the circuit too?'

'Not a chance, he was a real gentleman. Desange means "of the angels", and he was far too moral. He kept his killing for France, I don't know what he's up to now, but it'll be legit-imate, above board, respectable. Now can we shake hands, and both get on with our own business? I've got nothing against you, Akulov.'

'Thank you, that is much appreciated.' A thought occurred to Akulov. 'When was the last time you saw Basson?'

'Ages ago.'

'Five years ago, Tishina paid you to tell her when he contacted you.'

'She did.'

'Around that time you provided Basson with a pair of hand grenades.'

Gallacher nodded, he was looking nervous again. 'Yes. Two of them. They were duds, just like Tishina ordered.'

'He used one of them to in an attempt to kill an Italian businessman and murder his twenty-four-year-old girlfriend. When the grenade didn't work, he went on a rampage and shot six other people.'

'San Remo?' Gallacher looked down. 'That is unfortunate, but it's the nature of our business.'

'It is.' Akulov stood. 'I was there too.'

Gallacher pushed himself to his feet. 'Look, I'm sorry I couldn't be of more help, but that's all I've got.'

Akulov nodded and fired a round into Gallacher's chest, propelling him backwards onto his white settee. The former Legionnaire's mouth gaped open, reminding Akulov of the fish he'd watched the man place in his fridge.

'And that's all you get,' Akulov said as he fired a second round, this one directly into the man's heart.

Akulov walked away, got to the edge of the room then looked back, the place looked much better with a splash of colour.

Once outside the building, Akulov crossed the road and headed for the beach. He took the steps down from the promenade onto the sand and started to stroll. Making sure that no one was within earshot, he pulled an encrypted iPhone from his pocket and dialled the only number in its memory.

After three rings the call was accepted. Casey said, 'By looking at the time on my nightstand, I'm guessing that you are in Europe?'

'Correct.'

'So, what do you need?'

'I need to find a man called Lucas Desange. He's a former Legionnaire originally from the Ivory Coast. He served with Basson in Sarajevo.'

'OK, got it. You think he knows where Basson is holding up?'

'I have no idea, but I also have nothing else.'

'Right, I'm on it.'

'Thank you.'

'Ruslan, where exactly are you?'

Akulov looked up at the sky and imagined a CIA satellite high above, actively triangulating his exact location. 'On the beach,' Akulov said and ended the call.

* * *

Nice, France

The modest apartment did not have a sea view, but it was just a ten-minute walk to the beach. Through the open balcony window, Akulov could hear the calls of gulls mixed in with the hubbub of life passing below. He sipped his coffee as he listened to the stories the proud, white-haired woman told him of her son. How after they had left Ivory Coast he had studied hard at school before joining the French military. She sat next to Akulov on the floral settee and explained each and every image in the photo albums which lay across Akulov's lap. In the space of forty minutes, he had learnt both hers and her son's life story and seemingly seen a photograph which recorded every occasion. Akulov had feigned interest until that was, she had turned the heavy, plastic covered page to reveal a photograph of her son wearing the blue beret of the United Nations. Akulov had felt his chest tighten as his eyes fell upon an image of a much younger Martin Basson.

'Martin was a good friend to my son when he was in the Legion,' Madame Desange stated. 'He was a nice man, if a little too proud.'

'Do you know if your son has kept in contact with Martin?'

Desange's mother shrugged her heavy shoulders. 'Yes, they were close. Why do you ask?'

Akulov was posing as an American journalist researching an article on immigration success stories in France. 'It's just for a bit of background; I think it would interest our readers to learn a little more about life in the Legion, and how well Lucas adapted to it.'

'Ah, bon. Lucas has always had many friends, everybody liked Lucas, which is why I, first of all, found it odd that he should want to shoot people.'

'Shoot people?'

'You know, join the army.'

'I'm sure he only shot the bad people.'

'Killing anyone is a sin, regardless of what they have done.'

Akulov nodded, although he did not agree.

She closed the photo album, removed it from Akulov's lap then replaced it with a much newer looking one. 'This is where I keep the photos Lucas emails me about his life in Qatar. I have to get them printed.'

Akulov looked down at the photographs. There were images of Lucas Desange on a camel, in the desert, at a deserted beach and then posing in front of several local attractions which included an open-air souk.

'Look,' she said, pointing at a photograph showing what appeared to be a giant, steel-framed statue of an Oryx, 'this was taken at the hotel where Lucas works. It is a very large hotel, and Lucas is head of security. He has to speak English with all the foreign guests. When he arrives, he can speak English with you. He is much cleverer than me, I could never learn it.' She turned the page, and this time the Oryx appeared again but two figures stood in front of it, looking like Lilliputians.

'Lucas and Martin,' Akulov stated.

'Oui,' Madame Desange replied, 'Lucas did tell me that Martin sometimes visits him in Doha.'

The doorbell rang and then Akulov heard the sound of the key in the door.

'Mama!' a male voice called out.

Madame Desange clapped her hands together with happiness. 'We're in the lounge.'

Akulov heard the shuffling of feet and then what he took to be the sound of heavy shopping bags being placed on the floor. A moment later Lucas Desange entered, looking slightly greyer and heavier than he appeared in the photograph with Martin Basson. Akulov noted he had removed his shoes.

'I did not know you had company,' Desange said, a note of suspicion in his voice.

'This is Brian Imber. He's an American journalist, but he speaks good French. He's writing an article on successful immigrants.'

Akulov slowly stood and extended his right hand. 'It's nice to meet you, Lucas. Your mother has been telling me how proud she is of you.'

Desange shook Akulov's hand. Akulov noticed the grip was firm. 'Thank you, I hope she has not been boring you with her collection of photo albums?'

'Lucas, really. Can a mother not be proud of her only son?'

'She has been very helpful. I wonder if you would let me interview you?'

Akulov noted there was still suspicion in Desange's face. 'How did you get my details? It is not every day that I meet a journalist in my mother's living room.'

'Seumas Gallacher gave me your name.'

'Gallacher? That's not a name I've heard since I left the Legion. How is he?'

Akulov lied. 'I don't know, we only conversed on the phone. I have never met the man.'

Madame Desange clambered to her feet. 'I shall leave you two boys to it. I need to put my shopping away and start cooking.'

Akulov gave the woman a smile as she left the room. Desange sat in an armchair and Akulov retook his seat on the settee. Desange said, in English, 'Would it be easier if we conversed in your native tongue?'

Akulov replied in English, which wasn't his native tongue, 'Yes, thank you.'

'Very well,' Desange continued in English. 'First of all, can you explain to me a little bit more about who you are, what you are writing about and why you want to include me in this?'

Akulov held the man's gaze. 'First of all, I am not a journalist. Secondly, I am not writing an article. What I am is someone who needs your help.'

Desange's eyes narrowed. 'You tricked your way into my mother's apartment to ask for my help?'

'Yes, I did.'

'I work in Qatar. I'm here for five days to visit my mother. How did you know I was back in Nice?'

Akulov saw no reason now to lie. 'I was given your flight details by a contact in the State Department.'

Desange seemed confused. 'What do you mean? Someone in the French government is watching me?'

'Not the French, the American. In actual fact I am here on their behalf.'

'Are you trying to tell me you are with the CIA?'

'As I said, I am here on their behalf.'

'Can you prove this?'

'I know your flight details including exact seat allocation, which is not public knowledge. I can give you a number to call, if you like. You can speak to my contact.'

'I will, but after you have explained to me what exactly it is you want from me.'

'This is about Martin Basson.'

Desange blinked, he said, 'Who?'

Akulov picked up the last photo album he had been looking at. 'He's the man you are standing next to in the grounds of the St Regis Hotel in Doha. He is also the same man who served with you in the French Foreign Legion, who was injured whilst on a UN mission in Sarajevo.'

Desange's face registered first surprise and then interest. 'I see, that Martin Basson. What would you like to know about him?'

'I'd like you to tell me exactly where he lives?'

'Why?'

'Because Martin Basson is not the person you believe him to be. Martin Basson is a professional contract killer.'

Desange said nothing for a long moment before eventually he asked, 'Are you telling me my old friend is an assassin?'

'Yes,' Akulov confirmed, 'that is exactly what I am saying. His speciality is explosives. He was responsible for the Amsterdam bicycle bombing.'

Desange blinked several times, as though his brain was trying to comprehend Akulov's statement, and its implications. 'You can prove this?'

'Yes.'

'I see.'

Desange looked away, his gaze now fixing on some point out of the balcony window. Akulov understood the body language. Desange was replaying his memories of Basson in his mind's eye and trying to correlate what he knew of the man with what Akulov had now told him. The room had become quiet, except for the continued noise of Nice outside the windows and the sounds of Madame Desange busying herself in the kitchen.

Desange said, 'My mother was proud when I joined the Legion, because they were the best. Yet she was against me working in an environment where I was being trained to take lives. I tried to explain to her that if I ever had to take a life it was so I could save several others, perhaps thousands but she simply said to me that it was a sin even to take one, because we are not God but God's creation.'

'She told me the same earlier,' Akulov replied.

'I have always played down the operations I have undertaken, and I have never told her how many men I have been forced to kill. When you take a life, at least in my instance, a piece of you dies as well. It is a piece of your own humanity. This happens each time you kill until you have no humanity left.' Desange made eye contact again now with Akulov. 'There is a certain, unmistakable look the eye of a killer takes on, and by this I mean a killer who is devoid of all humanity. I first remember seeing this in Sarajevo, and until I met you, the last time I saw this was when I shared a morning coffee with my old friend, Martin Basson. Yet, you seem somehow different.'

'Sometimes a killer must repent and make amends,' Akulov said, not understanding why the words spilled from his mouth.

'This too I understand. This is perhaps what I am seeing in your eyes, yet this I have never seen in Martin. Tell me truthfully, what is it the Americans want from Martin Basson?'

'They want to stop him killing.'

'Do they want to kill him?'

'They do not.'

'But you do?'

'Yes. He murdered someone I cared for.'

'I understand, and I am sorry. You are asking me to give up one of my oldest friends.'

'Is he still the same man you knew before Sarajevo?'

'No. He is not.'

Akulov said, 'Are you going to help me?'

Desange said, 'Martin Basson lives in Doha. Most mornings we meet on the beach for coffee.'

21

DOHA, QATAR, TWO WEEKS LATER

Akulov's passport was American. It had been given to him directly by Vince Casey, not because he was working for the Central Intelligence Agency but because Casey wanted to make sure Akulov cleared the Qatari immigration checks without an issue. He was on a twenty-three-hour 'tourist stopover' in Doha before taking a connecting flight to Singapore.

Akulov exited Hammad International Airport with just his carry-on, his suitcase being safely held at a facility for first-class passengers. He stepped out into the hot, Doha April morning, instantly remembering the dry heat of the Gulf, and took the first Lexus limousine waiting in line outside. Akulov gave the driver his destination address and seconds later they set off. He had arrived at the strange time of the day which was after the morning rush hour and before lunch when the roads in the Qatari capital were not quiet, but no longer hectic. The driver chose not to speak to him, which Akulov appreciated.

A ten-minute blast down a smooth motorway brought

him the first glimpse of the Persian Gulf since he'd landed. On the left was empty desert dotted with the occasional concrete walled boxes, which Akulov imagined was the start of some type of new construction, or the extras and remnants from an earlier one. They passed a hotel on the right, which looked like an Arabian village, before leaving the motorway for the route which ran alongside Doha's corniche. To his left, mid-size skyscrapers jostled with older looking sand-coloured buildings and then a large construction with a passing resemblance to a stylised Sydney Opera House, stood proud.

The driver now chose to talk, his English was clear and the accent Pakistani. 'That is the National Museum of Qatar, it is built like a desert rose.'

Akulov nodded in appreciation, as the driver's eyes studied him in the rear-view mirror. 'Very nice.'

'Yes. Many, many interesting items. You should go to see it.'

On Akulov's right the azure sea sparkled. They were heading for the St Regis, but to do so they would have to go through the business area known as West Bay. The taxi passed a harbour containing replicas of traditional wooden dhows then a park with a gigantic Arabian coffee pot standing guard over it before entering West Bay's man-made canyons of gleaming office buildings.

Five minutes later the taxi made a right turn and Akulov found himself entering the grounds of the hotel, whose entrance was watched over by a pair of giant, ornate looking Oryx. The taxi swung into the space outside the hotel's lobby and a doorman rushed to open the taxi and welcome him. Even though it had been a first class courtesy limousine, Akulov handed the driver a handful of local Dirhams and then let the hotel employee take his bag from him. As he entered the hotel, he admired the scale of the architecture. It was far larger than anything he had experienced, except perhaps Las Vegas. Yet, here the place was on a beach and not a man-made road dedicated to gambling in the Nevada desert. Akulov crossed the marble floored concourse, and allowed himself to be checked in. He accepted the offer of an Arabic coffee and a date, before he was shown to his suite.

The suite came with a butler, and his was a Ukrainian and from Lviv. Akulov resisted the almost overwhelming urge to address his countryman in their shared tongue as he was travelling as an American doctor named Antony Smith. Once the butler had left, Akulov moved to the floor-to-ceiling windows and studied the view. The room was on the twelfth floor and had a dual aspect view which overlooked the Olympic-sized swimming pool below and the private beach beyond, in one direction, and in the other the artificial island of The Pearl which lay a kilometre away across an artificial channel.

Akulov checked his watch, this time not a cheap plastic Casio but a gold Rolex, more in keeping with his legend as well-heeled holidaymaker. He now had a little over twenty-one hours until he would be checking out of the hotel. With nothing planned, apart from what was scheduled for dawn the next day, Akulov decided to change, go downstairs and act like a tourist by familiarising himself with the pool area and the beach. He knew the others would also be arriving soon, if they were not there already.

* * *

Basson was awake before his alarm. He didn't know why but he somehow felt different. It was as though a physical burden had been lifted from his shoulders during the night. It was odd and he had no explanation for it. Pulling off his sheets, he padded to the balcony doors and opened them. The air at this time of the day was the freshest it ever became in Doha, and that was one of the reasons why he liked to be awake. He stepped onto the balcony and felt the residual warmth of the previous day's sun on the tiles and the ever-present layer of desert dust. The sea was a midnight blue mass, moving with the prevailing breeze, and the waxing moon hanging above it was doing its best to highlight individual waves as they passed beneath its beams. He had messed up not finding and killing Akulov, but at least his failure had mitigated this by his assassination of Valentina Tishina.

A sneer formed on his face as he remembered the sound she had made when his round had entered her chest, but she had been a formidable opponent. He rubbed the scar on his right arm. Although the bullet wound was now fully healed, it did give him, like his leg used to, the occasional twinge. However, on the plus side it provided him with more than enough material for 'old war stories' which the women he met in hotel bars seemed to like. Tishina was dead, and Akulov had once more become a ghost. Perhaps he really would be allowed to become an old, bold soldier?

The sound of the Fajar call to prayer started to echo from the local mosque, it was his cue to once more go for a swim. Turning back, he shut the door and took a clean pair of Speedos from his dresser, put them on and made his way downstairs. He collected his goggles from a hook in the hallway and noticed that the light in the maid's room was on. Rose would be preparing coffee and breakfast for him on his return, and of course after his swim he would be ravenous. Basson opened the back door and stepped onto the tepid sand, which within a few hours would once again be hot enough to scald the feet of the unwary. He took three steps into the water, controlled his urge to shiver by reminding himself that the water was no longer cold, and then ploughed under the silvery surface.

The dark abyss of the underwater world at this time of day excited him and challenged him. This close to the shore only the smaller nocturnal creatures darted about, but out in the gulf much larger predators were at play. He struck out for the centre of the channel between The Pearl and Katara Beach knowing that at this time of day the sea was his own personal plaything. He swam left, then moved parallel with both shorelines until he powered into the sea proper to bypass the still sleeping yacht club on the headland separating The Pearl from Katara, and Katara from the two five-star hotels sitting side by side, the St Regis and The Intercontinental.

With each stroke he could feel his fatigue and stress of the failed contracts easing from his knotted muscles, and his body started to relax. The words of his dead, Irish broker, played again in front of his mind's eye, that he should retire from the elimination business, that it was a young man's game, but at this time of day, these darkest hours before dawn when others felt hopeless, he felt invigorated and revived. He was going to find a new broker and start up again.

Basson powered on, feeling more alive than ever, he ducked under the rope cordoning off the edge of the safe swimming zone for the paying guests at the St Regis then less than a minute later trudged up the sand, panting with effort. He rinsed the sand from his feet and climbed the stairs. His former Legion comrade – Desange – met him at the top with his usual coffee and a towel.

'That was fast today, *mon ami*. It is like you are turbo-charged.'

Basson draped the towel around his shoulders and took the coffee. 'Merci, maybe really I am.'

'You've been away for a while, business or perhaps a little pleasure?'

'Desange, when you enjoy your business as much as I do, it is always a pleasure.'

'That is true. We must love what we do, otherwise what is the point? To get wealthy enough so that we may retire to do what we love but by that time we are too old to do it.'

'So which one are you, Desange, are you happy with your work or saving to retire?'

'I am just happy to be here, after all I have been through. We had some tough times you and I. But we survive, and we thrive.'

'We do.'

'There are not many I would call a real friend, but you have been one of them, Martin,' Desange replied and threw a mock salute.

'As have you, Desange.' Basson necked the remainder of his coffee. 'As always, I'll see you tomorrow, if I'm not dead.'

Basson retraced his steps first onto the beach and then into the water. The thought struck him that he had nothing to do, and nowhere to be. His broker was dead, he had no contract to undertake and enough money to never have to work again. Perhaps The Irishman had been right? Perhaps he should retire? No. He still had one mission to complete.

Basson pushed himself to get back as quickly as he could. He needed time to plan, and he needed time to prepare, and then he would find and finally slay the big, bad Wolf Six.

* * *

Akulov put the remainder of his possessions into his hand luggage and finished his cup of coffee. His time as a tourist in Qatar was almost up. The burner iPhone in his pocket vibrated. He took it out and tapped open WhatsApp. There was a message from the new CIA asset, the former French Foreign Legionnaire – Lucas Desange. It simply said:

> She is with me enjoying a surprise breakfast.

Akulov replied with a 'thumbs up' emoji and closed the app.

He moved to the floor-to-ceiling window of his suite and looked out across the water at The Pearl. The morning sun reflected from a myriad of windows as it rose, thousands of fiery orbs shining back at him. Akulov thought about the lives that lay behind each window, the young with their dreams, and the old with their memories. The rising sun brought hope for most, banishing the darkest hours, and the blackest thoughts. But he still had black thoughts which could not be banished by any amount of sunlight. He thought about the innocent lives cut short in Amsterdam; he told himself he was doing this for them but reluctantly had to admit that he was also doing it for himself. He turned, walked to the door and exited his suite.

* * *

Twenty-three minutes after leaving the private beach, Basson stopped short of the shore and let himself float in the dark waters as the sun started to blossom on the horizon. He watched his villa. More of the lights were on now but he couldn't see Rose, he imagined she was in the laundry room, but it made little difference where she was, she held no importance to him. He swam ashore and walked, dripping first into his garden. Removing his Speedos, he then quickly washed away the saltwater, using his external shower, before he pulled on a light, towelling Lacoste tracksuit, Rose had set out for him, and entered the villa.

His Filipino maid was not in the kitchen, but today his coffee was. He poured himself a cup from the large pot and felt the instant caffeine hit. It was far better than the dish-water Desange brought him, but then he reasoned he swam over to his old friend for the company and not the coffee.

Basson noticed a light was on in his office, the room that Rose did not enter without his permission. Vexed at this and the lack of a prepared breakfast, he left his empty cup and wandered out of the kitchen, down the dark hallway and into his office. His desk lamp was on, and it was illuminating something on the leather desktop. As he drew nearer Basson realised it was an envelope, and it bore the embossed logo of his friend's hotel. Could it be an invitation to a special event? Overtaken by curiosity, Basson picked up the envelope and opened it. There was a single card inside. Six words were written on it in a neat, legible hand:

Bang, Bang, You're Dead – Wolf Six

Basson looked around wildly, how was this card inside his house, unless? He pulled open a desk drawer. It contained a gun safe. He tapped in a six-digit code on the keypad. The steel lid slid back to reveal a Glock 17. Basson's hand reached for it when he abruptly felt a sharp pain, as though a thousand blades had sliced his skin, his body convulsed as his muscles contracted and he fell to the floor, landing on his antique, Persian rug. He saw a figure standing in the doorway. In its left hand it held a taser, and in its right there was a silenced 9mm Glock 19.

'Wolf Six!' Basson managed to hiss.

'I had forgotten how effective a taser could be, until one was used on me recently.' Akulov waggled his left hand, and the wires attached to the barbs in Basson's back shimmered. 'This reminds me of San Remo.'

Basson's muscles were on fire, but he knew it was temporary. 'You have come for your revenge, for that woman, Tishina. How very predictable.'

'Get up, Monsieur Le Bang-Bang.'

Slowly Basson got to his hands and knees, he reached out for the desk to assist in pulling himself up to his haunches and his eyes fell upon the Glock laying within reach, in the drawer. He unsteadily climbed to his feet, his left hand holding on to the back of his desk. He took a deep breath, and a sneer formed about his face. 'Where is the fire in your eyes, Wolf Six? Where has it gone? Did I extinguish that when I killed her? All I can see now is pain. And that makes me feel alive! The mythical, the unflappable, the unstoppable Wolf Six stands before me no longer resembling a Wolf but a beaten dog. Here I am, the man who assassinated the legendary Valentina Tishina, the mother of Werewolves, yet you can't pull the trigger. What is it, Akulov, have you finally realised that all of this, all our lives are a fragile illusion we have created? That nothing ever really matters?'

Basson threw out his right hand towards the Glock, it was his only play. Akulov fired. A single suppressed 9mm round slammed into the handle of the sidearm, throwing shards of its polymer frame into the air. Basson swore as a piece pierced his cheek. *'Putain! Trouduc!'*

Akulov remained impassive, and immobile.

Basson wiped his cheek. 'What now? Do it! Come on do it. Put a bullet between my eyes! Or perhaps you have simply lost your nerve?'

Akulov said, 'Taking a life isn't hard, when you've already given your own.'

Basson felt the anger well up inside him. The *connard* was toying with him, and he would not stand for that. He straightened up. 'Come on, pull the trigger, end me here and now!'

'No. Not here.'

'What? Do you want me to beg?'

'No,' Akulov replied, 'I want you to lead me to the dining room. It is a more civilised setting for a conversation.'

'The dining room?'

'Yes.'

'Well, why not. At least from there we shall see the view.'

Akulov gestured with his handgun. 'Move, and don't drip on the rug.'

Muscles aching, and cheek streaming with blood, Basson walked out of his office. The barbs and taser wires still attached to his back. Turning right Basson started to scan the hall for anything he could use as a weapon to strike Akulov. He shuffled along the hallway and drew level with the side of the ornate, marble staircase.

He had another 9mm handgun secreted in a second gun safe by the side of his bed, but he had no way of getting there before Akulov either shocked or shot him.

Or did he?

Basson allowed himself to stumble sideways. His left hand grabbed at the wrought-iron banister, he pulled with as much strength as he could muster, whilst at the same time driving up from both his powerful legs. Basson vaulted up and over the steel railings. The wires ripped from the barbs in his back as he scampered up the marble stairs. Heart pounding in his chest, Basson's feet fought for grip on the tiled steps. He heard the suppressed thud of a round but felt no impact just the sound of the round striking the marble. Arms hauling at the railings and legs pumping, Basson propelled himself further up the stairs, desperation turning to hope as only now did he hear Akulov's footsteps on the steps behind him.

* * *

Akulov dropped the taser and rounded the bottom of the stairs. Basson had already reached the halfway point, where a large potted palm stood on the landing pad between the two flights of stairs. He saw Basson push it, sending it tumbling down towards him in a flurry of soil, thorny leaves, and splintering ceramic. Cursing, Akulov stepped sideways, losing valuable time.

Climbing over the debris, he took two steps at a time, his tactical boots providing far more grip than Basson's bare feet and powered up the stairs. He saw Basson flash past above and to his right, through the railings on the landing. Akulov had studied the schematics of the villa, and he knew where the French assassin was heading. He could not beat him there, but then he did not need to. Arriving on the landing Akulov jogged towards the master bedroom at the far end. The door was locked, Akulov shot away the lock, then stomp kicked through it. Weapon up, he dissected the room.

Basson was crouching, half hidden behind his emperor-sized bed, retrieving an object from a metal drawer. Still moving, Akulov opened fire, a pair of rounds slammed into the top of the drawer, making Basson recoil and fall backwards.

But Basson had a Glock 17 in his hands. It was pointed directly at Akulov's chest. The Frenchman pulled the trigger. The retort of the unsuppressed round boomed and echoed off the marble tiled floor and bare, concrete walls.

Akulov continued to advance.

Eyes wide, Basson fired again, and again. A pair of double taps, in quick succession. The barrel flared, and the bullet cases were ejected, yet the rounds were having no effect on Akulov.

Finally permitting the rage he felt inside to the man who had murdered his broker bubble to the surface, Akulov placed his handgun on the credenza at the foot of the large bed and, unarmed, walked around slowly.

'Why won't you die!' Basson's words were anguished, confused, and his body was rigid as though Akulov had shocked him again, and in a sense he had. He fired again; again nothing.

'You can't kill what is already dead,' Akulov sent a quick straight kick into the French assassin's stomach, making him double over and drop his Glock. 'And part of me died the moment you murdered Tishina.' Akulov swung a simple uppercut, striking Basson on the jaw and forcing him to stumble backwards.

The Frenchman fell groggily against the glass balcony doors, blinking as though waking from a bad dream. Blood started to spill from his mouth, he spat it out onto the tiled floor. Akulov noted the sneer was now back about his face. 'You swopped my rounds for blanks? A cheap trick. So much planning, Wolf Six? Why not just kill me when you had the chance? Or perhaps you do not have that authority now that you are no longer a wolf but a domesticated lap dog for the CIA?'

Akulov made no reply as he abruptly stepped forward and launched a powerful side thrust kick into Basson's chest, which the Frenchman only partially blocked. The glass cracked and Akulov immediately struck him again but now with a crescent kick, sending the Frenchman crashing through the glass and onto the sun-drenched balcony floor outside.

Akulov paused as Basson slowly got to his feet. Arms up, he took on a fighting style which Akulov recognised. Swaying, he said, 'Come on, Akulov. Show me what you've got!'

Akulov feinted with his left leg then launched a right roundhouse at Basson, who managed to bat it away. Basson threw out his own kick, which Akulov absorbed by pivoting and raising his left thigh. Akulov now swung a left elbow, Basson ducked, advanced, and launched a snapping head-butt directly at Akulov's face. Wolf Six managed to twist away but the hardest part of the Frenchman's head made contact with his temple.

Akulov felt his vision start to grey out as he took a staggering step backwards, his boots crunching on the shattered glass. He blinked, and then saw Basson reach down and spring up at him with something glinting in his hand, a jagged dagger of broken glass. Turning sideways, Akulov knocked Basson's right arm up and away with his left fist, as he spun the Frenchman around to club the back of his neck with his right. The improvised weapon flew free from Basson's hand as he started to fall to his knees. Akulov sent a heavy kick into the man's stomach, causing him to roll across the balcony floor.

Unable to control himself, Akulov grabbed the man who had killed Valentina Tishina by the neck, hauled him back up to his feet and punched him heavily in the solar plexus. Unable to breathe, Basson made no attempt to prevent Akulov from dragging him to the balcony's edge. The ferocity of Doha's morning sun, and its myriad reflections rising from the sea made Akulov squint. Only now as Akulov started to lift him over, did Basson struggle to prevent himself from being thrown to his death.

'Stop! Stop!'

Akulov's orders were to deliver the Frenchman alive. That was his agreement with Casey. That was what would set him free from the CIA, yet he could not stop. He had set his own monster free. A monster he could not control, one which needed to kill Martin Basson.

'Please... no...'

Akulov had become deaf, the only sound he registered was the rushing blood of revenge ringing in his ears.

Basson toppled over the edge of the balcony.

Akulov, eyes closed, fell to his knees as Basson dropped to his death.

In his head he saw her, Valentina Tishina, as she had been when they had first met all those years before at the austere military office. It was another time; it was another life. Tishina had seen something in him, and he had known too that she was somehow special, but it was only now that he realised just how much so.

Akulov opened his eyes, tears fell. Blaming the stinging sun, he wiped them away and rose to his feet. And then he heard anguished groans from below. Looking down from the first-floor balcony, he saw Basson crawling his way through his sand garden towards the beach. Anger abating, to be replaced by disbelief Akulov suddenly realised he was thankful the drop was far less than he had imagined. He felt his burner phone vibrate; it gave a confirmation of the handover location. He noted it then turned on his heels, went back inside the villa and collecting his Glock, double timed it back downstairs and out into the garden.

Basson heard him approach and managed to get up to his hands and knees as he attempted in vain to escape. 'You've messed up... Wolf Six. The police will... be here soon. No one loosens off unsuppressed rounds in Doha... even if they are blanks. Let us end this fight. Call it quits. You flee whilst you still can!'

Akulov said, 'Get up.'

Basson fell onto his side. 'I have damaged my leg.'

'Get up, or I'll damage your head.'

With effort, and a grimace on his face, Basson managed to stand. 'And now?'

Akulov gestured back towards the villa with his Glock. 'Now we're taking your Bentley for a little drive.'

Arms across his stomach, Basson limped past him and down the side of the villa towards the garage door. 'Shall I open it?'

'That would help,' Akulov stated.

Basson typed a code on a pad and the rear door to the

double garage opened. Akulov let the Frenchman take a step inside then followed, entering earlier directly from the villa, he had already scouted the structure for weapons and found none. Nonchalantly parked in the middle of the two spaces was the British Racing Green Bentley Bentayga. Akulov produced the key fob from his pocket and blipped the luxury SUV's boot open.

Basson turned, a look of amusement on his face. 'You expect me to ride in the trunk?'

Akulov shook his head. 'No. I expect you to remove a pair of zip ties you keep in there and secure your own wrists.'

'You know me too well, *mon brave.*'

'I wish I did not know you at all.'

Basson leant into the boot, grunting as he did so. Akulov remained a safe distance behind, his suppressed Glock ready to counter any attack. Basson placed one tie around his left wrist and then brought his right hand towards it to attach the right.

'No. Behind your back.'

'You should have brought real cuffs; you and I both know that these plastic things will not hold for very long.'

'That is fine. We are not driving very far.'

Basson groaned again as he brought his arms behind his back, Akulov imagined he had several broken ribs, then wriggled his right hand into the plastic loop.

Akulov stepped forwards to tighten it then moved to the front passenger door. Opening it he said, 'Get in.'

Once Basson was in, Akulov pressed the button on the wall to open the large garage door before hopping into the driver's seat. He started the Bentley and enjoyed the growl of the engine as they pulled out of the garage, onto the drive and then immediately turned left on the deserted, suburban street. He had memorised the map of Qatar's Pearl Island and knew exactly where he was going.

'Wolf Six, I am thinking that if your masters wanted me dead, I would not now be in my own vehicle being driven by you.'

Akulov made no reply as they continued along La Plage West Drive. They entered the roundabout, joined the Pearl Boulevard and headed east. The traffic increased but it was mainly heading in the opposite direction.

'Tell me, is it the CIA who have ensured the Doha police are not on the scene?'

Akulov continued to remain silent.

Basson carried on. 'Of course, it is only they who would have the *wasta* to do so. Do you know what wasta is?'

'It's *Khrisha*,' Akulov replied.

'Exactly, you Russians have that word for it.'

Akulov let out a long, slow breath. 'I am Ukrainian.'

'My mistake, *mon brave.*'

Akulov was aware of the Frenchman's tactics. The method in which he was both attempting to be 'pally' whilst at the same time angering Akulov again. He imagined Basson would mention Tishina soon, and he imagined correctly.

'It has always been simply business for me, except for this last time.'

Akulov felt his fist tighten on the steering wheel and fought to relax it again.

Basson said, 'She betrayed me. She sold me out, I know that.'

Akulov could hold his tongue no more. 'Valentina refused to give the CIA anything. It was me. And you know this. The CIA want you for Amsterdam. You killed Americans.'

'What?' Basson seemed genuinely shocked. 'Those nobodies on their rented bicycles?'

'Everyone is a somebody.'

'Not to me.'

'And that is the issue, Bang-Bang.'

Basson shook his head and became silent. They reached the end of the boulevard where a grass and flower topped roundabout attempted to direct them back into the main residential part of The Pearl via the final cluster of beach-front villas, which were the most opulent so far. A minute later, Akulov turned the Bentley into a horseshoe shaped street, and then onto the drive of a sizeable, white villa which stood in between two others that were still under construction. The middle door of the triple-garage opened and Akulov drove inside the brightly lit interior.

He exited the Bentley, strode around to the other side, and opened the passenger door. 'Get out.'

Basson slowly clambered out, grunting and straining with effort as he did so. 'What is this place?'

'Walk to the door at the back, then turn left.'

Head darting around, Basson followed Akulov's instructions, and Akulov followed him.

They reached the interior of the villa which, like Basson's, used marble floor tiles, yet this one also had dark, oak panelling on the walls. 'Walk to the end of the hallway, then enter the last room on the right.'

'And what is in there, Wolf Six?'

'Your destiny.'

Basson entered the dining room and stopped abruptly. Akulov, two steps behind, now saw the reason why. He blinked not understanding who he was seeing, what he was seeing.

The space was dominated by a long, highly polished, mahogany table. Halfway down it on either side sat two men – Vince Casey and Mike Parnell. Yet they were not the reason why Basson had halted. It was not the presence of the two CIA men which had made Akulov freeze either, and caused his own eyes to become wide. It was the third person awaiting their arrival.

Past the table, the high picture window framed the Persian Gulf beyond, and standing in front of this – *contre jour* was a ghost.

Valentina Tishina's tone was flat and authoritative. 'Take a seat, Martin.'

Akulov opened his mouth to ask a question, but no words would come. He felt as though he was staring into the eyes of Medusa and slowly turning to stone.

Basson, voice croaky, said, 'You are alive? My contacts confirmed you were dead. How?'

'Highly expensive, custom-made Kevlar,' Tishina said, 'and the CIA.'

Basson spoke once more, a sudden unmistakable fury in his voice. 'What am I expected to do here, apologise? To beg for mercy? Congratulations, Tishina, you have found me, Wolf Six has delivered me, and this was all because of the CIA.'

Finally coming to his senses, Akulov used his left hand to push Basson into the chair at the foot of the table. Tishina took her seat at the head of the table, and Akulov approached her before taking up a position standing by her right shoulder. He still had his silenced sidearm in his right hand, ready if needed to kill Basson.

'Where are my manners?' Tishina pointed to each man in turn. 'Allow me to introduce Vince Casey and Mike Parnell of the Central Intelligence Agency.'

'We met in Harrisville. You were pretending to be with the FBI. What an unpleasant surprise to see you both again,' Basson said, with a sneer. 'What happens now, Valentina? Is this where I accept a deal from your CIA masters? To become a traitor to our profession, just like your lap dog Wolf Six did?'

Casey said, 'Basson, you became more than a traitor when you blew up those innocent American tourists in Amsterdam. You became a terrorist. As I am sure you are aware, the policy of the United States of America is that it does not negotiate with terrorists.'

Basson raised his head. 'Oh please. Why must everyone go on about those nameless, worthless nothings? On the grand scale of things what does it matter? What did they matter? Look at what I achieved. I destroyed the Dinescu crime family.'

'You deliberately detonated a twin device which killed civilians,' Casey said.

'Yet we achieved our mission objective. The client was happy.'

'The client was a madman,' Akulov added.

Tishina now spoke. 'Martin, you are aware that before I became a broker, I was a GRU operative. I was a killer, I was an assassin.'

'Of course, you were one of the best. You are legendary.'

'I have just accepted my first contract in twenty years.' Tishina rose to her feet and held out her right hand. Understanding the hint, Akulov handed her his silenced Glock 19.

'Wait!' Basson shouted, lurching to his feet. He addressed

the older of the two CIA operatives. 'Aren't you going to stop her?'

'No,' Casey replied, 'because I gave her the contract.'

'Please! It cannot end like this! I'll tell you everything, I'll give up everyone!'

'Just give up,' Parnell said.

With a classic, single-handed stance, Tishina squeezed the trigger. The round slammed into Basson's left kneecap. Yelling, he fell to the floor. Eyes wide he continued to howl and, hand clasped to his ruined knee, attempted to drag himself out of the room. Tishina fired a second round, it slammed into Basson's other knee. Basson fell onto his back.

Tishina slowly, and calmly walked towards him. She aimed the handgun directly at Basson's face, as a smile appeared on her own. 'Au revoir, Monsieur Le Bang-bang.'

EPILOGUE
ONE WEEK LATER

Monte Carlo, Monaco

Exiting the underground tunnel from Monaco's central station, Akulov emerged onto the bustling streets of the principality. Monaco was not his final destination today; it was a waypoint he was taking to ensure that he was not being followed. He turned to his right, crossed the street and headed towards Port Hercule. He spent the next half an hour walking around the crowded port and surrounding streets carrying out counter-surveillance measures. He had timed his route so that he arrived at a bus stop just as the vehicle pulled up. He bought a ticket, and it took him out of Monte Carlo, and out of Monaco into France.

The bus's last stop was central Nice. Akulov, however, alighted as soon as it reached the city limits. He walked down the hill to the harbour whilst the bus wound up the other side, continuing on towards the city centre. Akulov reached the quayside. This part of Nice bordered the old town and had a slower pace than Monaco. It too had a marina and the yachts, although large, were like toys in comparison to those in Monte Carlo. Here they competed with fishing boats for moorings.

His stomach rumbled at the sight of an old couple eating mussels outside a small restaurant. It looked like a good place, but it wasn't grand enough for the person he had a lunchtime appointment with, so he carried on walking until he arrived at the correct address. Akulov pushed the door open and stepped inside the restaurant. The interior was larger than he had expected, and three of its eight tables were already taken. One of these was circular. It was at the very back of the room, and at this sat Valentina Tishina. A wrinkled waiter greeted Akulov and immediately escorted him to Tishina's table. A place had been set up for him, which like hers, gave him a full view of the room.

Once the waiter had left, Tishina said, choosing to speak in English, 'You are still angry with me, aren't you?'

'I am not, but I was.'

'How many times can a girl say she is sorry?'

'Once, if she means it,' Akulov replied.

The waiter returned with a bottle of wine and, without being asked, poured a glass for both Tishina and Akulov. When he had left Tishina said, 'I've been coming here for years. It is a hidden gem. I always drink this same wine. They have the best Salade Niçoise. I have ordered you one.'

Akulov was not a fan of salads, in his opinion they should be reserved for rabbits, but nevertheless said, 'Thank you.'

Tishina raised her glass. 'What shall we drink to?'

'What would you like to drink to?'

'Life. Let us drink to life.'

Akulov raised his glass. 'To life.'

Tishina took a sip then returned her glass to the table. 'Casey made me an offer; he told me I could disappear. And I did for three months.'

Akulov nodded and made no reply.

Tishina continued, 'For those three months I was no longer myself. He put me in a safe house in the wilds of rural Portugal. I really thought I could leave everything behind, until one morning I woke up and realised that I could not. That really was not me. This is me, sitting here with you enjoying a glass of wine. And this is also me telling you that I have a new contract for you, one which I know you will not be able to refuse.'

'So, what is the contract?'

'I'll tell you tomorrow.'

Akulov was confused. 'Tomorrow?'

'I'll tell you tomorrow over breakfast.'

Akulov didn't know how to reply, so raised his glass to his lips and drank his wine.

* * *

MORE FROM ALEX SHAW

Another book from Alex Shaw, *Wolf Six*, is available to order now here:

https://mybook.to/WolfSixBackAd

ACKNOWLEDGEMENTS

Writing is a solitary process, which is why I am so grateful to those around me who have by turns inspired and supported my journey.

My biggest inspiration has been my wife Galia, for without her support I would not have been able to carry on my writing dream. I'd also be incapable of writing without my two sons Alexander and Jonathan, penning something they may one day read and enjoy spurs me on.

I need to thank my editor at Boldwood Books, Vic Britton, and my agents, Justin Nash and Kate Nash, for believing in my work and wanting to champion me and publish it.

I'd like to thank my friends both inside and outside of the book world for putting up with me, and for being vocal supporters. This is a long list, (and by now you all know who you are) and is not limited to: Neill J Furr, Liam Saville, Paul Page, Steph Edger, Stuart Field, Samantha Lee Howe, Alastair Sims, Alan McDermott, Tom Wood, Fred Finn, Jim Moreton, Jim Reynolds, Nick Furmidge, Michael Lynes, Glen R Stansfield, Ali Karim, Mike Stotter, Pater Rozovsky, Scott Lewis, Annabel Kantaria, Paul Gitsham, and 'superfan' Karen Campbell.

Lastly, I must thank you, the reader, if it were not for you I'd simply be talking to myself.

ABOUT THE AUTHOR

Alex Shaw is a member of the International Thriller Writers organisation and the Crime Writers Association. He is the author of three bestselling thriller series featuring Aidan Snow, Jack Tate and Sophie Racine. *Total Blackout*, the first in his Jack Tate series, was shortlisted for the 2021 Wilbur Smith Adventure Writing Prize.

Sign up to Alex Shaw's mailing list for news, competitions and updates on future books.

Visit Alex Shaw's website: www.alexwshaw.co.uk

Follow Alex Shaw on social media here:

X x.com/alexshawhetman

instagram.com/alexshawthrillerwriter

ALSO BY ALEX SHAW

Wolf Six

Kill Code

Boldwood

Boldwood Books is an award-winning fiction publishing company seeking out the best stories from around the world.

Find out more at www.boldwoodbooks.com

Join our reader community for brilliant books, competitions and offers!

Follow us
@BoldwoodBooks
@TheBoldBookClub

Sign up to our weekly deals newsletter

https://bit.ly/BoldwoodBNewsletter

9 781836 784043